Tristopolis Howling

JOHN MEANEY

Nulapeiron Press

ISBN-13: 978-1-8381217-1-6

BOOKS BY JOHN MEANEY

Paul Reynolds series
On The Brink

Case books (Case & Kat)
Destructor Function
Strategy Pattern

Josh Cumberland series
Edge
Point

Donal Riordan (Tristopolis) series
Bone Song
Dark Blood (UK title) Black Blood (US title)
Two For Tristopolis (short stories)
Tristopolis Requiem
Tristopolis Howling

Pilots universe
Absorption (Ragnarok 1)
Transmission (Ragnarok 2)
Resonance (Ragnarok 3)
Paradox (Nulapeiron 1)
Context (Nulapeiron 2)
Resolution (Nulapeiron 3)
To Hold Infinity

Standalone
New Jerusalem
Whisper of Disks (short story collection)

PRAISE FOR JOHN MEANEY

"A brilliant, inventive writer." *The Times*

"A spectacular writer. He makes SF seem all fresh and new again." Robert J. Sawyer, Hugo Award-winning author

"Cumberland leaps off the page, a trained killer whose anger and grief at his daughter's condition is brilliantly portrayed; the depiction of his simmering rage, barely held in check, and how he channels it, provides a masterclass in characterisation." *The Guardian*, reviewing Edge (Josh Cumberland book 1)

"What starts off as a simple missing persons enquiry develops into a full-blown coup against a fascist state... Set in a Britain extrapolated from today's violent streets, yet still highly recognisable, Edge is the first in what will hopefully be a long running series." *Total Sci-Fi*, reviewing Edge (Josh Cumberland book 1)

"Within five pages...I was completely hooked... the perfect blend of action and science fiction... I can only hope that there will be more." *The Eloquent Page*, reviewing Point (Josh Cumberland book 2)

"I absolutely don't want to live in the world [Meaney] has created. I didn't want to in Edge (the first book in the series) and I most certainly don't want to now. I do, however, want to read about it. It's relentless and gripping, with a brilliant balance between the personal and the political." *BiblioBuffet*, reviewing Point (Josh Cumberland book 2)

"Absorption is the best hard science fiction I've read this year, well written, exciting, mysterious, full of interesting characters and ideas..." *The Times*, reviewing Absorption (Ragnarok book 1)

"...the world building is phenomenal and the pace as chapters switch from time zones is just right, keeping the tension levels up. The female characters are particularly strong and literally jump off the page, particularly the WWII code breaker Gavriela. The novel is also steeped in historical accuracy and authenticity." *Terror-Tree.co.uk*, reviewing Transmission (Ragnarok book 2)

"Resonance is a book driven by big ambitions. Meaney has penned a story that aims to be epic beyond even the level of Dune or similarly famed series. Furthermore, the amount of research that has gone into the book adds a surprising degree of credibility..." *Starburst Magazine*, reviewing Resonance (Ragnarok book 3)

"Meaney's creepy death-haunted world lingers in the mind long after the book is closed... a smart and spooky read." *The Times*, reviewing Bone Song (Donal Riordan book 1)

TRISTOPOLIS HOWLING

DEDICATION

To Yvonne, my Wonder Woman, who in 2019 ran 146 races of half marathon distance or longer, including 9 full marathons and one ultra marathon, at the age of 65.

ONE

It was ten past twenty-five o'clock and Donal was pounding the heavy bag.

Outside the gym, visible through the arched windows, a quicksilver rain was falling from the always dark, ever-purple sky. The hissing rainfall on the roof accompanied the percussive thumps of Donal's kimodo-leather gloves smacking into the cylindrical canvas bag, over and over again.

High roof, empty gym, rain outside and him alone with a punching bag that took everything he threw at it. Perfect.

Punch after punch after punch…

Before zombiehood, he would have had to stop long before now, but as a resurrected man who'd brought his previous athletic discipline into his second existence, his endurance and ability to keep on generating power shot after power shot – jab-jab, jab-cross-shovel hook, repeat – went far beyond anything he'd previously dreamt of.

That, and the loss of any need to sleep, which was why he trained alone in the deconsecrated temple-turned-boxing gym while his beloved Mel slept the sleep of the innocent, or at least the bone-tired, after coaching everyone from kids and beginners to hungry almost-pros, not to mention her own conditioning workout early on and the skill work she fitted in between coaching sessions.

Correction: he was alone apart from the seven-strong family of flamesprites who lit the place, dancing in their sconces or occasionally taking up formation close to the rune-inscribed ceiling and whirling around in time to Donal's metronome-steady beating of the heavy bag.

One-two, one-two-three. Again.

Power from the whole body, mostly the core, starting from the big toe, arms just a delivery system, keeping up his guard and circling, always on the move.

Working, and loving it.

The sign outside read *Mel's Gym*, which was legally accurate and exactly right. In theory Donal earned money separately, but so far his cases barely brought in enough to cover the rent of his pokey office on the other side of Lower Danklyn.

Three hundred and thirty-three five-punch combinations thrown as he circled around the bag – some part of his mind kept automatic count – so he switched to southpaw and began to circle the other way as his inner tally reset to one, then incremented to two, starting the sequence once more.

At the far end of the gym, beyond the raised boxing heptagon, the tall door swung open.

An interruption.

Donal kept throwing punches but on the spot now, no longer circling, throwing his double jab with triple follow-up without looking at the bag, because his attention was on the opening door and the figure who stood there.

A woman's silhouette, shadow against shadow.

"No." The word came automatically from Donal's throat.

Zombies are supposed to possess conscious control of every reaction.

Skirt suit and shoes with practical heels, a hat adorned with what had to be a shining deathshrike feather, and that stance of fearless competence he remembered so well, except that it couldn't be, not her.

It just couldn't be.

"Who are you?" he said.

No more punches now.

Gloves down but psychological guard up, fully alert because this was utterly impossible.

A Magnus round had blown apart Laura Steele's head with a spray of grey mist right before Donal's eyes, nearly two years earlier.

Grey mist because her blood was black, she being a zombie, and in that confrontation Donal too had been fatally shot with his own weapon, and woke up to find Laura's zombie heart beating inside his own chest cavity, thanks to the quick actions of the black-garbed medic mages whose job and calling were to save anyone they could.

And Laura fell way outside that category, with her skull – her brain – destroyed.

She could never have survived.

Just couldn't…

"Who the Hades do you think you are?"

"Well who do you think, lover?" It was the old, familiar voice.

Enough to freeze Donal on the spot, and never mind the supposed ability of zombies to override reactions that were automatic and unconscious in ordinary living human beings.

Do something.

He unfroze and threw himself forward into a sprint, not worrying about the leather bag gloves which would prevent a strong grip, assuming he was going to grab hold of her sleeve.

Or maybe he was going to simply beat it to a pulp, this *thing* that had assumed the appearance of his violently murdered zombie lover, whose black heart beat inside his chest right now, and whose voice used to sound inside his mind thereafter, until he hooked up with Mel and his life – or unlife – changed once more.

A familiar voice in so many ways: exactly like Laura's.

And this apparition reproduced the sound exactly, even to someone with a zombie's enhanced sensory acuity regarding timbre and beat and, Thanatos damn it, the personality behind the words.

Donal moved.

The shadowy interior of the temple-turned-gym threw back empty echoes of his footsteps as he ran the length of the place, but she was gone.

No ordinary woman should have been able to do more than twitch in the length of time it took to sprint to the doorway at the far end, but she had already flitted to one side and exited as he pounded across the threshold and out onto the cracked and broken sidewalk, following her.

The street felt empty, slick with silver puddles and the sheets of falling quicksilver rain, while the rows of streetlamp flamesprites shifted fitfully in their black iron cages, doing their best to light the gloom.

No sign of her, the surely fake Laura, in either direction.

Impossible.

Donal looked up, squinting against the rainfall, seeing only threads of silver falling from the deep-purple sky. No levitating witches or mages. Not even a passing municipal scanbat.

He turned his attention downward, hunching into a low squat, pulling off his bag gloves and pressing the fingertips of his right hand against the sidewalk. The flagstones felt neutral. To a living human, they'd have felt cold.

Either way, there was no vibration, and no sign of a concealed manhole or similar, which he'd looked for before.

In life, in his original life, Donal had enjoyed running the catacombs beneath the streets, but this part of Lower Danklyn was free of all subterranean constructs, as far as he knew. Other than some really deep sewers, not accessible from here.

Nowhere for the apparition to have gone.

Either she'd teleported via quantally superimposed bilocation, or whatever the Hades mages called it, or she'd been a holomantic illusion. Another kind of mage trick.

Donal spat into the quicksilver rain, more a gesture from his childhood in the orphanage than any kind of actual biological process.

He'd had enough of mages.

Seven months ago, he'd killed an appalling female mage – not the same thing as a witch – called Calista Delfix, although not before her mercenaries and behemoths had brought terror to the streets of Tristopolis. And he couldn't have beaten her without Lamis, the mage who'd once been chauffeur-and-more to the previous police commissioner; but Donal hadn't been able to *trust* Lamis, not even then.

Too little regard for the lives of ordinary beings, human and otherwise: that was how mages operated.

Aside from the medic mages. And even then, there was something cold about the way they worked.

As Donal rose to his feet, wiping liquid metal from his face, he heard the muted growl of a car engine from beyond the end of the block, around the corner of Helwine Avenue. It continued, that sound, without diminishing.

Not moving off.

Tempting him?

He looked back at the gloomy, rearing, dark-grey former temple. His and Mel's living quarters were out of sight, in the tiny annexe that had once formed a presbytery.

At least, that was what Sister Mary-Anne Styx and the other Sisters of Thanatos would have called it, back in the orphanage schooldays whose influence had never left him, not really.

Tactical awareness was something he'd learned young, from Coach O'Brian – fully streetwise, despite that ever-ready grin – in a boxing gym at the AMA. Donal had honed that awareness in the Army, and recalibrated everything for the street as a TPD cop, first on the beat and finally as a detective lieutenant.

So he wasn't going to fall for any tricks.

Not if it meant leaving Mel unguarded.

The car's engine sound shifted, growing a fraction louder while remaining out of sight, as if it were edging towards the corner, being careful not to enter Donal's field of vision.

I don't like this.

His Magnus in its shoulder holster was hanging from a hook in the ex-presbytery bedroom. If Mel needed a firearm, she'd go for her own Draken first, a heavy piece with inlaid bone grips and a rather unusual double sight; but her more natural reaction would be to use her fists.

The unseen engine idled to a halt. Donal dropped his bag gloves to the sidewalk.

From the far corner, just out of sight, Laura's voice called out: "You need to go to your office, lover. Someone needs your help."

Hades. This was madness.

Because all his instincts told him that this was a genuine plea for assistance, even though every logical deduction and tactical analysis pointed to a very different conclusion.

Impossible.

But he wasn't going to leave Mel in place as a possible target. Not now, not ever.

"Alright," he called, his voice odd in the empty street. "I'll go."

"Good enough, sweetheart."

Heartbreaking, that voice. Smart and confident and always alluring.

The car's engine started once more and this time it moved off, the sound diminishing, and finally was gone, even from Donal's hypersensitive hearing.

He turned in the opposite direction, and squinted, focusing on the callbox despite the still-heavy quicksilver rain that hissed and spattered where it fell.

Viktor will help.

So would most of Donal's former colleagues, but the key point in Viktor Harman's favour – besides the twin deadly Grausers he invariably wore in shoulder holsters beneath his leather coat – was that Viktor's apartment block boasted a payphone in the ground-floor corridor.

Donal picked up his bag gloves from the sidewalk, smacked them against each other to flick the quicksilver off, and headed inside, not bothering to close the door behind him.

He headed for the collapsible card table near the boxing heptagon – referred to as a "ring" only during fights, not during training: that was considered bad luck – where Mel kept the ledger book, its vellum pages inscribed with the names and modest fees taken from the boxers, some with the special notation that meant she wasn't charging anything, because some of the kids and adults couldn't afford to pay.

The table also held a battered nine-sided cash box, which Donal was supposed to take to the presbytery before leaving the building – if he did, which wasn't often, not when most of Tristopolis was asleep, though why everyone felt they had to sleep at the same time of unchanging day was a question the Sisters of Thanatos had never properly answered, back when he had been young enough to ask about such things.

He opened the lid, extracted three heptagonal coins – two farthings and a single penny – and closed the cash box gently. The lock clicked softly but distinctly in the near silence, because the rain outside had eased.

While the flamesprites were back in their sconces, no longer dancing, trying not to draw attention to themselves.

"I think it's okay," said Donal. "I don't think there's any danger."

Not here, at any rate.

As for what waited at his office, that might be something else entirely.

In the callbox, still dressed in his training kit, Donal spun the cogs to Viktor's number and let the phone ring three times before hitting the hook to stop it. Then he repeated the process, and again, before waiting for a count of three hundred.

Back when he was alive, he'd have used a watch to count off the seconds, just to make sure, but these days he could do it in his head with accuracy.

He did wear a kind of watch: its display, currently resembling a miniature black pie with a sliver cut from it, denoted the amount of charge remaining in his zombie heart. But he already knew that he didn't need to plug in for the best part of four days.

"What do you want?" Viktor's usual form of greeting growled from the receiver.

"It's me," said Donal. "Were you awake anyway?"

The condo's housewraith would have risen through Viktor's apartment floor to notify him of the ringing phone: three rings, three times over. That was the arrangement for all of Viktor's inner circle of friends.

A small enough circle for him to identify the caller by voice alone.

"Just doing some light reading," came the growling answer.

Viktor Harman loomed tall and scared people even when he didn't mean to, but he read ThD-level texts for fun, or more precisely to follow a hard path of self-education without requiring external validation, like certificates or degrees.

"I have to go to the office," said Donal. "Which means leaving Mel alone, and I know she's a fighter, but this is a weird one."

"Possible ambush? You want backup?"

Far beyond anything a working cop should offer to a private investigator, especially one whose business was as new as Donal's. It could cost Viktor his badge if a shootout developed.

Donal said, "No thanks, my friend. I'm good on that front."

"I'll be there in two-fifths of an hour." Viktor hung up.

Donal nodded in the empty callbox, and replaced the receiver.

It was a fast Pneumetro ride from Viktor's neighbourhood to this one, but whatever the length of time, Donal wasn't heading out until he knew Mel was safe.

Which meant he had time for a sponge bath at the locker-room sink – zombies didn't sweat much, and a standing bath meant he could hear anyone approaching, better than a shower in the echoing tin stall – and a change of clothes: suit and tie so he wouldn't stand out among the few pedestrians abroad at this hour, plus the usual accessories: shoulder holster, loaded Magnus, and perhaps some extra rounds to finish off the ensemble.

If it hadn't been for the fake Laura, he would have been looking forward to finding out who or what was waiting at his office.

Or somewhere in the vicinity, or before that, en route.

Ambush?

He really wanted some answers.

The street stood dark and empty, his footsteps silent as he walked back to the gym – silent, except when he stepped in a quicksilver puddle with a liquid-metal splash.

He strode back inside the temple-turned-gym. It felt as if the spirits of previous worshippers and the things they prayed to were watching here and now, holding their ethereal breath; but he knew it was only his imagination, because if the intangible really lurked there, he would know it.

In part because he would sense their fear.

Of him, if they could read his mind.

Donal stopped at the corner of the street where it made an oblique angle into Helwine Avenue, aka Hel Ave. The mysterious woman had stood here for sure, but no resonance remained, no hint of scent or anything else that might have hinted at her presence.

Nothing.

He turned and looked back at the wide-shouldered silhouette standing near the main door of the boxing gym. A faint nod, a glint of reflected blue light from Viktor's round-lensed glasses, then Viktor shifted out of view, into shadows, guarding the building without being seen, and Hades help anyone or anything that tried to enter without warning.

So Mel was safe, or as safe as anyone could be.

Time to find out what was going on.

Donal hitched his tie, shrugged his shoulders to check the set of his shoulder-holstered Magnus, and set off in the direction of his office, ignoring the pentagonal entrance to the helically twisting pedestrian subway that would have saved him skirting around the perimeter of the next three blocks.

He continued steadily, walking rather than running, his footsteps fully soundless, his breathing non-existent.

Not required.

A wraith hooker slid out of a darkened doorway, wriggled her form to tempt him, then froze – to the extent a wraith could manage that – then rotated almost entirely out of the normal spatial dimensions, leaving only a wispy thread that slid back into the doorway and inside the building proper.

Wise move.

Donal carried on.

TWO

But he wasn't prepared for what greeted him at his office.

First, he went in the hard way. The tactically sneaky way.

Starting in the building's back alley, Donal leapt up to grab the first iron landing of the fire escape, hauled himself onto it, and climbed silently up the zig-zag sequences of rungs, all twenty-three storeys, up to the roof where two yellow-eyed gargoyles turned their stone heads, creaking, to regard him.

The nearer gargoyle widened its mouth, emphasising its curved, blunt-but-powerful teeth. A drop of glistening black venom grew on each incisor.

No thanks, mouthed Donal silently. *I've got this.*

The gargoyles gave slow, matching nods, turned their heads back to their original positions, and froze once more. The drops of venom shrank back inside the fangs of the gargoyle closest to Donal.

Around the rooftop perimeter, their twenty-one fellow guardians hadn't moved at all.

Donal stepped around quicksilver puddles – the rain had stopped completely, which was good – to the rooftop maintenance locker, whose protective hex relaxed at his approach, and allowed him to undo the lid's clasp. That was thanks to a modest bribe paid to the blue-skinned maintenance manager, who just happened to be a cousin to one Brian Fixtovax, the same Brian who ran the gun range at Tristopolis PD Headquarters on Avenue of the Basilisks.

Brian wasn't a friend, exactly, but he and Donal had done each other favours from time to time – sometimes major favours – which was good enough.

And Brian possessed an awful lot of cousins, here and there around the city.

Time to see what's what.

From the outdoor locker, Donal drew a heavy loop of black rope formed of pterashrike sinew, the same kind that he'd used in the Army during mountain training in what seemed like another life, and truly was, in many ways.

Or maybe achieving zombiehood was simply an exaggerated form of ordinary personal change, of the kind that came with aging.

In normal life.

Donal looped one end of the rope around to form a sliding noose, knotted in a Sorcerer's Hitch, although soldiers employed an earthier name for the same knot.

He looped the noose around the locker, which was fastened to the rooftop via pentagonal-headed bolts made of Illurian steel, as secure an anchor point as anyone might wish for. Then he lugged the remaining length of rope across the roof, playing it out from the heavy loop, before dropping the remainder with control over the side.

It swung a little, a damped oscillation, and soon enough hung steady.

Good enough.

At the rooftop edge, rope in his left hand, Donal checked his jacket was unbuttoned. There were pros and cons, because a gust of wind might make the fabric flap, but he needed to be able to reach his weapon fast. The Magnus itself felt secure in its shoulder holster.

Time to do it.

He turned and leaned out, back towards the street below, heels against the roof edge, both hands on the sinew rope, checking the feel of it. All good. He could walk his way down the building wall or perform a jumping abseil.

For the Hades of it, he took the second option.

Lightly jumping, both feet together, he descended via three long jumps – one, two, check the height and then the final bounce – swinging back to the wall and taking the impact with control, ankles and knees and hips bending, like a squat in a near-horizontal attitude, springing out slightly before growing still, hanging there in place, checking his position.

A lone purple taxi passed along the street below, nine storeys down.

No one else in sight.

The window to his office stood three feet to his left, lit from inside by a soft amber glow which had to be his desk lamp, which meant this couldn't be a hoax because he always switched off the lamp before leaving. And his office might be modest with a low rent to match, but he hadn't skimped on the hex protection for the door or the rest of the office, window included.

No runes glowed on the window sill, as they should have if an intruder had broken, somehow, through any of the barriers.

But still, the lamp glow.

Whoever or whatever awaited him clearly didn't care that he must know about the intrusion. His advantage was, or so he hoped, that no one would expect him to enter by the window.

Gripping hard with his right hand on the rope, he leaned left and tapped in a given sequence against the stonework near the window frame. An answering glow of scarlet runes arranged in a column indicated his request was accepted and acknowledged, which meant he could proceed as planned.

Both hands on the rope once more, he took in a deep breath – the first inhalation since leaving the boxing gym – and got ready to launch himself outwards by using three springy bounces to generate pseudo-elastic energy in his legs. And then he rammed his legs to full extension while swinging his body weight to the left, and as his velocity slowed to zero it seemed as if regular timeflow had ceased as well.

He was effectively hanging in empty air two yards from his office window and staring in.

To what looked like an entirely empty room.

Then gravity did its thing, the pendulum effect accelerating him directly towards the window – he'd calculated the angle just right – and as the window opening appeared to rush towards him, the window itself slid up with a solid thump, and then he was through the opening feet first and letting go of the pterashrike sinew rope.

It slid past him as he dropped with arching back, down to a squat on the floor, like the last part of a somersault, upper body coming forward, landing right in front of his desk, and he used the rebound to bring himself up to standing, his right hand whipping the Magnus out of its shoulder holster and pointing the gun at his office chair.

Which stood empty.

He swivelled, lowering his centre of gravity slightly, checking the room at all angles, including up and down – more than one kind of entity liked to hang from ceilings in wait, or spread out on a floor ready to grab a person's ankles and coalesce around their lower legs before bringing them down.

Nothing. No one.

He took two careful steps to the door. Marbled, semi-opaque glass, through which you could barely read the reversed Gothic letters of his trading name: *Riordan Investigations ULC.* No shadows moving in the corridor outside. No unusual glows or points of light either.

But when Donal turned back, an apparition was standing on his desk.

No. This never happens.

Except here it was: a huge white wolf with ruby eyes staring at him with mouth partly open to reveal its fangs.

"What—?"

Zombies' mouths don't dry up.

Except Donal's mouth had done just that.

You never saw such creatures, but you heard about them in whispers, or read about them in journalistic pieces in the *Tristopolitan Gazette* or its rivals, always in couched tones as if the simple act of speculating about their nature might be enough to bring ruin and disaster upon anyone who read the words.

Sightings were rare.

So very, very rare.

But they all had one thing in common: white wolves appeared for only one reason, and if it wasn't apparent at the time then it became obvious later, when you considered the circumstances in retrospect.

They showed themselves when the city itself was in danger.

Mortal danger.

Why here?

The wolf growled, and Donal's world went black.

And he woke up, prostrate on the floor, wondering what the Hades had just happened, and why – as the most immediate memory returned to him – he hadn't been torn into shreds of greyish meat, glistening with his black zombie blood.

Because it didn't want to kill me.

No other reason, because he'd clearly been defenceless yet survived unharmed. His chest ached as if he'd received a solid thump, but other than that, nothing.

Perhaps it wasn't hungry.

Donal went up to one knee, as if genuflecting in a temple. His Magnus was lying on the other side of his office, on the floor beneath the now-closed window.

No wolf on his desktop, however. Or anywhere in sight.

He placed one hand on the desk to lever himself up, needing the assistance because his mind was swirling and he really didn't feel steady enough for normal movement, even though he felt unharmed.

Apart from the pain in his chest, which faded almost entirely during the time it took him to get to his feet.

"I'm too old for weird stuff."

Except it wasn't age: he'd settled down, that was it.

In his mind, deep inside himself, he'd experienced a sea change when he and Mel bought the abandoned temple and refashioned it into a gym, performing most of the carpentry themselves, buying second-hand equipment where they could, registering the setup as a business and making their home together in the annexe. It was one of the reasons he hadn't taken up the Department's offer of reinstatement as a detective lieutenant.

He stood up properly now.

There was something on his desk that looked like a black glass skull, life-sized or a little smaller, but no sign of the white wolf he could have sworn was standing there before he blacked out.

Zombies never faint, of course.

First things first: he retrieved the Magnus from the floor, checked the weapon was intact, and tucked it back into the holster beneath his armpit, smoothed his tie and jacket, and prepared himself for whatever was going to happen the moment he touched the obsidian skull.

Which was… Nothing.

After a second, he lobbed the polished skull up towards the ceiling and caught it as it fell, as if he were getting ready to start a game of fastball. No flares of energy, no mind-bending distortions of reality or bursts of destructive hex: none of that stuff at all.

It might have been a cheap trinket, the kind of thing you bought at a souvenir kiosk after watching the game at Grimcore Park. Except that this was a memento of a far more significant encounter.

A white wolf in my office.

Not a phrase he'd ever expected to use, even in solitary thought.

He held the skull on his palm and stared into its empty sockets and tried to think of a smart remark to make, but nothing came to mind. Perhaps this had once been a real human being, their bone matter somehow transmogrified into black volcanic glass. He'd never heard of such a thing, but the idea felt much less weird than some of the things he'd actually encountered.

If this had been a case he was working on, he might have considered the skull his first clue. But no one was paying him, no client in sight, and his days of receiving a wage from the city lay behind him.

"What the Hades am I supposed to do with this?"

He placed the obsidian skull back on his desk, went around his desk and took his seat. Then he leaned forward and twisted the skull around, so it faced him.

"You're no help. Who killed you?"

"I don't remember," said the skull.

Donal's mouth opened but his mind had frozen.

Even in Tristopolis, he'd never heard of such a thing as a talking skull. He blinked, trying to work out if he'd seen the jaw move, but there was something slippery and blurred about his immediate short-term memory.

"What's your name?" Anything to keep the conversation going.

"Baladradian Chalintropovin."

Maybe the teeth had blurred, or vibrated, or something. The jawbone might have remained still, or it might have moved a little. There had been some form of motion, but Donal couldn't quite decide what it was.

"Was that your name or a Surinese curse? I couldn't tell."

Nothing now.

The skull was inanimate obsidian – black, polished and totally lifeless – the way it should have been all along.

Maybe dead things didn't retain a sense of humour.

I did. Sort of.

But Donal was only sort of dead. Or differently alive.

And not everyone's original personality persisted the way his did, or that he thought it did. That was something he'd always been aware of as a concept, at least as an adult in his first life, but he'd never thought to investigate further, to find out why or in which ways post-resurrection minds grew different from their pre-mortem phase.

His other priorities had shifted. Maybe this was something else he should devote some time to: the mysteries of zombiehood beyond his own day-to-day existence.

So what, I should go back to school?

Maybe his enhanced powers of discipline would extend to academic study. Part of him liked the idea of that: cracking open text books, gaining a degree or two, maybe even a ThD like what's his face, young Kyushen Jyu, who could analyse hex configurations and living minds the way Donal could field-strip a gun and snap the pieces back together with total confidence.

"Maybe Dr Jyu will know what to do." Donal smiled at the rhyme, and flicked his fingernail against the skull. "So screw you, too."

It didn't make the skull mad.

No reaction at all.

"Okay." Donal altered his tone. "If I keep this civil and mature, can we resume our conversation, Mr Chalintropovin?"

Nothing.

You're not going to be much help, are you?

He considered drawing his Magnus and blowing the skull apart into shards and sparkly dust. But maybe that would bring the white wolf back.

Assuming he hadn't imagined the apparition.

But the skull felt solid enough.

Three-fifths of an hour later, Donal strode back along the street where he lived, carrying the skull inside a purple canvas shoe bag slung over one shoulder. The bag normally contained an old pair of black sneakers, which he kept along with a threadbare tracksuit in his office in case he needed to fit in his workout during working hours.

The skull thumped his side gently on every step, which felt symbolic in some way. Something to do with nagging, and maybe a hint of pain to come.

Almost home, the *Mel's Gym* sign making him smile inside as always, just a little.

Viktor's footsteps sounded ultra-soft, almost silent, as he slipped out of the gym's side entrance and bared his teeth in something like a smile.

"All good." Viktor's tone was deep and gravelly, and his long face looked somber. "I had to kill a hundred ghouls single-handed, exorcise a pack of polterwraiths, strangle a dragonghast after pulling out its eyes, and stamp a cadre of combat mages into mincemeat, but otherwise nothing much."

Donal looked up and down the empty street. "Just a normal night in Lower Danklyn, then."

"Actually, I was wondering about that." A reflected spark from a streetlamp sprite slid across Viktor's glasses. "It's been dead quiet. I mean, nobody at all. Is it usually like this?"

"Huh. Good question."

Donal thought back to his journey, returning from his office. No one, among the few people out at this hour, had looked directly at him. Maybe the obsidian skull had emanated some influence in that regard, dissuading proximity, driving people who happened to be awake to stay indoors.

But earlier, when Donal had been heading towards his office, there'd only been that one sad street wraith plying her sordid trade who'd come out briefly to entice him. In all, the immediate area had felt even quieter than usual.

Maybe it wasn't anything to do with skulls or even white wolves, but some subliminal uneasiness caused by whatever it was that appeared here earlier in Laura's form.

"My other excellent question," said Viktor, "is what are you carrying in that smelly old bag? Are you taking up bowling?"

"Smelly? This is what I put my sneakers in normally, and they're only about seven years old. Fresh as anything."

"I'll bet. And the contents of the bag right now?"

Donal looked up and down the street again. He inhaled a little, just enough to emit a sigh, but changed his mind and said: "Come inside and I'll show you."

"Said the wraith to the politician."

"Thanatos. Now I remember why I've started working alone."

"Because you can't keep up with the smart remarks?"

Donal shook his head and led the way inside.

Wondering where the Hades these weird events might lead him.

THREE

One thing that hadn't altered in zombiehood was Donal's love of reading, the kind of books that entertained ordinary working folk rather than the literati.

While he waited for the rest of the world to wake up, he sat in one corner of the gym and resumed reading *Human: A Third Beginning*, yet another volume in the seemingly endless saga that he liked to return to when nothing in his real life (or unlife) was making sense.

The book was battered because he'd bought it second-hand as per usual from Peat's Bookstore, although the eponymous former owner had been murdered last year – Donal had tracked down the lowlife killer – and bequeathed it to his niece and nephew, who ran the place together now.

In the *Human* series, Earth wasn't phase-locked but rotated on its axis once a day instead of once a year. That fantasy version of the real world lacked a permanent Lightside: instead, every location experienced alternating light and dark on a daily basis.

Unsettling, and therefore intriguing to imagine.

The Sisters of Thanatos taught Donal and the other orphans to approach learning with critical thought and a downright heretical disregard for tradition by the standards of more venerable institutions. There was something called the Cataclysm Hypothesis that proposed a distant past in which the real Earth behaved like that fantasy version, accounting for the twenty-five-hour rhythm most species experienced in their bodily and mental processes.

Donal thought the notion far-fetched, but just plausible enough to render the *Human* books more solidly believable than perhaps they deserved.

The fight scenes were pretty good.

He reached the end of a chapter, sighed a little – in his previous life it would have been a purely unconscious act – placed the lizard-bone bookmark between the pages, and closed the book. After tapping it three times against his knee for no good reason, he placed the battered volume on the floorboards next to his chair, and picked up the purple canvas shoe-bag that he'd been keeping at his feet.

Perhaps if the skull remained covered up for a while, it would eventually prove more talkative when Donal decided to reveal it once more. Or maybe patience was the first thing that dead bones learned to embrace, if they retained some kind of coherent awareness.

Maybe, perhaps, possibly… He was working with the unknown again.

"You don't want the Department to handle it," Viktor had said, not quite a question, before departing an hour ago. "Not even the task force. Harald and Ruth included."

Meaning Laura's old team, now reformed and working on some new task that Donal wasn't entirely clear on. And didn't care to be, because he wasn't part of that team, not any longer.

"The wolf appeared to me," Donal had told Viktor. "That has to mean something, doesn't it?"

"Yeah, but do you have money to live on while you're investigating this for free?"

"Good point, but I think I'll manage. *We'll* manage."

One of the other team members might have made a remark about Donal being a kept man, but Viktor had just nodded, touched a finger to his forehead in casual salute, and stalked out without another word.

Heading straight to work without having slept. Or maybe not: superiors learned to grant Viktor a large measure of autonomy, for the sake of good results.

From the presbytery annexe came the sounds of Mel clattering in the kitchen as she put the coffee on. Donal smiled. This was his world now.

And no dead thing in a smelly shoe-bag – Viktor's description had been accurate enough – was going to change Donal's priorities.

Interesting, though, that Viktor had thought about money, because Donal no longer received a TPD salary, and he'd better bear that in mind if this looked like lasting a long time.

Whatever *this* was.

Mel was frying up lizard rashers by the time Donal reached the kitchen, with his shoe-bag-wrapped skull in hand. Two halves of a kimodo egg shell lay on a plate ready for discarding, with the liquid contents waiting in a plain ceramic jug.

Donal abandoned the shoe-bag on a chair and went to Mel.

"Hey, lover," she said.

"Yeah, hey." He kissed her.

And kept his arm around her strong shoulders as she returned her attention to the frying-pan.

"You want some of this?" she asked.

Zombies don't eat much. "I could manage a little. You want me to whisk the egg?"

"Well, now you're back, you might as well make yourself useful."

Donal slipped off his jacket, draped it over the chair he'd placed the skull on, rolled up his sleeves and tucked his tie inside his shirt. "So you know I slipped out for a while."

He unslung his Magnus and draped the rig on the back of the chair.

"I had to pee during the night," said Mel. "Your scary friend waved at me."

"That's not what you normally call it."

"Ha."

Donal fetched a whisk from the drawer and got to work on whipping the kimodo egg into a frothy mix.

When the food was cooked, Donal scooped a little of the scrambled egg onto his plate, and left the rest for Mel, who piled up a large breakfast. The flamesprites who'd been working in the stove flew up to the waiting wall sconces, adding to the illumination from their siblings on the other walls.

Donal and Mel possessed three kitchen chairs, mismatched but sold as a set in a charity shop run by the Ensorcelled Relief Foundation. They bought the chairs at the same time as the black table, which was topped with old, scratched hyperbeetle carapace.

As they sat down, Mel asked, "So are you taking up bowling, sweetheart?"

She nodded towards the third chair and the purple bag that clearly did not contain shoes.

"Let's eat first," said Donal, "and I'll show you afterwards."

Mel wrinkled her pug nose. "Okay."

Donal smiled. "Okay, then."

He poured some spicy sparklefruit ketchup onto his eggs, grabbed his fork and got to work on his first food for fifty hours, since he hadn't bothered eating yesterday.

Even so, he still left a little on his plate, feeling full before finishing the lot.

Mel ate faster than he did – faster than Donal would have eaten in his first life, for that matter – but there was more on her plate, so he still had to wait for her to finish. It was nice, just sitting here in their shared kitchen, taking these moments as precious, because they were.

"You're going to work 'em hard today," he said finally.

"Better believe it, buddy boy."

She dropped the plates in the sink with a clatter, while Donal poured two coffees, and they sat down once more.

"A white wolf," he said, "appeared to me in my office last night."

"Say what?"

"You know about the wolves, right?"

"Not really."

"Well, that's because you're Illurian, babe."

"And you Tristopolitans think this city is the centre of the universe."

"You mean it isn't?"

"Tell me what's going on, Donal Riordan."

"Yes, ma'am."

He gave her a sketch history of the wolves' odd appearances at times of crisis. "Including," he added, "killing a bunch of corrupted soldiers who were about to massacre truckloads of resurrected civilians, back when this city was falling apart."

"When Calista Delfix nearly destroyed the place, you mean."

"No, before that. When the Dark Circle mages infiltrated the city government and whipped up hatred against non-standard humans and your actual non-humans, all at the same time."

"So a really inclusive kind of narrow prejudice, then?"

"Yeah, you could say that." He waited a moment, then: "Last night, I was summoned to the office by an apparition that looked and sounded just like Laura."

Mel looked at him with her fearless fighter's gaze. "No need to ask Laura who."

Donal gave a tiny shrug. "I don't know if it was a tangible being or like a holomantic projection, kind of thing. Appeared downstairs, in the gym."

"So you didn't get that close."

"No." A pause. "I didn't shoot, either."

"Wouldn't have helped against a projection."

"I'd have found out what it was, maybe."

"And maybe left a bullet hole in the wall. And disturbed my sleep."

"Yeah…" Donal shrugged. "Actually, I'd left my weapon in the bedroom. But I could've thrown a medicine ball at the thing."

"I don't suppose she was here for training."

"No," said Donal. "*It* wasn't."

The muscles at the side of Mel's mouth had tightened. She nodded the same way she might before sparring: courteous acknowledgment while preparing to hit and be hit.

"Anyway, in my office," continued Donal, "the white wolf disappeared and I lost consciousness, not necessarily in that order—"

"Thanatos."

"—and when I woke up, I found it had left me a present. This thing."

He snagged the obsidian skull from the purple bag and placed the skull on the tabletop. And kept his fingertips on it for a moment.

"Mel Carson, meet, er, Baladradian Chalintropovin."

"Hey, Drad," Mel told the skull, and looked at Donal. "So it's got a name?"

"Of course I've got a name, you moron," said the skull.

"Call her that again," said Donal, "and I'll smash you into dust, pal."

He picked the skull up and rapped it down hard against the carapace-topped table.

"Ouch," said the skull.

"Donal, what the bloody Hades?" asked Mel. "You're talking to a glass skull."

"Obsidian, and if he insults you again I really will obliterate him."

"*Insults* me?"

"He called you a…"

Mel blinked, and blinked again. "It's an inanimate object."

"The Hades it is. Didn't you hear him?"

"Hear who?"

"The skull. Chalintropovin. He insulted you."

Mel shook her head.

Donal stared at the obsidian skull. "This isn't funny."

"I think it's hilarious," it answered.

The jawbone had moved, or at least blurred in some way. Donal was almost sure of it.

"I suppose you couldn't see the movement, either," he said to Mel. "Around the lower part, when he speaks."

Mel shook her head. "This isn't good."

"No. But the wolves are kind of the good guys, as far as anyone can tell from the stories."

"From what you said, no one knows a Hades of a lot about them. And the wolf might have given you this thing to destroy, right?"

"Huh. Right."

More likely to investigate, but Donal still didn't like the way the skull – he didn't want to think of it by name – had spoken to Mel. Even if it knew in advance that she wouldn't be able to hear his words.

Its words.

Donal didn't want to humanise the thing, because Mel was right: he might at some point need to destroy it.

Mel gestured with her chin towards the skull. "What are you planning on doing with it?"

"Well…" Donal flicked his fingernail against the polished obsidian, which remained unresponsive. "I've got a contact who might owe me a favour, and another who I probably owe several favours to, but might let me rack up another on account."

"Contacts. Like when you were an actual working cop, and civilians were willing to help the police department."

"One of the guys is a forensic Bone Listener at the OCML, Office of the

Chief Medical Listener, so maybe not quite a civilian. But yeah, I get your point."

As Detective Lieutenant Riordan, he had held official status while working on official cases. None of that applied these days.

"Who's the other one?" asked Mel.

"Say what?"

"The other contact," she said, "who might know how to deal with dead objects that insult the love of your life."

She beamed, and the atmosphere shifted in that instant.

"You got that last part right," said Donal. "That's exactly who you are."

"Yeah."

"Yeah."

They leaned across the table and kissed each other: soft, sweet and full of promises for later.

"Hey," said the skull. "Could you please turn me away before you do that slobbery stuff."

Donal ignored the thing.

The other contact was Dr Kyushen Jyu, which was why, an hour later, Donal was sitting in the rear of a purple taxi heading out of the city proper, or so it seemed, as they entered a wooded area where black iron trees rose on either side.

If you tilted your head against the window and looked up, the treetops seemed to blend directly into the deep-purple sky, as if the roadway ran along a tunnel through solidified darkness.

A winged shadow moved high up: an ambulance, headed the same way as Donal.

St Jarl's – strictly, the Hospital of St Jarl-the-Healer – was guarded by scanwraiths and high gates that swung open at the taxi's approach only because the wraiths had already finished sliding through chassis, seats and occupants, finding no suspicious hex or obvious malign intent.

One of the wraiths might have lingered next to Donal's skin for a few extra seconds, but slipped away just when he was about to introduce himself and ask the wraith what its name was.

If the wraiths had a problem with the obsidian skull of Baladradian Chalintropovin, currently resting on the seat next to Donal in the same purple shoe-bag as before, then Donal had no way of detecting their disquiet. He wasn't even sure they'd sensed the skull at all.

The taxi scrunched its way slowly along the extended gravel roadway to the parking area in front of the rearing towers and castellated buildings that formed the hospital. It reminded Donal somehow of the approach to Wailing Towers Penitentiary, except that here the gravel was formed of stones, not the knuckle bones of prisoners, living and dead.

Kyushen Jyu, pale and thin, was standing near the main entrance steps, along with two Night Sisters, neither of them Sister Felice, the only Night Sister whose name Donal could bring to mind.

But then, she'd been his primary care nurse after a particularly bad ensorcellment, and helped out later in an off-the-books operation against dark mages in the Energy Authority, so of course he would remember her.

It was Kyushen Jyu's thaumaturgical expertise that Donal needed today.

"Thanks, pal," said the driver when Donal handed over a seven-florin coin. "You want I should hang around for a while?"

"I might be an hour."

The driver shrugged, highlights sliding across his scales. "I'm off duty after this, home to the wife. I can drive back to the city for free, or you can pay me to drive back after I snooze for an hour right here."

"Fair enough." Donal remembered how he used to hate filling in expense forms. Now he wished he had a bureaucracy behind him, willing to reimburse every florin he spent, so long as he took a few minutes with pen and vellum to record the transaction.

He stepped out of the taxi, skull-in-bag dangling from his hand, and closed the door behind him without looking. His attention rested on Kyushen Jyu and the Night Sisters, one of whom was standing right next to Kyushen Jyu, inside his personal space.

Some people were insensitive to social niceties, and Kyushen Jyu had always been awkward, but less so on the last few occasions Donal had seen him.

"Lieutenant Riordan," said Kyushen Jyu. "This is Lynkse. And that's Sister Amber."

"Hi both." Donal remembered something he'd heard, back when they threw a barbecue to celebrate the official opening of Mel's Gym, and a handful of his former colleagues had attended. "Do you know Harald Hammersen, Sister Amber?"

"I'll say." She smiled, and blinked her vertically slitted eyes.

"She met him," said Kyushen Jyu, "when the Department was trying to trace your whereabouts, after Felice reported that your grave was empty."

Donal shook his head, remembering the time he came awake inside a buried coffin, coming out of temporal stasis and knowing straight away that everyone must have thought he was dead.

A normal human would have been destined for the necroflux reactor piles, but in that case someone would have detected the concealed amulet that produced the stasis hex, hopefully before they called down the shrikes to strip the flesh from his bones.

But zombie bones were far too wild for the reactors, hence graveyards and burial.

"Is she around to say hello to?" asked Donal. "Sister Felice, I mean. I ought to say hi. And I ought to mention to you that I'm not actually a lieutenant these days."

"I didn't hear that," said Kyushen Jyu. "If I didn't believe you were from Tristopolis PD, I wouldn't be able to throw my lab's resources at your feet, not without getting into trouble with my so-called superiors."

His smile was more confident than Donal had ever seen it. His voice sounded deeper, too.

Donal nodded to Sister Lynkse, who was clearly Kyushen Jyu's lover. She nodded back, not exactly smiling.

"Felice is busy in the ward," she said, her voice heavy with meaning.

A meaning that Donal had no idea how to make sense of.

Kyushen – suddenly Donal was thinking of him by his first name – cleared his throat. "Let me lead the detective to the lab, and we can get to work."

"Yes, you should do that." Sister Lynkse gave Kyushen's hand a surreptitious squeeze, then turned and slipped inside the building.

Sister Amber stared at Donal for a moment longer, shook her head, then followed Sister Lynkse.

Donal waited for a count of eleven, deliberately standing without moving, the bagged skull hanging from his hand. Then: "Is there something going on that I should know about?"

"Ahem. Girl stuff," said Kyushen Jyu.

"I don't get it. They don't even know me."

And Kyushen had never acted this warmly to Donal before. Donal had bullied him once into questioning a hex-protected prisoner, in a way that resulted in the prisoner falling into a Basilisk Trance that presumably persisted still, over a year later.

Donal had thought ever since that at some level, Kyushen continued to resent that episode.

"Lynnie and Felice," said Kyushen, "are good friends. Amber, too."

"Alright…"

"Sister Felice was visiting your grave." Kyushen shrugged his narrow shoulders. "Regularly. Probably the only person who ever went there, to the place where you were buried. That's the only reason anyone ever found out you were missing. *She's* the only reason."

"Oh," said Donal. "I… Oh."

"Right."

"I never knew she felt… Hades."

"Mm."

"No idea. I had no idea at all."

"When your grave appeared empty – actually just subsided, so you clearly hadn't managed to dig your own way out – she rang the Department on the cemetery phone. Got them out in force. Detectives and Bone Listeners and scene-of-crime diviners, the lot."

"Oh," said Donal again.

"So do you really want to talk to her today?"

"Er, what would I say to her?"

"Nothing useful, would be my guess." Kyushen pointed at the dangling bag. "So what have you brought for me to look at?"

Donal raised the bag, extracted the black obsidian skull, and held it out for Kyushen to see. "Meet Baladradian Chalintropovin. I know his name, its name, because the skull told me."

"It… told you?"

"Old Drad here" – the name Mel had come up with – "can be quite chatty when he wants to be."

It, he, Drad, the skull. Donal was going to have to make up his mind about treating the skull as an object or a conscious entity with a tangible identity.

Kyushen's eyes had widened, and his skin looked even paler than usual.

"Weeping Hades, Donal." He brought his hands up, palms forward, as if in self-defence. "Why would you bring a thing like that here?"

"What's wrong?"

"Cover it up. Cover it up *now*."

Donal stuffed the skull back in the bag, hearing a muffled: "Hey, don't be so rough," as he did so.

The skull's first words for a while.

"Wait there," muttered Kyushen. "I'll find something better to contain it. Something more solid. Shielded."

"I—"

But there was nothing more for Donal to say, because Kyushen was already running up the steps, his gait ungainly but effective, and he half stumbled inside the building before continuing, his footsteps clattering from an interior hallway, attenuating with distance until even Donal couldn't hear a thing.

He turned back to the purple taxi. Inside, the driver was slouched back, his cap pulled down over his eyes, apparently asleep.

Drad the skull was silent inside the purple shoe bag.

Wonderful.

FOUR

Professor Helena Steele was feeling her age, which was no longer unusual, though her ramrod-straight posture continued to fool everybody, as far as she could tell. Her visitor, Alkador Stern, reclining in the other armchair next to the pale green flames crackling in the fireplace, was her contemporary and one of the few people who acted as if they were at ease with her.

Or at least, not massively afraid. Perhaps a little nervous on occasion. But then their interests had never been at odds, not really. Not in their professional lives.

Not before today.

She wanted him at ease, although her intention was to deliver news that he might consider a blow, even a stab in the back. Except that she intended to say her piece in front of him, to his face.

"I've been thinking about retirement." She raised her glass of purple phosphosherry, in which tiny specks like silver stars floated back and forth, and took the minutest of sips. "What would you say to that, my friend?"

"My retirement or yours, dear Helena?"

"Either one. Well, no… My own, in fact."

"I believe the word *emeritus*, or *emerita*, translates as *put out to pasture*."

"I suppose it does. Maybe that's not entirely a bad thing."

The warmth of the fire on her skin and in her bones felt welcome.

My bones. Now there's a thing.

Thoughts of retirement couldn't help but hint at what followed, the end of everything. Not that her bones would make it as far as the reactor piles.

Or even to a graveyard, where zombies and similar minorities ended up, far preferable to her own eventual fate. The price of magehood.

"Who would take over the running of Mordanto?" Alkador raised his own glass, examined it, then put it down on the small table formed of interlocking chameleon skulls. "Don't even think of bringing me in. I'm happy where I am."

"Three people died in your labs last month."

"Quintober has always been an unlucky month in Collosso. Anyway, I've been considering my own exit strategy for several years, and my replacement, most wonderfully mentored by me, is about ready to step into my shoes."

Alkador raised one foot towards the pale-lime flames, warming it for a moment, and lowered it to the carpet.

Helena smiled. "I promise not to steal her."

"*Her?* I said nothing about gender."

"So of course I don't know about your protégée, Rina Dotrice, who scored top of her class every year while she was a student here, and rose quickly through the ranks – pardon the cliché – while working at the Centres for Curse Control in Fortinium, before you lured her to Collosso."

"Certainly the CCC's loss was our gain." Alkador smiled back at Helena. "And you can't have her."

"And my sympathies again on the other one, the fellow who came after Dotrice."

"I… Yes. Thank you. That was a tragedy. But the research we do… You know how dangerous it is, there on the frontiers of knowledge."

"I do know, old friend." Helena decided to let down her defences, just a little, for a change. "And in fact, I had a very different replacement in mind, in terms of someone taking over Mordanto. But young Kelvin Johannsson became a father eight months ago, and this is clearly the wrong time to dump a massive workload on his head. Even if he'd been qualified for longer."

Kelvin was in his thirties, but still the youngest living mage to have passed through the Agonies – strictly, the Antagona Ultima Reconstructions – to achieve the highest grade of mage master, as ranked by purely technical achievements.

All higher ranks, such as Helena's own, were a recognition of service as much as ability. Honorary in one sense, although available only to those who'd already traversed the painful path to expertise.

"I think I know who you mean." Alkador tapped his lips with his forefinger. "Shaven-headed chap, am I right?"

Alkador's vocabulary still betrayed his Glian upbringing, despite decades of living in the Federation. And of cultivating assets more than friendships, let's face it. He had amassed plenty of allies among senior mages; but not enough influence to counteract her power of veto regarding succession.

For his protestations about taking over Mordanto were disingenuous at best.

"You have the right man." Helena let out a small breath. "And he's the right replacement for me, but only if I can hang on long enough for him to become ready."

"If I do remember him correctly, then he's pretty young."

"Or we're pretty old, you and I."

"Well" – Alkador gave a small but genuine-sounding laugh – "I suppose there's no denying that."

He picked up his glass of phosphosherry and this time took a decent mouthful before putting it back down.

The pewter-coloured phone rang.

This was Helena's private study in the tallest eastern tower of Mordanto, where all calls were routed through the switchboard, staffed by empowered wraiths with mage supervisors on hand, and no casual caller was ever permitted access. Even so, Helena seriously considered ignoring the ringing phone.

But she sighed and gestured, and the old-fashioned device floated across to her. Taking hold of the stalk, she unhooked the earpiece – actually a genuine petrified pentacorn ear – and spoke into the fake baby dragon mouth mounted on the stalk. "Helena Steele."

"Ma'am, it's Kelvin."

The very mage they'd just been discussing. Helena might have remarked on it, were it not for the serious tone in Kelvin's voice.

And the fact that he'd chosen such a mundane communication method in preference to the usual channels.

"What's happened?" said Helena.

"I don't know fully. But I sent my best lieutenant to Möbius Park along with two assistants, to investigate a white wolf sighting, and as far as I can tell, they're dead. All three of them."

Meaning the mages, clearly: not the white wolf.

"So what are your plans?" Helena realised she'd transitioned to standing, without her cane, and without consciously rising from the armchair.

"I'm going to lead a full combat team to that location, departing three minutes from now."

And arriving within nanoseconds, because they'd doubtless be bilocating into place, after focusing waves of probability hex onto a precisely defined locus which, knowing Kelvin, would be tactically close to where the previous three mages had appeared, but not in the same spot.

The distance was several miles, which made precision focus a challenge far beyond most mages, even quantal specialists: the normal use for bilocation was tunnelling through solid walls, a few yards at most.

Once the superimposed twin locations were established, on the other hand, the spacetime separation between the two loci became irrelevant.

"You need to go yourself." She kept her voice neutral, neither instructing nor questioning, because she afforded him autonomy: he owned this problem, unless he chose to pass it upwards to her.

Or made some cataclysmic mistake, the kind that meant he would need a replacement, most likely because he had perished.

Alkador had risen from his chair also, the lines on his face deepening with concern. He might even be able to hear both sides of the conversation: Helena wouldn't put it past him.

Kelvin's voice in the earpiece grew harder in tone. "I do need to lead this mission. I'll log everything via my amulet, just in case."

"Then good luck," she told him. "I'll be following everything."

"Professor."

The phone clicked, but it took her a few thoughtful moments to hook the earpiece back into place on the stalk, cross the room, and put the telephone down by hand on her bureau desk.

She turned back to Alkador. "Something's happening in the grounds of City Hall."

"I *thought* I heard the words 'Möbius Park'. But why did he use the telephone, like a mundane?"

"Because the rest of his concentration was going into preparing hex shields, I should imagine."

Alkador's fleshy form shivered. "Combat. That never was my kind of thing."

"I know," said Helena gently. "But sometimes the choice becomes binary, between fighting and becoming a victim."

"I've always found a way to avoid conflict."

It was true. When Calista Delfix's forces invaded Tristopolis just a few months ago, Alkador had miraculously been holidaying in Surinam, touring the Plain of Horns on quadrosaur back, completely out of contact with Collosso. At least according to the senior aides that Helena had talked to at the time, desperate for allies in the city's hour of need.

"That's why I wanted to tell you in person," Helena told him now, her voice hardening just a little, "that I've specifically instructed that you *not* be considered as my replacement here, should something happen to me, or should I choose to step down before Kelvin is ready to take up the reins."

Because they both knew, despite Alkador's protestations earlier, that he did possess enough prominence, seniority and authority to form the most likely immediate candidate for heading up Mordanto Hospital and Thaumaturgical College, a two-century-old institution whose influence and research-driven expertise reached deeper and wider than its official name implied.

More so than l'Institutio Collosso, despite Collosso's greater age.

Helena did consider Alkador Stern an old friend, but with reservations, because of that one inherent flaw in his character, and not the sneaky way he'd been building up alliances in a manner designed for her to remain unaware, and the self-centred nature of his ambition.

The flaw was cowardice.

His expression shut down. "I see."

Part of Helena wanted to say *I'm sorry*, but the rest of her would have considered that a lie, so she held back.

Instead she said, "Whoever takes over from me will possess their own ideas on Mordanto's direction and identity. Ideas that will no doubt alter over time, as I'm sure you've found at Collosso."

Alkador didn't react to her acknowledgment of equality between them.

"But the thing is," she continued, "a small diversion of focus early on can lead down dark and powerful paths, because this is Mordanto, after all."

She didn't have to explain herself, but she'd known him for so very long, after all.

"Yes. Quite."

"Day to day, it's the individual mages, and every staff member, including wraiths and ghouls, who make up the institution's real identity. But policy and research direction can cause changes that seep down and permeate everywhere."

There were three known periods in Mordanto's history, two of them short lived, collectively called the Shadow Times, that should never be repeated, and would not, so long as Helena remained alive. Her and, by Thanatos, her successor, whoever that might prove to be.

"You don't need to lecture me on institutional identity, Helena Grimstone."

"My name has been Steele for a long time."

"But I knew you before, didn't I? Back when we were young and foolish students, and made so many mistakes."

"I've made peace with my memories, Alkador. Maybe you should try doing the same."

"Or maybe I have less to be sorry for."

Helena shook her head. "This is for another time. I do want to keep an eye on what's happening at Möbius Park. And, as you said, combat has never quite been to your taste, has it?"

"I certainly think I've outstayed my welcome. If I ever was truly welcome here, which quite frankly I now understand was never true."

His voice was chillier than Helena had ever heard it.

"Another time," she said.

"Indeed. I can find my own way out."

Something like a smile tugged at Helena's mouth. "No need."

She raised her hands.

"Don't you dare, Helena. Not like some bloody parcel delivery."

But the air was already thrumming, and sapphire sparkles were spreading miasma-like around Alkador's head and body.

"It's done," said Helena, and brought her hands together.

The sapphire sparkles imploded into a bright singularity, taking Alkador with them, and were gone.

As was her sort-of friendship with the man, half a century old and cut down just like that.

She turned away.

This was a long, long way from ranking among the hardest decisions she had made in her time leading Mordanto. But still...

And she wondered, for a moment, how many more tough choices she would have to battle through before she could finally hand over everything, the pain and the joy of it, to someone younger and strong enough to take her place.

Later.

Now, she raised her hands once more.

Time to find out what was happening in the deadly grounds of Möbius Park.

FIVE

Donal stood with his hand inside his jacket, lightly touching his holstered Magnus, while the scrunching sound grew steadily louder. Something heavy and ponderous was making its way around the exterior of the tower at the far end of the building that reared up to his right, as forbidding as ever.

From inside the purple shoe-bag, now at Donal's feet, came a muffled complaint. "I really don't like this. Have a heart, Riordan."

"I'm on my second heart already."

"Big deal. Consider the state I'm—"

Donal nudged the bag with his foot, and the skull inside fell silent.

Maybe because the scrunching sound felt closer.

It loomed, the hulking shape that made its ponderous way into view: four or five times the size of a human, as purple as the shoe-bag, its single flat, slot-shaped yellow eye shining without expression or obvious awareness, carrying a tiny box in its stubby-fingered hands.

Then Kyushen appeared from behind it, taking the lead, and Donal realised the box in the golem's hands was larger than he'd thought. Suitcase-sized, perhaps. It was the golem's bulk that diminished the apparent volume of the box.

That would be the container for Drad the skull, who seemed to have Kyushen worried, maybe even scared.

Donal lowered his hand and waited until Kyushen, trailed by the golem towering over him, drew close, step by crunching step, and came to a stop. The golem paused. Behind it, a churned-up trail marked its passage through the gravel.

Kyushen turned to look up at the golem. "Place the shield box on the ground."

The golem bent at the waist, placed the box on the gravel, and straightened up to its normal ready position, and grew still. Totally still.

"I didn't know St Jarl's used golems," said Donal.

"What difference does it make?"

"I honestly have no idea."

It was just that Donal had been friendly with wraiths and other beings for his whole life – for both lives – yet rarely found himself close to a golem, and had never, ever talked to one. He didn't even know if they possessed individual names.

Or actual sentient identities.

Black runes were inscribed all over the box, angular and odd, as if from a different runic system than all those other symbols that Donal had seen so often, he barely noticed them.

"You can pop the, um, thing in here." Kyushen squatted down awkwardly, fumbled at a catch, and flipped it up. He stepped back without opening the box.

"Okay." Donal swung the box lid up, revealing a satin-lined interior.

"No need to take the object out of the bag."

"I need something to keep my old sneakers in."

"Um."

Donal tipped the shiny black skull out, upside down, onto the velvet lining. The skull tipped over, the flattened, convex-edged back of its braincase uppermost.

"Hey. I didn't need a face plant, thank you."

"Stop complaining, Drad, or I won't turn you the right way up."

"My name isn't Drad, and you could at least—"

The skull's voice cut off as Donal dropped the lid shut. Instantly, the clasp snapped into the locked position all by itself, and the formerly black runes shone bright silver for nine seconds – a part of Donal's mind kept track – before settling down to a steady glimmer.

He stuffed the empty shoe-bag into his pocket, and looked around.

Several scanwraiths, barely visible, were rising up from the knuckle bone gravel. They drifted closer. One grew denser, rotating part of its – her – mass into the macroscopic spacetime dimensions.

I'm Ariana.

The wraith who'd lingered in the taxi.

"Donal Riordan."

What do you have in that curious container?

"The same thing I had beside me on the seat in the taxi." Donal gestured to the purple saloon car, whose driver appeared to be still asleep, although it seemed unlikely. Maybe he was used to golems and nosy wraiths.

I thought there was something odd about you.

"Really."

In a good way, Mr Riordan.

"If you're Ariana, then I'm Donal."

If you say so. You're not the person you used to be, but that doesn't make you safe in the current conditions.

"What do you mean?"

No one really knows the things existing in the crawlspace dimensions.

"Crawlspace?"

It's when they come out to play that you and the redbloods need to worry, friend Donal. And by worry I mean panic, really.

"Very cryptic. But thank you for your concern, Ariana." He was trying to be tactically dismissive, hoping the wraith might react against that, and actually come up with some kind of specific information. Maybe even something useful.

But he wasn't too surprised when Ariana began to sink back down inside the gravel. Her fellow wraiths had already slipped into the ground, presumably heading for their normal posts beneath the outer walls.

On the other hand, who really knew, with wraiths, what they were up to?

"Interesting." Kyushen was looking at Donal as if fascinated.

"What is?"

"You have a way with, um, people. Entities. I hadn't realised. I thought you were just dangerous and, well, kind of a thug, really. A hard man."

"Thanatos."

"I think it's the dangerous part that turns Felice on." Kyushen gave a boyish grin, something that Donal had only ever seen him give previously in the midst of some difficult research problem, surrounded with new esoteric kit in his research lab. "That's just what you might a call a hypothesis, you understand."

"And I think I liked you better when you were too shy to speak."

"The old days," said Kyushen, and shrugged.

As if it were decades rather than months in the past.

Donal shook his head and addressed the golem. "I think the box is ready for you to pick up now."

No reaction. The flat yellow eye might have been painted on stone. The golem as a whole could have been a statue, were it not for the fact that it had been moving only a couple of minutes ago.

"Maybe you don't know how to talk to everything," said Kyushen. "But we need the box down in my lab, and he's too big to fit through the main doors and walk down the corridors."

Donal regarded Kyushen's skinny form. They could carry the box between them, but he didn't trust Kyushen not to let go, and if the thing fell and cracked open, it might do more than annoy Drad the skull.

The shining runes and Kyushen's nervous caution, even fear, were obvious signals that the obsidian skull might hold dangerous capabilities, however much Donal felt like simply prodding it and kicking it about.

"That's a rubbish design." Donal pointed at the box with the toe of his shoe.

"The shield box? How so?"

"No carry-handle, right?"

"Ah," said Kyushen. "I think that's next year's model."

"With a smart mouth like that, maybe you should join the police department. Work with the scene-of-crime diviners and your actual investigators."

"Waste of whatever talents I've got. You really think you can manage the shield box, or should I call a couple of porters?"

"I've got it." Donal unbuttoned his jacket and squatted down.

It would have been easier in his shirtsleeves, but walking past patient wards wearing a shoulder-holstered Magnus probably wouldn't enhance the therapeutic ambience of the place.

Instead, he clasped his arms around the box, moved slightly to test its mass – heavier than he'd hoped – then drove upwards as if performing a deadlift in the gym: thinking of driving down with the heels and forward with the hips while actually causing the body to straighten up.

Holding the box hard against his chest so it wouldn't slip.

Not a deadlift, come to think of it, so much as a goblin squat, normally performed with a heavy barrel, but conceptually named after the way you'd lift a goblin wrestler, chest to chest, prior to twisting backwards into a throw.

Not that he'd even seen a goblin since his Army days, on overseas deployment. Mad buggers, the lot of them.

"That's embarrassing," said Kyushen. "Lifting the shield box. I really didn't think one man could manage it. I was kidding about getting you to do it."

"No sweat," said Donal, not meaning it.

The shield box might be heavy, but there was no point in admitting that this wasn't easy.

"There are seventeen steps up to the entrance." Kyushen gestured. "You can manage them?"

"Sure I can."

"Well." Kyushen turned to the golem and told it to return to its chamber.

Donal would have been curious to understand how to address a golem, but this shield box thing was growing progressively, subjectively heavier, so he took an awkward step, then a stagger, then more considered paces to the first of the shallow stone steps, where he spent a moment judging his position, and started up.

It's a good workout.

Telling himself that, rather than asking why exactly he was doing this, struggling up to the top of the steps and nearly tripping over the raised threshold into the pentagonal-tiled entranceway.

If anything, the physical effort made the psychological effort easier, entering the building, because if you stared too long at the tiles on floor, walls and ceiling, and asked yourself how it was that identical regular pentagons could be arranged into a flat configuration with no gaps between the edges, your entire sense of reality tended to slip into vertigo.

Despite his one prolonged stay here, back when he was a – what was the term that Ariana the wraith had used? – a redblood, right… Despite that, he could still be surprised by the features in this place: the little things, that you never noticed unless you truly looked.

"Turn left," called out Kyushen from behind him. "Down to the end of the corridor, then the staircase on the right."

Going down, of course.

Donal wondered if the hospital's original design had placed the laboratories in the deepest basement level, or whether some catastrophe caused by Kyushen or his predecessors resulted in banishment, as deep and far away from the treatment wards as possible.

But the shield box wasn't getting any lighter, so he adjusted the weight, feeling the strain in his back and forearms and pretty much everywhere, and walked on step by step, focusing on the effort.

Not thinking about any pretty Night Sisters with elegant bodies and entrancing eyes who might or might not be in love with him.

Definitely not thinking about that.

The laboratory hummed, filled with pitch darkness relieved by gloomy segments, and the soft golden glow of three-dimensional displays, of the kind that Kyushen used to analyse human mind patterns: equations and schematics, animated graphs and scrolling text in some language that Donal failed to recognise.

At the dead centre of the displays, the obsidian skull – it was hard to think of it by name right now – floated in place, slowly rotating, utterly silent.

The empty shield box stood in one corner. Apparently the skull was safe inside the scanfield.

Inside the displays, the glowing schematics looked tangled and overlaid in ways utterly different to the images that Donal had seen during police briefings featuring forensic evidence, and even when Kyushen interrogated that dwarfish prisoner, triggering a Basilisk Trance because of something that evil bastard Blanz – Senator Blanz, who was really a mage – had placed in the dwarf's mind.

"I'm looking at the pictures because the words are too hard for me, sort of thing," said Donal. "Except they're equations and stuff, not words, and I have no idea what they mean. But am I right in thinking they're odd?"

"You bet. Strangest thing I've come across." Kyushen looked up from some intricate apparatus that looked to be all wires and platinum framework, and shook his head. "It's at least as dangerous as I thought, maybe more so."

"Look, I don't want to risk the patients' health or anything."

"Oh, no. You brought this monstrosity here, least you can do is leave it with me until I've finished analysing it."

Donal started to smile, then: "Do you mean that literally? Leave it with you? Exactly how long do you think your analysis is going to take?"

"How long have you got? I could get half a dozen research papers out of this, provided I can borrow an eleven-dimensional thaumatic resonance scanner from somewhere. Maybe Mordanto, if you ask Professor Steele for me."

"She used to hate me, pal. I think she forgave me, or something, but we're still not friends."

"Oh."

Of course Donal carried Laura Steele's zombie heart inside his chest, except these days the beating black heart was his alone, no longer the source of Laura's post-immolation voice from time to time. Whatever remained of her had presumably blended into him, and altered him from before.

None of this could be easy for Professor Helena Steele to cope with.

If anything, she probably understood far too well what her daughter had been through; at any rate, Donal wasn't about to turn up at Mordanto's gates asking for favours, not now or in the future.

Which reminded him of the taxi driver, waiting up at ground level, assuming he hadn't already given up and driven back to the city proper.

"Look, I don't want to leave old Drad here."

"The fact that it talked to you is intriguing, Donal, and it's one of the reasons I really can't take it out of the hex field, because if it can attain that level of paracognitive manifestation with the tiny amount of energy presence I'm detecting, then I can't imagine what will happen when more flux seeps in from the compactified dimensions."

Donal blinked, trying to make sense of Kyushen's words. "More flux? *When* more flux seeps in? Is its energy increasing, or something?"

"Er, I thought you knew. Surely… Isn't that why you brought the skull here?" Kyushen's eyes were dark and shining, oddly lit in the gloom. "It's heading towards criticality exponentially, maybe even factorially – which is faster, in case you weren't aware – and I haven't figured out the timescale but I'm scared it might be soon."

"Bleeding Thanatos," said Donal.

"Well, yeah."

"Look, what do you know about the white wolves?"

"*That* old wives' tale? I've got real work to do here, if you don't mind."

"Well, sure. Go ahead." Donal gestured up towards the ceiling, approximately in the direction of the taxi outside the building. "I'm going to send my taxi back, so I can wait here for as long as it takes. Can I bring you anything from upstairs while I'm there?"

Wondering whether he should talk about the wolf that had given him the skull in the first place. Perhaps he ought to keep that part to himself, at least for now.

"Coffee and a doughnut from the staff room would be nice," said Kyushen. "Scarab cream if there's any left. Amber brought in a box from Fat'n'Sugar this morning."

Donal shook his head. It was just like being a cop again.

"I'll see what I can do," he said.

He headed out of the lab and back up the stairs, moving a lot more easily than coming down with the shield box earlier.

Outside, as Donal approached the taxi, the driver cranked down his window and leaned out. "You about ready to go, pal?"

"I think I need to stay longer, so you'd better take off." Donal reached for his wallet. "Let me pay you something for the wait, though."

"No need. Working stiffs like you and me, we don't got the money to splash around."

"You got that right."

"Look after the farthings, and the florins will look after themselves." The driver scratched the scales on the side of his face. "Well, that's what they say, but I'm pretty sure there's more to it than that."

"If you ever find out, let me know."

"I might do that. You own that new boxing gym, right?"

It was where he'd picked up Donal earlier.

Donal smiled. "My much better half is the owner, and she's the main coach. I help out a bit. You wanted to come and train?"

"Not me, but my boy. He needs to learn how to look after himself. Has a hard time in school, looking different from the other kids."

"Mel's great with the kids," said Donal. "Take your boy along, watch some of the training. See what you think." He paused, then: "You come across a gym where they don't allow you to watch a session, that's not the kind of place you want to train in. You or your boy."

"Appreciate that."

"And mention my name if I'm not around. I'm Donal."

"Kapeltin. That's Kapeltin Katurah. My friends call me Kap."

"Good to meet you, Kap."

"Likewise, Donal. Take it easy."

"Yeah. Don't take no wooden florins, right?"

"Got that straight." Kap started the engine and shifted the taxi into gear, and tipped the peaked cap he wore. "Easy, pal."

The taxi rolled in a wide, gravel-crunching semicircle around Donal, and headed for the gates which swung open, with no wraiths in sight this time.

Donal turned back to the main building.

It took a few minutes to find a staff room. Kyushen had referred to *the* staff room, but in a complex as big as St Jarl's there had to be quite a few. This one was on the second floor near to the Acute Enscorcellment Ward, which brought back memories of Donal's own time here.

"Can I grab a coffee and doughnut for Dr Jyu?" he asked the Night Sister who stood behind the counter, sipping what appeared to be a freshly made cup of helebore tea.

"Sure." She gestured to a coffee pot. "That stuff is well stewed by now. Somebody ought to drink it, and it sure isn't going to be me."

"Cheers." He found a cracked mug, which didn't seem right in a hospital, but used it anyway.

"You're fetching it for Kyushen Jyu, you said."

"He's in the lab." Donal finished pouring. "It's not for me."

Zombies' lack of appetite was well known, so he pretty much assumed that the Night Sister would understand he wasn't trying to pinch a freebie.

"Um… We've met, haven't we?"

"Have we?" Donal stopped and looked at her.

Her vertically slitted green eyes widened. "You were that detective who killed the diva under ensorcellment. But you weren't, um, resurrected then."

"Back in my redblood days." Donal gave a half smile, dismissing the memory of what he'd done while enscorcelled: an automatic reaction held over from his treatment in this very place. "A term I've only just learned today."

"Well, yes. Everyone calls me Callie."

"Donal Riordan. Pleased to meet you again, Sister Calico."

"You *do* remember."

"Sort of." More the name than the person.

There was a movement at the door, and Donal turned.

"Felice," said Sister Calico. "Look who's here."

Sister Felice stared at Donal with unblinking eyes.

Donal took a breath as if he were still a redblood – the word had lodged in his mind, alright – and spoke first: "You saved my life a second time, calling it in from the graveyard phone."

"You got yourself out of there."

"Actually a mage did it, and I wasn't awake for the process. But if the task force hadn't been looking for me, thanks to you, I'd have died for real in Illurium. I was saved by one of the cops that followed me, a real sharpshooter. Right place, right time, kind of thing."

In fact, Donal had needed to slam the sniper round into Blanz by hand, because of a protective hex field that froze the round in place just before it pierced Blanz's body, but distracted him enough to weaken the invisible hooks that had torn at Donal's flesh, trying to hold him in place.

Donal had used a palm strike to drive the round in fatally, which meant the bastard who killed Laura was finally dead, but Sister Felice wouldn't want to hear about that.

"Well, good." Felice put her arms around her torso, as if hugging herself.

Donal brought his attention back to the moment. "So thank you. I don't have the words."

Neither one of them had moved closer to the other.

"This is nice," said Sister Calico. "A reunion like this."

Felice glared at her, then gave a slow blink.

"Maybe you should catch up properly," continued Sister Calico. "What time does your shift finish, Felice? Fourteen o'clock?"

"I'm not free. But you're, er, doing alright, Lieutenant Riordan?"

"Sure. But I'm not actually a detective lieutenant any more. Or any kind of cop."

"A private eye is a kind of cop, isn't…" Felice's voice trailed off.

So she'd been keeping track of him, after all.

"I guess you could say that."

"Let me pour you both some tea," said Sister Calico. "And there's a packet of crawfish cookies no one's opened yet."

"I've got to get back to the ward," said Felice.

"Not without a break." Sister Calico picked up a kettle. "I'll just—"

That was when a banshee wail split the air.

"Alarm." Felice's ears flattened.

Another banshee joined in, screeching just as loudly and pitched even higher, followed by a third, then a fourth.

"Basement level!" Sister Calico had to shout against the noise. "The labs!"

"Thanatos," muttered Donal, though the banshees drowned the sound.

He dropped the coffee mug as he launched into motion, swerving around Sister Calico and running past Felice, who half raised a hand, but whether it was to stop him or something else there was no time to find out because he was already in the corridor and accelerating hard.

Sprinting down the stairs, taking four treads at a time until he reached ground level where this stairway ended. It took another five seconds to hurtle along the corridor to the basement staircase.

Down again, slipping once but correcting himself before disaster, balance awry because the banshee din was oppressive here, vibrating every organ in his body, and in his previous life he couldn't have made it this far without having to stop and stumble away.

Last corridor to the lab, and he poured on the speed, then decelerated with an effort, trying not to go too far, to skid to a halt on the polished floor before he reached the roiling, black and silver barrier of pure hex or *something* that filled the corridor in front of him, and seemed to pierce the floor, ceiling and walls, leaving no gaps.

The field bulged a little, slightly convex, and if it comprised part of a sphere's exterior, then the spherical field was huge.

And centred on Kyushen's lab.

This is my fault.

Donal's sense of geometry these days worked with finer precision, by orders of magnitude, than in his first life. And he knew, with almost absolute certainty, where the real centre of this sphere was positioned.

Not just the lab, not just the workbench Kyushen had been using, but the sample object he'd been analysing.

That Thanatos-damned skull.

I should never have brought it here.

At that moment, the banshees' siren wail cut out.

Total silence followed.

SIX

Commissioner Sandarov's desk was vibrating.

"It's okay," he told it. "I'll keep you safe."

The desk trembled a little, then became quiescent. Sandarov squared the blotter pad and inkwell stand and the cube containing his family photographs, and patted the desktop.

He was in shirtsleeves, his jacket draped across the back of the chair, his cuffs turned up.

"You couldn't be in a safer place," he added.

A skeleton clock with quartz crystal eyes ticked off the minutes. Sandarov watched the stained metallic bones swinging the scythe in its three-second rhythm: back, pause, and forward stroke. Usually he found the motion soothing more than ominous, but today felt different.

He still had a little time before his visitors arrived, so he pushed back his chair and stood, and walked to the window.

Looking down through the glass, he reminded himself – yet again – why he did this job. Political and bureaucratic power, the daily tedium of pushing vellum and the twice-a-month glad-handing of politicians and rich businessfolk, were the price he had to pay for serving Tristopolis.

Most definitely the price, not a reward.

One hundred and eighty-seven floors below, the forbidding length of Avenue of the Basilisks looked narrow, the vehicles and pedestrians tiny, just one more feature of the great baroque vastness of the city, *his* city – in the sense of pledging himself, not in notional ownership – stretching as far as he could see.

By leaning forward, not quite pressing his nose against the glass, he could see far off, at the distant midtown boundary, the two-thousand-foot-high skull where the nine-lane Orb-Sinister Freeway entered the great skull's left eye socket. In the opposite direction, though it was mostly obscured by the spike-encrusted Lathonic Towers and the forbidding silhouette of the Umbral Stellation, stood the mirror-complimentary skull whose right eye socket, impossible to see from here, formed the entry point for the Orb-Dexter Freeway, which Sandarov drove along every day, to and from home.

Routine, unlike his imminent meeting.

With a sigh, he turned back to his desk, unfolded his cuffs, fetched his kraken-bone cufflinks from his pocket and fastened them in place. He smoothed down his tie, pulled his jacket from the back of his swivel chair, and slipped the jacket on.

The grandfather clock, running a minute late compared to the skeleton clock across the room – as if trying to delay the inevitable – moaned softly.

"Hush now," said Sandarov. "They'll be here soon, and that's that."

At that point the inner door shields split apart at their sawtooth joins and rotated back into the surrounding wall, leaving just a plain black door from which, a second later, a diffident knock sounded.

Sandarov walked back to his desk, sat down, and called out: "Open."

Nothing happened.

"I said *open*."

There was a shiver, then the door clicked and swung slowly inwards, revealing two figures: a woman, her skin glistening – the exact colour of freshly spilled blood – and dressed in black leather, the same shade as her waist-length hair; plus a male companion.

He had pale skin and limp blond hair that reached to his shoulders, and he wore a puff-sleeved white shirt-tunic and black trousers tucked into boots, like some pirate from a children's play, were it not for the eerie cloud of frost that surrounded him.

In the background, Sergeant Yorak was retreating, his blue skin almost white with nervousness. He'd have been the one who knocked to announce the visitor's presence, and strictly speaking, by normal protocol, he should have hung around to announce the visitors by name.

But then again, this wasn't exactly a normal appointment.

"Hellah." Sandarov raised his hand in greeting, knowing better than to offer a handshake. "And Klaudius. It's good to see you up here."

"I'm sure," murmured Klaudius.

"Hardly," muttered Hellah.

Sandarov retreated behind his desk. The two waiting visitors' chairs consisted of iron frames and soft flame-proof cushions, and were entirely non-animate, fetched several hours ago from storage by Sergeant Yarov, looking nervous even then, because he understood the significance of replacing the usual furniture with these things.

After his two visitors sat – Hellah on the left, from Sandarov's point of view, and Klaudius to the right – Sandarov took his own seat and leaned forward, elbows on his desk, glad to notice that his hands looked steady, a long way from his inner trembling.

The air surrounding Hellah seemed crisper and warmer than was natural, while frost-mist continued to waft gently around Klaudius, but for all their differences in appearance, their eyes appeared identical: heptagonal orange irises, and the penetrating stare of people who'd seen things, on a daily basis, that even Tristopolis's finest could barely imagine.

"So how *is* life," Sandarov forced himself to ask, "on the minus two hundred and seventy-third floor?"

"You don't actually want to know." Klaudius crossed his legs, and tilted his head to one side. "Really, Commissioner."

"Or you could come down and visit." Hellah's smile was pure spite. "See for yourself how the other half lives."

"The other nought point zero zero zero zero something percent," said Klaudius.

Hellah's gaze remained fastened, unblinking, on Sandarov. "My brother can be so literal. It's one of his least endearing qualities."

"At least I have *some* good points."

"I'd like to come down and stay a while." Again it was an effort to maintain composure and a steady voice, maybe even a touch of amusement, but Sandarov knew it had to be done. "But without an intact mind and, you know, remaining alive, I wouldn't be much good to the Department."

"Wimp," said Hellah, while Klaudius smiled.

"Sure." Sandarov glanced at the office door, and after a moment, it swung shut with a defiant click, even though it should have closed as soon as the visitors entered. "But we know there's something going on. Everyone's felt it."

Even the wraiths who worked the elevator tubes, and visited every level within the vast tower comprising Tristopolis PD Headquarters, refused to so much as hint at what they were sensing down below. Most were taciturn by habit, but even the more friendly wraiths, a few of them downright talkative in normal times, were staying silent.

"Felt what?" said Hellah. "What the Hades could they perceive all the way up here?"

"Them sensing anything at all" – Klaudius kept his tone mild, perhaps simply to annoy his sister – "means we're failing to keep a lid on things. I suppose we should do better, Commissioner."

"I'm not, what, berating you." Sandarov blew out a breath, less steadily than he would have liked. "Not criticising. Just asking what the situation is, and what I can do to help."

Hellah snorted at that, looked away and gave a scornful laugh.

"Or," continued Sandarov, "you might at least provide us with some information about what's happening."

"You can't imagine," said Hellah.

"I'm guessing one of the denizens is getting, um, restless. Something like that."

"Restless." Hellah shook her head.

"Not entirely inaccurate," said Klaudius. "One of them is more affected than the others, for sure."

The entities that lived deep below HQ – if *lived* was the right word to describe their continuing existence – remained largely unknown quantities, even now that Sandarov was Commissioner, with access to all sorts of previously unavailable files describing creatures and forces within his city that he found it hard to read about, never mind experiencing even a touch of them in person.

"So this entity," said Sandarov. "Does it have a name?"

"Sure," said Hellah, and opened her mouth once more, allowing something else to come out of it.

A vibration that shook the air, blurred every object; a resonance from a hollow void; a roar-screech-howl beyond anything Sandarov had imagined could exist; and a dread sequence of syllables that spoke of tragedy and abominable disaster, to a backdrop of anguished cries from his desk and every other animate item in his office, as the quartz eyes of the skeleton clock exploded in its skull, spraying shards and splinters across the room.

Hellah closed her mouth and silence slammed down.

"That's the short version of its name," said Klaudius. "The long version would most likely bring the building down."

"Er…" said Sandarov.

He'd never felt entirely out of his depth as Police Commissioner until this moment.

"And it really isn't happy." Hellah crossed her legs, mirror-opposite to the way Klaudius was sitting. "If I didn't know better, I'd say it was frightened."

The siblings sat there, saying nothing more, allowing that to sink in.

"What in the name of Thanatos," said Sandarov finally, "could scare an entity like that?"

Klaudius looked at Hellah, then turned back to Sandarov. "The walls are cracking open, in the deepest levels."

"Are you saying the building's in trouble?"

"Not structurally at the moment. What I mean is, it's a kind of message. Or symptom. Or diversion of normal energy vortices. There's more than one way to analyse the phenomenon."

Sandarov rubbed his face. "Maybe I should have brought Professor Steele in on this meeting."

"Who?" asked Hellah.

"Head of Mordanto," said Klaudius.

"Oh, *mages*. Fat lot of good they'll do."

That worried Sandarov even more than the startling effects of uttering the entity's name. An entity that itself was worried about some kind of greater threat or danger, if Sandarov was understanding things correctly.

"Is there any way you can guess at the nature of what's wrong," said Sandarov, "in words I might understand?"

Hellah's blood-red face twisted in a sarcastic smile.

"My sister is trying to look superior," answered Klaudius. "Which she is, of course, but in this case, we don't know the details yet. Or even whether we want to attempt finding out."

"Mostly because I don't want to die." Hellah's orange eyes began to glow: twin seven-sided rings of flame. "I'd even rather my brother stay alive."

Klaudius's eyes brightened into similar heptagons of fire. "Something we both agree on, Commissioner, my fiery sister and I."

Something told Sandarov this meeting was in danger of ending abruptly, before he'd found out anything other than confirmation that things were going to Hades in the deep subterranean levels, which hadn't caused real trouble in decades, maybe even centuries.

"Who in the city," Sandarov found himself saying, "*is* able to help you? Who or what?"

At that, the orange fire in both pairs of eyes dampened down to a glimmer.

"There is something," said Klaudius. "Either help, or its opposite."

"There *may* be something," said Hellah.

"We don't know what it is" – Klaudius gave a shrug that looked false, as if he were trying to disguise his real anxiety – "but there's a kind of resonance effect that we can pick up."

Hellah shook her head.

Klaudius said: "The Commissioner wanted us to use words he might understand, remember?"

"Well. Sure." A dismissive red-handed wave. "Go ahead, then."

"Outside the city centre proper." Klaudius looked down for a moment, then straight at Sandarov. "Thirty-seven and two-ninths of a mile from here, at a bearing of one-nine-four degrees, twenty-one minutes and five seconds."

"Did you want him to repeat that?" asked Hellah. "And how many times?"

Sanderson glanced down at the blotter on his desk. The digits and symbols were more shakily rendered than usual, but his desk had performed its job well enough.

"No need," Sandarov told Hellah. "And as for what's there…" He blinked, several times. "South-south-west, approximately, and around thirty-seven miles. Okay, I've got it."

"I suppose we'll need a map," said Hellah sourly, "and a little divination spell that even a witch could manage."

"Actually," said Klaudius, "I do believe the Commissioner has figured it out already."

Hella's orange eyes brightened again. "Really?"

"I know my city," said Sandarov. "And there's nothing much that lies in that direction, not that far out. So little chance of my making a mistake."

"Do tell," said Klaudius. "If you would, Commissioner."

"It's actually a hospital. Although I've never been there myself, I do know where it is."

Hellah and Klaudius looked at each other, with matching flame eyes.

"Called St Jarl's," added Sandarov. "We sometimes ferry hex crime victims there. Ensorcelment cases, that kind of thing."

"A hospital," said Hellah. "Where they heal things, or try to."

"Right," said Klaudius. "Whatever our friends down below are sensing, healing doesn't have a Hades of a lot to do with it."

Hellah looked at Sandarov with those blazing eyes. "They're not really our friends, Commissioner, so don't let my brother's irony blind you to the other danger here."

"I don't understand."

"She means," said Klaudius, "that if they grow any more perturbed, they may decide to break loose of this place, and make their way out through the city."

Sandarov felt the blood drain from his face. "They can't do that."

Hellah gave another of her short, spiteful laughs. "Think again. Ordinarily – well, no, ordinarily they wouldn't even care about moving from where they are right now – but where they might otherwise just swim out along the compactified dimensions…"

"Like wraiths," interjected Klaudius. "But thousands of times larger and commanding energies more like something a hundred thousand wraiths might manage. Maybe even more."

"… this time they won't go that way," continued Hellah, "because that's where the danger is coming from. So they'll stick with the macroscopic dimensions."

"In other words," said Klaudius, "what you think of as everyday reality."

"Yeah," muttered Sandarov. "I got that part."

Something shook his intestines. The skeleton clock with the shattered eyes paused and missed a stroke, while the grandfather clock sounded an off-pitch *bong* although it wasn't the top of the hour, or anywhere near.

Some wave of energy or whatever, rising upwards from the depths below them.

"Constructive interference," said Hellah.

"Magnified that ripple," said Klaudius.

As they looked at each other, the orange flames in their eyes seemed to circumnavigate their heptagonal irises, Hellah's travelling widdershins, Klaudius's in the opposite direction, so they looked again like mirror images of each other.

"It's getting worse down below, then." Sandarov made it a statement more than a question. "Tell me what I can do."

"Pee in your underwear," said Hellah, at the same time that Klaudius muttered: "Panic."

"I'm open to serious—"

"No, we need to go." Klaudius's eyes dimmed, out of synch with his sister's for a moment. "Quieten things down if we can."

Tension lines appeared on Hellah's face, and for the first time Sandarov felt sympathy for her, facing daily dangers and stresses he could never appreciate.

"Take care," he said. "Both of you, be careful down there."

After a second, Hellah gave an abrupt, wordless nod. Klaudius was already rising from his chair. "Alright, then."

The office door swung open before Sandarov could even turn in its direction. Hellah's mouth twitched at the corner, as she stood up next to her brother.

Another moment of hesitation, then the siblings strode out of the office, Klaudius marginally in the lead, to the open plan area beyond, which from Sandarov's position behind his desk looked to be deserted, despite the fact that a full shift was supposed to be on duty.

Frightening though they were, Klaudius and Hellah looked small and fragile as they entered the corridor beyond, heading for the bank of elevator tubes.

And all Sandarov could do was watch them go.

"No," he muttered. "There *is* something. St Jarl's. I'll send a team to—"

Sergeant Yorak half stumbled into the office, looking out of breath, his blue face glistening with sweat. "There's a major incident of some sort at City Hall. Massive hexplosions in Möbius Park, reports of casualties, possibly some dead Mordanto mages."

"*What?*"

"Rapid response teams are en route. Some officers from Robbery-Haunting were in the vicinity, and they're calling in reports, but so far they can't tell exactly what is happening, either."

As per his training, Sandarov took three deliberate breaths before answering. "Alright, Sergeant. Grab a vacant operations room, or turf out a team if you have to. Organise central command and control here, get whoever is senior on site to establish local command near Möbius Park, decision-making priority to whoever is on the ground."

"Sir."

"Do that now, and I'll be with you in a few moments. Go *now*."

"Yes, sir."

As Sergeant Yorak bolted out of the office, Sandarov tapped his desktop and said, "Drawer three, please. Right hand side."

It slid open before he finished speaking. Sandarov reached inside and drew out the dragonwing telephone, its nacreous surface shifting with highlights, and a hint of dark specks swimming deep inside.

He lifted the handset, and heard the humming of defensive line sprites.

"Give me Professor Steele. Aleph One priority."

The second time in his career that he'd needed to make such a call.

"Helena Steele here." The patrician tone cut like a crystal knife through the panic in Sandarov's head.

"Professor, we have a problem. Do you have mages working an emergency situation in Möbius Park?"

"That's in hand, Commissioner. I was about to transport myself there in person, just to check."

"It's not our only problem. There's something else happening at the same time."

"Something else?"

"The… *things* that live here, below the minus two hundred and seventy-third floor, are terrified. And something's happening, related somehow, at St Jarl's right now."

"That's not good. That's really not good."

Sandarov noticed his desk was trembling once more. He laid his palm on it, trying to calm the poor thing down.

"I'm setting up a coordinating team," he said into the phone. "I wonder if you could come over in person."

"I'll be right…" came from the receiver.

A sapphire point of light erupted in the centre of Sandarov's office, burst outwards and flared away to nothing, leaving an erect, straight-backed woman with white hair, dressed in a plain but elegant skirt suit, carrying a platinum-topped cane.

"…here," she said.

Professor Helena Steele.

Sandarov, frozen in place with telephone in hand, should have been relieved at her arrival, and would have been, were it not for his momentary glimpse of emotion in her clear grey eyes, right before she shut her expression down.

He'd never seen her scared before.

SEVEN

Donal hadn't worked with Levison since the Diva case, but standing here in a third-floor corridor in St Jarl's, with institutional paint on the walls and rune-inscribed parquet flooring beneath their feet, the strong smell of beetlewax polish all around, and that flat, deadening feel to the air, they might almost have been back in a precinct, if not HQ.

And Levison hadn't changed a bit.

His suit might have been the same one he wore on protection detail in the Théâtre du Loup Mort off Hoardway. He looked as if he hadn't shaved today, but that was misleading, because he always looked that way a few hours into his shift.

The two uniforms who'd arrived with Levison were new to Donal, and Levison hadn't introduced them. Probably the only thing that had gone differently, now that Donal was no longer a lieutenant with the Department.

One of the uniforms was currently standing watch down below in the basement level, as close to the darkness-enveloped lab as she could get, while her partner was outside the building in the patrol car, monitoring the radio.

"How's Tilly?" asked Donal.

"Hades, pal. You got Thanatos-knows-what growing down there in the basement, inside a sphere of black energy or something that's got the technical experts confused, scared totally witless, and you're making small talk?"

"Witless or something that sounds similar, right. Is Tilly still keeping you under control?"

"Of course she is. Although I had two tarantula cream doughnuts for lunch the other day, but don't tell anyone."

"I'd be too scared to. Your wife is a fearsome woman."

"Tell me something I don't know. When I told Fred and Freda you had a licence for that piece under your jacket, I wasn't lying, was I?"

"I'm legal," Donal told him. "The two uniforms are related? They look nothing like each other."

"Nah, they got assigned together ages back, just coz someone was amused by their names being identical, nearly. It kinda stuck. They work well together, too."

Donal nodded, pushed his hands in his pockets, and tried to work out how he felt about this situation. Whatever was happening inside Kyushen's lab – and whatever had happened to Kyushen himself – was on Donal. No getting away from that.

And not much point, he decided, in holding back what he knew. There was no client to protect. Maybe his own reputation, given that Kyushen had dismissed the white wolves as an old wives' tale, but so what?

Breaking through the black-and-silver barrier – which *was* spherical: extrusions into other rooms and corridors on the floor above the basement indicated as much – was a job for thaumaturgeons or mages, maybe witches, and certainly not a private investigator operating a long way out of his depth.

Donal decided to start at the beginning. "You ever meet Laura Steele?"

"Commander Steele? She had quite the reputation." Levison glanced at Donal's chest. "Talking about fearsome."

"Yeah, it was her heart they put inside me when I got shot." Donal blew out a breath. "Me and Laura, after I transferred to her team and before Blanz shot me, we weren't just colleagues, you know?"

"I heard she left you a fortune in her will, posh apartment in Darksan Tower, the lot. Except you gave it all away, right?"

"The Unity Party were confiscating zombies' bank accounts, and I'm pretty sure mine was one of them, when the city had all that trouble. And I signed over the apartment to Adam Obsidian and Ruth Zarenski, both task force cops, before the UP could take that too."

Levison shook his head. "Don't know 'em. Or much about that task force, either. Look, I need to know what happened today, alright?"

"Ah, I'm trying to tell you. You know Laura died, true death, when Blanz shot her in the head" – a brief mental glimpse of that destruction, grey mist in the air before Donal's own world went away – "which is why her heart was there and available when the medics opened up my chest on site, not that I was awake for that part." He stopped, seeing Levison's appalled expression.

Levison recovered, and gave a wry smile. "I don't remember you being this talkative."

"Maybe because I haven't had colleagues to talk to for a while. Colleagues or, well, friends."

"Uh-huh. So what exactly does your deceased, previous superior officer, with whom you had an inappropriate personal relationship, have to do with the thing in the basement here?"

"Did you say *whom*?"

"I've kept up the evening classes. So what's the story?"

"I was working out alone in the boxing gym last night. The place I got with Mel, Imelda Carson, who I'm with these days. Sorry, *whom*."

"I got the invitation to the opening, Donal. To the barbecue. But Tilly was sick."

Something clouded in Levison's eyes, and Donal realised that things weren't perfect in his home life after all. Tilly's fearsomeness was part of what Levison clearly loved her for, his grumpy complaining just a cover for tenderness; but now, Levison was hurting inside.

Donal softened his voice and guessed: "She's got some medical condition, does she?"

"Yeah." Levison rubbed his face. "Look, just tell me, will you?"

"Some apparition that looked and sounded like Laura, exactly like her, told me to go to my office, and when I got there a white wolf looked at me, or something" – Donal ran his hand through his hair, remembering – "and when I woke up there was a black glass skull, obsidian kind of thing, lying on my desk, and no sign of the Thanatos-damned wolf."

Levison's mouth dropped open, wordlessly.

"And the skull talks to me," added Donal, "but Mel can't hear a thing or see its mouth, jawbone, move. Sarcastic sense of humour, too. I mean the skull, not Mel. Although she has her moments."

"Sweet screaming Hades. So you took the skull here?"

"For Dr Kyushen Jyu to investigate. He's helped us out before." Donal pulled his hands out of his pockets and shook his head. "I mean he's helped the Department. He's a ThD, not an MD."

Donal heard a sound and turned. The uniform they'd left outside, Fred presumably, was hurrying along the corridor, coming this way. He looked like someone trying not to run.

"What's up?" asked Levison.

"Message from Commander Bowman, says the scene will be secured shortly. And, er, they want Mr Riordan" – Fred shot a glance at Donal – "back at HQ. Something to do with the Commissioner."

It was Donal who'd called in a report from the Chief Thaumaturgeon's office here on the third floor. Since Donal was out of his depth regarding the phenomenon in the basement, it had been his only possible course of action.

Which logically meant he was less use to an investigation than any of the St Jarl's staff, who all knew vastly more about hex-related matters than he did. Hex or whatever this was.

"I've told you everything," he said to Levison. "I'm a civilian as far as this case is concerned. Or any case, actually."

"And a helpful witness, right?"

Donal shook his head, but not in denial. Levison had him there.

"So I'll radio back," said Fred. "Say you'll be right along."

"Sure," Donal told him. "I'll need a ride, though."

"The Commander said not to worry about that. You or me."

"What does that mean?"

Fred shrugged inside his uniform. "Beats me. I figured pressing the Commander on details was like a, what, sub-optimal career-advancing move."

"It's a good job I left the Department," said Donal. "All this elegant language and all, you guys are getting far too educated for me. Sophisticated, even."

"Screw a bunch of sophisticated." Levison looked at Fred. "Anything else? Don't worry about the witness here overhearing. He's going to behave himself and do the right thing."

"Oh." Fred blinked, his attention on Donal. "You're *that* Riordan. Now it makes sense."

"What does?"

"Er, the Commissioner said to act respectful but, um, expect loyalty and don't take no for answer."

"Thanatos," said Donal, while Levison chuckled.

A group of medics, some in black medical coats, others in business suits, appeared at the far end of the corridor. They looked like a deputation, striding faster this way on sighting Levison, all of them frowning.

Half a dozen Night Sisters trailed the medics, Felice among them, none of them looking happy either.

"What's happening outside?" called a heavyset woman at the front of the advancing group.

She might have been the Deputy Chief Thaumaturgeon, although Donal hadn't been paying much attention to names and titles a short while earlier, when he burst into the admin area and told them to call Avenue of the Basilisks right away, deliberately opening his jacket so everyone could see his holstered Magnus; although if bullets could solve every problem, he might have dealt with the intrusion in the lab singlehandedly, and avoided all this ruckus.

"Outside?" Levison looked at Fred, who shook his head, clearly having no idea what this meant.

Donal was already moving, heading for the main stairs fast, because if something was changing then the time for talk was over.

He was first down the staircase and out through the impossibly pentagon-tiled vestibule to descend the outdoor steps, jogging to a halt with gravel crunching beneath his feet, feeling the closeness of the air pressing heavily against his skin, before he processed the strange turbulent pattern twisting in the dark-purple sky.

A group of five black pteracopters, in a V-shaped formation, burst out of the centre of that disturbance. They hung in place for a moment, then the lead pteractopter began a vertical descent almost directly above Donal, while the others split into two pairs, each pair heading for a clear area, beyond the east and west wings of St Jarl's main complex: dark and crenellated and punctuated with gloomy, pointed towers.

The nearest pteracopter commenced its landing procedure.

The air pounded, shaking Donal inside, but he forced himself to squint upwards while everyone else was cowering away from the downdraught, and he realised the descending 'copter was armoured and equipped with twin Spellstorm missile launchers, bulky and pregnant with death, mounted on either side of the fuselage, or whatever you called it on a pteracopter.

Maybe overkill, maybe not.

Depending on what the Hades was producing that black-and-silver energy field centred on the skull in Kyushen's lab. What it was, and what it was up to.

As for the people inside the pteracopter, Donal knew what he was going to see even before the 'copter touched down on its skids and the occupants launched themselves out while the thing was still rocking.

Black suits, white shirts, black ties, wraparound shades, and stone-faced expressions to match. Lithe, no-nonsense movement.

Donal found himself smiling.

"What the Hades?" Levison, puffing, came out of the main doors behind Donal, followed by three Night Sisters – including Felice – who must have run faster than the rest because they'd started at the rear of the group.

Donal nodded to Felice, but directed his words to Levison. "You can relax, bud. The feds are here."

"Just what I needed."

One of the thaumaturgeons burst out of the doorway. "What exactly is going on out—Oh."

"Right." Felice sounded almost amused. "Federal spellbinders."

The thaumaturgeon blanched.

And shifted out of the way, like everybody else including Donal, as the spellbinders headed wordlessly into the building.

Nobody else's business now.

The pteracopter's rotors continued to whip around, and after a moment Donal realised that, inside the semi-darkened hexiglass of the 'copter's cockpit or flight cabin or whatever it was called, the pilot was gesturing, stabbing an urgent forefinger in Levison's direction.

"Hey," called Donal, attracting Fred's attention but not Levison, who was staring at the main St Jarl's entrance that the federal spellbinders had used, moving fast without appearing to actually run up the steps.

Or maybe Levison was looking at the St Jarl's staff, none of whom seemed tempted to follow the spellbinders back inside.

Presumably the patients were in other medics' care, or else the assumption was that the wards and operating theatres and all the rest were either outside the danger zone or at such high risk that no extra presence could help them.

Fred tugged Levison's sleeve and pointed at Donal, and when Levison turned, Donal gestured towards the pteracopter. Levison jogged over, holding the lapels of his jacket shut against the draught, and was soon engaged in a shouted exchange of brief words with the pilot.

Donal would have been tempted to try and lip-read, but he'd never properly learned the skill, so instead he turned back to the building in time to see Sister Lynkse come out shaking and crying, and half stumble down to join her colleagues, several of whom circled around and hugged her; and Donal cursed inside himself because she was Kyushen's lover and petrified with fear for him, and that was Donal's fault.

Levison came over and shouted into Donal's ear: "You need to get in the 'copter. Fly to HQ."

It wasn't what Donal wanted to do, because all of his training and experience was telling him to take sudden and violent action right now, except for the wiser part insisting that there was no effective move he could make besides detaching and observing, waiting for an opening to occur.

You learned it in the boxing ring and in the midst of battle and sometimes on the street: occasionally, waiting and watching formed the only course available, and the trick was to do it with a proactive, aggressive frame of mind.

"Thanatos damn it," he muttered, not loudly enough for anyone to hear above the pteractopter's din; but Levison twitched his mouth and withdrew all the same.

Donal headed for the 'copter.

A minute later, Donal was strapped in and staring out of a side window as the gravel drive dropped away below. Beyond the building's wing on that side, he could see one of the other landed pteracopters, its rotors still, and part of another 'copter beside it. No sign of the federal spellbinders who'd travelled inside: they must be in the building, doing whatever they had to in order to "secure the scene" – which could mean pretty much anything when the feds were involved.

As St Jarl's swung out of view, Donal caught one last glimpse of Levison talking to a sobbing Night Sister who had to be Felice – Donal was almost sure of it – then Levison was reaching inside his jacket and coming out with handcuffs.

Progress in the case? Something Donal could help with?

But there was no point in trying to talk to the pilot who looked intent on flying the 'copter, her features stone hard, an awful lot like the spellbinders who'd entered St Jarl's, and Donal wondered if she was an agent too.

They straightened up and headed towards the heart of Tristopolis.

None of this felt good.

EIGHT

The Vixen was a low, dark car with fins, the kind of car no one got in the way of, not if they had any sense.

She was headed out of the city proper, her amber headlights cutting into the darkness of the straight F-779, the federal highway that effectively bisected Black Iron Forest if you looked on a map, but only because maps tend to highlight travel routes and not their surroundings.

In fact, she was the only vehicle in sight, and had been for quite some time, even at the speed she was travelling at. The forest's vastness eclipsed and swallowed the insignificant line of the highway, rendering it irrelevant to the actual reality of the surrounding world.

The road didn't cut through the forest: not at all. The forest barely tolerated its minimal existence.

Heart-rending howls sounded from time to time amid the trees, audible even over the Vixen's rushing slipstream, occasionally accompanied by glimpses of amber eyes, not too dissimilar in shade from the Vixen's twin headlights. Those glowing eyes flickered inside the forest, their owners running fast, always dropping back into darkness after a time.

The Vixen hurtled on.

It was several hours before she reached the Tartrous Trail, slowed down and almost halted, then growled her engine and took the Trail, speeding up again, leaving the federal highway behind.

Even if someone were looking for her with scanbats or pteracopters or the like, which seemed massively unlikely in any case, they would never spot her now.

An hour later, she exited the Tartrous Trail in favour of another road, unnamed and even narrower, heading deeper and deeper into Black Iron Forest, most of whose trees were indeed jet black, while others glimmered silver-white or were largely transparent, as dark as the deep-purple sky overhead, occasionally flaring with wild sprite fire but otherwise scarcely visible.

Next to a low hill, the Vixen rolled to a halt.

Her engine moaned and grew silent.

All around, the forest air felt still, as if the trees were holding their collective breath.

No life here. Or at least, not the kind that the Vixen might wish for.

At some point, decades past, someone had dug into the hillside to create a subterranean cottage; but now it stood empty, its once-strong metal door crumpled and rusted, discarded on the ground, the remains of ripped-apart hinges hanging in the doorway.

Darkness inside. Black windows like a skull's empty eye sockets.

You might have expected some wild creatures to have made their homes here, even if temporarily, but from what the Vixen could sense, even insects and spiders steered clear of the ruin.

Twisted wands of metal dotted the ground, loosely circling the hill. The remains of protective wards, blasted by hex too powerful to stop.

And on a leaning post, a moss-covered notice bearing the federal Salamander-and-Eagle insignia declared the property a crime scene, under the legal jurisdiction and protection of the Tristopolitan authorities, for a period lasting until the 1st of Pentember 6607.

But that was twelve months ago.

No one had cared enough to come here since.

A dark lake lay beyond the hill, so the Vixen started her engine and rolled slowly towards it, bumping her way off the track and onto uneven soil that lay thick with black grass. She drove all the way to the muddy edge, until her front tyres almost touched the still, viscous-looking water.

She could do it.

Roll in further and let the waters roll over her, and allow it all to stop. Let everything stop.

And wait for rust and dissolution to come, if it ever would.

Yes, she could do that.

But she preferred a more definite ending, a gesture more in keeping with her sometimes fiery nature. If you could call it a gesture, given that she preferred to end her existence away from anyone else's sight, and if no one ever discovered her dead remains, that was perfectly fine with her.

Still, the dark lake tempted her.

In the end, it was the thought that this journey was a pilgrimage, yet to be completed, that took her away from thoughts of immediate self-immolation, because there was one more place she had to visit, and contemplate, think hard about the past, and consider all the decisions that had taken her to her current predicament.

To a point where she deserved to die.

It took another hour and three-sevenths to find her way back along the nameless road, then the Tartrous Trail, and finally to rejoin the federal highway.

There, she headed north-northwest, not the straight-line path an airplane or pteracopter might take, but the shortest route a land-bound entity could follow if she were headed for the capital of the Federation, the most important city in terms of government; even though the Vixen, like all Tristopolitans, felt in her heart that her own city was, in some true sense, the capital of the world, never mind the Federation.

Something might have slipped across the sky to the south, some flying shadow, but the Vixen no longer cared. She knew what she was doing now.

Opening up her throttle, she roared along the straight dark, otherwise unlit highway, her amber high beams blazing: one last thundering ride before the end.

Heading at maximum speed towards Fortinium.

To the place where her sister Laura had died.

NINE

The pteracopter's cabin continued to pulse with thunder as they passed over landmarks in the city: landmarks that Donal recognised. There stood the familiar two-thousand-foot-high skull pierced by the Orb-Dexter Freeway plus ramps to and from a profusion of lesser roads.

And passing down below, almost directly beneath the 'copter, a vast dark tower that Donal had never seen from this angle, yet recognised immediately.

The address was One, Avenue of the Basilisks, and already it was receding behind them as the pteracopter thundered on.

"Hey!" Donal shouted above the din, and tapped the pilot's shoulder, lightly because he didn't want to distract her too much. "We've gone past Police HQ."

The pilot glanced at him, gave the minutest of head shakes, and returned her attention to the world ahead.

For all his zombie acuity, Donal had no idea what that head shake meant: whether she couldn't hear him or could hear every word distinctly, but didn't want to talk about matters that were none of his concern. Perhaps because from her point of view a passenger mattered no more than some item of inanimate cargo.

Although she wore a jumpsuit and lacked anti-trance shades – perhaps the cabin's tinted hexiglass performed the same function as far as the outside world was concerned – the attitude settled a question in Donal's mind: she was an agent, a federal spellbinder, for sure.

And as for their destination, well, he'd find out when they landed, so that was that.

Except that a minute later, he was able to guess where they were going, or at least intending to go, from the firework-like flickering of definite hexplosions – small ones, like grenades or mortar fire – and lines of tracer bullets whose silvery, pulsing light could only mean enchanted spell-piercing rounds, all of it taking place in a dark stretch of open ground within high walls right in the heart of Tristopolis, because that was Möbius Park down below.

Möbius Park, in whose grounds stood the centuries-old edifice that was City Hall.

The park was guarded, or supposed to be guarded, by subterranean ectoplasma wraiths of the nastiest sort, who stripped flesh from the bones of any unauthorised visitors and occasionally, it was rumoured, took down innocent passers-by outside the park walls, when there was no one else around to observe what happened.

Vicious and horrible, so where the Hades were they now, if open conflict was occurring below? Unless they were part of the problem, but Donal couldn't see that happening.

The pilot took the pteracopter lower and closer, assessing the mage fire beneath them, then commenced a straight-line descent to a spot inside one of the tall gateways filled with curved, nasty-looking fangs.

"Dragon Maw Gate," said Donal as his seat rocked with the controlled impact of touchdown. "And no iceghouls in sight."

Whether the pilot could hear him, Donal had no idea, and didn't really care. It took him an entire seven seconds to detach his safety belt's necromagnetic fastenings, roll sideways out through the hatch as it folded open automatically, land in a crouch and jog clear of the still-spinning rotors whose downdraught beat at his head and the back of his shoulders, even as he felt relief from escaping the pteracopter cabin and returning to fresh air.

There should have been iceghouls checking out new arrivals, not to mention those ectoplasma wraiths waiting to deal with anyone who failed to pass the iceghouls' checks or attempted to sneak past, but none of that was happening.

He glanced back at the pteracopter, whose rotors continued to turn in place, the pilot scarcely visible behind the tinted hexiglass. Maybe the Spellstorm rocket clusters mounted on both sides of the 'copter weren't aggressive overkill, after all.

Donal turned his attention to the ground in front of him, moving faster now.

He reached for his holstered Magnus but stopped, because whatever enemy action was taking place, it probably wasn't something he could affect by shooting at it; while on the other hand, presenting a hostile image to any friendlies – like combat mages currently under fire – could result in Donal's sudden immolation.

"A sub-optimal outcome," he muttered to himself as he came to a halt, thinking that maybe he wasn't so different from cops like Fred and Levison after all.

Which begged the question: why was he here?

"Riordan," said a voice that might have been entirely in Donal's head, and added: "Ahead left, there's a copse, a group of trees, and that's where we are."

"I know what a Thanatos-damned copse is," muttered Donal. "I may be a Lower Danklyn boy, but I ain't stupid."

Sister Mary-Anne Styx and her colleagues in the orphanage school had seen to that. Whatever else his childhood had lacked, there had been books and boxing; and that had always been enough.

"I'm a friend of Mage Kelvin," the voice continued. "Well, more of a colleague. Subordinate, even. Er, Kelvin would contact you directly, but he's a little busy now."

"Wonderful. If you see someone with a gun in their hand, don't chuck any hex. It'll be me, most likely."

By the time Donal finished the sentence, he'd drawn the Magnus without slowing down, running now with his elbow close to his body, in a decent position to turn through any required angle and fire using the instinctive shooting method, in contrast to extending one or both arms to consciously aim at whoever or whatever was attacking you.

It mightn't do any good, not when the dark air was exploding in sparks and oddly coloured flames – green and indigo as much as yellow-orange – most likely as trivial side effects of the real mage-level conflict; but any small chance trumped zero.

The air felt colder than it should have done.

Soon he gained the cover of the trees, black twigs snapping at his face but not enough to do real damage, with the exception of a vicious-looking bone-thick branch that whipped in his direction, and which Donal blocked with the butt of his Magnus, feeling the shock run through his arm. He slipped under the branch and simply ran on, heading into the heart of the copse.

He considered firing back into the tree just to teach it a lesson, but wasting rounds went against his training, so he dismissed the idea, forgetting it completely.

And then he was jogging to a halt inside a dark clearing, a dell containing seven, no, eight mages, two of whom lay unconscious or dead on the grass, while another looked to be strapped into an odd-looking stretcher, moaning and weakly struggling against his bonds.

Mage Kelvin, shaven-headed and strong-featured, was working busily inside a fiery framework of white-gold light, runic symbols glowing in the air, shifting and sliding in rows and columns as he gestured and manipulated energies using Thanatos-knew-what techniques that Donal could sense only as weird vibrations inside his skin, and slivers of ice sliding directly along his nerves.

But he could read the mage's expression easily enough, and knew this fight was going badly.

A younger mage with a shock of coppery red hair gestured at Donal. "I called you. Over here."

The voice was simultaneously different from and yet identical to the one in Donal's head, less than a minute earlier.

Mages. The world rarely made sense when they were around.

"What's going on?" Donal reached the beckoning mage. "And what's your name?"

"My—? I'm Anderl. Anderl Havoch. Pleased to meet you, Donal Riordan."

Donal shook his head at the incongruous courtesy. "I thought I was going to see the Commissioner at HQ. Or at least Commander Bowman."

"HQ?"

"Tristopolis PD Headquarters. At Avenue of the—"

"Oh, *police*. That'll come later, I suppose." Anderl ran a hand through his unruly red hair. "Kelvin's creating a manifold map, or trying to."

"Am I supposed to know what that is?" Donal glanced at the three unwounded mages standing nearby, two men and one woman, their faces blank, surrounded by a faint sapphire haze. "Or what they're up to?"

"Keeping us from dying, for a start," said Anderl. "You wouldn't believe the energies at play out there."

He gestured towards the trees, or more likely the direction in which City Hall lay out of sight. At that moment, a greater explosion lit the sky, like the climax of some firework show, but accompanied by waves of iciness slamming through the air.

Then a billowing sheet of light appeared next to Kelvin, and Anderl tugged at Donal's sleeve then pointed, clearly unaware of how close he'd just come to getting a Magnus smashed into his teeth.

"See?" Anderl grinned, showing those teeth in a way that looked boyish. "A manifold map."

"Wonderful. How does that help?"

"It allows Agent Chambers to pinpoint the weak areas. Except everything's shifting about so much, I'm not sure it'll help her."

Donal looked up as thunder moved overhead. From underneath, the pteractopter looked hard and menacing, the twin Spellstorm clusters, each bearing nine of the eponymous missiles, looking as lethal as they actually were.

"Is Federal Agent Chambers a pilot, by any chance?"

"Oh, yes." A twitch from Anderl's mouth. "I thought you knew."

"And is she intending to use—"

Massive vibrations accompanied the tearing apart of air, diagonal columns of sundering from pteracopter to ground, and a roaring upward explosion of concurrent detonations: pure destruction at its simplest, rawest best.

"—the Spellstorms." It was no longer a question.

The ground pulsed and Donal, adjusting balance, grabbed young Anderl's sleeve to keep Anderl upright. They were lucky the impact point was at least half a mile way.

This was a big park.

"Whew. Thank you, Mr Riordan."

"Any time." Donal let go of Anderl's sleeve.

Around them, the park grew quiet. Even the trees stopped moving, agitated and angry – or frightened – though they'd been just seconds earlier.

Mage Kelvin straightened and smiled as the glowing runes and lines surrounding him faded away, until only an after image, or something very like it, remained.

A buffered, ghostly almost-image that could probably be summoned back to full strength with minimal delay: the mage equivalent of a round in the chamber. Most likely. Not that you could ever be sure, with mages.

"Donal. How very good to see you."

"Kelvin." Donal hadn't realised they were on first name terms, but he could go with it. "Likewise."

He held out his hand, and after a half second pause, Mage Kelvin – or simply Kelvin now – returned the gesture and they shook, while Anderl watched, blinking in obvious surprise.

"This thing is more, well, serious," said Kelvin, "than what we got up to in the Energy Authority that time."

"I don't see any captive, mindless children being used as fuel."

A hissing intake of breath from Anderl caused Kelvin to look at him. "I need you," said Kelvin, "to summon scanbats for an overflight, to check ground zero. Can you do that?"

"Um, yes, Mage."

"Then do it now."

"Right away." Anderl turned away and began to create a glowing framework of his own, narrower and weakly glimmering in comparison to Kelvin's manifestation.

To Donal, Kelvin added: "I'm pretty sure we've driven it underground, by which I mean the compactified hyperdimensions, not mud and rock. But only for a while."

"Oh," said Donal, trying to parse meaning from the words. "What do you mean by *it*?"

Besides something so powerful that even a missile strike of eighteen Spellstorms fired together couldn't kill it, because Donal was pretty sure that Chambers had launched all nine missiles from each cluster, both clusters at once.

"Well, that's the key question. And if I were half the mage people think I should be, I'd have a brilliantly incisive answer to give you right now, but I don't."

"Too many sleepless nights," muttered Anderl. "That's what happens when you have babies. My mother produced twins when I was sixteen, and I was never so happy as when I left home, five months later." He spoke without looking away from his framework of yellow light, which shone a little brighter now. "Even though I was headed for the Zeroth Trials along with all the other Mordantelle would-be recruits."

That would be the basic training academy linked to Mordanto proper, in some complicated fashion Donal didn't entirely understand.

"Anderl," said Kelvin.

"I'm doing it. Co-opted a flock from TPD eyries, which were closer than our own. No alarm resonances. The ground looks clear."

"I'll need to check a scanbat myself before we examine the ground in person."

From all this mage talk, Donal extracted one thing: whatever the threat was, it frightened a senior mage enough to need double checks before even venturing onto ground from which said threat had almost certainly departed.

"I'd like to know why I'm here. And" – Donal looked down at the Magnus in his hand, then reholstered it beneath his jacket – "what the Hades you expect me to contribute to… whatever it is you're up to."

"There's a threat to the city." Anderl held up a hand as if to stabilise his framework of light while he looked at Donal. "Isn't that enough?"

Kelvin sighed. "That's enough from *you*."

"Yes, Mage."

"Unless you require another solitary spell, you'll remain silent now."

Anderl nodded and returned to his work, whatever it was. His lips had tightened. Clearly *solitary spell* wasn't meant in a pleasant, take-a-quiet-break kind of way.

Mages.

Too certain of themselves, and they weren't the only ones.

"Me and Mel, she's my partner," said Donal, "we do our shopping in Tillyghast Groceries, in a little alleyway off Serpentine Twist. Maybe a mile from the Danklyn end of Hoardway Extension."

"Excuse me?" Kelvin glanced at Anderl as though the younger mage might elucidate, but Anderl was keeping focused on his work.

"So next time," said Donal, "when we're at the cash register and the ghoul on duty asks for money, I'll just say it's okay, I've been helping out mages. So the ghoul will just hand over the groceries free of charge, and wave me and Mel goodbye. Right?"

"Ah."

"Right, ah. Because that's not going to happen. Funny how people being paid a salary keep expecting me to work for free, helping them. With *their* work. That they're being paid to do."

Kelvin looked up. Without Donal hearing it, a scanbat had manoeuvred into place directly overhead. Seen from this close, it resembled a person-sized moth as much as a bat, including the insectile head.

"I'll do it." That was one of the other three mages, the woman, who'd been engaged in some other facet of the battle that involved all three of them being immersed in a single conjoined sapphire glow: a shade of blue light that Donal associated with mage teleportation, although he might have been mistaken in that.

"Are you sure, Carolina?" Kelvin asked the mage.

"I've enough strength left. Besides" – with a half smile – "we'll all feel safer if you maintain vigilance, Mage Kelvin."

Kelvin nodded his shaven head. "Go ahead."

Donal knew what would happen next. The scanbat would descend until its head and the mage's head occupied the same volume of space, the phenomenon that Tristopolis PD training manuals described as quantal superposition, without explaining how the Hades such a thing could occur in real life.

The scanbat's surveillance perceptions would merge, somehow, with the mage's own memories: the mage would remember every observation, as though she had made the flight herself.

It was fascinating, but Donal had seen it before.

"See you," he said.

And he turned and walked away.

No one called out from behind him.

Good.

Wise move on their part.

Donal made his way among the trees. As he reached the one whose branch had whipped towards his face earlier, the tree flinched, the imprint of the Magnus butt visible on the branch's bark.

"Don't worry about it." Donal patted its trunk. "I was scared too."

He exited onto an open stretch of black grass, cropped lawn-short by maintenance ghouls who were nowhere in sight, no more than the ectoplasma wraiths and iceghouls, and of course he couldn't blame them.

Even indentured beings were bound by contracts with work conditions, and remaining in place while disaster exploded all around wasn't necessarily covered in the agreement. Although come to think of it, for the ectoplasma wraiths, as security staff authorised to kill, it probably was.

Off to one side he could see a team of SWAT officers looking in his direction. They were probably the source of the tracer fire he'd seen earlier, from the pteracopter. He raised a hand.

Surprisingly, one of the officers waved back.

Donal stopped and focused hard, squinting a little as the distant officer pulled off his helmet and tugged down his goggles to throat level.

"Adam Obsidian," Donal called out. "Good to see you."

Not sure if his voice could carry that far.

Regardless, Adam waved again, then turned back to his team, ignoring Donal now.

Since when had Adam transferred to a Sorcerous Weapons Assault Team? It was a good fit for an ex-Marine – the same ex-Marine whose sniper skills had saved Donal in Illurium – but the last Donal knew, Adam had been working plainclothes as part of the—

Never mind. Nothing to do with me.

Not these days.

Donal reached the fangs of Dragon Maw Gate, ironbone fangs that reared hard and impenetrable as ever, and he stopped.

And stared very hard.

"I'm not in the mood."

After a second, the fangs ground open, screeching as if they needed oiling.

"Good choice."

He exited onto the street outside.

TEN

Commisioner Sandarov prowled his office until his agitation transferred to the furniture once more.

The desk had evinced a nervous disposition ever since he acquired the thing on being promoted to captain, back in the day; but now even the grandfather clock, normally staid, even stoic, was swinging its pendulum erratically.

Perhaps it missed the skeleton clock, currently down with the maintenance sorcerors having its crystalline eyes replaced or regrown or whatever the Hades they did. Sandarov didn't want to know.

"Sir?"

"What?" Sandarov whirled, thinking it was lucky that he didn't wear a firearm on the job these days, because he might have whipped it out in that moment, although hopefully not fired: there's a point where nervous energy flips from being helpful to disastrous, and shooting Sergeant Yorak would have been tragic.

Particularly for Yorak.

"Um." A gulp, as though Yorak understood what Sandarov had just imagined. "There's been an arrest. Commander Bowman is going down to, er, observe the interrogation right now."

"Good. Who's the suspect?" No need to ask which case Yorak meant, not with Professor Helena Steele's appearance and disappearance earlier, and the ongoing situation in Möbius Park.

Reflected highlights shifted across Yorak's shaven blue scalp as he shook his head. "A Night Sister from St Jarl's. It's hard to credit, really."

Sandarov looked at him carefully. "Are you saying it's a bad arrest?"

"Apparently she confessed to something. To Sergeant Levison, there on site. At St Jarl's, I mean."

"But you think there's something odd about it."

Street smarts were invaluable on the beat and during plainclothes investigations at crime scenes and going door to door. Yorak's time on foot patrol, when he'd been a raw junior officer, resulted in performance reviews rating him as barely adequate despite his natural empathy with members of the public.

That was a polite bureaucratic way of labelling him incompetent on the mean streets but a potential asset for the Department if utilised in other ways.

The more Sandarov's role as commissioner required dealing with admin and bureaucracy, the more he came to admire – or at least recognise with gratitude – Yorak's ability to grind through detail and organise masses of paperwork, and extract pertinent conclusions from reams of tedious information.

Mountains of inscribed vellum that would have had Sandarov putting a bullet through his own head if forced to wade through it all.

"Sir, you know the old saying, that a Night Sister can do no wrong?"

"I remember locker room talk about girls in uniform. Not the kind of banter I encourage, Sergeant."

"No, sir. But it's actually… You know we, I mean the Department, help carry out the criminal background checks for student Night Sister applicants, in collaboration with the Ministry of Retribution."

"Uh, huh. Court documents, kind of thing."

"And arrest records, sir. Well the thing is, transferring the results into the format required for the College of—"

"Is this going somewhere meaningful, Sergeant Yorak?"

"I just mean it's literally true. The saying about doing no wrong."

"What?"

"A Night Sister is incapable of carrying out an action she believes to be immoral. She cannot do it."

Sandarov considered this. Between selection processes and education procedures, when you added in neurospell scanners and modification thaumaturgy, maybe you could instil such rigorous behavioural standards for real.

Perhaps it wasn't so different from military service, taking soft civilians and hardening them up through seven months of basic training, until you had people tough enough to survive battlefield drills and finally the real thing.

"So you're saying they can't act immorally? And that applies to every single Night Sister?"

"Yes, sir."

"Is that the same as saying they can't act illegally?"

"Um…"

"I think I'll go down and take a look for myself."

"Yes, sir."

It had been an effort for Sandarov to stay out of the operations room, knowing full well that his presence would have been counter-productive at best.

Like the locker room talk that he discouraged: sometimes the banter between working officers reached Entity Resources violation levels as a natural consequence of the awful stuff they dealt with day to day; and the higher a visiting officer's rank, the more likely the intrusion was to dampen the creative friction: the very friction needed to crack the case open.

So he'd kept to his office, maintaining that necessary separation, while wishing it were otherwise.

To put it another way: he'd been waiting for an excuse to get involved.

The operations room that Yorak had set up was on the same floor as Sandarov's office, but the questioning was taking place seventeen storeys down, so that was where Sandarov told the elevator wraith to carry him as he stepped into the vertical shaft.

Yes, Commissioner.

Not all wraiths maintained formality, but the ones who did seemed to be the most efficient. Or maybe that was a biased observation, given his own high regard for discipline.

Sandarov nodded his thanks as he stepped out onto the 170th floor.

A minute later, he entered an observation room, where a lean, fiftyish athletic man with pale skin and cropped rust-coloured hair – Commander Bowman, looking almost as he had before resurrection – was standing close to what appeared to be a threshold leading to the interrogation chamber, although if you tried to cross that threshold you'd fall back with a thump and perhaps a bloody nose, because a solid wall blocked the way.

Solid, but transparent to the point of invisibility, though only from this side.

"Commander," said Sandarov as Bowman turned. "Any progress?"

Only a pale Night Sister with entrancing blue eyes currently occupied the interrogation chamber, her wrists linked by slender platinum chains to hex bolts in the tabletop, the table itself being formed of solid stone petri-welded to the chamber floor.

Giving prisoners time to mull over their situation formed a standard part of questioning.

"We're getting there, Commisioner. I've got Detective Zarenski asking the questions, because she's known to the suspect, whose name is Sister Felice."

"Is that wise?" Sandarov kept judgment out of his tone, knowing that Bowman, with his resurrected person's sensory acuity, would understand this to be a simple question, not an accusation.

"Sister Felice came forward to confess. She may not even have committed a crime, although" – Bowman gestured to the interrogation chamber – "if she's responsible for what happened in Möbius Park as well as St Jarl's, there'll be a charge of negligent homicide at least."

"And how does she know Detective Zarenski?"

"Ruth, that's Detective Zarenski, was part of the team that Donal Riordan put together to bust open that thing at the Energy Authority. Sister Felice was one of three civilians that Riordan co-opted to help."

"Okay…"

"The other two being Dr Kyushen Jyu, currently trapped inside some kind of hex field or worse at St Jarl's, and Kelvin Johannsson of Mordanto. If you can call him a civilian." Bowman glanced at the captive Night Sister, then turned back to Sandarov. "Mage Kelvin is leading the major Mordanto response team at Möbius Park right now, after a first three-person team was killed. Or so we think."

"Are all these links suspicious in themselves, or is it just that these people all knowing each other got them involved in the same thing?" Sandarov rubbed his face. "Ugh, that's clumsily put. What I mean is—"

"I understand, Commissioner. So far, it looks like the only wrongdoing is Sister Felice's own actions. Wrongdoing or misjudgement."

"Hmm."

There was a tap on the door that Sandarov had entered by, then it swung open to reveal a long-haired witch carrying a five-ring ratskin binder emblazoned with the federal Salamander-and-Eagle, the insignia glowing the same soft silver as the rat skull amulet that the witch wore at her throat.

"Commissioner. Commander."

Sandarov knew better than to ask for her name. He nodded instead, while Bowman inclined his head respectfully, not quite bowing.

The witch faced the transparent wall, opened her binder and held it in both hands, revealing vellum pages that looked blank, save for today's date written as a heading in cursive purple script.

"Very thorough," Sandarov told Bowman.

"Thank you, sir."

Not everyone would have thought to bring in a witch for this.

Every cop was trance-shielded and otherwise trained in hex spotting, spell listening and the like, but only to a degree. A fully certified observer – Sandarov guessed the witch possessed truthseer capabilities also – would pick up on odd resonances in the suspect's words or thoughts.

Not just reading between the lines of their responses to questions, but actively searching for signs of possession or ensorcellment, any hints of coercion, even the deep subconscious kind that the suspect might prove unaware of.

Preventing miscarriages of justice formed a side effect that Sandarov approved of, though he knew the practice was really due to the Ministry of Retribution's deep institutional desire to always find the actual guilty party in every case.

Different emphasis, same result.

Sister Felice turned her head to look at the opposite wall, remained still for an elongated moment, then looked this way, gave the tiniest of smiles, and returned her attention to straight ahead, her gaze distant and perhaps a little sad.

Two detectives entered: a lean man with seventeen o'clock shadow and seen-it-all eyes, and a hard-faced woman with short hair.

"Levison and Zarenski," said Bowman.

"Have they worked together before?"

"No, sir. But they're both experienced, and smart."

"Fair enough."

The detectives pulled out bone-frame chairs, scraping them across the stone floor, and sat down facing the suspect, Sister Felice.

Here in the observation room, the nameless witch took a half step forward, towards the invisible dividing wall.

"Something wrong?" Bowman had noticed even before Sandarov.

"I don't know." The witch transferred her open binder to her left hand only, and pressed her right hand against the wall. "I'm not sensing resistance or subterfuge on the suspect's part. But there is… something."

In the interrogation chamber, Detective Zarenski picked up where, Sandarov guessed, she'd previously left off, before taking a deliberate break.

Letting the suspect worry alone.

Now Zarenski scowled. "Tell me again where you bought the skull, Felice."

Using the suspect's first name without a title. Classic.

Except they weren't strangers to each other. Sandarov had forgotten that for a moment.

"Parasite Alley, Gregor's Emporium."

"We're trying to understand." Levison kept his tone mild. "What happened there, exactly?"

"What do you mean?" Sister Felice blinked, and the pupils of her eyes narrowed, not quite to vertical slits. "I paid twenty-nine florins, more than I could afford but that was the price, and the guy who owned the place, I suppose you might call him a bit greasy, put the skull in a wormskin bag and handed it to me." A puzzled shrug. "What else would you expect?"

"How did Mr Stevanovic look when you left him?" Zarenski's voice sounded as hard as the impregnable walls that had contained so many suspects and prisoners over the decades and centuries.

"Did he try to do anything to you?" asked Levison sympathetically.

Sister Felice exhaled, the backs of her hands on the tabletop, palms upward, the picture of resigned helplessness. "I already confessed that it's all my fault. This Mr Stevin-what's-it told me to be careful because discord spells are, what, unstable in uncontrolled circumstances, I think he said."

"And that meant he deserved to die?" Zarenski's question formed a flat accusation.

"What?" Sister Felice drew her hands back until the chains clinked and grew taut. "Nobody died. I mean… Not there. Not in the shop."

Levison reached into his jacket pocket and drew out some blue-and-white photographs that he spread out across the table, pictures uppermost, like revealing a hand of cards.

"Gregor Stevanovic," he said. "If you put all the body parts back together in the right way, his wife, sorry, his *widow* and his daughters might just recognise him."

Sandarov glanced at the witch's open binder, the previously blank vellum now inscribed with the detectives' words along with the suspect's responses.

As Sister Felice said, "I don't…" before her voice trailed off, the words drew themselves cursively on the vellum page in the witch's binder:

I don't

The witch looked so intent that Sandarov hesitated, on the point of asking whether the suspect's look of horrified shock felt genuine, but he didn't want to interrupt. In part because a soft red glow was growing in the formerly empty eye sockets of the rat skull hanging from the witch's throat.

Levison had switched from sympathy to accusation, and maybe that had wrongfooted Sister Felice; but the problem was, a Night Sister dealt routinely with trauma, maybe more than the average police officer, so she wasn't going to shriek and break down the way a soft civilian might.

Not at the sight of photographed body parts, at any rate.

"I was trying to free Donal of that woman who's so bad for him, and I thought I was doing the right thing but, but—" Sister Felice began gasping.

"Calm down," said Zarenski.

But her tone wasn't sympathetic enough, while Levison had already lost rapport by deliberately switching his attitude from support to accusation, when he laid down the photographs.

"Commander, I don't want to micro-manage," Sandarov found himself saying, tasting the lie in his own words, "but can they bring this back under control?"

Bowman shook his head, then: "I'll interrupt if I have to, but this is the wrong time to undermine Zarenski and Levison's authority."

The witch wasn't saying anything, which was no help at all, while her rat skull amulet's eyes were glowing redder and brighter by the second.

"Okay." Sandarov could have overridden Bowman's decision, but he welcomed the pushback, because it was too easy to throw your weight around and screw up your subordinates' work by failing to grasp all the details and nuances they were dealing with.

On the other hand, those Thanatos-damned rat skull eyes…

"Something's happening inside the Night Sister's head," said the witch.

"I'm on it." Bowman was heading for the door already, while Sandarov was still taking in the situation.

"Can you stop whatever it is?" Sandarov asked the witch as Bowman exited the room.

The witch almost threw the open ratskin binder to him. "Take this."

"Got it." Snatching the binder and slamming the thing shut.

Never mind his lofty rank as Police Commissioner. If he could help best by making a nice pot of helebore tea all round, or even sweeping the Thanatos-damned floor, then that was fine by him.

Let the witch do her work, and get out of her way. And clear anything else away that might slow her down.

Blazing scarlet now, the rat skull eye sockets at her throat.

Sandarov could only watch as Bowman burst into the interrogation chamber at the same moment as Sister Felice reared up, clutched at her heart as best she could with manacled hands, the clash of slender platinum chains almost musical…

"No," said Sandarov.

…and Sister Felice collapsed, falling awkwardly and breaking at least one of her slender arms, most likely both, because the crack as her limbs struck the edge of the table as she fell went right through Sandarov, making him want to throw up.

So pretty and fragile-looking, although Night Sisters were stronger than they looked, but Sandarov felt as if some eldritch wraith had reached inside his body and hooked out his stomach, and the feeling that swept down through him was guilt as much as shock.

Along with the conviction that a Night Sister who'd volunteered a confession probably deserved kinder treatment than being chained to an interrogation chamber table.

Zarenski was already crouched by the fallen Sister Felice, raising her up a little while Levison, hand shaking, was attempting to unlock the slender-chained manacles.

Bowman turned and slammed the heel of his palm against the scarlet pentagonal call-button set into the wall by the door.

Too slow. Their reactions were too slow.

Two duty wraiths rose up through the floor of the interrogation chamber, turning straight away to the limp form of the Night Sister. One of the wraiths extended a ghostly limb-like extrusion deep into Sister Felice's torso, as if grasping her heart.

"Is she still alive?" Sandarov's voice barely sounded like his own.

"I don't know." The witch was clutching her rat-skull amulet in one hand now, while the amulet's empty eyes shone a steady, baleful red.

"Thanatos, I've really screwed this up." His department, his responsibility, everything on him. "If she's dead—"

No one in the interrogation chamber should have heard him, even though the door to this room and the chamber hung open, but Ruth Zarenski looked up as if she sensed everything, her eyes not quite focusing on the spot where Sandarov stood, but close enough, given that the wall remained fully opaque from her side.

"She has a pulse," said Zarenski. "But it's fluttering."

Sandarov shook his head, blinking hard.

Wondering what else was going to go to Hades today.

Ten seconds later, the building shook, despite being a solid tower over two hundred storeys tall and reaching even farther to subterranean depths, while out in the corridor someone screamed.

Sandarov's day had just grown worse.

Big time.

ELEVEN

Donal still felt anything but calm and civilised.

He took the Hypoway from Mistreach Tower Station, sitting by himself at one end of an ovoid carriage that rattled along the translucent sky-tubes that became grimier and more scratched the farther he travelled from the environs of Möbius Park and City Hall and the richest parts of downtown Tristopolis.

Other commuters kept clear of him, preferring to strap-hang than sit nearby; and right now he didn't care.

Soon enough, the capsule was slowing at a high-tower platform less than a mile from his destination, so he decided to exit early. He descended all seventeen flights of exposed, rust-red metal steps where winds howled ceaselessly – he'd never known it otherwise, not here in Screamworthy Heights – while down-and-out wraiths circled the open tower structure as they always did, for reasons he'd never managed to discover.

Lonely, perhaps, preferring the vicinity of passing strangers to floating inside solid, lifeless stone. Or the emptiness of the other, smaller dimensions.

No one else was climbing or descending the exposed stairs, as was usually the case, which was one reason he'd chosen to leave the Hypoway here, because he wasn't fit company for anyone right now. He needed to walk the streets alone.

And so he did.

Lower Danklyn was home, not just now with Mel, but for most of his life apart from his Army days, although those days formed more than an interlude. More like a major separation between phases of existence.

He knew the neighbourhood – likewise Danklyn Deeps and Lesser Colereach which adjoined Lower Danklyn – and he knew the people. They were rude and crude often, vicious at worst, brave and tough-skinned and wisecracking at best, and they were his kind of Tristopolitans.

Anyone or anything threatened them, he'd be out there fighting alongside everybody else, which was why the words spoken by that red-headed young brat of a mage still echoed in his mind: "There's a threat to the city. Isn't that enough?"

If Donal were independently wealthy, then he could afford to be vigilant for any danger or wrongdoing, but there was a reason *vigilant* and *vigilante* came next to each other in the dictionary.

Years ago, as a uniformed officer new to the streets, Donal had watched as his sergeant, old Davidov, turned a blind eye to a youthful street gang fleeing the building where they'd pummeled Bat-Ears Polanski half to death.

"It's what old Bat-Ears gets his own hard men to do. To poor fools who fall behind on the vig, the vigorish. Know what I mean?"

So call it street justice, exactly what a pitiless loan shark deserved, except that a few weeks later, the same tough young guys had killed another man who might have deserved everything he got also… if only he'd been guilty of what they thought he'd done.

But he'd been entirely innocent, working elsewhere at the time of his alleged crime, toiling in the laundry of the Janaval Hotel, an upmarket establishment a long Hypoway ride away, and forming another world entirely, especially if you happened to be a paying guest, not staff.

And the crime he'd been accused of, as some half-wit locals admitted later, mumbling in court, hadn't actually occurred at all.

Sergeant Davidov took early retirement on a reduced pension the day after the judge delivered her verdict on the gang. Neither Davidov nor Donal had spoken a word about letting the gang escape, though the episode hung between them during long periods of duty before the court case as they walked the beat together; and for sure, nothing made its way into any official report.

But no one tried to stop Davidov retiring, either.

All of this ran through Donal's head as he strode along familiar cracked sidewalks, past a stretch of purplestone tenements that had seen better days, into an area of dark grey ramshackle apartment blocks and five-storey houses converted into three-dimensional mazes of single rooms, with a diverse mix of inhabitants best described as lively.

Turning into his street, focused on the ambivalent images running through his head as much as on the actual surroundings, speeding up a little as he—

"What?"

—faltered and stopped entirely, hand whipping inside his jacket, grasping his holstered Magnus but holding it there, not drawing, because not every problem could be solved by shooting and violence.

Or by turning away – turning a blind eye – either.

But it roiled and glistened, the silver and black membranous-looking phenomenon that enveloped – like a distorted bubble – the whole of his home, the deconsecrated building now called Mel's Gym, and she would have been inside when this barrier appeared, trapping her inside.

At best, holding her captive.

While at worst—

"No," he said. "No, no, no, no…"

It was dome-shaped, pretty much: the upper portion of a sphere, except that if the field really was spherical, the centre lay well below ground, which was probably significant but not in any way that Donal could make use of.

Mel. You can't be in there.

But where else would she be right now? Not out running, not so soon after that tremendous breakfast. She preferred to do roadwork later if at all, because of her years working in places where getting out onto the streets wasn't always possible, and not all during busy working hours, while a simple jump rope could fit in your coat pocket and all you needed was a few square feet of floor space.

Her words, living in his head.

Donal stopped close to the barrier, having edged closer automatically, knowing this was his fault but the time for guilt wasn't yet, because he had to get Mel out of there.

He punched the barrier, fast and hard and—

Stupid.

—nothing was there, no barrier but the stone temple building, and overhead the same wooden sign, *Mel's Gym* in cursive script that they'd paid a proper sign painter called Paulie Delgasso to create, because neither of them felt confident of doing it right themselves.

The barrier had popped out of existence.

"Mel!"

He ran to the side door, twisting the old iron ring-lock and almost falling inside, desperate, needing to know if she was alright.

"Hey." Mel was there. "Donal? What's wrong?"

She was with two of her younger boxers, but Donal didn't care. He hurried over and grabbed her and pulled her tight, squeezing her against him, the side of his face pressed against hers, his eyes closing as the awful tension dropped away.

"Thank Thanatos." He kissed her ear, and squeezed her again. "Oh, thank Thanatos."

"Donal?" she said as they disengaged. "That was nice, but what's wrong?"

"I thought you were trapped in here."

"Trapped?"

He stepped back a little, holding Mel by her strong upper arms, not willing to let go, not yet.

"I thought something weird had happened to the building." He looked at the two young boxers – a boy and a girl, aged ten or thereabouts – and smiled at both of them. "Hey, sorry to interrupt your training."

"That's alright," said the boy.

His scales glistened, and a fleeting thought came to Donal: if that taxi driver, Kap, brought his son here to train, he'd certainly find company.

Donal let go of Mel, who smiled.

He turned to face the boy. "You didn't notice anything weird just happen, did you?"

Donal wasn't sure what to hope for, because he didn't want to be falling into craziness and hallucinating visions that were totally unreal… but he didn't want Mel trapped inside some dangerous phenomenon, either.

"Nope." The boy shook his head, his black eyes free of worry.

"Just a crawlspace energy thing." The girl looked standard human, and her words sounded innocent of guile.

"What kind of energy thing?"

A small shrug. "I don't know."

"Something odd happened?" said Mel. "What was it, Anya?"

"Well…" Young Anya's eyes snapped into a momentary state of featureless dark blue, maybe indigo, then back to normal human eyes. "Just a thing."

The change had been fast and transient, like a camera shutter, open and closed, just like that.

"How, er, how long did it last for?" asked Donal.

Because the barrier field, or whatever it was, might have snapped into existence just as he turned into the street, or it might have manifested earlier, any time since his previous departure.

Except that people out on the streets would have noticed, if it had persisted for anything beyond a few seconds, or a minute or two at most.

"Just a little while." Young Anya shrugged. "I counted Mixadriptotrix twenty-nine times."

Counting seconds by naming a Surinese raptor you'd never want to meet in real life: nothing had changed since Donal was the same age as these kids right now.

"Is there any kind of energy thing still happening?" Mel sounded mildly interested, but she'd be as alert to danger as Donal, because nothing was going to happen to these kids while she was around to guard them.

And in the long term grant them the gifts of strength and toughness and knowing how to fight – three very different things that went together nicely – because the absence of adversity wasn't peace: it was setting kids up as future victims.

Which Mel would not allow.

Another reason for Donal to love her, as if all the other reasons weren't enough already… which they were, many times over.

Young Anya shook her head. "It popped."

"The dome," said Donal. "Popped like a bubble, did it?"

"Uh-huh." Anya nodded, an exaggerated motion, as if the gesture were newly learned… or needed emphasis if other people were going to notice it.

"Do you know where it came from?"

She'd already mentioned the crawlspace dimensions, and that wasn't really the issue, because what Donal really needed to know was who or what created the thing, and why.

"Resonance." Anya took care pronouncing the word. Then she blinked, this time in the normal fashion. "Like a memory, I think."

"Donal…" Mel's fingers brushed his sleeve, as she crouched down to Anya's level. "Would your auntie know more, Anya, if you talked to her?"

"Uh-huh." Another nod.

"Maybe I'll pop in to see her with you, on the way home from training, is that okay?"

"Sure." A grin. "She'd like that."

"Good. So we'll carry on. Last few drills and a cool down." Mel rose to standing. "And after we've finished, I'll walk you home while Uncle Donal takes the next group through training. I mean Coach Donal."

"Er," said Donal.

"You might as well get changed, Coach," Mel told him. "A third of an hour, and Anya and Billy and I are done here, and the others will be starting to arrive."

An hour ago, Donal had been flying in a pteracopter piloted by a federal spellbinder, and talking to a mage on first name terms. Now he was about to teach a bunch of kids how to box and generally look after themselves, in the neighbourhood he'd grown up in.

"I can't think of anything I'd rather do."

"No." A very adult twinkle showed in Mel's eyes. "I'm sure you can't."

"Later," said Donal, smiling.

And headed towards their presbytery-apartment, feeling more settled inside than he had been for hours.

Thirteen hours, in fact, since the pseudo-Laura had appeared here and quickly vanished.

Forget her.

Time to concentrate on his immediate responsibilities.

Simple priorities were everything.

TWELVE

The Vixen screeched to a halt, feeling her tyres burn, her engine-heart thumping and growling, her chassis aching in a way that ought to have been pleasant, like an ordinary human filled with elation following a long-distance run; but worry and regret ruined everything.

She couldn't burn away the guilt, no matter how fast she hammered down the highway. There was no escape for her: not like that.

Nor should there be. She didn't deserve an easy way out.

But something odd was glimmering ahead of her. Rock sheared as questing tentacles pushed upwards from the road surface, shattering solid tarmac and splintering empty air, or seeming to.

The Vixen couldn't quite perceive, in her present state, the exact nature of this shocking intrusion into reality, but she knew it for a threat. Knew it with zero doubt.

And she didn't want to die this way.

I wanted to end it all.

But not like this. Never like this.

Way in the distance, beyond the spreading, forking disruption in macroscopic reality immediately ahead, the image of her destination broke up into shards, into random fragments like reflections in a shattered mirror: the towers of Fortinium, capital of the Federation and the city where sweet Laura – her dearest, only sister – met her death.

Cracks in reality twisted and curled like a grabbing, seeking hand, and a sudden realisation dropped through the Vixen's transmission, her clutch locking solid, brakes seizing as her pistons skipped a beat. Then she disengaged her gearbox to neutral as her engine revved, hard and fast and quite uncontrollable.

Panicking, because she knew exactly what the phenomenon wanted. Why it was manifesting here and now, of all the times and places in the world it might have chosen.

It's after me.

And not in gratitude for her helping it, inadvertently, to reach this reality. This was a thing of rage and destruction and… hunger.

It didn't do warm feelings.

Thanatos. What have I done?

Even more damage than she'd realised, for sure.

The sound of cracking tarmac grew louder behind her, and the road trembled beneath her tyres, and she knew there was no escape in either direction. She was going to die the most agonising of deaths right here on the open highway, where she should have been at her safest, secure in her element.

More sundering of reality: the beginnings of a building-sized dome-like nothingness rising from the shattered road, and a partial glimpse of an elliptical void within the convex distortion, like a giant eye within some distorted, immaterial skull; and the Vixen was bizarrely reminded, just for a second, of the pair of two-thousand-foot-high skulls through whose empty eye sockets the Orb-Dexter and Orb-Sinister Highways ran respectively, back in central Tristopolis.

And they weren't the only giant remains that the Vixen had seen in her varied life. For a moment, she held the thought that perhaps this non-material being resembled those titanic pseudo-human remnants for a reason, the kind of thing her mother – damn her to Hades – would call a morphological resonance.

It rose further, this thing in front of her, until a second ovoid sort-of eye was visible, then a gaping abyss-within-confusion that might have formed a mouth, then more: until something like a vast head and shoulders had smashed its way upwards from the road and surrounding verges; and it reared above her, huge and angry and redolent of *other*, of some hellish mode of being beyond anything even the Vixen, with all her special knowledge, had dreamed might exist.

She beeped her horn twice, then twice more, louder the second time, sounding her defiance: *screw-you, screw-you,* hoping the entity understood what she thought of it. Would continue to think of it, even as it crushed her bodywork and twisted her chassis and sucked the energies out of her until the final blackness granted mercy.

If it did. Perhaps this giant, evil thing would continue to savour the core of her mental being, keep her shattered thoughts and some kind of awareness burning inside its twisted vastness, for in this world, death wasn't always the end.

Or more precisely, there might be agonising years or decades or possibly even centuries to torment you, before true oblivion finally snuffed you out.

The talon-like hand curved overhead, looking more solid in those last few seconds before reality went away, and the Vixen squeezed her headlights shut, then snapped them open once more in a final, hopeless gesture of defiance.

Something huge and red and tinged with orange, the colour of blood and flame, streaked overhead and was gone, heading in the general direction of Fortinium but surely not planning to stop, not flying at that speed.

Faster than any plane or bird the Vixen had ever seen.

The giant hand held still above her, and the vast apparition hardened in place, like ice, then turned its great head to follow the flying redness, before turning back to look down at the Vixen.

Void-eyes staring all the way through her.

No…

The vanished flying redness might have used wings, might have stretched longer than two giant freight trucks, trailing a longer, slender tail as it flashed through the sky; or it might have possessed some other form impossible to truly see. But its appearance had affected the apparition about to kill the Vixen.

It looked right through her, but it gave her information too, because those eyes made of void stuff shone with something she recognized because she herself was filled with it.

Fear.

The great entity about to kill her felt afraid.

Not of me.

Her engine cut out, just like that. This was too much, too huge for her to fight against, and all she could do was let everything go and allow death to happen, however it intended to take her.

No movement from the entity.

You can kill me now.

All her burdens were evaporating, liberated by helplessness. And hopelessness. No more struggle to endure.

Void eyes, regarding her.

Knowing her. Judging.

I've nothing to hide.

And nothing to fear, because the worst was upon her.

The end.

It took several seconds for her to realise she was still alive, and the entity was turning away and diving down, like a swimmer submerging in water, except there were no waves and a great smashed hole remained, severing the highway, splitting it all the way across.

She leaked a little transmission fluid in relief, just a squirt, and felt no shame in it.

I thought I was dead.

Had been absolutely sure of it, in fact.

As dead as Laura.

Oblivion, and she'd welcomed its imminent appearance, but it hadn't happened.

The death I totally…

And the tail end of her thought melted into nothingness, not quite forming the word *deserved.*

Because the thing that had intended to kill her, that huge entity that rose up from the road while breaking it apart, was *not* the being that entered this region of reality because of the Vixen's stupid meddling, of her taking Night Sister Felice to see that idiot, Gregor Stevanovic, who'd promised to provide an icon suffused with a disruption spell, the kind of hex that could compromise any kind of human communication or relationship… unless the people involved were truly, deeply right for and committed to each other.

As for the entity that had been about to crush her, along with the flying red and orange thing that flashed by overhead and inadvertently saved the Vixen's life, as far she could tell… Neither one of those formed the real threat.

Two entities, appearing so far from Tristopolis yet originating there, at least in this reality.

But neither of those huge, dread entities had travelled this far simply to hunt down one tiny car-person fleeing down a highway, speeding towards her own imagined destiny at the place where sweet Laura had died.

None of that held much relevance for those entities. None at all for the red flying thing: that was certain. The other had recognised this scared Vixen for what she was and what she had done, and nearly given her what she deserved, but it hadn't come all this way specifically to hunt her down.

Which meant…

Neither of them was the thing breaking through from the compactified-dimensions route that led here from Beyond.

Most likely the two fleeing entities had already been living in the macroscopic dimensions, or mostly so. Dear Laura had long ago muttered things about the dread beings existing in a kind of voluntary subterranean house arrest, deep below the forbidding tower of Police HQ on Avenue of the Basilisks.

Whatever the Vixen had allowed to enter the world, it had scared both of those fleeing dread creatures.

They'd been here because they were fleeing from Tristopolis. As for the entity who'd been about to kill her: her death would have been secondary, a small recompense for the total disruption of that entity's existence.

She knew that now.

Whatever I've done, it's even worse than I thought.

Only a few minutes ago, she wouldn't have believed that possible; but now she knew, and there was no avoiding the implications.

She fired her ignition, let her pistons hum for half a minute, and slipped gently into first gear. Rolled to the edge of the gaping hole, shifted to reverse and steered as she moved back in a curved line.

Then moving in first gear again, turning, keeping slow to analyse the state of the roadway.

More cracks and holes marred the tarmac that previously lay behind her, but an area off to one side remained intact. Just enough room to roll past the disruption, provided she didn't mind rolling her wheels through black grass for a short stretch, and the ground looked level enough for her to make it.

Beyond, the highway stretched back, unbroken as far as she could see, all the way to her city of Tristopolis.

She rolled slowly, slowly past the broken stretch, then eased onto the tarmac proper, appreciating the smoothness of the dark surface and the sure grip of her tyres.

Time to get a move on.

And try to fix things, if she could.

A minute later, she was hurtling at over a hundred, driving fast and hard back towards Tristopolis, no longer caring how this might end. Knowing only that she would try her best to make things right.

Travelling faster now.

THIRTEEN

Donal finished the session by getting the young boxers to applaud each other and by extension themselves.

During the training, he'd taken a couple of opportunities to teach the difference between a partner and an opponent – and on the street, an actual enemy – which boiled down to knowing when to take it easy drilling and sparring, and when to try and knock the other guy's head off, especially when the same person loomed in front of you both times.

And in the case of an enemy, going for the throat, using elbows and forearms and knees as extra weapons, and making tactical use of obstacles on the ground, the drop of a kerb or the solid hardness of a brick wall, along with keeping peripheral alertness and staying on the move, so you could slam multiple attackers into each other or place them in each other's way, and usually to redefine your goal as going *through* a bunch of them and getting clear, instead of trying to put all of them on the ground.

He was careful how he framed these things, very careful, but they formed lessons the kids needed to learn, every one of them.

And there was value in knowing from tangible, solid experience that you could fight through getting your nose broken or your ribs bent out of shape, and conversely of learning viscerally that sometimes when you smashed an opponent's nose into bloody flatness, they wouldn't even blink as they came back at you with ferocious intent.

But none of these youngsters had reached the stage of needing to enter that particular crucible in order to progress. Not yet.

A couple were getting close, though. Perhaps later in the year, Mel would want to organise some matches with other clubs. It might prove useful all round.

Bright laughter and fist bumps accompanied the kids' exit, some still damp-headed with sweat, even though a structured cool-down was a mandatory part of training, more so than Donal remembered from his own youthful days at the AMA with Coach O'Brian.

"Good work," he called out as the last of them filed out, and the tall door swung shut.

The sound echoed in the now-empty, otherwise silent gym that still felt full of sweat and adrenaline and physicality: of discipline and striving and facing up to fear.

Harder to do when the problems are complicated.

Donal allowed his smile to fade, because however fine a job he'd made of the training, and however important his and Mel's contribution to these kids' lives – something he would never learn either way: that was the way of things – larger conflicts loomed in the background, including at least one vast threat capable of frightening mages.

And of killing them: there'd been fatalities at Möbius Park, before Federal Agent Chambers launched those Spellstorm missiles from her pteracopter and the enemy, whatever it was, had at best made a tactical withdrawal, and at worst simply left the vicinity because it wanted to shift elsewhere, not much caring what humans tried to do to it.

Donal had a bad feeling that the latter was most likely true. Mage Kelvin Johannsson's nervousness had spoken volumes.

So why should I be able to do anything about it?

No reason that he could think of, except for an indirect factor that he might easily misinterpret: the white wolf had appeared in his office, no one else's, and given him the obsidian skull of Drad, aka Baladradian Chalintropovin, thereby bringing disaster to Kyushen at St Jarl's, and causing mages to think that one resurrected ex-cop turned struggling PI might have something to contribute in the middle of disaster.

Wonderful.

The tall door at the far end swung open, and for a tenth of a second Donal thought it might be the pseudo-Laura returning, but for all her icy zombie strength, Laura had never possessed shoulder muscles or an athletic stance like that.

"Hey, babe," he said.

"Hey yourself," said Mel.

"What's wrong?"

She came forward, shaking her head. "Anya's witchy aunt picked up a trace of a resonance on Anya, whatever that really means. So the good news is you weren't hallucinating."

"And the bad news is, I'm guessing, that something really weird must have happened, to leave a trace on someone inside the building."

"Yeah, something like that." Her grey eyes swirled as she took hold of his shoulders. "She's unlicensed, the aunt, but she's got real abilities."

Donal slid his arms around Mel's waist.

"I'll be careful," he told her.

Their real conversation was several steps ahead of their actual words. Both of them knew what needed to happen next.

And it wasn't going to involve young Anya's witchy aunt.

"Ammunition," said Mel. "Take plenty of rounds."

"I'm not sure it's that kind of problem."

"Really?" She kissed him, soft and strong, their lips seeming to blend into each other, as if they were a single person, not two. Then: "Something big and bad is manifesting in your city, *our* city, out of all the places in the universe it might go. Tristopolis, my love, isn't actually the centre of the cosmos."

"Ah."

"Right, ah."

"You're a smart dudette, Imelda Carson."

"You're not so bad yourself, Mr Riordan."

He was tactically trained but in many ways, so was she. Which meant her reading of the situation was accurate, although neither of them could tell what the plan of battle might turn out to be, or whether any plan was doomed to shatter against reality, given the magnitude of what the city faced.

But Mel was right.

Somewhere, somehow, a person was responsible for this.

I'll find them.

Time for Donal to go to work.

Back in suit and tie and shoulder-holstered Magnus, he travelled an extended route by Hypoway and Pneumetro halfway across central Tristopolis, in ovoid carriages that were by turns grimy and scratched and shaking or smooth and shiny, depending on which line he happened to take for each section of the journey.

Maybe a taxi would have been better, but this way he could tell, with a greater likelihood of getting it right, if he was under observation from anyone other than perhaps a real mage: with those buggers, you could never really be sure what was happening.

Which might have made his destination questionable, were it not for one factor: Mage Lamis was a slippery, devious bastard, but he'd risked his life to save the city. Or maybe just to destroy his turncoat protégée, Calista Delfix.

Either way, he'd been known to act on the side of ordinary people, even if his reasons lay a long way from anything Donal might recognise as sensible motivation.

Donal got off at Gallway Depths, and followed a twisting, helical pedestrian tunnel down to a subterranean level that existed, if he remembered the numbers correctly, three and a half furlongs beneath the bottom of the River Umber, almost half a mile below the elevated station where he'd exited.

Wraiths slipped in and out of the solid bone-and-steel walls, going about their business – whatever that might be – and paying no attention to Donal, or none that he could detect.

He took his time walking the downward slope, in part because it was darker here, due to the sparsity of flamesprites and the impoverished illumination of the few who were serving out their indenture in these surroundings. But it gave him time to marshal his questions and arguments in advance of coming face to face with Lamis.

With a sheaf of possibilities loosely rehearsed in his imagination, and trusting that when the moment came, his experience and intuition would make everything right.

Not exactly a philosophy of life, but maybe part of it.

The steel door formed an eleven-sided polygon, and looked more like a hatch inside a submarine than the entrance to a mage's apartment. But then, what exactly did a mage's home look like?

Donal had zero experience: for all the different social circles his working life had taken him into, the domestic arrangements of true professional mages were a totally blank area.

His hand started to slip away when he raised it to knock, but he'd come up against this kind of spell before and simply forced his fist through the repulsion hex and thumped three times, as hard as he could manage.

Then stepped back, and waited.

Maybe I should count Mixadriptotrixes.

Or more properly *Mixadriptotrices* in the plural, as Sister Mary-Anne Styx would have insisted back in his schooldays, forming the word in elegant copperplate with chalk on purpleboard, while dangling a knotted whip from the other hand, because the greatest lesson of all she taught was discipline.

Donal took a swivelling, angled step backwards to avoid the hatch – really, that was the best word for it – as it swung open towards him. Inside hung darkness, save for the green-and-blue glow of runes inscribed ring-like around all eleven segments of the threshold; and something in the air similar to a static charge indicated that stepping inside without a clear invitation would most likely prove agonising at best.

And probably fatal, or effectively so: termination hex or Basilisk Trance, take your pick.

"Good to see you," came the familiar sepulchral voice. "Come in, Lieutenant."

"Thanks, but I don't actually hold that rank these days."

"No matter." The runes flickered. "You're recognised, and can enter safely."

Donal nodded, trusting the invitation but not making the mistake of thinking it a permanent, ongoing form of permission. He was welcome today, but if he came back tomorrow, there would be no guarantees.

Something passed across his skin as he stepped inside, but it was no worse than being checked out by scanwraiths at St Jarl's. Or Möbius Park, under normal conditions.

"There's trouble," he said into darkness.

"Well, of course there is."

"If you mean I wouldn't just pop in for a beer and, what, to talk about spikeball and what the Gauntlets' chances are this season, then get over it. We're not friends, but we are on the same side when it comes to trouble."

Blue light slowly strengthened, revealing Mage Lamis dressed in an actual heavy robe, sitting in an armchair, wearing wraparound shades as usual, holding an open book in his left hand.

Of course he'd been reading in total darkness. And no actual eyes lay behind those shades, only empty blasted sockets. But...

Mages.

Odd buggers, the lot of them.

"You should know," said Lamis. "You're pretty odd yourself."

"I wasn't aware I was subvocalising."

"Maybe you weren't."

"And maybe mages like to exaggerate their powers. Cultivate an image, kind of thing."

True mind-reading was beyond their capabilities: Donal was *almost* sure of it.

"Well, I did need your help against Calista." Lamis closed the book and put it on his lap. "There's no beer in the fridge, but I've helebore tea of several varieties, and some Surinese dark blend coffee already ground up in the percolator."

"Coffee would be good," said Donal, covering his surprise.

Inside his head, he replayed the tone and rhythm of Lamis's words. Sepulchral as always, but the subtleties of prosody – of timbre and vocal cadence and all the rest – formed a powerful hint.

It had never occurred to Donal that mages could get lonely.

Although he understood none of the details, he'd gained the impression that Lamis was persona non grata among the more respectable, traditional portions of mage society. Perhaps there was some kind of story there.

From somewhere out back, a click sounded and a percolator began to drip. Lamis hadn't so much as twitched, but he'd somehow caused it to happen.

Underestimating him would be a mistake, even under these new circumstances, with his acting friendly and hinting at vulnerability.

"Sit down, Mr Riordan. If you please."

There was an empty armchair obliquely facing Lamis. It hadn't been there a moment ago.

"Sure." Donal sat down and leaned back, hands on the arms of the chair, ready to lever himself up at speed if required.

The smell of dark, strong coffee rose from a small table to his right. A steaming mug stood on a black embroidered doily. Lamis's mug, on his chair-side table, rested on a coaster made from a single polished scale.

Neither table, nor the items upon them, had been there when Donal took his seat. In the armchair that hadn't been there when he entered the apartment.

"Fast percolator," he said.

"Indeed." Lamis raised his mug and took a sip.

It would have been rude not to follow suit, so Donal did. The coffee was strong and bitter, the best he'd tasted for a very long while.

"You're not very busy, are you?" He placed the mug back down. "The coffee's excellent, by the way. Thank you."

"What makes you say that? About not being busy, I mean."

Donal gestured. "If this represents the pinnacle of mage expertise, then you'd all be working in posh restaurants as chefs. Or bartenders. I expect you can put together all sorts of cocktails just by snapping your fingers."

A cavernous chuckle sounded in Lamis's chest, the first sign of amusement Donal had ever detected in the man.

"You have me to rights, Mr Riordan."

"Call me Donal." Surprising himself.

"Well… And I'm Lamis, of course. That is my first name."

"You have another?" Donal had addressed him as Lamis in the past, in fact, not knowing what else to call him.

"Grimstone," said Lamis.

Something stirred deep inside Donal. Not so much a memory as a distant emotional response from another time.

Lamis gave a cold-looking smile. "In fact, I'm Dexter Lamis Grimstone, so strictly speaking, Lamis is my middle name. But it's what I always go by."

It was Donal's day for getting to know mages better. First Kelvin, now Lamis.

"Some weird things are going on," he said.

"I know. You walked away from Helena's young protégé at Möbius Park, and I laughed harder than I have done for years. So thank you for that."

"You mean from Mage Kelvin. And that implies you were there, or else watching from a distance."

"The latter, Donal. From this very armchair." Lamis patted the arm with one hand, and reached for his coffee with the other.

Donal watched him take another sip, his own coffee no longer relevant.

"I'm glad I gave you something to laugh about, Lamis. What I don't get is why you found it so amusing."

"Because the Mordanto way is to assume everyone will trip over themselves in eagerness to help clever mages, grateful for the privilege."

"Indeed." Donal flattened his voice. "And I seem to recall, you got me to help you in much the same way."

"I rescued you from the grave and wrote you a rather large cheque, although I've a feeling you gave the money to someone in Illurium."

"To two people, who deserved it," said Donal. "I'm surprised you picked up on that."

"The point is, I didn't expect you to work for free."

There'd been clothing provided and some other things also, including a Magnus similar to the one beneath his armpit right now.

"Yeah" said Donal. "And I appreciate it. But this time, I can last a short while without income, and whatever's happening, I think normal existence is about to be suspended without warning if no one does anything about it."

"That might well be the case," said Lamis.

"And?"

"And what, exactly?"

"I was hoping you'd come up with something helpful."

"Ah. And how much were you intending to pay me, Donal?"

"Thanatos. Sweet bleeding Hades."

And then he laughed, and after a moment Lamis joined in. Laughing like old friends.

The way normal people might behave.

"You got me," added Donal. "Well and truly."

"I certainly did."

"Maybe we should leave it to the cops and Mordanto, after all. The ones on salary."

"You said it yourself." Lamis's voice remained deep and sepulchral, yet lighter than before. "Normal existence is about to be suspended, maybe permanently, without some kind of massive intervention."

"Yeah… I was thinking, whatever the threat's nature, something drew it here. Someone called it, on purpose or by accident."

"That's highly likely," said Lamis.

"So give me a hint of how to track them down, why don't you."

"I can't do that from here."

"Really?" Donal gestured to the coffee mug on the table beside his chair. "You made these things just appear."

"Actually, I made a forced quantal measurement that altered the past so that I'd already placed the furniture there by hand prior to your arrival."

Donal stared at Lamis's face, focusing on his wraparound shades. "Say what?"

"There are severe limitations, otherwise I could have altered Calista's past so she was never born, or died tragically young, or something. Maybe had her taken from her evil mother by the authorities, early enough to make a difference."

"Yes, but…" Donal touched the mug.

It still felt hot.

And real.

Yet it came from a past he did not remember experiencing – actually had not experienced, if he understood Lamis's non-technical explanation correctly.

"Farseeing works differently," said Lamis, "and quantal bilocation does allow for what you might call teleportation, but again under huge constraints."

All those lectures at the police academy, and the world of mages remained a confusing, hidden mystery.

"Maybe you fell asleep in the classroom too much," added Lamis.

"You did *not* just read my thoughts."

"No, of course I didn't."

Donal himself had picked up other folks' subvocalised musings – those of ordinary humans, call them redbloods – from time to time, since gaining zombiehood. Nowadays he possessed far more control of his own self's inner processes, but perhaps even his massive self-awareness and highly sensitive hearing still missed things: subconscious processes that worked the same way now for him as they had in his first, ordinary life.

Subvocalising his thoughts, so someone with preternaturally sharp hearing might pick them up.

That must be it.

"If you say so," continued Lamis, and gave a slightly reptilian smile.

"Enough."

"Yes." A different kind of smile. "So what about those Gauntlets, then?"

"Huh?"

"Everyone says they're going to be relegated to the second division, but they've signed Gunnarrson and Beckwith, and taken on a new strength and conditioning coach. Even though we're two-thirds through the season, I think Marge Ojimdo can turn her team around."

Donal rubbed his face. "I really didn't mean it about the spikeball."

"Yes, I know."

"So are you going to point me in the right direction, or what?"

"No."

"What?"

"I'm going to come with you, Donal." Lamis took another sip of coffee, then spread his hands apart.

But nothing fell, because there was no coffee mug.

Neither did a table stand next to Lamis's armchair. Nor its counterpart next to Donal.

"Sweet Hades, Lamis."

"Friends stick together."

"I don't think we're—"

"Of course we are."

Sapphire-blue fire rose up all around, and Donal was tumbling forward into a blazing pit, and everything flared up in overwhelming brilliance as he dropped into a vortex wilder than anything he might have tried to imagine.

Falling, but not alone.

Lamis, now wearing a dark suit instead of the robe, but still with the wraparound shades, was diving alongside Donal into the swirling sapphire vortex of light and cold fire.

Falling faster.

Towards a distant white spot.

White, becoming nova bright, while Lamis grinned hard enough to show his teeth.

You should be careful what you ask for.

Mages.

You never knew what they might do n—

Reality exploded.

FOURTEEN

A thousand people died within a second of the huge hand appearing.

It rose above the sprawling tenements of Conklyn Wilds, half transparent and cupping the air like a swimmer's hand rising out of water in the front crawl, except this hand stretched half a mile in length or more, and the curved fingers terminated in talons, and it grew more opaque as it descended on the buildings and smashed them into shards and dust.

Most perished without suffering, in that instant.

A hovering scanbat perceived the entire incident by chance, from its position a hundred feet above Darkplay Park, which was fortunate because otherwise there would have been no reliable record at all, not since the rooftop surveillance mirrors had been removed from across the city – although there had been few enough even in that system's heyday, in a district as impoverished as Conklyn.

Mage Kelvin Johannsson, trying to concentrate while strapped into a vibrating seat in a thunderously loud pteracopter piloted by one Federal Agent Chambers, was struggling to gain a complete overview of central and southern Tristopolis, doing everything he could to detect or predict the next intrusion into macroscopic reality of the being that he'd taken to calling the Void Threat.

Because in tactical meetings with his fellow mages, he needed to call it something, and that seemed to fit.

Naming something doesn't always mean that you know what it is.

All his hex equations and spell-space modelling spoke of resonances he'd never seen before, side effects of the vast entity's origins beyond the normal regions of the compactified dimensions colloquially known as crawlspace, where wraiths either wholly lived or rotated mostly out of, so part of their mass-energy existed in the macroscopic spacetime dimensions while the rest remained in crawlspace.

But every reading from today's intrusion hinted at an origin in a chilly Beyond, an unknown and unknowable region lying on the far side of contiguous crawlspace, where no human, neither mage nor witch, could travel or function or even perceive the surroundings.

That was where the Void Threat came from: a reality linked to this continuum by some pathway or bridge existing only among the compactified crawlspace dimensions.

And that was so far beyond even the most advanced theoretical modelling at Mordanto that Kelvin didn't know where to start in terms of mounting a defence, never mind some form of counterattack to strike against the enemy.

Andrei. I will keep you safe.

Eight months old, and right now Natasha, Kelvin's beautiful shaven-headed wife, was cradling Andrei in a shawl embroidered with protective runes, which Kelvin knew because even here, in a banking noisy pteracopter high above the city, he could see his wife and child via quantal tunnelling of distant photons into his peripheral vision.

To maintain that link required the conjuration equivalent of an isometric hold, a static strength exercise: perhaps as extreme as a gymnast's iron cross on the rings; but he would keep the link in place for as long as he could, because that was why he was really here.

Keeping Andrei and Natasha safe meant everything.

"There's something down on the river." Federal Agent Chambers' voice sounded in Kelvin's headphones, which he'd almost forgotten he was wearing.

"I don't see it."

"Left below, by Shatterway Quay."

He must have misheard, even with the headphones, because a second later he realised the odd phenomenon wasn't *on* the river: it was *in* it. Something pale and dimly visible was moving below the black surface of the wide River Inkflow, a mile from where it merged with the greater Umber.

Heading out to sea? That would be perfect, or rather the best that he could hope for: the Void Threat shifting its attention far from Tristopolis, making it somebody else's problem, which perhaps formed a bad way to think.

But it would also give him and his fellow mages a breathing space, some time to consider ways of combating a threat so vast that right now, anything they could come with up felt tragically inadequate at best.

I'm scared.

He could organise, with Helena Steele's authorisation and influence and technical help, a massed counterspell involving the conjoined efforts of virtually everybody at Mordanto and among their affiliates and allies. But right now, the more he considered the options, the more he felt sure that any such counter-offensive would in fact prove counter-productive: snagging the attention of the Void Threat as a simple annoyance, causing it to turn its full concentration on destroying Tristopolis.

Like destroying an ant nest, or worse: perhaps as reflexively fast and effortless as swatting an individual insect out of existence.

To attack the Void Threat might bring about the ruin of Tristopolis.

Sudden extinction.

Maybe there are no good choices.

It was a harsh thought, but perhaps an accurate one.

"I'm taking us lower," came Chambers' voice in his headphones.

"Yes, let's do that."

But the pteractopter was already descending at a forward downward angle, whether Kelvin approved or not.

The thing beneath the river was accelerating.

"Thanatos," muttered Chambers, working the joystick and the pedals in complex ways.

A spume of water flew upwards towards them.

"Let me—" Kelvin formed mudra gestures with both hands as a way of concentrating the neural patterns in his brain: neural cliques architected by hard years of discipline into configurations able to resonate with necromagnetic fields, like the one generated by the torc he wore around his neck beneath his tunic.

But Chambers reacted faster than Kelvin could create a defensive spell, twisting the pteracopter away from the upward-rushing column of water, though not fast enough to avoid spatters like heavy rainfall – aqueous, not quicksilver – as the column fell back into the river from which it had been formed.

Something squawked in his ears, and he realised that the pteracopter's radio signal had been diverted, shared, so he could, for the moment, hear what Chambers heard over the external channel, and in turn listen to what she said to the operator on the other end of the signal.

"—known origin, out to open sea possibly, repeat possibly."

"Roger that," came Chambers's reply. "Question: pursue or break off? Please advise."

Despite the noise and shaking and the dire threat below and the peripheral vision of his precious Andrei and Natasha, Kelvin felt his mouth twitch with amusement, because Federal Agent Chambers wasn't asking for instructions.

She might request advice, but she would act with total decisiveness after making up her own mind.

Kelvin wished he could act so confidently. So quickly.

It would help if I knew what I should do.

Professor Helena Steele had hinted more than once that she wanted him to make mistakes by taking on new responsibilities with minimal guidance, because only by friction with complicated reality could anyone grow hardened and tough enough to lead. But right now, any mistake could cost a million lives, maybe even more.

Too much responsibility.

On the other hand, with the Void Threat here among them, maybe nothing they could do would make a difference. In that case, there was nothing to hold him back, either.

He closed his eyes.

In his memory, or pseudo-memory, he was staring from a steady vantage point high in the air above Darkplay Park: the viewpoint of a hovering municipal scanbat, whose perceptions had been absorbed by Mage Carolina with exquisite precision, subsequently shared with him by quantal merging of her hippocampus with the parietal lobes at the rear of his brain.

In his mental vision, the giant, taloned hand came down once more, smashing the tenements of Conklyn Wilds again into dust clouds and rubble. One strike, and then it transitioned back to an immaterial state as it disappeared beneath the shattered ground.

One *stroke*, not strike: it really did look like a swimming movement, one portion of the being's self becoming material for less than a second, before it moved on beneath the surface.

Kelvin brought his attention back to the moving paleness beneath the Inkflow's rippling waves.

Sorry. I love you.

He dropped the quantal connection to his wife and son, needing all his resources for the next part.

"—able to track—" Chambers' voice, fading into then out of his awareness.

Never mind.

Focusing.

I need to touch your thoughts.

Not mind-reading, but neural-flow-to-neural-flow resonance: he wouldn't be able to understand the thing's thoughts, but perhaps he could gain a taste or hint of its mind set and worldview. Try to gauge its intent, knowing he was likely to fail but needing to make the attempt, because everything lay under threat right now.

Natasha. Andrei…

For their sakes, he had to put them out of his mind, just for the duration.

Focusing harder.

Silver fire that only he could perceive filled his mind and body: an intricate, barbed, rotating structure of energy flux that few non-mages even dreamed might exist. A key part of the more powerful, esoteric techniques practised by Mordanto's finest.

And painful.

So very painful.

Filling every nerve with agony, because that was the price you paid to operate as a true adept in ways that had little to do with uneducated superstitions, and everything to do with the interface between reality's true, deep, quantal nature and dynamic neural patterns created by rigorous internal discipline, honed by pain and experience, directed by theory as inscribed in reams of thaumic field equations.

It *hurt.*

"—right, mage? You look—"

Ignore.

Hurting harder than he'd ever experienced before.

A moving target inside the river's waters, but neither the motion nor the distance between them should have made a difference, not to the questing hex configuration he was struggling to conjure into being.

Something else was making it harder to—

"Thanatos!"

He reeled back in his seat, gasping as the attempted contact broke and his neurological lattice of internal silver fire broke apart and shattered into smaller fragments of agony inside him and was gone.

Warm blood trickling from his nose. Pain inside his eyeballs.

"Talk to me, Mage. What's happening?"

"Sorry." He looked at Federal Agent Chambers. "I tried to make… contact. With the thing down in the water."

"Damn it to Hades." She brought the pteracopter level, the culmination of some hard manoeuvring that Kelvin could barely recall in retrospect, and hadn't really felt at the time. "What did it do, Mage? Break your quest hex?"

Kelvin shook his head. No one should have been able to detect what he'd been attempting, but then again, Chambers was clearly a federal spellbinder: he'd worked that out before.

"Partly it was fear," said Kelvin. "Its fear, not just mine."

"Excuse me? Did you say *it* was afraid? That thing hammering along beneath the surface of the River Inkflow?"

"It's not the same entity that destroyed Conklyn Wilds."

"The Hades it isn't. I can smell the void on it from here."

Definitely a federal spellbinder.

"You can, and I felt it, tasted it, when I tried to make contact. It's from the same place as that other entity, but it's not the same one."

For one thing it was smaller.

An awful lot smaller.

Which meant the other one was vast indeed.

"And you say it's afraid?" said Chambers. "Of what, the other entity?"

"I've been calling it the Void Threat."

"Okay, good name. It works."

"And whatever that entity is in the river below us, it's trying to get away from the Void Threat, because it's scared."

"I've run out of Spellstorms, but I'm not out of options. You recommend letting the thing reach open sea?"

"That's what it's aiming for," said Kelvin, "and yes, I think we should let it go."

There might be dangers to shipping later on, but the greater Void Threat entity was a clear and present danger to the whole of Tristopolis, while the fleeing creature below might simply take refuge in the mid-ocean depths and stay there. Maybe even start to feed off herds of feral behemoths, which would if anything make trans-oceanic voyaging safer, removing one of shipping's greatest current threats.

"That's my judgement," said Kelvin. "Send someone else to keep track of its movements, if you can spare farseer operatives to act as spotters, otherwise just let it go completely."

"Roger that."

A click sounded in Kelvin's headphones, and Chambers continued to talk using her headset microphone, but inaudibly to him. The pteracopter's continuing roar blocked all other sound.

He might have tried to decipher her words by lipreading and mental resonance all the same, but besides the possibility of professionally offending a federal spellbinder, he felt simply too tired to make the effort.

Such a hard day already.

And he still wasn't ready to confront the Void Threat directly.

"I don't think any of us are." Chambers' voice, back in his headphones.

Leaking thoughts wasn't something Kelvin did normally. Federal spellbinders trod a different path to expertise than mages followed, the result being more specialised but also tougher in several ways, and a great deal more violent.

Not to mention ruthless.

But he wouldn't underestimate Federal Agent Chambers' sensitivity, either.

"The thing is," he told her, "if the scared thing we were tracking isn't the immediate danger, what we ought to be worrying about is—"

"Is where exactly the Void Threat is lurking right now." She reached for her headset and clicked a button. "Be advised, Control. Be advised. Entity in river is not, repeat not the main threat. Primary is elsewhere, repeat elsewhere."

Deep purple sky and the long vista of Tristopolitan towers swung left to right across Kelvin's vision as Chambers turned the pteracopter smoothly around.

"Am returning to South Central to resume grid search of—"

Something smashed behind Kelvin and the shock slammed his head back against the seat then forwards as the pteracopter cabin tipped, and Shatterway

Quay slid back into view below, alongside the river which was dark and placid-looking because that was not the source of the threat.

"Tail rotor's gone," shouted Chambers. "We're going down."

The merest hint of contact with a descending, taloned hand: that was all it had taken to destroy the pteracopter's integrity most likely by accident, because the greater contact came now, as the massive hand smacked down onto and into the River Inkflow, crashing tsunami-level waves into existence on either side, replacing placid waters with chaotic foam as it grabbed and caught and squeezed its prey, so dreadfully, lethally hard.

Even now, while panic and fear of imminent death clutched Kelvin's heart, the sound of that eldritch scream travelled right through him, shook every organ, and made him cry out with grief and shock.

That lesser entity was never going to make it as far as the ocean.

"Hang on," said Chambers as the foaming river grew large beneath them.

Falling and twisting, and Kelvin was trying to form an exit for them both as blue sparkles twinkled around the cabin, but he was far too tired and the world had morphed into a sickening, juddering kaleidoscope, impossible to hang onto.

Trying, but—

Natasha, I love you.

And his son, so young.

Andrei, I hope you—

"This is it, Mage."

Impact.

A maelstrom of blue fire surrounding him, absorbing him, his nerves exploding with an agony surpassing even his attempted resonance with the fleeing entity which was squealing now – he couldn't see anything but blazing sapphire, but he felt this too, and it was awful – as it died, that lesser creature from the crawlspace Beyond.

Split apart by talons and the otherworldly hunger of the thing that fed on it. Kelvin felt this, felt awful death crushing the smaller entity out of existence, and he knew that he himself was lost.

Andrei.

Never to see his son get into scrapes at school, find romance and study and make stupid mistakes as he turned into an adult and in turn perhaps had children of his—

Nova brilliance as the end appeared.

Natasha…

The greater part of him, his grounding in the world, his reason for everything he—

Explosion.

And strong hands holding him by his clothing, lowering him face-first to what looked like cold wet roughened concrete, and a part of him wanted to laugh but the whole thing had been too much so he closed his eyes instead and allowed it to slip away.

Let go of reality, so hard.

Peaceful oblivion.

FIFTEEN

Donal was a Lower Danklyn boy at heart, but as an adult he was a Tristopolitan who knew and loved more than his own immediate neighbourhood, so when he fell onto damp concrete, going down onto one knee but raising his head fast to check his surroundings, he knew immediately where Lamis had taken them.

Shatterway Quay. No mistaking the place.

He stood up slowly, taking it all in.

Spider-cranes and rust-streaked shipping containers in rows and stacks, and everything sopping wet although his own suit was dry, apart from the patch where his knee had touched the concrete, while the River Inkflow was churning, awash with white foam as if the entire thing were filled with detergent and stirred up violently by giants.

"Pretty much what happened," came the familiar sepulchral voice.

"What the Hades?" said Donal.

Lamis, standing tall, pointed down to the ground. "Both creatures went straight down into the earth, in a mostly immaterial state, or there'd be a lot more devastation."

"That's right." A woman's voice, behind Donal.

He turned. "What's happening? Who are—"

She wore a dark jumpsuit, and with one hand she was holding up a shaven-headed kneeling man whose head drooped forward, emphasising his polished scalp. But the woman's eyes were focused on Lamis.

"You're welcome," Lamis told her.

An abrupt nod from her, then she turned to the man she was supporting, who groaned his way into consciousness, and allowed her to help him to stand. He rocked, though, so the woman kept hold of him.

"Kelvin," said Donal. "What's happened?"

"He'll be alright," said the woman.

In that moment, he recognised her, though he'd last seen her face through the curved, tinted hexiglass of a cockpit or cabin or whatever the correct term was for a pteracopter. A federal 'copter in this case, armed with Spellstorm missiles until she'd fired the lot at the entity in Möbius Park.

"Federal Agent Chambers," he said, remembering the name he'd been told.

"Huh. And you're Riordan, right? The guy I flew from St Jarl's."

"Right." Donal gestured. "This is Mage Lamis."

"I know." Her tone was hard, and so was her expression.

Lamis turned away as if ignoring her. The direction of his gaze was difficult to judge with the wraparound shades, but he seemed to be looking at the still-churning river.

Foaming, but less so than a few seconds earlier.

"Two creatures," said Donal. "You said *two*?"

"The thing in the park," said Chambers. "Mage Kelvin calls it the Void Threat, so we're adopting that as the official operational designation. That thing, plus a smaller entity the Void Threat just killed."

"And absorbed." Kelvin spoke with a wince, as if just forming the words brought a migraine upon him.

At least he was standing without Chambers' support now.

"We were in the pteracopter," said Chambers. "In serious trouble, heading for a crash and unable to auto-rotate. Trying for a bilocation jettison but failing until assistance came by, by chance."

Kelvin blinked as he focused on Lamis's tall figure. "Oh, no."

"Yes, quite. We'd both be dead," Chambers told him, "if it weren't for him."

"I… Thank you, Mage."

Lamis turned back to him and gave a small, tight smile. "That was hard to say, wasn't it? But you're welcome."

Donal rubbed his face, not much caring to interpret the personal tensions and history among mages and federal spellbinders, not when the ordinary Tristopolitan populace remained at risk.

"Wait a minute." Federal Agent Chambers possessed grey-green eyes, hard and cold and staring now at Donal's chest. "What's this?"

After a second, Donal worked out what she meant.

"I'm a licensed investigator," he said. "My concealed-carry permit is up to date."

The extra rounds he carried on his belt were unusual, but this was an unusual day, and carrying ammunition remained legal in itself.

"I should have seen it before." Chambers looked at Kelvin, then at Lamis, and gave a tiny head shake. "But you both missed it too. Entirely."

Maybe she wasn't talking about firearms or bullets.

Kelvin tilted his head, and winced again.

"You should be in hospital," Donal told him. "There could be some concussion there."

"A couple of minutes ago," said Kelvin, "I was in a pteracopter with Federal Agent Chambers piloting, and now the pteracopter is in pieces at the bottom of the Inkflow. So I think I'm in pretty decent shape, considering."

"Up to you," said Donal. "You're a grown-up. Do you know what Federal Agent Chambers is on about, by any chance?"

"I do not."

Distant sirens sounded, and three black ambulances were spreading their bat-wings as they descended towards Blameway Stadium, by the looks of it. Most likely intending to land on the extensive parking lot rather than the sports ground, though you never knew.

No way of knowing how many casualties were out there.

But Shatterway Quay, this part of it at least, remained deserted apart from the four of them: Chambers, Lamis, Kelvin and Donal himself.

And if the other three all turned against him, Donal didn't fancy his chances. Not against the kinds of energies and deadly hex they were capable of deploying.

"I don't get it." He addressed Chambers directly. "What's your problem here?"

"Open your shirt," she said tightly. "I need you to undo your tie and unbutton your shirt to your waist. Do it now."

Lamis straightened, though Donal wouldn't have thought it possible, given his already erect stance.

"You should do what she says, my friend."

"Oh, Hades," said Donal.

Not knowing what was happening, but certain he wasn't going to like it.

Carefully, not taking his eyes off Chambers, he unknotted his tie, smoothed the two ends downwards, and undid his buttons one by one.

Nobody smiled, but then he already knew this was not a joke.

Federal spellbinders weren't exactly known for fun and giggles. More like serious expressions and sudden death. Judgement and justice in an instant, while mercy never got a look-in.

Never. Not when the feds were involved.

Without being asked, Donal pulled the halves of his shirt wide open, revealing his chest. The air felt perfectly fine against his skin, although a redblood would find the conditions cold.

"When was the last time you recharged?" said Chambers.

"Say what?"

"Your heart. When was the last time you plugged it in?"

Oh, sweet Thanatos.

This really wasn't going to be good news.

"Yesterday afternoon," he told her.

"You took a twenty-one-dimensional relic to St Jarl's." Kelvin winced again. Maybe it was a broken rib or a shattered tooth: his body language was hard to read. "When did you obtain it?"

"If you mean Drad the skull, then I guess about one o'clock, or a little after." Donal had no idea how a shape could possess twenty-one dimensions, but the obsidian skull was what he brought to Kyushen at St Jarl's. "Someone, something, came to see me at home a little after twenty-five o'clock, so about an hour after that, in my office."

Kelvin, Lamis and Chambers appeared to exchange glances, though in Lamis's case, with the wraparound shades, it was hard to be certain.

"I think we need to hear the whole story," said Lamis.

Chambers' mouth tightened. Maybe she didn't like the *we* in Lamis's suggestion, but if anyone here was on Donal's side, it was him.

So it might be a good idea to keep on with the assumption that Lamis was a key part of what they were doing. Except right now Donal was standing on Shatterway Quay, dressed in a suit with his shirt open to the waist, and he didn't understand where they were going with this.

"Perhaps we should take a closer look first," said Kelvin, "and hear Donal's story afterwards."

Using his name at least, not depersonalising a potential threat.

Oh, Thanatos.

Now he understood what they were on about.

"Is there something in here?" He placed a hand on his chest, above his heart. "Something concealed?"

When he came around in his office, lying on the floor, he'd felt a pain in his chest, right enough. But by the time he'd struggled to his feet, the pain had dissipated, and like an idiot he'd thought no more about it.

He realised that Lamis and Kelvin were moving their hands through identical, synchronous patterns of motion, and after a second, glowing violet and orange lines appeared in the air, primarily outlined rectangles with rounded corners, hanging there, stacked in layers, while runes inscribed in blue-tinged light circled all around.

Donal knew he wasn't going to like this.

Whatever it was.

Federal Agent Chambers was taking a different approach. From one perspective, she appeared totally unchanged; yet at the same time, somehow, her skin attained a kind of hardened whitish sheen, a bit like porcelain, no, like enamelled steel.

She took a step forward, and in that instant, what had been her eyes became twin glowing lights of emerald green.

Donal had never heard of such a thing, but then again, when federal spellbinders went into action, the only survivors afterwards tended to be the feds themselves. Witnesses, if any, were sent straight to trauma witches for counselling, which for all Donal knew involved cleansing said witnesses of memories that revealed tactical operation details.

Arguably for the sake of the witnesses' sanity: he could see how that might make sense.

Not liking this at all.

"*Open. Up. Now.*" Strange eldritch tones, barely human, came from Chambers' mouth. "*Do. It.*"

Donal pressed his chest and nodded at the same time. Dug in, twisted, and pulled it open: a flap of skin and myofascial tissue in its relaxed state – normal elasticity would resume when he sealed his chest back up again – with the pectoral muscle fibres, also preternaturally relaxed and extensible, stretched apart by the implanted black threads whose job was to do just that; plus the hinged sections of rib levered open.

Revealing his steadily beating, glistening black heart… and the silver crab-like metal object clasped around it, with three ruby ellipses on its back that might have been decorative markings, or might be eyes, looking at him and forming judgement.

Donal held totally still, staring at the thing he'd been carrying inside his chest without realising.

I am such a moron.

And with no idea how this was going to turn out, because this was totally new territory.

Not even sure whether this was an animate object or inanimate-yet-hexed, or something totally different.

In my Thanatos-damned heart cavity.

"It must have been the wolf that put it there." He spoke without looking away from the silver thing with the three ruby eyes upon its back: he'd decided it *was* watching him somehow. "I should have known."

Or maybe something situated a long distance away was watching through those eyes. Which couldn't have seen anything while his chest was closed up, so perhaps the plan had been for this thing to break its way out at some strategic moment.

Claw its way into open air and intervene in whatever was going on at that time. Maybe after shredding Donal's heart, either incidentally as part of its escape or intentionally as part of the plan.

"Wolf?" said Kelvin.

"White wolf, in my office." Donal glanced at him, then returned his attention to his opened-up chest. "Gave me the skull. At least, I thought it did."

Maybe he'd misinterpreted everything up to this point. If he could carry this thing around inside him without realising, what else might he have missed?

There'd been a white wolf and then it was gone when he awoke, and it was when he pulled himself to his feet that he'd seen the obsidian polished skull upon his desk.

Which to be fair, was more or less where the white wolf had been standing when Donal swung into his office through the open window.

Glowing white and green in front of him now.

That was Chambers, attaining some altered state that Donal realised with a sudden shock was entirely defensive, intended to protect her from whatever energies the thing inside his chest might attempt to deploy.

That scared him.

Likewise the growing three-dimensional lattice-like construct formed of violet and orange lines of light, reinforced and bound together with moving, blue-outlined runes: two mage conjurations joined together into a single protective shield, intended to guard Kelvin and Lamis for as long as the silver crab-like construct in Donal's chest remained a threat.

He hadn't liked it earlier. Now he was really worried.

This was inside my chest while I had breakfast with Mel. All that time.

A cold fury settled inside him.

Not allowed.

White wolf or Drad or someone or something else: it didn't matter who implanted this object. They'd violated his and Mel's privacy, and potentially endangered Mel, which he would *not* allow to continue.

So this was it.

He grabbed the silver crab-thing with his right hand, and pulled, but it would not come free and only massive zombie self-control enabled him to stop his scream before it began, because this *hurt* – burned internally in some way he had never experienced before.

"Oh, no, you don't."

So he changed tack. He wouldn't try to pull the thing free while ripping his own heart apart, because that would be counter-productive.

But I'm not letting you stay there.

He squeezed.

Some resurrected persons might hang onto pseudo-life while entirely neglecting their physical selves, even though mental state and physical being remained wrapped up together, for zombies exactly as for redbloods – he really had adopted that term in his mind – so that everything about those zombies' inner existence remained impoverished compared to the splendour they might have experienced.

And others went in the opposite direction.

Discipline was a harsh word to some people's ears, but to Donal, discipline was his greatest friend and ally, the only constant in his changing world, the thing that kept him together, kept his identity intact no matter what happened.

Zombie focus plus natural discipline plus the necrochemical processes of resurrected life combined to take athleticism to elite levels, and Donal had always been a runner and a boxer. Just squeezing a fist for impact a thousand times a day develops some kind of strength: the press-ups and chin-ups simply add to the core effect.

Too bad I'm not a wrestler.

He squeezed the silver crab-thing in his chest.

Or a climber. Even a bricklayer.

There were people with stronger grips than him, but not a huge number, and one of the main differences between redbloods and zombies was the number of energy systems in the body: redbloods possess three, two of them acting on a timescale of seconds while the third, aerobic process can keep going for hours; but no one can sprint a marathon.

No redblood, at least.

But resurrected athletes rely on a single necrochemical process for all forms of energy, which meant that for Donal, as he tried to crush the metal thing implanted inside his chest, although he squeezed hard enough to make his inner forearms burn, he could keep this going for hours if he had to.

I will not *give up.*

Squeezing harder, and maintaining it.

Not while I'm alive.

Minimal tension in the rest of his body, enough to keep him standing, while everything else went into his grip: the tendons in his hand, the muscles of his forearm; but the biggest factor had to be his strength of will.

Simply squeezing.

Pain, burning: irrelevant.

Focus.

Just the squeeze.

Nothing else.

The world shrinking away and darkening, everything narrowed down to primeval simplicity: squeeze to live, or fail and die.

A fraction harder, beyond what he'd thought possible.

Burning harder than ever, the sinews in his forearms, the tendons in his thumb and fingers, and none of it mattered because focusing his strength was everything.

Something shifted, and the pain flaring in his heart went beyond anything he'd ever felt before: deeply internal and *personal* in some new and shocking way.

Doesn't matter.

In fact it gave him a boost, because it meant he was affecting the metal crab-thing, and if it was trying to make him give up by inducing this pain, then too bad: this was his game now.

Owning it.

Squeezing and squeezing and squeezing: simply that.

"—out!" Some kind of distant warning shout.

No matter.

Yes. Harder.

He wouldn't have thought it possible, but he found another level of tension and determination, and buckled down.

Red glow from beneath his clenched hand.

Ignore.

Brighter now, but he didn't care.

Keep—

Something shifted.

—going.

He clenched even harder.

Yes.

Insisting, despite a glow as strong as molten ore, and pain inside transcending agony to some new layer of suffering, because none of that was relevant.

Yes…

And then it went, the integrity of the crab-thing. Gave way and began to crumple and something vital broke inside the metal carapace and that was it.

The thing imploded.

Red light was everywhere, and the burning.

"Riordan!"

White glowing hands clutching at him.

"Got it," he said, or imagined he did.

Flare of redness and heat, then…

Nothing.

SIXTEEN

Spinning.

First the blue vortex with Mage Lamis and now this whirling redness and none of it making perceptual sense, as if someone had disconnected his senses from reality and given everything inside him a vicious, violent stir inside a cauldron, and kept it going.

No.

Slapping his chest cavity shut even as he fell inside chaos, after flinging away the wreckage of the crab-thing that had lurked inside him. His own body existing and making sense, no matter what the state of his whirling, blood-red surroundings.

Ferocious, scarlet chaos.

It's changing.

And he fell out into cold reality once more, into the real world, landing on his feet with his right hand inside his jacket but not checking his heart, not needing to, because he knew his chest cavity was fully sealed, even though he'd performed the action in a glowing maelstrom.

With maximum speed, he drew the Magnus right-handed, let go of it and turned, catching the handgun in mid-air with his left hand – whose muscles remained fresh – and grew very still as he took in the curved rows of eyes focused on him.

Red eyes, all of them.

And the building interior: semi-circular tiers of creamy marble like some kind of amphitheatre, with Donal standing on the ground-level stage, while his lupine audience of hundreds poured all their attention onto him.

White wolves everywhere, with eyes the colour of shining rubies.

Two old wolves stood level with him: even larger than the others, and exactly how Donal knew they were older, given that every wolf here possessed white fur, he could not have said. Perhaps it was the wisdom in those eyes – but not a human wisdom.

The she-wolf growled – they were a mating pair, no, a *couple*, though again Donal had no idea how he knew that – and part of him knew this for purely wolf-speak, not like the few human words that Tristopolis PD's deathwolves uttered with difficulty.

And yet another part of him heard the she-wolf's utterings as purely human language.

"This must play out," she said.

Beside her, the big he-wolf growled. "We could help the humans. Directly and in force."

"At what cost? And I don't just mean how many of our lives."

Donal lowered his Magnus.

He transferred it to his right hand and reholstered it, without taking his eyes off the she-wolf in front of him, retaining peripheral awareness of the curved banks of other lupine eyes focused upon him, ruby red and highly intelligent with an apex predator's focus.

Any one of them could tear him apart in seconds, and never mind the Magnus and the extra rounds clipped to his belt: he was sure of it.

And this Council – again, he held odd knowledge in his head that he had no memory of learning – comprised two hundred and seven of the white wolves' representatives, not counting the two elders who ranked foremost among them and ruled via guidance, not imperative dictates, and never with selfishness or individual self-interest as a motive.

"We've revealed ourselves before," growled the he-wolf.

Several of the watching white wolves stirred, as if agreeing with the observation.

"As individuals, or at most a few together," replied the she-wolf, his wife. "And rarely."

"We can battle as a pack." Her husband bared his fangs. "And as a meta-pack, if we call everyone together."

"You want to bring the Cataclysm forward?"

"I want to end it, my dear."

"As do I, my love. But not before the optimal time."

The he-wolf turned his massive head to regard Donal. "Do you consider yourself brave, little human?"

"I try to do what has to be done." Donal's throat felt dry, and the words came out harsher than intended. "Everyone gets scared. Everyone."

A wave of low rumbles passed through the rows of watching wolves, and it seemed to indicate amusement, like a wry or gentle chuckle.

The white wolves were magnificent. Maybe Donal should bow or go down on one knee, or something.

"Excuse me," he said, and turned away.

He buttoned up his shirt, knotted his tie, straightened everything and hitched his belt, and fastened one button on his jacket. It compromised his ability to draw the Magnus fast, though only by a fraction because he practised closed-jacket draws as part of his training.

Still, he felt the wolves would understand a human gesture of respect. They probably understood more about people than people did themselves, regardless of the colour of a person's blood.

He turned back and gave the tiniest of bows to the watching wolves: an audience of judges, not spectators.

The she-wolf turned to her husband. "You see?"

"Yes." The he-wolf dipped his head. "In this, you were right."

This Council could become a War Council if required, and in some sense it already was, and always had been. More knowledge, new to Donal yet feeling old, as if he'd known the facts since childhood.

"What can I do?" he said.

It felt as if he were offering to pledge service, as he'd once sworn to uphold the defence of the Federation on enlisting in the Army, and when he swore to uphold law, order and forceful retribution at the start of his career with the Tristopolis PD.

His heart seemed to beat faster, which for a zombie was supposed to be impossible.

"You can't defeat the Void Threat," said the he-wolf.

The wolves had plucked the term from Donal's mind, or else it was Donal's way of understanding the wolf-speak reference reframed for his human self – his resurrected human self, but he wasn't sure his zombie status had much to do with it.

"Not alone." The she-wolf dipped her head. "On this, we can all agree, little one."

Not even Sister Mary-Anne Styx at the orphanage had called him that, yet it felt right in these surroundings.

Overhead, the marble interior formed a domed ceiling. The thought of surroundings made Donal wonder about the location, not to mention ways of exiting this place; but he would not act with discourtesy if he could help it, so he brought his attention back to the two elder wolves before him.

About to ask whether they could help him fight the Void Threat, he stopped the words before uttering them, knowing it would be a mistake.

"Will it harm your cause," he asked instead, "if the Void Threat is defeated?"

Again, the low rumble among the watching wolves. Not quite a lupine version of a chuckle this time, but a sound of approval all the same.

"It will be useful," said the she-wolf, "if your kind removes the entity from physical existence."

Not necessarily a euphemism for killing, Donal understood. Getting the Void Threat to flee back to its original dwelling space would be good enough, although the wolves didn't particularly feel that the entity deserved to live.

They just didn't think that Donal's kind was up to killing it.

Whatever "your kind" meant.

The he-wolf growled and pulled his lips back from his fangs once more, and spoke. "She means all physical and wraith-like Tristopolitans, not just humans."

"Understood, sir." Donal nodded.

He'd been perturbed when Lamis had appeared to read his thoughts. Here, it felt totally natural, even relaxing.

And "wraith-like" included sprites and ghouls: the meaning was utterly clear. But getting every individual of every kind in the city to fight together en masse to defeat the Void Thing...

That seemed impossible.

"You cannot defeat it," said the she-wolf.

"But the Summoner can send it back." The he-wolf's eyes glowed strongly as he spoke.

"The Summoner?" said Donal.

"Someone placed it in your lair," the she-wolf told him. "Our operator found it there."

"My lair... My office?"

"Yes," said the he-wolf.

And his wife had meant operator in the sense of *operative*: one of their kind, a white wolf acting as a lone soldier in potentially hostile territory.

"Did...?" Donal stopped.

The operator, the wolf in his office, had come to investigate the skull, and had decided to do nothing other than allow Donal to take possession and let the game play out.

Whatever the game was. Whoever the unseen player or players might be.

So much I don't know.

But the wolves didn't know who was behind all this any more than he did, or so it seemed.

Donal wanted to ask about the Cataclysm that she-wolf had mentioned, but something told him not to. The wolves hadn't brought him here to tell him all their history and intentions. They weren't even intending to help humanity and other sentients directly, from what he could tell.

Even the he-wolf, Donal realised, didn't want an all-out attack from the massed ranks of wolves drawn from the entire continent.

Or possibly his suggestion meant drawing white wolves here from all over the world. There was a level of understanding that Donal couldn't drill down to, for all the clarity of wolf-speak-to-human-speak translation that was happening inside his mind.

When the he-wolf had suggested a mass attack of white wolves, he'd chosen it as the least bad of the available options, all of them predicted to be disastrous.

As Donal glanced up at the two hundred and seven pairs of watching ruby eyes, he understood the seriousness of their deliberations – planning the next step in some type of ongoing campaign that perhaps had lasted for centuries – and realised this was something like a once-in-a-human-generation event, or maybe rarer.

He didn't feel up to representing humanity, red- or black-blooded, never mind the other kinds of citizen who enriched Tristopolitan life and that of the world beyond. He was an orphan from Lower Danklyn who'd tried to bring a tiny bit of justice into his vast city, and simply live an ordinary life: no more than that.

But he was here, him and no one else.

So deal with it.

"The skull," he said. "Baladradian Chalintropovin. That's the Summoner?"

"That name, Chalintropovin, belongs to the human portion of the composite."

"Oh," said Donal.

He knew a wraith called Aggie, short for Aggregate, with a unique and definite personality, yet she'd previously been two separate wraiths, who fused and changed when one rescued the other from a trap comprised of ferocious energies whose nature Donal didn't entirely understand.

Aggie was neither of her forebears, but possessed a definite identity, so clearly an entity could form by an act of composition; but Donal had never heard of a human and a non-human entity merging in such a way.

"More than two." The she-wolf's eyes glowed stronger. "Perhaps nine in total, though we cannot be sure."

"Nine different types of entity? Or one human and eight of the same non-human kind?" Donal shook his head, realising the answer couldn't help him, not directly. "Never mind. I presume I need to return to St Jarl's, where I left the skull?"

"Yes," said the he-wolf.

"I know mages and others who might help me." For some reason, Donal didn't think he should mention federal spellbinders explicitly in these surroundings. "If they need to know about entity types, they'll be able to figure it out, I expect."

"Yes," said the she-wolf.

Donal looked up at the massed ranks, the steady ruby-coloured eyes, and felt similar to the way he reacted on seeing another fighter or cop or soldier: a deep recognition of similarity based on attitude and posture and related body language, without requiring a single word of conversation.

For all their differences, he and the white wolves possessed something in common: deep inside, a matter of attitude and bearing and perspective on the world, at a level so real and fundamental that he would find it difficult, even embarrassing, to articulate the concepts in ordinary words.

"I'll do my best," he told them.

They lowered their heads en masse, and a feeling of awe swept down through Donal's body

I don't deserve to be standing here.

But he was here, so he bowed in return.

"We can send you to the place you call St Jarl's," the she-wolf told him, her eyes simultaneously gentle and wise and ready for lethal violence in an instant. "Or to the docks from where we fetched you."

That would be Shatterway Quay, where Lamis and Kelvin and Federal Agent Chambers might be still standing, although if they'd departed via the sapphire vortex or some other means, there was no point in going there now.

And it lay over thirty miles from St Jarl's, which would leave Donal with another journey to make, and more time to waste.

As if I knew what to do in St Jarl's.

He'd been powerless before the black-and-silver sphere of nothingness before, and he felt no different now. Which meant he needed allies.

"The dock," he said. "Send me back to Shatterway Quay please, ma'am."

The she-wolf drew her lips back in something like a smile.

"Yes," she said.

"You will find a way," said the he-wolf.

To penetrate whatever phenomenon had trapped or obliterated poor Kyushen Jyu: Donal understood what the he-wolf meant.

"Thank you, sir." Donal inclined his head towards both of the elder wolves. "I'm honoured."

He said it, and he meant it.

And then the redness fell upon him.

The ultimate dismissal.

SEVENTEEN

Donal sat up with a start, finding himself on the concrete of Shatterway Quay, his back and the back of his legs damp – no, more than that: truly wet – because he'd been lying on this dock that remained soaked with water, the result of the Void Threat's one-sided battle against a lesser entity in the river.

Somehow, he knew that as clearly as if he'd seen the confrontation unfold: seen it with his own eyes.

"Donal." The familiar sepulchral voice of Lamis. "You're alright?"

He was standing with Kelvin off to Donal's right. There was no sign of Federal Agent Chambers.

"What happened?" asked Donal. "How come I was lying on the ground?"

He rose to his feet, turning, his suit fabric clammy and wet against hamstrings and calves and the back of his shoulders.

"You crushed the metal construct in your chest," said Kelvin, "and then collapsed. Chambers went to phone for an ambulance."

The nearest phone booth might be a mile away. There were certainly none in the dockyard, not unless Chambers broke into one of the site offices – which of course she might.

"And she took the construct with her," said Lamis. "More to the point. She'll be dissecting the remains herself, I should think."

Donal's jacket was still buttoned, but twisted. He straightened it, checked his tie knot, and angled his neck from side to side, more a gesture from his first life than an actual necessity for loosening up his muscles.

"Hey!" A distant female shout.

From a spiralling ramp off a footbridge, Federal Agent Chambers came jogging over, her gait easy, her expression serious.

"You've woken up," she added, checking Donal out. Then she turned to the mages. "That monitor construct disappeared from my hand."

"Disappeared?" said Kelvin.

"With a flare-up of red light as it went."

"Are you... Well of course you're sure." Kelvin ran a hand across his shaved scalp. "Entirely the wrong necromagnetic frequency for spillover from geodesic manipulation, so it must be some other..."

The words faded from Donal's awareness as he looked back at the patch of concrete where he'd been lying. Every second of his meeting with the Council of White Wolves remained vivid in his mind. Surely no hallucination could persist so tangibly afterwards.

It could *not* have been a dream.

"You sealed up his chest and did up his clothing." Chambers gestured at Donal, though her words were directed towards Kelvin and Lamis. "Might have wanted to leave him opened up for the paramedics to work on."

"I'm fine," Donal told her.

But Mages Kelvin and Lamis were looking at each other and shaking their heads.

"We didn't touch him at all," said Kelvin.

"Indeed," said Lamis.

"But we only looked away from him for a second."

Donal pulled wet trouser fabric away from the back of his legs. "I came awake in this state, but I don't think I was really unconscious or—"

"What the Hades is that?" said Chambers.

Her skin took on something of that white, enamelled steel appearance once more, as if poised to complete a transformation into living armour.

A red glow emanated from Donal's right hand.

"Oh," he said.

When he raised his hand, his knuckles uppermost, the source of the redness became clearly visible.

A silvery ring encircling his second finger, a red ellipse glowing inside its setting. And two more, he realised as he turned his hand over and spread his fingers: three ellipses in all, set equidistantly around the ring's circumference.

"It's a present," he added, and pulled his mouth to one side in a half smile.

Chambers shook her head. "It's the monitor construct, reformed."

"And the real monitors behind it are our friends." Donal turned to Lamis. "None of us can defeat the Void Threat, not even the combined forces of Mordanto and the feds, uh, federal spellbinders, or even a battalion of Death Dragoons, if they could get here in time."

Behind the wraparound shades, Lamis's expression remained unreadable, but his voice grew deeper and colder than ever. "What makes you a sudden expert on the nature of this thing?"

"You think the Void Threat got at me, somehow?" Donal shook his head. "Didn't happen."

"Yet my question stands."

"The friends who gave me this" – he raised his right fist to show the ring, and the ellipse grew brighter for a moment – "told me enough to get us started, but no more than that."

He glanced in the direction of the dark River Inkflow, though its surface looked placid once more and the Void Threat and its now-dead prey were long gone.

"I know a little about the nature of the Void Threat," he added, "but it's only a starting point and I'm just an ordinary ex-cop turned private citizen trying to play a small part in saving the city."

"Pretty speech," said Kelvin. "Very modest."

"And accurate." Chambers sounded impatient, although her skin had regained its normal, non-defensive appearance. "Riordan knows Death-all about trans-dimensional geodesics and crawlspace topology, so we're wasting time standing here and talking about it."

Donal felt his eyes narrow as he looked at her.

"You *know*," he said. "You're not curious about the people I called my friends, the ones who gave me this ring, because you already know exactly who they are."

"I worked it out." Her voice tightened. "Except the white wolves aren't people, and you're a Thanatos-damned fool if you haven't worked that out yet."

Kelvin sucked in a breath, and Lamis might even have twitched the side of his mouth: his version of a normal person gasping in shock.

"Interesting friends you have," said Lamis.

"You should know," Donal told him.

Darkness moved overhead: black bat-wings spread beneath the perpetually deep purple sky.

"Ambulance," said Federal Agent Chambers. "I've no way to abort the callout, but whatever kind of help we need right now, it isn't medical."

The docks were extensive, and a single overflight was sufficient for the ambulance's driver – or pilot, for Donal had never decided, and paramedics were not talkative beings, so their preference remained unknown – to decide on a clear length of concrete for landing.

Soon enough, the black ambulance flew down to land, furled its wings on touchdown and commenced deceleration, braking to a halt in a surprisingly short distance, leaving wheel-marks along the glistening wet concrete.

"We need to get to St Jarl's," said Donal. "The ambulance is one way, unless you mages can snap your fingers and whisk us there, just like that."

"If it were that easy," said Kelvin, "no mage would need to walk anywhere, and you'd see us popping into and out of existence all over the city, day in and day out, just to go shopping and the like."

"Huh." Maybe Donal had grown blasé over the past few hours. Of course it couldn't be that straightforward.

They probably needed hours or more to recharge in between transitions;

and both Lamis and Kelvin were senior mages: that much was certain. Most likely the majority of mages couldn't manage such feats at all.

"I thought Mordanto employed housekeeping staff for matters as mundane as shopping," said Chambers.

"I was being hypothetical."

"Sure you were."

Donal looked from Chambers to Kelvin to Lamis. "This is going to be fun. Since we're all getting on so well."

"Up yours," said Chambers.

"A modicum of politeness might help," said Kelvin.

Which made Donal shake his head, because he could take more of Chambers' sarcastic attitude than Kelvin's attempt at smooth diplomacy.

Two beings with grey skin and black uniforms were approaching from the ambulance, their nictitating membranes working overtime on their dark eyes, as if they were trying to work out which of the standing humans was supposed to be the patient in need of emergency treatment.

Paramedics. Life-savers, genuinely brave in the service of ordinary folk, yet entirely lacking in actual empathy as far as Donal had ever been able to tell.

"I'm feeling much better," he told them. "Sorry. It wasn't a hoax."

Chambers said: "Doesn't matter. We need your ambulance. Federal business."

The two paramedics looked at each and other shook their heads.

"Not—"

"—possible."

A green glimmer rose in Federal Agent Chambers' eyes, at the same time as Kelvin and Lamis formed spellcast mudras with their hands, and Donal unbuttoned his jacket to reveal the holstered Magnus.

"Oh."

"Ah."

"*Exactly*," said Chambers, with just a hint of otherworldly harmonics in her voice.

Enough to make the two paramedics step aside, one to the left and the other to the right, leaving a clear path towards the low black ambulance. It was long and predatory-looking, and the best way to travel so long as Chambers could pilot the thing.

"Of course she can," said Lamis.

Donal tightened his right fist and clamped down on his thoughts. This mindreading would have to stop.

Chambers led the way with the two mages right behind her, but Donal hesitated, looked from one paramedic to the other – really looked – and saw not just their trembling, but the way that the trembling increased as Chambers and Lamis and Kelvin drew closer to the ambulance.

The paramedics' grey-skinned faces were hard to read, which Donal had always interpreted as a lack of emotion in their kind, but he'd been proven wrong several times over in the space of less than twenty-five hours; and this particular old mistake was overdue for correction.

"Wait," he called out to Chambers. "The paramedics need to come with us."

"We don't need them," said Chambers. "Come on, Riordan. Or I'll reconsider whether we actually need *you*."

She and the mages had stopped, turned back, and frowned in synchronised impatience as if they'd rehearsed it.

"It's isn't all about us," Donal told her. "They can't be separated from their ambulance." He gestured towards the paramedics. "Not for any length of time."

"Don't be—" began Chambers.

"He's right." Lamis cut her off. "Separation might prove damaging, possibly not, but it would certainly be most painful. I can see that now."

His wraparound shades might conceal blasted pits for eye sockets, but insight was his speciality. It was embarrassing that a mundane, albeit a resurrected one with enhanced acuity, had spotted a phenomenon that he himself had missed.

"Don't worry about it," Donal told him. "All mages tend to underestimate mundanes."

Lamis jerked, and Kelvin stared at him, then at Donal. "You picked up on a mage's leaked thought? On *Lamis's* thought?"

A hint of glowing green in Chambers' eyes.

"The enemy is somewhere below the city," said Donal, "ready to rise up and smash the whole of Tristopolis into rubble without a sweat, and our only hope is to get the thing at St Jarl's to communicate with that real enemy, the Void Threat, and send it back where it came from."

If there was anything Donal had in common with a federal spellbinder it was a deep understanding of the tactical and strategic need for aggression, directed at the appropriate target – and how that need affected priorities, and differentiated between necessary action and wasted time.

Standing around discussing esoteric concepts fell into the time-wasting category, especially since Donal had little desire for introspective analysis, and none at all for doing it with an audience.

A federal spellbinder ought to understand that much.

Chambers nodded, and the green glimmer faded, bringing her eyes back to their normal grey-green hue.

"Noted," she said. "Everyone, get into the ambulance, including you two paramedics. We need to move."

They made their way to the ambulance in a ragged group.

The long black vehicle could easily hold a dozen people in comfort, maybe nineteen or twenty at a push, so room wasn't an issue, and neither was the weight: ambulances could fly with all sorts of wounded entities inside, or ensorcelled humans channelling all kinds of hex that sometimes manifested as physical mass, which made an ambulance possibly the most tactically useful type of vehicle to possess in odd, dangerous circumstances.

Donal had never heard of a private individual owning a second-hand ambulance, but if he got through this current struggle and managed to scrape up enough money, maybe later he could investigate the possibility of getting one himself.

He wondered what Mel would have to say about that.

Perhaps he ought to find out first, before making any kind of actual plans.

A minute later, he was sitting on a sideways-facing bench seat in the rear of the ambulance – on the left-hand side, so the front of the vehicle was to his left – opposite the two grey-skinned paramedics, who were almost expressionless but hinting at glum depression, and a cheerful-looking Mage Kelvin, whose eyes had come alight in a human, even boyish way.

"I've never ridden in one of these before," he said. "It's quite a treat."

Donal shook his head, but couldn't help smiling.

Up front, Lamis was sitting next to Chambers, who of course was at the wheel, and at whatever other controls were situated there. Donal had never really tried to get a good look.

The paramedics simply sat opposite Donal in silence, their eyes nictitating in synchrony from time to time, looking nowhere special, apparently lost in their thoughts. The details were impossible to read.

"We're headed for St Jarl's," Donal told them. "And it is a real emergency, or we wouldn't be doing this."

No reaction.

Well, no matter. If a deeper apology were required later, he would consider it then, and maybe give them a metaphorical slap upside the head instead, for not reacting in a more positive way.

Or maybe a physical slap. Sometimes simpler is better.

The ambulance's twin engines rumbled, vibrating the seat beneath Donal along with the rest of the vehicle.

"How high do you think we'll fly?" asked Kelvin, as if he were ten years old.

"Behave yourself," said Donal, "or you won't get an ice cream later."

Kelvin laughed.

It was the happiest sound that Donal had heard in a long time, and he grinned almost as broadly as Kelvin when the ambulance began to roll forward, accelerate hard, and tilt its front upward as the bat-wings spread out to either side; and the wheels lost contact with the ground.

Both paramedics lowered their heads as if ashamed, as the vehicle rose and the damp darkness of Shatterway Quay fell away beneath them, and over a minute passed before the ambulance levelled out, flying high above even the tallest towers of Tristopolis.

So huge and vast, Donal's baroque, twisted, full-of-life city, where existence was complicated and you had to be tough-skinned and street smart and determined to survive – the opposite to quiet rural life – and every inhabitant was different from yet similar to every other Tristopolitan; and you could crack wise about the place all you liked, but in the end, this place mattered; and there was nothing to do when the city was in danger except fight for its survival.

The two paramedics looked up at him, and their nictitating membranes slid across their eyes three times in synchrony.

"Yes. We—"

"—understand."

Then they did something that Donal hadn't realised their kind was capable of doing. In unison, they smiled.

Curved needle-like fangs revealed themselves in those smiles, and the paramedics' fingers, which ended in talons rather than nails, elongated themselves, just enough to indicate their lethal potential.

"We will fight by—"

"—your side."

Kelvin looked as surprised as Donal felt.

"Thank you," was all that Donal could say.

The city's towers continued to slide past below and off to either side, beneath the always-purple sky that looked as if it stretched to infinity, and even though you knew about the millions and millions of inhabitants, it remained impossible to contemplate every single one of them as an individual with their own birth and death and complicated life in between, every one of them defining a subjective world, a universe, while every such universe was doomed in the end to extinction.

But not today. Not for everyone en masse.

Tristopolis deserved to live.

EIGHTEEN

Off to the ambulance's right – straight in front of Donal in his sideways-facing seat, as he stared past the paramedics' shoulders – a column of fire shot upwards. It was orange and startling against the deep purple sky and dark city backdrop.

Slender in appearance from inside the ambulance at altitude, it had to be hundreds of feet high, maybe a thousand, as near as Donal could judge.

"Did you see that?" he called to Chambers and Lamis up front.

"There's another to port." Chambers spoke in a clipped voice, not trying to project her voice back. "I'm going to take us higher."

Donal glanced out the window behind his shoulder, and saw that she was right: another fire-column, perhaps further away, was arrowing up from among the buildings.

He would have thought that simply accelerating forward was the best way to get them past any additional fire columns about to manifest themselves – not increase altitude as Chambers had decided to do – but perhaps a federal spellbinder had some idea about the nature of the fire. Donal was clueless in that regard.

To either side, the two existing columns continued to burn with no sign of turbulence or twisting apart or, for that matter, any clouds of smoke.

A soft keening sound arose from both paramedics' throats in unison.

Maybe they sensed casualties below, and the perception triggered a deep desire to fly the ambulance down to ground level and try to help. It was understandable, but most likely getting to St Jarl's would let Chambers and the mages do something about the greater Void Threat that was probably, somehow – maybe indirectly – behind these new eruptions of fire.

And certainly threatened the whole of Tristopolis, not to mention the further carnage it might wreak across the rest of the Federation and the greater world once Tristopolis was destroyed.

There was an odd look in Kelvin's eyes, and for a second it seemed that the world had blurred the way it did when you took a hook punch out of nowhere and it smacked you in the temple or the side of the jaw: it looked as if multiple Kelvins were occupying the same space, or almost the same space, superimposed upon each other; and then the effect snapped out of existence, and Kelvin looked like himself once more, singular and solidified.

"Turn back!" he shouted.

"Hard to starboard." Up front, Lamis was addressing Chambers. "Any way you can."

Lamis had been Commissioner Vilnar's driver, before the Commissioner was killed in City Hall. Perhaps it accounted for the authority in his voice now, although Vilnar's cars had been ordinary ground-based limos, as far as Donal knew.

Perhaps the job had been more than an excuse for a police commissioner to keep a trusted mage close at hand without any of the administrative procedures and safeguards hampering the usual employment of consultants, which was what Donal had assumed the setup to be.

Maybe Lamis really possessed some expertise in handling vehicles in emergency situations, even vehicles in flight.

"Thanatos." Chambers reacted and the ambulance banked right and downwards.

Donal's stomach felt empty all of a sudden, and he clutched the nearest chrome handles to hold himself in place on the bench seat, in danger otherwise of falling across the aisle, either onto the paramedics' laps or potentially hitting the opposite window.

Then it happened.

A vast sheet of flame spread upwards and out before them: a giant curtain of fire stretching from left to right of the ambulance's original trajectory, filled with twisting shapes suggesting mouths and tortured eyes, and rearing thousands of feet into the air, far higher than the altitude the ambulance had been flying at.

Stretching miles to either side, the flames.

Chambers was taking them down, banking past a high tower and into a canyon between buildings, following a miles-long straight boulevard that might have been Shameway Divide, but Donal felt too disoriented to be certain.

What the Hades is going on?

The paramedics stopped their keening noise and looked to the front of the ambulance, their dark eyes growing wider than ever. In the pilot's seat – driver's seat, whatever – Chambers seemed to stiffen, then she gave a sharp, almost microscopic nod.

Donal glanced at Kelvin, who raised an eyebrow. He'd noticed it too.

Some kind of silent communication from paramedics to federal spellbinder.

They were hurtling along the Divide – Donal grew certain of the street's identity – at the level of the highest tower pinnacles flowing past on either side. Here and there, to both left and right, small clouds of startled gargoyles were rising into the air, flapping their stubby wings that looked far too small and dense to be effective for flight; but they were ascending all the same.

Was Chambers looking for a place to land? Or simply flying away from the vast new obstruction, this barrier of flame, and planning to ascend once more, as soon she had a new trajectory determined?

An explosion burst sideways out of a building on the left. Chambers banked right then left again, and they were past it, descending almost low enough to touch car roofs with the ambulance's wheels. Donal wondered how long she could maintain this altitude without crashing into something.

Not liking this.

The two paramedics' bodies seemed to be vibrating, and their twin gazes were fastened on what appeared to be the back of Chambers' head, even as the flying ambulance tilted and briefly rose, then descended back to level flight within the artificial canyon formed of buildings; and the paramedics might have rocked in their bench seat but nothing was going to divert their attention.

Helping Federal Agent Chambers fly this Thanatos-damned ambulance for sure, because if they were up to anything else, the two paramedics would be dead: no one messes with federal spellbinders and lives to tell the tale.

Everyone knows that.

Then came what the paramedics and Chambers must have been looking for: a clear stretch of roadway up ahead, where a few scattered cars had pulled up onto the sidewalks and stopped, and all other vehicles had swerved into one or other of the side-streets, leaving Shameway Divide itself devoid of traffic.

Really not liking this.

The black wings made snapping sounds on either side, their lower surfaces cupped into concave configurations that Donal had never seen before, and caused the ambulance to shudder as it dropped faster than he'd expected; and when the tyres stuck tarmac, the suspension springs bounced hard enough to fling Donal upwards from his seat.

His head thumped against the ceiling and he dropped back onto the seat and the ambulance was screeching as Chambers fought to slow it down in time – yes, there were parked vehicles and scattering pedestrians up ahead: a longer clear stretch would have been too much to hope for – and in under three seconds Chambers had brought the whole thing swinging sideways to a howling halt.

Blue-grey smoke rose from the tyres, along with the stench of burning rubber; but the ambulance was still and otherwise intact, or seemed to be, and no one inside was injured.

"Hades," said Donal. "Could you do that again, Agent? I couldn't quite see what was happening."

No one laughed, or even smiled.

Not everyone has a sense of humour.

The wings on either side folded into the ambulance's body, and both paramedics slumped back on their bench seat, their chests rising and falling in time as they caught their breath and tried to recover.

Some people might think it strange, but Donal was beginning to think that nothing could surprise him these days, not after everything he'd been through during his career, especially in the last few years.

White wolves, though…

Since he'd regained consciousness – or something – on the dock with his suit and shirt buttoned up and his tie reknotted, even though the mages hadn't taken their eyes off him long enough for him to do such a thing unobserved, part of his mind had been engaged in analysing memory, in trying to decipher the nature of his experience that felt so very real.

The circumstances implied that his entire meeting with the Council of White Wolves had spanned just an instant in time.

Either that or it had occurred inside his mind in real-time while he lay on the dock unconscious, then instantaneously changed the state of his clothing and placed the silver ring adorned with red ellipses on his finger just as he woke up.

Both seemed logical possibilities – within an esoteric frame of reference, at least – and he couldn't think of a third option, which meant the other possibilities were even more insane; and it seemed to him that his first guess must be true: that he'd physically been elsewhere and experienced a minutes-long duration of time, while the whole interaction actually took only an instant in the normal world's timeframe.

It seemed the least bizarre of all available options, every one of which felt crazy.

Chambers and Lamis had already exited the ambulance from either side up front, while Donal had been thinking about the Council of White Wolves. Here in the back of the ambulance, the two paramedics were rousing themselves, back to something like normal, and turning towards the rear doors as though they, too, had decided to get out.

But Kelvin didn't look as if he was going anywhere.

Injured?

For a fraction of a second, Donal thought it might be a Basilisk Trance, which would have been horrific. Kelvin was sitting in place with a gentle expression on his face and defocused eyes trained on nothing at all: not so much lost in thought as simply disconnected from the world.

But his muscles showed none of the rigidity that went with imprisonment in a Basilisk Trance. He didn't look distressed in any way.

And then he blinked, glanced in Donal's direction and then stared back into empty air, and said: "Yes, he's here."

The paramedics were watching with interest.

"What's her name, the Night Sister?" said Kelvin. "Okay. I could try to transport him directly to your—Oh."

A few odd moments followed, with Kelvin nodding to no one there, then he finished with: "Understood, Professor. I'll do that. And good luck to you, too."

Then he blinked the communication trance out of existence, because that was clearly what he'd been up to. Unless he was delusional or ensorcelled, but Chambers or Lamis would have detected that – even though they were outside on the street – and taken some kind of action by now, if that had been the case.

Kelvin looked at Donal, and his gaze was normal now. "You should probably go to Avenue of the Basilisks. To your headquarters."

"Not exactly mine, these days."

"Yes, quite. But I mean Police HQ, where someone called Sister Felice is either a witness or a prisoner – I'm not entirely clear on that point, because I'm getting this from Professor Steele, who's been on the phone with Commissioner Sandarov. Although she was there in person earlier, in the Commisioner's office, if I understood correctly."

The ambulance interior felt cold, imbued with some kind of clinical, chemical fragrance that Donal hadn't noticed before. Maybe something had been spilled in the hard landing; or maybe it was his state of mind, fastening on details that hadn't been relevant while they were dodging flames and explosions in the air.

"I know Sister Felice," he told Kelvin. "And so do you. She helped on the Energy Authority thing."

"Ah, yes."

"She's based at St Jarl's."

"Right now she's in a cell or something. Professor Steele says she needs help, but I don't know what kind. Except that I think it's within my purview."

Purview. Thanatos.

There was a knock on the window behind Donal. It was Chambers, crouching down and looking inside, her face hard with impatience.

"Let's get out," said Donal. "And then we can all work out what to do."

"Sure." Kelvin roused himself, edging to the rear door which swung open as he reached for it. "Thank you, Mage."

He was addressing Lamis, who was standing out on the street, and who'd pulled the rear hatch open from outside.

Kelvin shuffled along the bench seat then gingerly hauled himself out through the gap, as if he'd aged by several decades in the space of minutes, and out onto the street.

"I'll be alright in a minute or three," he said, rubbing his face.

"Take your time." Donal slid out after him and stepped away from the ambulance, rotating slowly to take in what was happening.

An odd sensation filled the air as if it had grown ionised before a storm, and everything felt heavy and quiet, while the shouts and siren sounds were distant, as if they were happening in a dream.

Close at hand, Shameway Divide was quiet and felt deserted, as if everyone were home asleep; but instead it was strewn with abandoned cars.

And, over a mile away down the length of the canyon-like boulevard, in the direction from which Chambers had flown the ambulance here, reared that great wall of tortured flame, filled with writhing shapes suggestive of agonised mouths and suffering eyes, as if a thousand human beings had transformed into giant-sized flamesprites and merged – or been imprisoned – inside a single blazing conflagration.

Yet it wasn't spreading or advancing, simply standing there and burning; and despite its distance, Donal could feel some of its warmth upon his face.

"That's not good," he said.

"Very astute," muttered Chambers. "I can't think why Tristopolis PD sacked you."

"No one sacked him," said Lamis. "He was buried in a cemetery and left there, presumed dead. Presumed killed in the line of duty, in fact while engaged in an act of bravery. And I believe they offered to reinstate him on his return."

"Huh." Chambers flicked a glance in Donal's direction. "Alright. Noted."

Kelvin approached them. "There's a Night Sister at Police HQ, an acquaintance of Donal's, who's been in contact with – I mean physically touched – the skull that's producing the distortion field at St Jarl's."

So had Donal, but everyone here knew that, and it hadn't helped so far.

"In contact?" said Chambers. "How, exactly?"

"She purchased the skull, after asking the storekeeper for an artefact housing a particular kind of hex configuration, and she might know something more subconsciously that might help. An interrogation witch has tried to get information out of her, but—"

"Witches." Chambers sounded dismissive. "Right. Maybe she's worth talking to, this Night Sister, or maybe we should just go and talk to the storekeeper, or else to try to get past that bastard thing" – she gestured towards the giant wall of flame, which still appeared to be going nowhere – "and hammer our way to St Jarl's as fast as possible."

"Have you tried any kind of hex involving entanglement?" asked Kelvin, and looked at Lamis. "Or any form of compactified-dimensions translocation? I mean in the last few minutes."

Both Chambers and Lamis blinked. After a second, Chambers' expression tightened, while Lamis's long features remained immobile and unreadable; but his silence was a reply of sorts.

Wonderful.

"Are you suffering from inadequacies in the hex department?" Donal had to say it. "Problems with performance?"

But the words came from established patterns of professional banter, from being used to working alongside hard-nosed cops in dangerous and nasty situations: a levity more apparent than actual. He was feeling anything but light-hearted.

"Professor Steele told me." Kelvin addressed Chambers and Lamis directly, ignoring Donal, which was probably understandable. "Every likely geodesic and manifold is blocked or turned back on itself. And some pathways are taken up by, well, entities more concerned with getting away from this vicinity than maintaining their normally invisible, marginal existence."

Sometimes Kelvin could act like a schoolboy, especially when something delighted him. On other occasions, his words mixed pretentious phrasing with concise but highly esoteric descriptions. It was a wonder that Donal still liked the guy.

He had mixed feelings about Sister Felice, too. And wasn't the point of all this to get as much expertise as possible – actual experts in person, like these three individuals – on the ground at St Jarl's?

Which made him wonder what all those highly qualified thaumaturgeons and the like were up to right now. Maybe they were making some kind of progress.

But there was no way of knowing either way, not from here. He took it for granted that the fire entity – or entities, or whatever the manifestation actually was – would have destroyed every phone line it intersected.

"Can't we just fly over that thing?" He pointed at the wall of fire with the tortured, twisting forms inside. "It's high for sure, but it doesn't seem to be growing any higher."

"It would destroy any craft or vehicle that tried." Chambers shook her head slightly. "Give me a moment, alright?"

Kelvin raised an eyebrow, Lamis remained impassive, and Donal simply watched as Chambers walked up to the two paramedics, stood unusually still for several quiet moments, and then she shook their hands, one after the other, entirely in silence.

Silent, but some kind of communication had been taking place, all the same: Donal was sure of it.

Chambers returned to the two mages and Donal. Behind her, the paramedics simply climbed back into the black ambulance – to their normal seats up front – and started the twin engines.

"They're going to look for casualties," said Chambers. "Drive at ground level, administer first aid where they can, take any bad emergencies to Fearblame Clinic or St Aethelred's, whichever they can get to."

The ambulance got into motion, took a curved path around the four of them – for a second, the nearer paramedic looked out at Donal, and seemed to give the minutest of nods which Donal returned, hopefully fast enough for the paramedic to notice – and then the ambulance was heading down Shameway Divide, but not too fast.

Three blocks down, it swung left and was lost from sight.

"We could have used the wheels," said Kelvin.

"Any kind of vehicle will do us," said Lamis. "They need the ambulance for their work."

Whether they'd recovered their energies or not, neither of the mages could transport themselves or others via the blue vortex phenomenon – whatever it was exactly. That much, Donal had understood from Kelvin's words.

Also that Kelvin had been communicating with Professor Helena Steele, head of Mordanto and mother to the dead Laura whose heart beat inside Donal's chest. Donal didn't know how he felt about that.

But introspection could come later, if at all.

Here and now, there was something else he didn't understand the nature of, and it was right there in sight, a mile from here, blocking Shameway Divide and rearing tall and stretching who-knew-how-many miles to either side.

He pointed at the wall of flame. "Does any of you know what the Hades that is? Something to do with the Void Threat thing? It can't just have popped up by coincidence."

Tactical assessment. Chambers turned to him and nodded. She would understand the need to analyse fast, decide fast, and act even faster.

"It hasn't travelled far to get here," she said, wrinkling her nose. "Not recently. I can't smell any trace of the Beyond on it."

By travelling she didn't mean crossing land inside the Federation or immigrating through the usual borders: that much was obvious.

Also, the nose wrinkling made her look cute, just for a moment. Donal pushed that thought firmly back into a recess in his mind.

"I know it," said Lamis in something like his usual sepulchral voice.

Like, but not identical: Donal had never detected fear in him before.

"Oh, no," said Kelvin. "Oh, dear Thanatos. I'm sorry, Mage."

Chambers was frowning. She clearly didn't get it, any more than Donal did.

"You *know* that thing?" she said.

Lamis reached up, and did something he'd done only once before in Donal's presence: he took off his wraparound shades, and revealed the blasted pits where his eyes should have been.

Ruined sockets, that looked as if they'd been burned in an inferno, even though the rest of Lamis's face remained unmarked.

"I had a brief encounter with the entity." He turned his face from Chambers to Kelvin to Donal, seeming to focus on each in turn with the burned, empty ruins where his eyes should have been. "When I worked with the late Commissioner Vilnar."

The underlying meaning was obvious. That flame-being, whatever it was, had taken Lamis's eyes.

"You mean it lives beneath Avenue of the Basilisks," said Donal.

The others looked at him, as if surprised that he would speak, what with him being the only mundane among them.

"I was a cop," he said. "We know what's what. Get over it."

And ready with his tactical assessment, too.

He continued, "That thing is way more powerful than you by yourself – sorry, Lamis, but you pretty much just said it yourself – and I'm guessing the three of you together wouldn't do much better. Is there any way to travel *beneath* it, via the catacombs?"

Chambers had already said it was impossible to fly over. Had it been possible, she wouldn't have let the paramedics regain possession of their ambulance.

It had been a long time since Donal had run the catacombs for training and enjoyment. Although running probably wasn't an option: Chambers looked fit enough to keep up, but neither of the mages appeared particularly athletic. And Lamis wasn't exactly a spring lizard.

The corner of Chambers' mouth twitched, even though Donal could have sworn he hadn't leaked his thoughts.

But Lamis was shaking his head. "Its preferred base is deep, deep below ground." The deepness of his natural tone emphasised the words. "Think of it as keeping its feet inside lava unless absolutely necessary."

He replaced his wraparound shades, adjusted them, and turned to look at the vast fire entity. Reflected, distorted flames danced on the shades' dark lenses.

"So it extends a long way down," said Donal. "Alright."

Meaning the catacombs were out as well, as a means of getting beyond the thing.

"We can't travel directly towards St Jarl's," said Chambers. "It's a miles-long detour to either side, and that way" – she pointed – "the only possible route might well reach out to sea, meaning we'd need to commandeer a boat to get around the end of the fire entity."

"Or another aircraft." Donal thought he was stating the obvious, but in a tactical analysis session, simply assuming that other people had the same understanding as yourself was a great way to get people killed.

"Right. Or submarine, if we could possibly get one." Chambers let out a breath. "Unlikely. If we go the other way, we should be able to reach Avenue of the Basilisks, but the problem is that right now, I'm not sure Police HQ itself is going to be accessible."

Donal looked at Kelvin. "Is she right?"

Kelvin shook his head. "I was talking with Professor Steele, but she'd left Police HQ sometime earlier. Before that entity appeared." He gestured towards the wall of fire. "I have no idea how to assess the probability either way, because I don't know enough about the entity's, um, let's say geometry."

Being non-technical for the mundane. Right.

"Lamis," said Donal. "I'm sorry, but you know more about the thing. If we reach Avenue of the Basilisks, is part of that entity likely to be blocking the way to HQ?"

Even with the wraparound shades, you could tell that Lamis was frowning, which was like a normal person running round in circles in total panic mode, unable to process what was happening.

At least it hadn't been a stupid question. Here the fire thing manifested as a barrier, a vast sheet or wall of flame, but near its origin, or presumed origin, it might maintain some kind of connection direct to the subterranean levels beneath the Headquarters tower. A complicated shape.

Therefore a shape that might block the way into the tower.

After several moments, Lamis said: "The minus two hundred and seventy-third floor grants access to the dwellings of all the entities that manifest there. I don't know the exact number for sure, but the figure of seven hundred and seventy-seven often crops up in the ancient scrolls and necroflux diffraction patterns from the old guardians' fossilised bones."

"Er," said Donal. "What?"

He'd thought that nothing could surprise him any more.

"Seven-seven-seven," said Chambers. "That figures."

Donal had been asking about the fire entity. The idea that there might be a multitude of others, perhaps equally powerful and dangerous and unknowable, hadn't crossed his mind. That was despite his long-held but vague knowledge of entities, plural, living deep beneath HQ.

Ignoring Chambers' remark about the exact number – mystic numerology didn't interest Donal at all – the implication was that even if the fire entity hadn't blocked entrance to HQ, other beings might well have done just that.

St Jarl's or HQ.

Simple choice.

He drew his Magnus, checked the load, reholstered.

"I'm going to try for Avenue of the Basilisks," he said. "Anyone coming with me?"

Three sets of eyes – or in Lamis's case, some conjured equivalent behind his wraparound shades – targeted Donal.

"You ever heard of chain of command?" said Chambers. "How did you last long enough in Tristopolis PD to make lieutenant?"

"Pure luck," said Donal. "And these days I'm freelance, in any case."

Meaning outside the hierarchy, for better and for worse, because there were really were pros and cons.

Chambers' mouth twitched.

"Lead on, fearless leader," she said, and everyone's mood shifted.

Lamis tilted his head to one side by a fraction, while Kelvin gave a boyish grin, almost as wide as in the back of the ambulance, and said: "This could prove really exciting."

Wonderful. Not.

Doesn't he realise how serious this is?

Maybe it didn't matter, so long as Kelvin continued to function professionally as required.

Or maybe there was something else going on.

"No." Chambers had stepped close to him, almost without his realising, and her next words sounded in his mind even though her lips remained utterly still: "Don't speculate. I'm keeping him focused, on task, instead of worrying about his family. It's a fine balancing act, and I need you not to ruin it."

Donal blinked.

Sweet Thanatos.

And clamped down his thoughts harder than ever, trying not to leak the faintest of hints for either mage to pick up, not to mention Chambers herself.

A federal spellbinder could manipulate the mind of a senior mage without his knowledge? Donal had never, ever, picked up even a hint of such a thing, not in all his time in the Department.

And if anyone had suggested the possibility, he'd have thought them mad.

He gave a tight nod. "So you're with me? Headed for HQ?"

"Yes," said Chambers.

Kelvin looked at Lamis. "You know you want to."

Whatever Chambers was doing, perhaps it would help reinstate Lamis in Kelvin's eyes, a process that might have already begun earlier on Shatterway Quay. Maybe Donal should encourage that, even without knowing what Lamis might have done in the past to become a pariah among his own kind.

Perhaps he owed Lamis that much.

Lamis nodded.

"Right then." Donal turned, placing his back towards the fire entity blocking Shameway Divide, and thought about the twisted topography of the streets nearby – there were regions of grid layouts, both rectilinear and triangular, throughout Tristopolis, but this district here featured more of the tangled spaghetti or bucketful-of-twisted-worms style of urban planning.

"Second turning on the right," he continued, "then there's an alleyway we can cut through, and once we're on Crickety Arc Lane we might even be able to pick up a taxi."

"Or hotwire a parked car," said Chambers.

"Isn't that a federal crime?" said Donal.

"It would be." The corner of her mouth curled up. "But we're the good guys, so that's okay."

"Alright."

They started off, walking in the middle of the road for now, in the absence of any moving traffic. All of the pedestrians who'd been fleeing earlier were already gone.

I think we're going to make it.

The road in front of them exploded.

NINETEEN

In the distance, the Vixen could make out a vast wall of fire. It dwarfed the towers of central Tristopolis, and stretched for miles, although she could not estimate how many.

All my doing.

Not the entity she'd caused to be summoned into this world, but still a destructive being that would normally be tucked below Police Headquarters and minding its own strange business. She wasn't certain of the thing's identity, but Laura – dear Laura, who she missed so much – had introduced her once to a fearsome Guardian with blood-red skin, name of Hellah, and in a basement parking garage, Hellah had allowed the Vixen to play with a baby dragonlet.

The little creature with its tiny, cute wings had been formed from the imaginative conjuring of a flame entity, a being similar in nature to the fire phenomenon now raging across city streets and doubtless destroying buildings, even without moving from its current location.

Perhaps it was enraged, that wall of fire in which semi-human face-shapes writhed, but the Vixen thought it unlikely. Almost certainly, it was threatening to break loose entirely… because it was afraid.

I can't fight it.

She knew her limitations. Had always known them, and yes, her transmogrification into vehicular form had pushed back the boundaries of her power, enhancing them greatly, at least according to her own system of values – oh, the arguments with Laura over that point beforehand, and the tears from her beloved twin when the process was complete – but not enough, nowhere near enough, to challenge any of those entities that the Guardians watched over but could never truly contain, not against those entities' will.

Not individually, and certainly not collectively, for a horrible realisation was seeping through the Vixen's hydraulics and causing her transmission to shiver: if the threat she had attracted into this world scared one of the normally subterranean entities to burst out of hidden confinement and into the world at large – even to this extent, without truly attempting to go on the rampage or simply move fast to get away from here – then what of the others?

What if the threat she had brought here from Beyond caused *all* of the entities normally beneath Avenue of the Basilisks – deep beneath the tower that was Tristopolis PD Headquarters – to break free in panic or even rage?

Even if they could fight the thing – even if – then that confrontation would wreak havoc on the city and every normal being who lived here, wraiths and ghouls included, because if anything had grown clear to the Vixen it was this: the danger could advance along any or all of the spacetime dimensions, macroscopic and compactified alike.

She had never believed in anything like a true Armageddon until now.

But maybe there's a way…

What was it Laura used to say? "You don't fight a suspect, Vickie, ever, unless you can help it. You remove their power before they even start to use it."

Dear, sweet Laura had been talking about arrest procedures and the like, including the notion that pre-emptive "shutdown" as she called it – without a trace of humour in her voice or eyes, so different from her younger self – was the least damaging option for the person being arrested as well as for the officers and vulnerable public alike.

For power read motivation.

If the Beyond entity goes back where it came from, maybe all the others will go back to normal also.

It was obvious, really. She should have realised it hours ago, back on the F-779 and nearing Fortinium, when those two fleeing entities appeared, the red one in particular being in flight in every sense of the term.

I could ask Mother for help.

Just the thought of it brought tears to her wiper nozzles, but she squeezed them shut and wiped her windscreen twice, back and forth in slow deliberate arcs, and consciously slowed her revs to regain emotional control.

"Hey, get me away from here."

A hand outside, on her driver's door handle.

"Come on…" Wrenching at her chrome.

She snapped the door open, knocking the man back, then whipped her door shut again, fast enough to dislocate his fingers if he hadn't let go… but he had. Then she upped the power and dropped her gearbox into first, right on the edge of engaging her clutch.

Slowly, she turned her front wheels so that any leap into motion would take her front wing into the stranger's legs and torso. His eyes grew rounder and larger than she'd ever seen in a human before.

She growled her engine louder.

"I'm sorry. I—" He turned and stumbled back on the sidewalk and then began to run, or at least to make some panicked, uncoordinated attempt at such a motion.

The Vixen remembered Laura's lover, Lieutenant Donal Riordan, back in his first life, athletic and resilient even then. So different from this frightened, pathetic excuse for a human being.

He's only scared, that's all.

And part of the Vixen must have hated Donal or been jealous of what Laura had with him, for far too short a time. Or something. The Vixen's motives for helping Sister Felice were now a mystery to herself, the outcome of muddled thinking and lack of mental discipline, exactly the kind of thing that Laura would have hated.

And criticised her for incisively, with a sister's insight, a twin's shared understanding of the weaknesses they had in common.

She lowered her revs, dropped her clutch, and rolled towards the man, then past him, and slowly came to a halt.

And popped her back door open.

For a second the man hesitated, then he stepped forward, stopped once more, and glanced back towards the rearing wall of fire in which giant grotesques faces seemed to writhe. The sight of it made up his mind, by the looks of it: he slid into the back seat and pulled the door shut.

The Vixen allowed him to do it.

"I… Thank you. My family's in South Kings, near Kraken Avenue, you know? I just want to get there and see that they're—"

With gentle acceleration, the Vixen got moving once more.

"—okay, that's all."

Moving faster now, but keeping the motion smooth, because the last thing she needed was this guy having a panic attack and damaging her back seat. She wasn't vain but neither was she a tramp: her unblemished upholstery was a mark of self-care and appropriate self-discipline, nothing more.

And she'd rather keep it that way.

So she upped her speed but kept everything steady, maintained greater than usual distance when she found herself in some sort of traffic about a mile from West Kings, took a shortcut at her backseat passenger's suggestion – he was called Brindle, Freddy Brindle, so he told her, regardless of whether she actually wanted to know – and she was careful on the turns, and on avoiding the occasional pedestrian crossing the streets at random, their attention on the distant danger of the fire entity instead of more immediate concerns.

Soon enough she was in South Kings, and gliding to a halt about halfway along Kraken Avenue, which Freddy Brindle said was perfect.

"Thank you," he said yet again. "I'm sorry I panicked and, um, wasn't polite. I understand you're a… Well. Anyway. Thank you."

She opened her rear door, waited for him to nod and slide out, and carefully closed her door once more, with a gentle click of her lock.

And flickered her headlights once.

Freddy Brindle waved goodbye.

Go well, and keep your family safe.

She rolled on.

Began to accelerate, no longer with a vulnerable passenger on board.

Alright. I know where I'm going now.

Mordanto was out, because Mother would… Well, because of Mother.

Accelerating really hard, and pedestrians now were stopping to stare at her as she hammered along the streets, swerving around slower vehicles when she came across them – still, the place was far quieter than it should have been – and soon enough was driving through what appeared to be countryside, but wasn't.

Meadows covered in purple grass stretched for a mile or more on either side of a razor-straight carriageway, but however rural it might appear at first glance, Worriesome Common lay well within the boundaries of Greater Tristopolis.

The Vixen had jogged around the entire perimeter on foot quite a few times, back when she was plain Victoria Steele; and one of the first things she had done post-transmogrification, once the pain had faded, was to hammer around the Worriesome Loop roadway in top gear when almost everyone was asleep, roaring along the near-deserted tarmac and feeling the joy and power of her new form, which she'd underestimated if anything, in those pre-transmogrification days when she'd merely dreamed of it: for the good as well as the pain of changing were more profound in practice than she had ever imagined beforehand.

Soon enough, the jagged towers she was looking for became visible behind the stands of black iron trees.

I never thought I'd be here again.

Because her transmogrification had proved harder and infinitely more painful than she'd been able to envisage in advance, even with all of Laura's warnings, this place remained ineradicably linked with memories of agony.

The unmarked outer gates of the institution proper were shut.

That's not supposed to happen.

She rolled up to them and halted.

Flicked her headlights once, twice and finally a third time, and waited with her engine softly idling, placing her gears in neutral and wishing she could do the same with her innermost feelings, because right now she felt dominated by turmoil.

The threat from Beyond, the other entities frightened into a state where they themselves might bring ruin upon Tristopolis and everybody in it, and the personal damage she herself might have inflicted on Sister Felice – enabling twisted actions on the part of someone driven by resentfulness and jealousy: that was what the Vixen's "help" had done for the poor Night Sister – and even Donal Riordan, who possibly didn't deserve interference in his life, despite that Mel he'd taken up with, and the question the Vixen should have asked herself previously stood starkly obvious in her mind right now, as if painted in large letters.

What business was any of that of hers?

I'm such a—

The gates lifted slightly, parted with a reluctant squeak, and ground their way inwards, drawing back across the serpent-vertebrae gravel driveway, more like some kind of hunter's trap being primed to snap shut on a prey creature than any kind of welcome.

I could still go to Mordanto.

But that was stupid. Of course she couldn't.

When the gates were opened wide enough, she rolled forward, scrunching the polished vertebrae of perished serpents beneath her wheels, wishing she could enjoy the feel and sound of it, but nervousness was growing inside her, and she kept her speed low for more reasons than simple traction.

She was only a few yards in when the gates swung shut behind her with a clang. The sound seemed to hang in the heavy air, overlaid with strange resonance, for far too long.

Onward.

Bloodghouls hung from blue steel trees on either side of the driveway that stretched a third of a mile to the courtyard and the main doors of the central building. Every ghoul in turn leered at the Vixen as she rolled past.

She didn't care. There was too much other stuff to worry about.

Soon enough, she came to the curved open courtyard, her headlight beams swinging across the freestanding sign as she followed the courtyard's arc. The lettering glittered briefly, but she needed no lighting to know what it said, for the sign had been here for many decades.

L'Insitutio Collosso
Chrd. 6429 FE
per dolor ad cognitionem

Nostalgia and bitterness swirled inside her in equal amounts, and she wondered whether she should have come here at all. Her engine skipped a beat, even though her pistons were supposed to be healthy.

I'm an idiot.

She was about to throttle up and drop back into gear when sapphire sparkles began to swirl in the courtyard right in front of her, so she cut her ignition completely and relaxed her hydraulics, knowing she was committed now.

Blue light blazed, and then the figure she was expecting had materialised less than two yards from her radiator grille, but then the old mage never had understood how to keep an appropriate distance from subordinates and clients and patients and, well, anyone really.

"Well, well." The tones were unctuous. "It is so good to see you again, my dear."

He placed his hand on her bodywork, just above her left headlight, and smiled at her.

"I'll have my assistants help you freshen up," he added, "and we'll talk in a few minutes, alright?"

She gave a soft toot of acknowledgement and acquiescence.

Then pattering footsteps sounded, and three men and three women, all of them looking terribly young, came hurrying down the outer steps from the main doors.

"Professor Stern," said the lead assistant. "How may we help?"

"Get our guest ready, and I'll see her in the West Hall shortly."

"Yes, Pr—"

But Alkador Stern was already glowing blue as sparkles coalesced around him, and in a second he had vanished once more, doubtless translocated to his study or somewhere equally private, where no one could see how much effort two translocation shifts in rapid succession might have cost him.

Always keeping up appearances.

Not that she'd expected any different. And it might be that the older he grew, the more Stern's powers represented an empty façade rather than true strength and actual ability – the words *spent force* rose from nowhere in her mind – and there was a level of creepiness in the man that for some reason Mother had always been blind to, at least as far as the Vixen could tell.

It was just that she had nowhere else to go.

TWENTY

A wall of dust stood maybe thirteen feet ahead of Donal, stretching to either side, terminating at the building walls: cracked walls that remained standing, despite the explosive force that had torn upwards from beneath the road, followed by a dark winged form erupting from the newly blasted pit and arrowing straight up skywards and entirely out of sight within three seconds.

Donal didn't need to count Mixadriptotrixes to track duration, not these days.

The roiling dust was taking its time to slow and settle down to the broken ground. At least the invisible barrier was holding it at bay, so that Lamis and Kelvin and Chambers and Donal himself remained unmarked by the stuff.

He'd assumed at first that Kelvin had cast the barrier in place, but after a few moments Kelvin had turned to look at Lamis with silent respect, while Chambers simply frowned with her skin starting to glisten, perhaps a sign that she'd been about to armour herself against the dust and debris.

"There's got to be a better way than this." She looked around in every direction, including upwards and down at the ground. "If things keep breaking loose from beneath Police HQ, there won't be a building standing for us to get to. And the city won't need to worry about destruction from the Void Threat, because the whole place will be in rubble regardless."

"Bilocation," said Kelvin. "We can get there directly."

Donal squinted at him, though the clues were more in the vocal undertones than visible body language: there was more to this suggestion than the surface words.

"I thought you mages," said Donal, "needed to recharge your batteries or something."

He tapped his chest above his zombie heart, to show he understood the concept perfectly.

Plus there was supposed to be some kind of interference in place, something blocking bilocation transitions or whatever they were called, if Kelvin's words back in the ambulance had meant what they'd seemed to mean.

"We do." Lamis's voice was a deep rumble. "And you're right, of course, young Kelvin. I'm old and I've served my—"

"No." Kelvin raised a hand. "Your skills are extraordinary, Mage. The geodesic blocks are beyond my ability to traverse, but not beyond yours. I can see that now. For you, the barriers are surely surmountable. So… It will be my honour."

Chambers reached out and grasped Donal's sleeve. "Don't move, Riordan."

"No." Lamis formed a one-handed control gesture, some kind of hex-manipulation mudra. "I forbid—"

"Too late." Kelvin bowed his shaved head. "It's done."

As Kelvin toppled forward, Lamis moved fast – faster than Donal would have thought possible – and caught him.

Then Lamis snarled, or something like it, kept hold of the slumping Kelvin in one arm, and reached the other hand out to Donal and Chambers.

"Quickly. Two second build-up."

Chambers tugged Donal, maintaining her grip on his sleeve, but Donal was already moving forward. They came together, all four of them, in nothing like a group hug: just people who needed to get something done.

Lamis's hand fastened on Donal's shoulder as the blueness brightened all around them, and reality began to spin, enveloped in the vortex.

Sapphire light, everywhere and pressing as if solid, and a part of Donal's mind remembered one of the mages – it was hard to remember which one as reality swirled – remarking that a red glow, as in the White Wolf equivalent of this mage-adept process, was the wrong colour for spillover energies, or something like that, which made Donal wonder what the significance of this blueness really was; or perhaps he was simply trying to hang onto a random thought as a safeguard against disintegration, because there were dangers in this process that he'd not appreciated before.

Previously the transition had been short-lived, but this process now was taking time, though how many seconds had passed, Donal could not have said – which by itself was a dangerous indication – and he was sort of conscious of the other three individuals with him, but in a vaguer way than before.

And then the blue light began to burn inside him, or that was how it felt, and it was a bad surprise. The previous transition had been painless, but this was really starting to hurt.

Something's wrong.

Then Lamis's hand, which had remained on Donal's shoulder, tightened hard, reinforcing coherence and bringing both Lamis and the unconscious

Kelvin into focus, falling feet first in formation, and Chambers was with them, but there was something odd about her too-white skin.

Lamis's lips parted although sound could not exist here, Donal felt sure, and in that moment Chambers squeezed his arm and then let go, relinquishing her grip in what had to be a deliberate act, and she fell aside in a blizzard of blue light and in an instant dropped out of sight.

Blueness brighter than ever.

All around.

Something's really not—

Explosion.

Yet another one, in a day that seemed defined by things blowing up or flying apart.

And they tumbled out into darkness.

It took a few moments to readjust. They were in a large, unlit room with a decent-sized window; but it was devoid of furniture. They were high up – the window overlooking the dark cityscape revealed that much – and alone, with no immediate threat in sight.

Lamis was struggling to hold Kelvin up. "Help me."

"Thanatos. Here." Donal took Kelvin's weight, and lowered the younger mage to the floor. "He's still breathing, but only just."

"Not unassisted." Wraparound shades could not conceal the lines in Lamis's face. "I'm keeping his lungs going, or more precisely his diaphragm and intercostal muscles, and he needs a critical care facility or he'll die."

Donal rose to his feet. "He gave you his life energy to power the transition, right?"

"Energy, yes. Life force, if that's what you're thinking off… Then no, of course not." Lamis shook his head. "What kind of superstitious nonsense did you learn at school? There's no such thing as life force."

"Yeah, I know." Donal rubbed his face. "Trying to make sense of mage stuff isn't easy. Where have you brought us?"

"It was supposed to be the Commissioner's office. Kelvin made his sacrifice and I did my best, but I'm not at all sure where we've ended up."

Lamis was continuing to look down at the comatose Kelvin, at least as far Donal could tell with the shades and all, and there was the matter of keeping Kelvin's breathing going by some kind of invisible but no doubt tangible manipulation, stimulating the breathing muscles directly.

Which meant it was up to Donal to look around and figure out where they'd ended up.

He pressed his left arm inwards, checking the feel of the holstered Magnus – all okay – and took two steps towards the window, then stopped. Turning, he checked the closed door: massive and armoured, with a giant sawtooth vertical join, implying that the door could open like a sideways mouth with fangs, and slam shut hard and fast if needed.

Under other circumstances, Donal would have smiled.

"You did it," he told Lamis. "We're on the 187th floor. You took us to the Commissioner's office, alright."

"It doesn't look like—Oh."

"Yeah. Commissioner Vilnar was a good man. I guess Sandarov didn't want to move his stuff in here when he took over. Whether that's respectful or something else, I got no idea."

Lamis's already lined forehead wrinkled further above his shades. "You don't know the new man?"

"By sight, yes. A couple of the guys I've worked with, guys I trust, said he was the best replacement that anyone could've found."

But that was all. It felt weird to be back here in an empty dark office that looked larger than before, and where his footsteps, as he walked to the window to confirm his knowledge, echoed coldly.

That was of course Avenue of the Basilisks down below.

He turned back and strode to the armoured door, waited a second, then pressed his palm against the metal. "My name is Donal Riordan. I've been here quite a few times in the past, just not recently."

Even to his zombie touch the door felt cold.

"I appreciate how you must, er… Look, I know you served the old man well. I'm sorry I couldn't save him when, um, when it happened."

Donal had been there, in City Hall, reluctantly but playing along because Commissioner Vilnar had wanted him to start developing political skills. As if someone like Donal could rise high in the Department, high enough to need contacts and favours, both owed and owing, with civic officials and influential businessfolk and all the rest.

In the past now.

It occurred to him that he hadn't actually said what he wanted. "Um, could you open up, please?"

Nothing.

"I need to get out," he added. "Police business. Emergency. I need to *help* people, okay?"

A total lack of hum or resonance or any kind of motion, any sign that the animate door had heard him. Or perhaps it was no longer animate. Perhaps it had died – or rotated its sentient substrate into the crawlspace dimensions, for such intelligences were approximately wraith-like – on hearing the news of Commissioner Vilnar's death.

Lamis was the obvious person to deal with this, but when Donal turned back to the centre of the room, he saw Lamis sitting cross-legged next to the supine Kelvin, and Lamis's head was bowed, his shoulders slumped in a tired way, a depth of fatigue that Donal had never seen in him before.

Using all his strength to keep Kelvin breathing: it was obvious.

Nothing today was turning out the way that Donal had expected. It was time to redefine his objectives, re-examine the situation, plot the next few steps that ought to lead in the right direction… and execute them, hard and fast with necessary aggression. The voices of drill sergeants and Academy instructors echoed in his memory from across the years.

When in doubt, rely on trained procedures.

Lamis and Kelvin and Donal himself – there was no way of knowing about Chambers – had come here because Felice was somewhere in the building, with some kind of knowledge about the cause of all this.

Professor Helena Steele, Laura's mother, had communicated as much to Kelvin via some kind of remote sharing of thoughts or projecting of words or whatever the Hades it was that mages did to talk across long distances without any actual telephones or cables involved.

So the first immediate goal was to find Felice. Getting out of this room was not so much an objective as a means of achieving one.

Okay, good. So how do I do that?

Appropriate questions were a start, but the real trick was finding useful answers.

The door was armoured. So was the window, quintuple laminate with three of those layers hex-shielded, and breaking in from the outside would have been nigh-on impossible. But from the office interior… that was different.

Back in the day, as a detective lieutenant, Donal had been known to exit from his own office through the window when he'd felt the urgency. Back when he'd had an office here: an office in which he kept a rope and gloves.

Nothing like that here.

He strode past Lamis and the comatose Kelvin, reached the window, and found the cog fastenings which he spun to the unlocked position. It took three tugs from a half-squat stance to jerk the window loose enough to open, but once it was free, the pane slid upwards easily enough.

Behind him – he glanced back – Lamis had angled his bowed head slightly, aware of the opening window but unable to divert any more attention from keeping Kelvin alive, as far as Donal could tell. Just one more reason to get on with this and stop delaying.

He grabbed hold of the sill, muttered Mel's name once to himself, and swung himself over, and hung there from both hands, the balls of his feet against the outer wall below the sill.

Madness.

In the distance, orange flames shot up: flames that might be offshoots of the great fire entity that had blocked their way before, that miles-long wall of flames that would be visible from around the corner of the building. Here, cold turbulent breezes threatened to grow stronger by the second.

What are you doing, lover?

A wraith had slipped out of the solid wall below, and slowly ascended to hang level with Donal.

"Aggie? I was just hanging around. About to do some climbing, that's all."

The strain in his almost-straight arms was minimal, apart from his fingers and forearms which had to remain taut and hard as hooks, or he would fall.

Silly man. I've missed your daft jokes.

"I just wanted to reach another window where someone might let me in."

Or kill you, if they didn't recognise you.

"Well, yes. Or that."

Aggie floated in space, ethereally bouncing up and down, unaffected by the turbulent air.

I sensed a vortex spillover coming from Arrhennius's old office, and here you are.

"There's a mage inside." He had to raise his voice, almost shouting, as the breeze strengthened to become a wind. "Two mages, and one of them is critically injured. They brought me here. I need to see a suspect called Sister Felice, a Night Sister, but can you get the mage some medical help?"

Avenue of the Basilisks, the sidewalks and road itself, looked a very long way below. Vertigo had rarely afflicted him in the past, but it wouldn't take much to knock him loose from his hold on the sill, and drop him into the void.

The wraith called Aggie wasn't precisely his friend. She was an amalgam of two: the long-lived Gertie had indeed been friendly and talked in that bantering, teasing fashion; Xalia had been a colleague, a friend of Laura's more than Donal's, far younger than Gertie but a tougher kind of wraith altogether.

You're wondering if I'm as friendly as I'm acting, aren't you?

"Everything's different now." Donal was still hanging in place, ready for the next move, knowing he couldn't stay like this. "I'm not even a cop these days, you know?"

I know.

If there was one thing that Gertie and Xalia had possessed in common, it was a fierce determination to defend the Department. Dependable or dangerous: it depended on your perspective, on who you were and how she read your intentions.

Donal's analysis of Aggie just popped into his head, and his intuition about what to do next appeared even faster, and he went with it.

He released his grip on the 187th floor window sill, and toppled backwards, into empty air.

Falling, face towards the blank deep purple sky, air cold against his back where it pressed but not hard enough to save him.

Dropping fast.

Hoping he hadn't misjudged her.

Faster still.

TWENTY-ONE

In the event, they didn't need a third party to get Donal inside the building. Aggie caught him before the acceleration built up too far, which was good: had she waited until he was close to the ground, she would have had to decelerate so fast that she might as well have let him hit the sidewalk.

Greyberry jelly on concrete: that would have been his fate.

Instead, they bobbed in place, Aggie cradling him like an overgrown baby hundreds of feet above Avenue of the Basilisks, then they drifted closer to the HQ wall, shifting laterally to a window where Aggie dematerialised part of herself, becoming sufficiently insubstantial to reach through the solid glass and stone and unlock the window.

"I can pull the actual windowpane up myself from here."

Or you can be a good boy and let me deal with it.

"Okay. Thanks."

I don't know why I put up with your nonsense, Donal Riordan.

"Because you're a sweetheart, Aggie."

Sure I am.

"Well, yeah…"

The glass pane slid up and Aggie carried him through the opening and into an open plan office where only three harassed-looking uniformed officers were working, amid a sea of unstaffed desks and unanswered ringing telephones.

Donal saw the ceiling growing closer as they came further into the room, and wondered why Aggie was rising while still holding him.

She felt softer and warmer than he remembered.

If you want to know who this is, ring Entity Resources and ask about Lieutenant Donal Riordan.

"I'm Riordan," said Donal. "But—"

Hush now. I'm putting you down.

"Okay."

He wasn't with the Department these days, but if the officers here assumed that he was – because of Aggie: everyone in HQ knew exactly who she was – then the rest of what he had to do here should be easy, or relatively so: find a named suspect or witness, whichever she was, and go talk to her.

Aggie tilted him as she descended, so his feet touched the beetle-chitin parquet flooring first, and she grew less substantial without slowing the downward motion, fading as she slipped slowly down into the black floor.

"Thank you," he called as the last of her disappeared from sight.

"Hades of a day," said one of the uniforms.

"Tell me about it," said Donal. "Someone's brought in a witness or suspect called Sister Felice, a Night Sister. You know anything about it, or did Aggie bring me to the wrong floor?"

The three cops looked at each other. Two had phones in their hands, which they ignored.

"Infirmary, down the corridor." One of them shook her head. "But you can't go in there."

Three infirmaries were situated in the building, in part because of the diversity of beings who might require treatment. The two above ground were on the 23rd floor – Donal hadn't fallen that far – and the 103rd, which had to be where he was, and which also meant he'd fallen more than eighty storeys and survived.

Thanks to Aggie responding to his impulsive decision to let himself fall.

"I have to." Donal gestured with his chin towards the window, or more precisely the world outside. "She might know something to help stop all that."

The same cop stood up. "Sir, you'll die if you go anywhere near. It's all to do with the levels below. You know." She pointed to the floor. "*Way* down below."

Everyone knew the subterranean depths were filled with eldritch dangers and unpredictable beings of great power. For most officers in the Department, that was all they knew; and it was enough.

Donal stood firmly in that category.

"Thanks," he told her. "But I'm going to have to try."

"Then good luck, sir."

She didn't say *you'll need it*, but her tone implied as much. Then she glanced over at the unoccupied desks and still-ringing phones, shook her head, sat back down and raised her own handset to her ear. "Okay, look, ma'am. We can only suggest staying in place until the roads are cleared. You need to—"

Donal tuned her out.

Time to find out what he could.

He strode fast along aisles and corridors, pushed his way through two sets of double doors, then a third, and came out on the central landing where the rows of open elevator shafts stood. They were empty and seemed not to be in use: maybe everyone was already where they needed to be.

But even as Donal thought that, a wraith shot up inside the furthermost shaft, carrying a determined-looking medic and some kind of silvery apparatus whose geometry, even though he'd simply glimpsed it, challenged Donal's perceptions of angles and perspective.

"Good on you, Aggie."

She was surely taking help up to the 187th floor, where Lamis and the comatose Kelvin were trapped inside the former Commissioner Vilnar's old office.

Aggie had most likely fetched that medic from the 23rd floor infirmary, which meant the uniformed cop's warning had been germane: the infirmary on this floor, the 103rd, had been inaccessible or somehow too risky, or otherwise no good as a source of help.

Too bad it was the place where Donal had to go.

He crossed the landing and halted before another set of double doors, and held out his left hand palm first, close to the door without actually touching the solid polished bone it was made of. The air felt distinctly warm, but entirely lacking in traces of smoke or a smell of burning furniture or fittings or, thank Thanatos, people.

With luck, that meant no danger of a sudden backdraught and gouts of flame triggered by the simple act of opening a door.

He took hold of the handle, ignoring the heat, gripped hard, and wrenched the door towards him.

Opening onto madness.

Sheets and columns of flame were writhing here, inside what should have been the infirmary's reception area but was already half destroyed, melted or broken, while in the corridor beyond, a normally elegant body was twisting in mid-air as though held up by a tormented wraith, although Donal could sense nothing there at all, which meant it wasn't actually a wraith as such: unless they materialised to a significant extent, they couldn't hold up a solid object of any kind, including a twisting, tortured Night Sister who seemed to be screaming but in utter silence.

It was Felice, and something had hold of her.

But there was someone else standing this side of the flames, with her hands raised and sparkling with spillover hex the exact same colour as the fire itself, while her skin, bathed in the fiery light, was glistening scarlet, like freshly spilled blood, and her clothes and hair were identically black, while something other than sight or sound, some kind of deeply felt vibration, told Donal that she, the red-skinned woman, stood at the centre of a field of power, the kind of energy that no human should have been able to handle.

Her eyes, when she turned to snarl at Donal, were twin heptagons of fire.

"Get out of here, zombie."

Donal tilted his head from side to side, although his neck didn't really need loosening. He was as ready for action as he'd ever been.

Strictly speaking there was no such thing as a citizen's arrest, although people used the term. But there was a law granting pretty much that right, and if you were one of the few people who knew its official name in the statute books, you could employ a more impressive form of wording, one that the would-be arrestee might actually pay attention to.

"I'm arresting you," he began, "under Article 917B of the—"

"The Hades you are." She swept a hand in his direction.

Fire shot up from floor to ceiling in front of him and spread, circling back to meet the walls, forming a barrier between him and the woman and the ruined reception area beyond.

What in the name of Thanatos do I do now?

Well, what had he been planning to do before Aggie turned up unexpectedly and carried him down here to the 103rd floor?

The proximate goal was to get to Felice. That was the first step.

"Death, Death, Death," he muttered.

Time to go climbing after all.

TWENTY-TWO

The thing that had been Kyushen Jyu was howling in agony, in a hellish realm where reality twisted and spread out along too many dimensions for his poor human mind to grasp.

He was smarter than anyone he knew, at least these days when he no longer carried out postdoc research under the auspices of two Strossfeld Prize laureates at the Bohr-Mann Institute in Grossdämonsburg; and some part of him understood exactly what was happening to him, as his consciousness continued somehow to fire along what should have been geometrically untenable neural configurations: the stuff of his being, his self, continually rotated, translated, dilated, contracted and generally pulled apart in a universe no human was ever meant to experience directly.

It hurt so very much.

His visual awareness was drowning, flooded with sheet lightning that shone green and blue and purple and blazed with other eldritch colours for which he had no name. For which no one back in the normal world had names. And worse: amid that shining, shifting kaleidoscope of impossibility, dark unlikely shapes were moving, apparently with purpose.

They could have killed him, pretty much in an instant, if he'd been worth the bother.

Part of him wished they would do just that: blot out his agony before his mind splintered into a chaos no power anywhere could ever put back together again.

Sound existed in this place, but travelled along so many axes, all of them mutually orthogonal, as to render the harmonic mix and frequencies, the otherworldly equivalents of timbre and pitch, far too complex for his auditory processing to parse in any way at all. A loud mess filled what should have been his sense of hearing, and there was no way he could think of to shut it out.

He could certainly never make sense of it, not that cacophony.

But he did retain some proprioceptive awareness, a sense of where his muscles were, of orientation and position and all the rest, and perhaps that was the worst of all, not just in hammering home the strangeness and pain of his situation, but also his helplessness.

For his body was spread out like an insane piece of abstract sculpture, existing in at least eleven dimensions and possibly a good deal more, which meant confusion ranked alongside agony in his current overwhelming predicament.

How do you move even a finger, never mind a limb or your entire body, when the world is too complicated for you to grasp?

Of course the real question lay even deeper at the heart of his agonised mind, where he didn't want to face it, but equally, could not avoid it forever.

Why was he still alive?

How was he alive?

He doubted if he could ever be sane again, but something was keeping him integrated – at least to this extent – when this new reality should have twisted his subatomic components apart, splitting them along axes that remained curled up and tiny and literally imperceptible in normal reality, converting everything that had been Kyushen Jyu into a multitude of whatever force particles existed here in this continuum, spilling out along every one of the orthogonal dimensions of this terrible place.

A spontaneous, instantaneous explosion should have killed him.

This isn't possible.

Yet clearly he was here, and hurting.

Howling as the pain grew even worse.

Seconds or aeons tumbled past, and Kyushen no longer knew or cared about anything beyond the world of pain, could form no thought beyond the endless question of when this torture might end.

Yet something changed. A coherent though shadowy shape, some sort of pseudo-organic configuration, appeared to be moving amid the perceptual chaos.

Moving with purpose.

Drawing near.

Come to kill me at last?

Part of him wanted it. All of him wanted this agony to end.

<<You're human also. Yet you're in this place.>>

Words that were not sounds but something else, uttered by a very different kind of voice.

I can't stand this.

He writhed in ways that made no sense to a three-dimensional mind, and it hurt beyond imagining but he could not help it.

The shadow configuration drew closer still, its means of locomotion impossible for Kyushen's fragmented kaleidoscope of a mind to perceive or analyse.

<<Let me help you.>>

Kyushen twisted.

No. What are you?

He wanted the pain to end, but not by dying. Suddenly, he wanted more than anything to live.

<<You can call me Drad. That seems to be easier for small minds to grasp.>>

Closer again, much closer, that impossible shadow being.

What are you doing?

Extruding some kind of limb, perhaps a tendril or cluster of tendrils: reality was too complicated here to make proper sense even of multiplicity, of cardinality. Of number itself.

<<Or Baladradian, if you want to be a little more formal.>>

What?

<<That's my name, Dr Jyu. Or do you even remember that that is *your* name? You look awful, by the way.>>

I… am… Kyushen Jyu.

<<Good. And I'm afraid this is going to hurt.>>

After so much agony, how could anything be worse?

I don't care.

Then the tendril inserted itself into Kyushen's mind, and he began to realise the depths of his mistake, for now he cared very much indeed.

Howling harder even than before.

Beyond the worst of human imagining.

TWENTY-THREE

The cavernous gold-and-green garage bay was tall – the ceiling hung forty feet or more overhead – and the entire place was shining, well-lit and comfortable. Even better, the washdown with hoses and warm, foamy water – it took five of the institute's students, dressed in dark-green coveralls and working as a team, to do the work on her – followed by a deep soothing polish, felt luxurious. So it took a while for the Vixen to realise what a bad mistake she'd made in coming here.

An easy mistake, of course, because l'Institutio Collosso had been her home and refuge in the past, not to mention a place of rebirth and transformation, of transmogrification to her current form: to the form – after all the confusion of childhood and adolescence – she had finally realised she was meant to inhabit.

For her younger self, the institute was a place of healing and becoming. But emotions were one thing, and logic was another. Laura, dear dead Laura, her counterpart in so many ways, who'd become a driven cop and a resurrected woman – revived after that calamitous event that no one in the family ever, ever discussed – would have framed the discussion in terms of tactics and strategy and achievable objectives, of aggression as a good thing; and it was funny because of the two of them, identical twins as far the outside world was concerned, the seemingly conservative Laura had been – in so many ways – the wild one.

It wasn't Victoria-turned-Vixen who'd communed with feral cats on rooftops and in alleyways and parks ever since she was a little girl.

Or who'd deliberately chosen a profession where placing herself in harm's way – for the sake of others – was part of the job.

Laura. I wish you were here with me.

No one to share her thoughts with. That was the real problem, wasn't it?

We were different, but at least we understood each other.

And now she was literally alone, as the five students finished tidying away the cleaning kit, hex-locked the storage cupboard – for no good reason, surely – and bowed to her before leaving through a small, human-width doorway to an inner corridor.

The door, of polished green chitin, clicked shut. The sound echoed strongly in the large, mostly empty space of the huge garage.

No sounds or sense of presence came from the courtyard outside, from beyond the large sliding doors that were also locked, so no enemy in the larger world could see her or get at her. It should have made her feel safe, not trapped.

I've been so Thanatos-damned stupid.

Which wasn't news, was it?

She fired her ignition, felt the smoothness of her pistons, the strength in her hydraulics, the suppleness of her couplings and steering, the unarguable power of her transmission. There was something wrong about the way Professor Alkador Stern had welcomed her back, something that went beyond social awkwardness and a lack of interpersonal skills, beyond even a mild touch of creepiness; and he might wield total authoritarian power over the students and faculty and operational staff in this place, but she herself was a long way from helpless.

People who set traps should be careful of what they catch.

Trap?

The word had come from her subconscious, but it tasted right in her mind. In coming here, she'd rolled right into a trap. She felt intuitively certain of the fact. Stern had some kind of plan for her, and the sprucing up by his students – young men and women entirely lacking in inside knowledge, simply following instructions – had been intended to put her at her ease, to make her guard drop along with her actual, active defences.

He's played me for a fool.

Not just her.

Me and Felice.

And if the city managed to survive the current cataclysm, the last thing Alkador Stern would want was two living beings capable of testifying against him in an unforgiving court of law.

He's going to kill me.

No, that was wrong.

He's going to try to kill me.

Better.

Because she might end up dying anyway – Hades, she'd been intending to take her own life earlier, after realising just how badly wrong her plans had gone, her and Felice's – but if she had to go, she wasn't going to go alone.

So, tactics.

Like Mortwood Park.

She blinked her headlights, remembering the park and days of innocence, so very long ago.

Hide and seek, away from their parents, and Laura dropping from a branch as Victoria-as-was slunk around the trunk in their game of mutual tag, where both of them were "it" and targets at the same time.

"Got you again, Vicky!"

Because straight up is the last direction people look in when the chase is on.

Now, the Vixen flexed the centre of her chassis and transmission from side to side, then up and down on alternating sides like a slow wriggle, in ways no inanimate automobile could ever copy. She might look and feel for the most part like a vehicle, but there had always been more to her than that.

The flexing capability meant she could do the next part without crumpling her bodywork or – with luck – even scratching her paint. And she'd done it before at speed, in fast-moving circumstances: just not when going up against mages.

She growled her engine, disengaged and re-engaged her clutch with ease, and rolled slowly but deliberately in first gear towards the solid inner wall, rocking a little as she worked her tyres through the beginning of transformation, like a pianist wriggling her fingers before touching the keys.

And she arched back just a little as she neared the wall, the shallowest of curves, but with her elongating tyres that was just enough to reach and fasten black rubber against the wall and roll up, like sticky fingers fastening and releasing as her tyres took her up the vertical wall, first the front wheels then the rear wheels as well, her extensions spreading inside the solid wall, spreading and forking out at finer and finer scales like tree roots, down to a scale where the ordinary forces holding matter together worked on the stuff of her tyre-tendrils also, allowing her to grip, release and move.

"You could climb like this on a slick, wet surface in a vacuum," Mage Annabel Treese had told her, here in this very institute, towards the end of her post-transmogrification habilitation programme, when they'd started on advanced techniques like this.

Annabel had been kind, but apparently unhappy here: she'd transferred to Mordanto shortly after Victoria-turned-Vixen left Collosso to start her new life.

The Vixen had never driven in a vacuum, but she'd climbed walls for sure, although not often. If she'd wanted to spend her life aloft, she wouldn't have gone for wheels instead of pliable limbs or even wings. But she knew how strong her tyres' grip could be, and how long she could cling in place if she had to.

A very, very long time.

And with a predator's patience, if required.

Within minutes she was upside down on the ceiling, pretty much at the centre, with all four tyres splayed darkly against the smooth chitinous material, fastened in place with total security and no chance whatsoever of falling.

At some point, of course, she would drop, and fast. Releasing her tyres in sequence so gravity and torque would turn her the right way up as she fell.

I'm ready.

But not until her prey walked right beneath her.

TWENTY-FOUR

From the outside ledge that Donal stood on, chest close to the wall and both hands clinging, it was a long drop to the street below: he'd pass a hundred and two storeys, not including the one he stood level with at the moment, before impact with the sidewalk and the end of everything.

So he'd better not topple off, because people were depending on him, the nearest being Sister Felice, presumably still suspended in mid-air and twisting in agony next to a barrier of fire, all of this nearby, a matter of yards away within the building, a civilian being tortured right where she should have been safest: in the heart of Police HQ.

It was a matter of traversal, of keeping going sideways without falling off, of making steady progress and above all not panicking. But at least he'd snatched a brass hex claw from a maintenance cupboard before climbing outside from the near-deserted office area.

After retreating from the flame barrier that he had no hope of passing through directly.

The claw hung heavily in his jacket pocket, distorting the cut of it but – with luck – not enough to tear its way loose, because it was the claw which had allowed him to open a locked window in order to get out, and should be enough to get him back in through some other window beyond the flames thrown up by the red-skinned woman, whoever the Hades she was.

Sideways at a steady pace: step to the side, bring the other foot up, and repeat, all the while crimping his fingers and releasing and snatching new holds on the ornate dark stonework, while the uncertain wind tugged at his jacket, at him, and he dared not turn his head far enough to check what was happening across his city, how far the disasters had spread.

Mel. I need you to be safe.

But she was capable and strong. Survivor's qualities. He had to trust in her abilities.

Concentrate.

So, steady sideways progress – step out, step up; step out, step up – and trying not to fumble the ongoing changes of handholds, remembering not to breathe – good job he wasn't a redblood any more – because his chest was close enough to the building wall as it was: too close and he'd be rebounding off and then he'd be toppling and done for.

Call it a shuffle, really, but so long as he kept going, who cared?

A stronger gust of wind fell upon him, and all he could do was hang in place, eyes squeezed shut in case of dust, and wait for it to pass, which a mere twenty-nine seconds later was what it did.

Such a long drop below.

He tried not to rock in the wake of the wind's passing.

Succeeded.

Carry on.

Windows were sparse at this part of the exterior, but here came the first one, except that even before he reached it the orange glow was fierce and he could feel a little of the heat. Where the horizontal ledge became the window sill, at a protruding stone border, Donal knew he would have to be extra careful not to touch the glass, not with the strength of the fire inside.

Civilian-grade glass, without such heavy-duty hex protection, would have blown out or maybe even melted long ago.

Orange flames inside, obscuring everything else: no sign of the writhing Felice or the black-haired, black-clad woman with skin the colour of blood. Slowly, slowly, Donal edged past, taking extra care while rounding the window's stone border that led to more unbroken wall, deliberately not hurrying, thankful once more that zombiehood allowed him consciously to shift around the internal architecture of his mind, including the deliberate control of behaviour that would have been reflex, learned or innate, back in his original life.

All impulses? Really?

It was a weird question to pop up in his mind, here when the slightest twitch in the wrong direction would send him sailing into space. But odd thoughts do crop up in the midst of ongoing action: he'd learned that as both a cop and a soldier, and discussed it once with a veteran firefighter over whiskeys in a Direside bar, an old grizzled guy who'd said he'd experienced much the same thing during significant callouts.

As for fire: there was plenty of that inside, and all Donal wanted to do right now was avoid it.

No impulses or intuitive actions at all? For sure?

Pretty insistent for a fleeting thought.

He reached for the next handhold, stopped, and withdrew to the previous protrusion where he crimped his fingers hard and held himself in place, and waited.

Not for anything in the outside world, but for the notion that was forming in his head. Notion or question: one of those, at any rate.

Why did you let yourself fall earlier?

Aggie had caught him, but the act had been an unconscious leap of faith.

And what about your reaction to the first white wolf?

In his office, dry-mouthed before the lone wolf, and again when he faced the entire Council of White Wolves, their name capitalised and formalised in his mind in a way that felt entirely right. The first wolf, when Donal was unconscious, had implanted the, what, the monitor device that he now wore as a ring on his right hand.

He checked, and the ring's three inset ellipses were blazing scarlet, as if detecting some great power nearby, which – given what he'd seen of the blood-red woman inside the building – was not exactly startling news.

And neither, when it came down to it, was the realisation that he himself had continued to change over time: the immediate post-resurrection Donal had been a more calculating man than his redblood, earlier self; and now he'd become more intuitive once more, or so it seemed: more like his original personality.

Surely a natural integration, nothing else.

Like his unthinking reaction when the apparition that looked exactly like Laura had started this whole thing in motion…

"What the Hades does it matter, for Thanatos' sake?" Speaking aloud to no one at all, on the exterior of a tower maybe a thousand feet above the ground. Speaking to the wind.

Introspection of this kind had always felt useless, in every stage of his existence. He'd settled into a new phase of life. So what?

Just keep going.

First things first: get to Felice, get her clear of whatever had hold of her, and then, second step, try to find out what she knew; then take it from there.

Another window was drawing close, but this one felt different.

Good…

Or was it?

No flames, no orange glow. That *was* good.

But as he grew closer, it looked grey, the window – strangely grey – but then again this was high up with no illumination, the city cloaked as ever by the deep purple sky above, and there were limits to everybody's visual acuity, even a zombie's.

At first, he noticed that the window wasn't hot, or even warm. Closer still, continuing his sideways shuffle, he realised that the hard stone his fingers were hooked on felt chilly, and when he finally drew near and reached the edge of the window, it looked less like hex-protected multi-layered glass and more like a block of ice.

I don't like this.

So the world was throwing up surprises, as it always did. No matter. Steady forward progress was the name of the game. Or in this case lateral progress, careful as he edged around the side of the window, slowing right down as he placed his hand against the ice-cold glass and confirmed every suspicion: it was frozen solid for sure, and the big question had to be how much ice was packed inside, reinforcing the glass.

Carefully, carefully, he reached for the hex key in his jacket pocket, careful to keep the fingers of his other hand well hooked in place on a decent hold, his knees slightly bent and his feet mostly on the ledge, which here seemed covered with frost and would therefore provide minimal friction against any horizontal movement of his feet.

Not good, not good, not good.

Exact in his movement, he brought the brass claw against the edge of the window, found one of the lock points – with these things, you only needed one such point to make the process work – and twisted. The glass shivered but did not move.

Again.

He repeated the motion, and this time several cracks appeared in the icy coating.

Alright. It'll work.

Third time with the claw, and the window shook and broke free of the ice and slid upwards, with shards of ice falling, two of them hitting the ledge on which Donal stood, each leaving a spray of ice before bouncing and toppling into the void.

He replaced the claw in his pocket, stared at the ice that still blocked the way inside, and carefully lowered his centre of gravity, examining the ice block before him and the edges of the window opening, before deciding what to do.

With his left hand rotated inwards – thumb turned down and palm out – he took a solid hooking grip, jamming his way in, forcing his fingers into the restricted space between ice and stone on the left side of the opening. The slipperiness of the ledge beneath his shoes might be a problem, so his handhold needed to be strong.

And with his right hand, he reached inside his jacket.

To an amateur with a hammer, everything looks like a nail.

Yeah, right. But sometimes the hammer is the right tool for the job, no matter who is wielding it and how diverse the contents of their toolbox might be.

The Magnus was a tool of sorts.

"I thought you were just dangerous," Kyushen had told him back in St Jarl's. It felt like a long time ago. "And, well, kind of a thug, really. A hard man."

And sometimes that was exactly what it took to solve the problem in front of you. With one hand you hung on for safety, and with the other hand, well, you went with the viciousness and violence.

Hanging there one-handed, in an ice-blocked window opening on the 103rd floor of Police HQ, Donal trained his Magnus at point-blank range, steadied himself without needing to breathe, squinted his eyes for some measure of protection, and squeezed the trigger.

Ice exploded in front of him, but he hung on.

Again.

He fired three more shots before the whole thing blew apart and the way inside was clear, if littered with icy debris.

Gotcha.

Gun in hand, he slipped inside the building and landed in a straddle stance, ready to shoot, scanning in all directions.

The immediate office was empty, but relatively small, and the partly open door in front of him led to a corridor where someone was definitely moving.

With his left hand, Donal wiped his face.

You're in. Keep going.

Time to find Felice.

Before leaving the office, he reloaded the Magnus. In the absence of knowledge of what he was about to face, a full load with hex-piercing rounds was a sensible precaution, but he wasn't going to make the hammer-therefore-nail assumption.

There was every possibility that, whatever waited outside in the corridor for him, the threat wasn't going to be the kind that you could make go away simply by shooting at it.

On the other hand it might be *just* that kind, so a full load it was.

He stopped at the open doorway, lowered himself a little, and peeked around the doorjamb, just a one-eyed glimpse to reconnoitre, and pulled back slowly, although the man outside had been standing with his back to Donal.

A man, dressed in white and black, in a costume that should have looked like a fancy-dress pirate getup but instead had seemed – even in that instant – to suit him entirely. Maybe there was something subtle about the fabric and so on, the hallmarks of professional tailoring, that made all the difference.

Or maybe it was the clouds of icy mist and fog that swirled around him, here inside the Headquarters building, in a wider area at the end of the corridor.

And the ice-covered corpses of half a dozen officers splayed upon the frosty floor.

What the Hades?

No flames, no blood-red woman.

Wondering just how badly he'd been misreading the tactical situation.

And what, exactly, he needed to do next.

I've got a fully loaded Magnus, at least.
Sometimes you just go with what you know.

TWENTY-FIVE

Donal's plan boiled down to this: shooting an empty-handed civilian in the back. Nothing else made sense.

Around the corner, at the end of corridor, lay six dead officers covered in ice – and those were just the corpses that he'd managed to glimpse from here. In the wider, open-plan area beyond the corridor, there might be many more.

Along with Felice, out of sight around that corner, still writhing in mid-air, most likely. And there was his justification: a civilian, Felice, alive and in clear danger. There could be some other explanation for ice-covered corpses that didn't make the man, the pale stranger dressed in white and black, an actual murderer… but none came to mind.

Still, Donal held back.

I've taken action before, on a lot less evidence.

Maybe he was afraid. Perhaps it was the fact that he no longer carried a badge. Or maybe just clambering around the outside of the building, after all the events of earlier, including white wolves and multiple instances of teleportation – translocation, whatever – had simply wiped him out.

He was a resurrected human being, not a tireless machine.

Cupping his left hand beneath the Magnus butt, he got ready to swing around the door jamb into the corridor. A glimmer of red on the frosty open door startled him, until he remembered the ring on his right middle finger.

Glowing stronger now. As if he needed the warning of danger.

I could call the wolves, maybe.

It was a monitor construct, in Federal Agent Chambers' words: the device formerly concealed inside his chest. The white wolves said nothing about refashioning it as a ring – or anything at all, in fact – but there it was on his finger, ever since they'd transported him back to Shatterway Quay.

Could he use the ring to call them directly, and if so, how? Just talk to the ring? What did the words *monitor construct* really mean?

Stupid. All that talking would do for sure was tell the stranger outside that there was someone here. As if the gunshots hadn't warned him already. But even if talking to the ring worked in terms of making contact, would the white wolves really come, and fast enough to make a difference?

They hadn't sworn to help him. In fact, the allegiance was the other way around – he had pretty much signed up for their cause, without knowing what it truly was – a fact that puzzled him a little in retrospect.

Federal Agent Chambers had said, clear as anything, that she didn't trust the white wolves, while implying she knew much more about them than he did.

Felice is out there, in trouble.

So this was it.

He could take action now or climb back outside, retreat, and try one way or another to fetch reinforcements, or even replacements: leaving others, the city's paid professionals, to do the job.

No.

Action now.

He rolled around the corner.

The man had turned, so Donal could see his face: pale skin, long pale hair, everything bloodless except for the eyes: twin heptagonal irises of golden fire, exactly like the blood-red woman who'd thrown up the barrier of flame before, the barrier Donal had bypassed by climbing around the outside of the Thanatos-damned building.

Not mages, but something else. And there were two of them.

And no chance of taking this one by surprise, not now.

"The Night Sister," called Donal. "Are you the one that's holding her?"

"You don't get to intervene," answered the stranger, "in matters you don't understand."

"I'll take that as a yes."

"Take it any way you—"

Donal whipped up the Magnus and fired seven times, as fast as the mechanism could handle, and then a vertical sheet of ice was slamming blade-like through the air directly at him so he dodged left, bounced off the wall and sprinted forward, holding the Magnus directly in front of him despite the weight, and firing four more shots, percussive bangs in deafening sequence, but for all the running and the powerful repeated recoil, his aim was good for every shot.

He fired again until all thirteen rounds were spent and he was face to face with the pale-faced stranger who was standing there still, half-smiling until Donal whipped the Magnus upward beneath his pointed chin, snapping his head back, and Donal continued by collapsing his right arm to drive his right elbow directly into the stranger's larynx and that, finally, caused a reaction.

Clutching his throat, the pale man staggered back, and Donal kicked him left-footed, hard, thrusting into the right side of the bastard's body, catching him in the liver, which dropped him to the floor, curling up like a foetus, his eyes squeezed shut in agony.

There were icy splinters of metal on the floor: the hex-piercing Magnus rounds that the stranger had somehow nullified and shattered; but old-fashioned bodily impact had been another matter entirely.

The stranger was in agony, but with abilities like his, he might be more dangerous now than ever, and for sure would have lost any remaining inhibitions on using his most deadly powers the moment Donal struck him. A civilian most likely wouldn't understand – would assume the danger was past, not greater than before – but tactically there was only course of action open to Donal now, and so he took it.

A solid kick to the bastard's chin, and he was out of it.

Blood trickled from his mouth, perhaps because his teeth had severed the tip of his tongue. The chances of a broken jaw were high.

Donal counted thirteen dead officers littering the floor, their postures awkward and splayed, their corpses coated with frost and ice.

"Felice!" he said, catching sight of her.

Thirteen corpses and one beautiful Night Sister, still alive, still floating in mid-air and undergoing torture.

Whatever the pale man had done to her, it hadn't ceased when Donal knocked him out.

He strode towards Felice, intending to snatch her clear of whatever invisible force was holding her.

"No!" The female voice was muffled. "You'll kill her if you try."

Donal turned.

For a split second he'd assumed that the faintness of her words was caused by partial deafness from the shots he'd fired himself, but though his ears were ringing slightly, he could still hear the rustle of his sleeve as he moved, the sounds of his shoes on the floor, which meant his hearing had reverted almost to normal already, just one more welcome symptom of zombiehood.

There was a wall of ice standing between him and the approaching woman, and that had been deadening any sound from her side of the ice; but the ice was also melting, splitting open in places, which was probably why he'd been able to hear anything at all.

Distorted by the rippling ice, it was hard to make out her features, but the colour of her blood-red skin was clear enough, along with the blackness of her hair and the matching black clothes.

The Magnus needs loading, remember.

It was a matter of training and practice: Donal could reload his weapon, all seventeen rounds, very fast indeed; and so he did, right now.

By the time the woman was able to step through the melting ice barrier, Donal had the reloaded Magnus aimed steadily at the centre of her upper body.

"I'm on your side," she said. "And I'm glad you didn't kill Klaudius, even if he deserved it."

"Who the Hades are you, then?" Not letting the gun waver by even a fraction.

"My name is Hellah, and I normally live and work on the minus two hundred and seventy-third floor of this very building."

Donal, for all his zombiehood and reduced need for oxygen, sucked in a breath.

"So you understand what my job is," she continued, her heptagonal irises softening to lambent orange flames no brighter than a Lucifer stick for lighting a kitchen stove, if you couldn't afford a flamesprite. "Mine and my brother's."

"Your brother." Donal didn't look down at the pale, unconscious man, because the greater danger now stood right in front of him.

"Yes," said Hellah, "and he appears to have been ensorcelled."

Donal shook his head, still keeping his Magnus aimed steadily at the woman's – at Hellah's – sternum.

"Convenient excuse," he said. "You threw fire at me, remember?"

"I threw up a barrier to keep you safe from my brother."

"Huh."

It was a good answer. Also a smart one, from someone who might be as devious as a mage, or more so. If anything, the reputation of the Guardians who lived below was altogether darker, twisted and considerably more dangerous than that of Mordanto's adepts, even the most senior of them.

Hellah was looking at him oddly.

That was a strange thought regarding a woman with seven-sided polygons for irises that burned with orange flame, but there *was* something thoughtful and insightful in her gaze nonetheless; and when she tilted her head to one side, she softened her voice to suit.

"You of all people, Donal Riordan, should understand how ensorcellment can make anyone do anything. Do things they would normally shudder to contemplate."

"I don't…"

"Oh, but you do. The signs are still inside you, for those who know how to look."

Something strange happened next.

"No," said Donal.

And when he blinked, the world blurred, and the inner corners of his eyes began to sting.

"I really don't…" he started to go on, then stopped.

Realising what he was doing.

Zombies don't cry.

But there were tears in his eyes, starting to trickle down his eyes.

"I..." He lowered the gun. "I'm sorry."

And his shoulders shook as he sobbed.

Thanatos. How could I?

Remembering how he'd flensed the dead Diva's flesh from her bones, in the depths of his ensorcellment, not realising the strangeness of his own thoughts and actions; and how a team of armoured cops led by Laura Steele – their first meeting – had crashed into his inherited cottage in Black Iron Forest – inherited from the grandfather he had never known, and who'd made no attempt to rescue his grandson from institutional life in the orphanage – and how those cops had stopped Donal before he could enjoy the songs laid down within the Diva's bones.

Memories that normally didn't stop him dead, that he could normally dismiss – if they surfaced at all – without experiencing more than a hint of emotion, thanks to the treatment he'd received at St Jarl's, where his primary post-op carer had been Sister Felice, so sweet and elegant and, so he'd believed, purely professional in her attitude towards him.

"Put the gun away," said Hellah, and her voice was very gentle.

"Alright." He reholstered the Magnus beneath his left armpit, and adjusted his jacket.

"The Night Sister's name is Felice? Sister Felice?"

"Yes."

He didn't think she'd picked the information from him by listening to subvocalised musings. People said there was no such thing as true mind reading, but then again, they also said that when it came to the Guardians, normal rules were anything but applicable.

And that's what she was: one of the human Guardians – human or humanish – who lived among the greater entities below and kept endless watch over them. Currently there were just two of them, or so it was rumoured, and presumably the other Guardian was the nasty piece of work that Donal had just knocked out. Her brother Klaudius.

"Let me see what I can do," said Hellah.

Her skin was no longer just the colour of wet blood: it appeared to be truly wet, glistening as if liquid, fresh blood formed a coating on her skin. The flames in her eyes intensified, and began to blaze so much that Donal had to turn away.

Felice's suspended body jerked into stillness. Her back was arched strongly, her mouth open as if frozen in a scream, her fingers ending in extruded claws as if she'd been trying to claw her way out of whatever invisible field was holding her in place.

Hellah gestured, and the air glowed orange.

"Catch her," she said.

The orange winked out and Felice simply dropped.

Thanatos.

And Donal caught her, amazed at his own speed, before she could hit the floor.

Felice. You really are beautiful.

He laid her gently down on the black, still-frosty chitinous surface. She remained unconscious, but her expression grew peaceful and her claws slowly retracted, and very softly she began to snore.

Donal straightened up and turned to face this Hellah properly. "Your brother did this?"

"Under ensorcellment, as I said."

"Yeah? And if his powers are as strong as yours, who the Hades could lay a compulsion trance on him?"

"That's a really good question, Mr Riordan."

"And *that* is what people say when they're buying time to think of an answer."

"Oh, but I don't have an answer." Hellah gave a grim smile as she shook her head, her face still glistening as if covered in fresh blood. "Not yet. When I do find out who's responsible, I'm going to hurt them. For a long time, and slowly."

Donal blinked. "I think your brother's lucky, having a sister like you."

"And Felice is equally… Oh, but her feelings for you aren't reciprocated, are they? Even though you think she's elegant and beautiful."

"Well, I'm not blind." He looked down at the still-sleeping Felice. "Did you pick up on her feelings earlier? Or right now, while she's still out of it?"

"Just now. If I'd seen her earlier, I might have been able to prevent this disaster, and save those poor people's lives." Hellah gestured at the fallen officers.

"She knows something about the causes behind all this." Donal gestured towards the window, meaning the city outside. "The Void Threat as well as the things you normally look after down below, the things who are getting loose."

"Most of the resident entities remain exactly where they should be." Hellah's voice had hardened. "The handful who got loose are the weaker ones. The ones Klaudius and I couldn't spare attention to in the normal way, as we try to keep the others bound in place. Call it triage. There's a third category, the ones who aren't frightened of anything, that I'm simply leaving alone right now."

Decades worth of arcane lore and study lay behind her words: that was obvious. And maybe that was understating the depths of meaning Donal had no hope of comprehending.

"But *Void Threat* is an interesting term," continued Hellah. "A mage's term, but accurate enough, all the same."

"I've met all sorts of interesting beings recently." Donal raised his right hand to show her the still-glowing ring. "You see?"

She didn't react to the sight of it, but kept her gaze trained on his face.

"What have your mage friends said about stopping this Void Threat, if anything?"

"There's something called a Summoner, a black glass skull inhabited by a, er, composite being, kind of thing. The human part is called Drad, I mean Baladradian Chalintropovin, but… It might be able to coax the Void Threat into returning to wherever it came from. At least, I think so. Maybe."

Saying it aloud made Donal realise the weakness of his plans, of what should have been the backbone of his strategy for dealing with this catastrophe. He could end up back at the hospital with mages in tow and still find it impossible to penetrate the black-and-silver barrier or communicate with Drad at all.

And there was no telling what had happened to poor Kyushen, trapped inside and probably dead by now.

"At St Jarl's." Hellah almost spat the words. "That's the source of all the geodesic disturbance, right?"

"Probably." It sounded similar to words that Kelvin had used earlier to Lamis. Donal had picked up hints of meaning, no more than that, from hearing the mages' conversation. "A friend of mine, Dr Kyushen Jyu, is trapped inside some sort of spherical barrier there, along with the skull. At least I hope he's still alive."

"You can't know that, though. The chances are against it."

"He's a researcher. ThD, not MD. One of the best in his field, according to the medical types." Hoping that might make a difference.

"Nevertheless." Hellah's skin was looking drier now, but still red as ever: simply more matte than gloss. "You need to get there, you and as many mages as you can summon, for all the good they'll do."

Tension lines appeared in her face.

"Seems to me," said Donal, "you're more powerful than a bunch of mages."

"I am." She looked down to the floor. "But it takes two of us to keep our charges quiet at the best of times."

Not seeing the surface she was standing on, but the eldritch denizens of the minus 273rd floor, a very long way below.

"You mean you can't leave," said Donal.

"Not this building." Hellah looked at him, and gave a fleeting half smile. "But I have to leave this office and go down to where I belong, and take my brother with me."

"If he's ensorcelled, he won't help you, will he?"

"I can keep Klaudius out of things. In coma, for as long as it takes. Then if you succeed at St Jarl's before all Hades breaks loose below, I'll be able to reverse the ensorcellment, and get Klaudius back to normal. But only when the Void Threat stops disrupting the continuum and my other charges quieten down, so I've no other distractions."

Donal looked at the still-sleeping Felice. She looked elegant and, well, delicate. Although that was probably an illusion: she was a Night Sister, after all.

"She's been thinking about you," Hellah went on. "A lot. But that's all I can tell you. I can't probe any deeper – no time now – and that means you'll have to question her in the ordinary way."

She squatted down, took hold of her unconscious brother by his waistcoat lapels, and stood up, raising her brother to his feet. Then she dipped and swung him across her shoulders in a decent fireman's carry.

"Er, good luck," said Donal.

"And you." Her eyes blazed orange for a second. "I haven't met anyone like you for many years, maybe ever."

"What do you mean?"

Unreadable undertones swirled beneath her words. "Everyone else is afraid of me."

At that she turned as easily as if the unconscious Klaudius across her shoulders weighed scarcely anything, and strode out towards the open, empty-looking elevator shafts.

Where she didn't stop to wait for a wraith, but simply stepped into an opening and dropped from sight.

Hellah and her brother Klaudius were gone.

Sweet bleeding Thanatos.

This felt like one of the strangest days of Donal's existence, and it wasn't over yet.

"Mmm..." On the floor, the beautiful Felice began to stir.

Maybe she'd be able to answer his questions, but a new flaw seemed to have opened up in his plans: obvious now after his interactions with the awe-inspiring Hellah.

He wasn't a mage, and the situation was so dire that even the most senior mages had been unable to shut things down.

So what the Hades was he supposed to even ask Felice when she woke?

"Donal?"

And the time for wondering was past. "Sister Felice. How are you feeling?"

"I'm... Why am I lying on the floor?" She sat up, rubbed her arms, then stopped as she processed the sight of dead police officers all around the place.

"An ensorcelled Guardian did it," said Donal. "But he's been dealt with."

"Guardian?"

"There's only two these days, as far as I know. But they're... Never mind." Donal stopped, listened hard, then quickly placed his Magnus flat on the floor and stepped back.

And knelt down, and raised his hands.

"Donal...?"

At that, armoured officers poured out of the elevator shafts: two SWAT teams aided by wraiths. "On the floor, on the floor!"

Donal lay on his chest and said nothing as they jerked his hands behind his back and fastened on the cold, hard cuffs, very tight, while wraiths swirled all around, aggressively alert.

What more could go wrong today?

TWENTY-SIX

Commander Bowman arrived with the first team of detectives. The SWAT officers had used an empty pharmacist's office at the end of the infirmary as a temporary holding cell for Donal. No attempt at conversation, simply orders: go in, sit down, put your hands flat on the table.

And stay there.

Donal didn't ask questions or try to talk back, or even look around as they led Sister Felice to another room, after checking the rest of the floor and verifying that everything in sight was secure.

Then, the commander's arrival. He must have been waiting for the all-clear signal from the SWAT teams.

Bowman's complexion was similar to Donal's, and for good reason. The flatness of his tone when he spoke, though subtle, was a definite signal, zombie-to-zombie, signifying that Donal's resurrected status wasn't going to get him any preferential treatment.

"What happened to those officers outside?" said Bowman.

"A Guardian called Klaudius killed them." Donal kept his own voice level. "The other Guardian, his sister Hellah, has him unconscious back down on the minus two hundred and seventy-third floor. He's been ensorcelled, apparently."

"Ensorcelled? A Guardian?"

"That's what Hellah told me."

Bowman looked at him for a long moment, neither breathing nor blinking, then turned to one of the other detectives, a long-faced woman unknown to Donal. "We can do without the cuffs, Sergeant."

"Sir?"

"Undo the cuffs. Riordan's not going to be any trouble."

Donal said, "Mage Lamis transported me and Mage Kelvin to Commission Vilnar's old office. Aggie, that's the wraith, was taking medical help up to him, the last I saw. Kelvin's in a bad way. Lamis had to stay with him, just to keep him breathing."

Federal Agent Chambers had started the translocation with them, but let go and exited to some other location deliberately. Donal could explain that part later, but the important thing was to establish that he'd appeared here in something like an official capacity and with good intent.

He held still as the detective sergeant undid the cuffs and took them off him. Then he nodded to her. "Thank you."

She stepped back without replying, and tucked the cuffs into her jacket pocket. She didn't look like someone who'd worry about ruining the line of the garment. Or cared what anyone else might think about it.

"That doesn't quite explain," said Bowman, "what you're doing here."

"I was trying originally to get back to St Jarl's," answered Donal, "with the mages plus a federal spellbinder. The artefact or, well, object that I took there, a black glass skull, might be the key to sending back the Void Threat."

"Void Threat?"

"Something from the parts of spacetime that normal folk like us don't know anything about. It's big and nasty, and it's apparently the reason that the entities down below HQ are getting worked up."

Bowman said nothing. The sergeant looked as if she wanted to say a great deal, none of it polite or pleasant, but took her lead from Bowman and restrained herself.

"You want me to get any more technical," Donal went on, "I'll just be repeating words the mages used, so don't expect it to be accurate or anything."

"And how exactly are you involved?" said Bowman. "How did you get this skull thing in the first place?"

"I don't know." Donal wanted to rub his face, but he also didn't want to show agitation in front of Bowman or the sergeant; so he made the urge go away. "I'm not entirely sure, but I think Sister Felice had something to do with planting it in my office for me to find. I was just about to ask her when the tac teams arrived. They're good, too. Swept the place at record speed."

Outside, the whole of Tristopolis remained at peril. But getting emotional here would only get Donal slammed inside a cell until he calmed down; calm professionalism was the way to get the Department on his side.

In his first life, he'd have used steady breathing to keep the sense of urgency under control.

Bowman picked up a fossilised three-horned trilobite, tapped a fingernail on one of its splayed fangs, and set it back down among a collection of interesting body parts preserved in amber.

"We tried to question the Night Sister earlier," he said. "*We* including a truthseer-licensed witch and Commissioner Sandarov in person, and two experienced detectives. The Night Sister fell into something a lot like a

Basilisk Trance, which is why we sent her here, to the infirmary."

Donal shook his head. "Klaudius had her suspended in mid-air, torturing her or something. Why, I have no idea. Or exactly what he was doing to her, for that matter."

"And yet she seems perfectly okay right now."

"That's the other Guardian's doing. Hellah. She evaporated the, er, whatever it was her brother conjured up. Whatever hex field, kind of thing, that was holding Felice up in the air and making her suffer."

"*Felice*, is it? Good friends, are you?"

"She was my primary post-op carer a long time back, in St Jarl's. It's all in my record, Commander." Donal looked up at the sergeant. "I mean my Entity Resources record, from my years with the Department."

He didn't know her, therefore she maybe didn't know that he had been a cop.

"That doesn't really answer my question," said Bowman. "How close are you, exactly?"

"Not at all. I didn't... My friends at St Jarl's told me earlier this morning, before everything went to Hades, that Felice had a, er, thing for me. And Hellah confirmed it, kind of, just before she went back down below with her brother. But it was all news to me."

This wasn't the kind of calm and detached professionalism he'd been going for. Leaning against the wall, the sergeant shook her head. Maybe she was thinking the same thing.

"Have you ever been to Parasite Alley?" she asked.

Donal focused on her, wondering what the point of the question could be. "Not since I was a beat officer," he said. "And that was a long time ago."

"So if I ask the wraiths around Gregor's Emporium whether they recognise your photograph, they won't recognise you, right?"

"Not unless they've got really long memories."

"But you do know the place."

"I remember the old man who owned it. He was a fence, also a snitch, but only when he heard about the really nasty stuff. Burglaries and the like, he kept his mouth shut, provided none of the victims got hurt."

"He was your informant?"

"Not mine. Sergeant Theodus, as he was then. He retired years ago, and as for old Gregor..." Donal shook his head. "There's no way he could still be alive. Or if he is, he's certainly not working. Like I said, this was years ago, and he was ancient even then."

"Gregor Isaak Stevanovic was murdered last night, and he didn't die easily."

"The middle name wasn't Isaak, it was Ulyssess. Sergeant Theodus used to call him Gus, from his initials." Donal gave a small deliberate shrug. "So this'll be a son or nephew, most likely."

The sergeant looked at Bowman and nodded. "My sister says the Night Sister's story is consistent with this. She's babbling a bit, by the standards of a medical professional." And, with bitter humour: "A grown up Night Sister tinkering with love spells, that's what this boils down to."

Donal raised an eyebrow but didn't ask. If they'd wanted him to know about the sergeant's sister – whatever that was all about – they'd have explained it already.

He was here on sufferance at best, and in custody if he put a step wrong: that was obvious, and never mind that he'd once been a detective here himself. Thirteen dead officers and a city-wide emergency made for a serious perspective and a need for fast, even vicious decisions.

"A love spell," said Bowman.

"Near enough," said the sergeant. "Or an out-of-love spell to make someone available, more precisely, with a side effect of making them more likely to respond to, um, advances. Enhancing a rebound effect, apparently."

Bowman shook his head.

"The kind of disruption hex," the sergeant went on, "that primarily messes up an existing relationship with someone else, unless the two people involved are really, what, meant for each other. True love, kind of thing."

She didn't sound like someone who believed in the concept at all.

"Wait," said Donal. "You mean Drad, the skull, was supposed to make me, what, break up with Mel? She's my partner, by the way. We live together."

The sergeant blinked. "Please tell me you don't mean Mel who owns the boxing gym in Danklyn."

"Er, that's where we live. The apartment at the gym."

"Thanatos." She looked at Bowman. "My young niece works out there. My sister, that's my *other* sister who's my niece's mother, has only good things to say about the place."

As she was saying that, another woman came to the office door. The newcomer was identical to the sergeant.

The sister.

One of the sisters, of which there were at least three, if Donal had understood correctly. This would be the one who'd been questioning Felice.

The newcomer nodded to Bowman. "Sister Felice didn't know anything about disrupting geodesics in the crawlspace dimensions, or any of that."

Twins, and totally identical, even down to the subtleties of voice.

"Thank you, Sergeant," said Bowman.

And identical ranks as well. Donal wondered if the commander had any way of telling the two of them apart. But this was no time for idle social questions.

"Someone duped Felice." Donal needed two things: to understand, and to demonstrate his understanding, showing that he could be an asset. "That's what we're getting at here, isn't it? Duped her and Gregor Junior alike, in all probability. Is an obsidian skull *supposed* to be good for sneaking in a whatchacallit, disruption hex?"

The twin sergeants shrugged in unison, a gesture that should have looked more disconcerting than it actually did.

But Bowman said, "According to the *Encyclopædia Arkana*, it's a traditional Surinese totem, and a prime target for Surinese mischief-makers because it's ideal for just that, for sneaking in a disguised hex. The obsidian obscures the hex configuration from witchsight, even from most mages."

Both sergeants blinked, and Donal did likewise.

"That's pretty impressive, Commander," he said.

"Flattery will get you nowhere. I can read. Big deal."

Of course Bowman had started to question Felice earlier, or observed while the other detectives did it. Perhaps they'd managed to get some information out of her before the pseudo-Basilisk Trance – or whatever it was – had descended on her.

Enough to send Bowman to the appropriate article in the encyclopaedia, at any rate.

"Hellah, that's the Guardian," said Donal, "told me to get to St Jarl's with as many mages as possible, though she wasn't actually optimistic about the chances of them managing to get anything done."

The twin sergeants stirred.

"What exactly is the hex—"

"—contained in the skull?"

One of many good questions that Donal had partial answers to at best. He stirred on the hard chair, no longer feeling comfortable, wanting to be on the move again.

Whatever it was that Felice had been expecting the skull to contain, she'd been misled. And presumably, so had the dead shopkeeper. Either that or he'd been a minor, disposable partner in the conspiracy.

"An actual composite being," said Donal. "That's what the skull contains. Like a wraith, a little bit, I suppose, and from the same weird dimensions that the Void Threat comes from. Or some other region nearby, or something." He shrugged. "A personality, at any rate. Human, although that's apparently just a portion of the whole thing. Maybe the human part is the mind of someone who's long dead? I just don't know, that's the thing."

"A personality." Bowman's voice was flatter than ever. "Not a hex spell at all."

"Right, a personality with a name. Baladradian Chalintropovin, though I've been calling him Drad. Sarcastic bugger. Although…" Donal paused, glanced at the twin sergeants, then: "Mel can't hear it – couldn't hear it, when I showed her the skull – or see its mouth or jaw move. But I could."

"And this Drad," said Bowman. "Is he responsible for tricking Sister Felice into thinking the skull just contained a relationship disruption spell?

Or did someone else put him in there? Someone or something."

"Thanatos, I don't know."

All this background could be key to moving ahead and solving the city's major problem; or it could be a waste of time, when they should have been trying to get to St Jarl's as fast as possible.

Bowman sighed, which for a zombie was of course a conscious act. "The reports from St Jarl's, which we were getting regularly until half an hour ago when the phone lines went down and every radio's thaumionic valves overheated, described some kind of barrier centred on the lab where a researcher had started working on the skull. Do you agree with that assessment?"

"Yeah." Donal let out a breath of his own. "The researcher was, is, Kyushen Jyu, who's helped out the Department a lot in the past. I hope to Thanatos I haven't killed him by giving him the skull, but I might have done just that."

"And how is this supposed to help combat the Void Threat? And why didn't you tell anyone in authority about this earlier?" There was an edge to Bowman's voice now. "Like when you arrived at St Jarl's in a taxi driven by a Mister Kapeltin Katurah. Or even before, by ringing from your office or your home, the converted temple in Lower Danklyn."

Even as a redblood, Bowman had been a stickler for fine detail, according to the colleagues who'd known him back then. Zombiehood had clearly sharpened his focus.

This was the part Donal really hadn't wanted to talk about. But he had to get out of here, had to do something to help, however futile. However low the chances of turning back an entity as vast and powerful as the Void Threat that could so easily destroy Tristopolis at any moment.

And turning it back was the best they could hope for. Destroying it… No. Absolutely no chance whatsoever.

"Do you know where it is right now?" he asked. "The Void Threat. Are you tracking it?"

Somebody would be. Whether they were able to report their observations to anyone here in HQ, that was another matter. Assuming communications were as disrupted as Bowman had said.

"It went out to sea," said Bowman. "Headed away from the city in a north-north-westerly direction, swimming in a straight line – it you can call it swimming. Fast, anyhow. We've had spotter pteracraft following it."

"Well, thank—"

"And a short while ago, apparently, it turned back. Coming at a slow but unchanging speed. Even if it stops before reaching land, there's likely to be a tsunami predicted to kill at least fifty percent of the population, and probably a lot more. Ninety-something percent casualties is most likely."

Which begged the question of what would happen if the Void Threat kept on coming and took out its rage on the towers and tenements occupied by beings so much tinier than itself. Maybe no one would survive at all.

Not even the wraiths, who could certainly rotate out of the normal spacetime dimensions sufficiently to let crashing water and breaking buildings pass right through them, but couldn't possibly escape a huge and dangerous entity raging in all the dimensions simultaneously, the crawlspace dimensions included.

I'm going to have to tell Bowman everything.

Even Kyushen had thought the white wolves were an old wives' tale, while Federal Agent Chambers clearly accepted them as real but not friendly, certainly not trustworthy.

Slowly, careful in case either of the sergeants reacted badly, Donal raised his right hand and rotated it so that the palm was towards him.

"See this?" he said.

Both sergeants blinked, exactly in synch. This time the effect was spooky.

"See—"

"—what, exactly?"

"Er… The ring that's glowing red?" He formed a fist and pointed it towards Bowman. "This thing?"

Bowman shook his head.

Thanatos. They can't see it.

Earlier, Donal had said or at least implied something about the ring or the white wolves, back when he was talking to Hellah, but she'd kept her attention on his face. Hadn't so much as glanced at his hand when he'd raised it, much as he'd done just now.

The mages and Chambers saw it easily.

But mages and federal spellbinders weren't the same as Guardians or ordinary redbloods, or even zombies.

Bowman's the same as me, though.

"Okay, hang on." Donal thought about it. "Give me a moment."

He tugged on the ring.

Come on, damn you.

It wouldn't budge, of course. He thought, then: "Can you watch this and listen carefully? I mean really carefully."

Slowly, he moved his fist near the edge of the chitin-covered table – the tabletop glimmered with reflected red light, but apparently only as far his eyes were concerned – and he gently tapped against the hard surface.

"I heard that," said Bowman. "It sounded like metal, but your skin never touched the tabletop."

The twin sergeants looked at each other.

"An invisible—"

"—ring. Seriously?"

And they turned identical scornful gazes on Donal.

"White wolves gave it to me," he said.

There.

He'd said it, in only six words. Told them about the wolves, the stuff of tabloid legends and dismissed even by the likes of Dr Kyushen Jyu, and maybe in the process losing every last bit of credibility, assuming he retained any at all.

What happened next was up to Commander Bowman.

I just want to save Mel.

Not even sure if they were going to let him out of here. He might be able to fight his way out in theory, but not without the whole thing escalating to lethal force – at some point someone would draw a firearm, and the chances of no shots being fired would collapse to zero, almost certainly – and he couldn't do that, not under these circumstances.

Not when he didn't even know what he should do once he got to St Jarl's, if he ever made it that far.

Bowman picked up the desk telephone, a pewter lizard sculpture – or transmogrified corpse, more likely, given the fine detail – with cogs where the claws should have been. He spun the first five cogs only, which meant an internal extension elsewhere in HQ.

"It's worse than we thought. We've hit an actual omega-class crisis. Ah, no, I never thought I'd say those words, either." A pause. "Yes, that's right."

He replaced the handset with the softest of clicks, and looked at Donal.

"You've got no idea, Riordan, just how bad this is."

Donal relaxed his shoulders and steadied himself.

Waiting for Bowman's next move.

TWENTY-SEVEN

The Vixen dropped from the ceiling. She released the grip of her left side tyres first, causing the lofty garage interior to swing past her vision as she rotated, then her right side tyres gave the tiniest of squelching sounds as she withdrew their fastening filaments and regained normal smoothness as she fell.

Neither of the men below her so much as glanced up in the last split second of their lives.

She'd judged the timing just right, and as the two mages reached the point right beneath her, she struck them with her underside: a sickening crunch of split skulls and then her valves gasped and hydraulics bounced with the impact of all four tyres on the ground, pretty much simultaneously, the closest to a perfect landing she could have wished for.

There'd been no way to create a non-lethal impact, but she'd sensed the build-up of hex before the two mages entered the garage from the rear entrance – although they'd done their best to conceal that build-up – and the resonance leakage had told its own story: she'd only done to them what they'd intended to do to her.

Neither one of them was Professor Alkador Stern, but the Vixen didn't think that two mages, reasonably high up in the adepts' hierarchy to judge by the intensity of hex they'd been controlling between them, could sneak around l'Institutio Collosso with murderous intent and without either Stern or his watch-mages detecting them, not to mention the bloodghouls roaming the grounds and hanging from the trees outside.

Bad mistake coming here.

Whether she meant herself, or the two crushed mages underneath her chassis, she wasn't entirely sure. The important thing was getting out of this place, and these two might be able to help her, depending on the amount of visible damage she had caused them.

So she rolled clear in reverse, as carefully as possible – an ankle crunched beneath her front tyre as she backed off, but never mind – and cast her yellow gaze downwards, squinting her headlights.

One of the skulls had split quite badly, but the other was more just… distorted. Flat on the top in a way that would have looked almost inconspicuous, if it weren't for the popped-out right eye and bleeding ears.

Still, though the Vixen was neither mage nor witch in her own right, she could in her present form – although she would need to alter state in a rather painful fashion – manipulate hex just enough to effect some temporary, purely cosmetic repairs.

Enough for the corpses to look reasonably intact, to appear alive for a matter of seconds, no more. Camouflage was called for, even though getting out of Collosso was normally easier than entering, certainly easier than arriving uninvited and with ill intent.

Her actual arrival, as welcoming and easy as anyone could get, had made her think she was truly welcome here; but it had really been the pleased welcome of a leering hunter whose prey had walked – or rolled, in her case – straight into his trap.

Alkador Stern. I can't believe I trusted you.

Maybe it was that betrayal which accounted for her total lack of sympathy towards the two mage corpses lying on the garage floor in front of her. Knowing Stern, these two had arrived here as schoolchildren, pretty much, and had grown into adulthood amid total indoctrination; but at some point you had to consider adults as responsible for their own behaviour and not as victims of their upbringing.

Or maybe it was the fact that the whole of Tristopolis was at risk because of her complicit actions, so that pre-emptive lethal defence against a pair of nameless mages was just one more tiny part of the entire mess surrounding her.

I can't extrude again.

Well, she was going to have to, even though there had been too little time to recover from her driving and previous exertions, including her extruded manifestation in Lower Danklyn that perhaps indicated the moment she'd really crossed the line.

The moment she did something that dear, dead Laura would have hated for her doing.

And which she was about to do again, because she could see no other choice.

Here we go.

She popped open her doors, switched her engine off, and concentrated.

This was going to be hard.

Some seven minutes later, she had manifested her human form, linked to her engine core via the most slender of thaumoplasmic threads, and to save time she'd reformed herself in the exact same clothing as before: the severe skirt suit, the sharp hat with the shrike feather at the exact same angle as one that the real Laura used to wear.

Back when she'd been Victoria, once childhood had passed, her taste in fashion had been less conservative than Laura's. Perhaps it had simply been to annoy Mother. Maybe that was the root cause of everything.

What was that about taking responsibility as an adult?

She strode elegantly – because part of her was still trying to be Laura more than her own earlier self – and kept her knees together as she crouched down, pressed the first dead mage's eyeball back into place, and squeezed his skull a little to reshape it.

"Good enough." Not quite Laura's voice, but then she wasn't actually trying to maintain the pretence this time.

Two dead men. Not much of an audience.

She hauled the dead mage partly upright, dragged him along the floor while leaving a narrower trail of blood than she'd expected, and manoeuvred him into her driver's seat, or more precisely seated him behind the steering-wheel which no one controlled but her.

Blood on her upholstery, but that was the least of her worries right now.

The second mage took more work, but the Vixen would look more convincing with two human forms inside her, so she manipulated the shattered head between both manifested hands, an amber glow surrounding her as she worked the structural hex, knowing that in making use of it, she increased the chances of someone detecting her and raising the alarm.

At some point, Alkador Stern would send someone to check up on the two mages, when they failed to report back. If the Vixen had thought Stern was likely to come here in person, she might have tried to devise some ambush capable of taking out even him, the head of Collosso.

No, he wouldn't come himself.

Delegation and deviousness were his tools of power. It had taken her a long time to realise that, along with the totally self-centred nature of his true objectives whenever he acted, but eventually she had seen through his pleasantries and patrician accent and avuncular bonhomie.

Seen what he really was.

Alright. Good enough.

Soon enough, she had two corpses sitting on her front seats, heads propped up by headrests, one with his hands fastened to her steering-wheel, though it was the wheel maintaining a grip on the dead man's fingers and thumbs, not the other way round.

Very realistic.

Not.

But maybe sufficient to pass a cursory check, and that might be all it took to get her out of this place.

Okay. I can release this extrusion now.

She looked down at her temporary human hands, turned them this way and that, and tried to work out if she missed this, her original form. If she'd done the wrong thing in making the change.

In coming here to Collosso the first time.

Maybe…

But then she remembered the thrill, even today in her hours of fear and suicidal desperation, of roaring along a highway at full power, commanding energies no ordinary bipedal form could possible handle, not to mention the way she'd dropped like a spider from the ceiling and crushed the two murderous mages who'd come for her, which as mere Victoria she never could have managed.

Strength. No, more than that: toughness.

I am me.

She knew who she was once more.

Now I just have to make things right.

She closed her eyes, relinquished that aspect of her vision, and pulled her extruded self back into her engine core, closed her doors tightly, and just rested there quietly on all four tyres, placing all her attention inside herself.

Regaining calm – and readiness of strength – for the things she had to do next.

Okay. I'm ready.

She turned on her ignition and widened her headlights to high beam, stronger than ever.

Time to move.

TWENTY-EIGHT

Donal needed to regain control of the situation, or at least of his own actions: if there was a quick way to set the entire city back to rights – if the situation were that simple – he or someone else would have done it already.

But there was something he needed to know before acting.

"What's an omega-class crisis?" he asked Commander Bowman.

You could sort of guess, naturally, but there was something specific in the way Bowman had used the term on the phone, and Donal thought it might have something to do with the white wolves themselves. Or maybe it was indirect: indicating a crisis so bad that even the wolves had decided to get involved.

The more interesting question, which he couldn't ask directly – not if he expected an answer – was who, exactly, Bowman had made the call to.

"What it sounds like," said Bowman.

Okay. No more information was coming Donal's way.

The twin sergeants exchanged glances. Maybe they'd recognised the extension number that Bowman had rung. Donal could certainly reconstruct it from memory, in spite of the angle he'd observed from, and despite the fact that Bowman had spun the cogs back to neutral sevens all the way across, as soon as he'd finished the call.

52976. The extension could be anyone's.

Someone would be able to tell Donal whose it was, provided he asked nicely. Maybe Eduardo, if he was still the perpetually on-duty desk sergeant in the main foyer at ground level. At any other time, Donal would have known one way or the other about Eduardo, because that would have been his way into HQ, not via translocation or whatever the Hades it was.

Mages. More trouble than they were worth.

I'm going to have to make a move here.

Bowman was staring at him. "Alright. You've won a place at the top table, through sheer bloody-mindedness."

Maybe the moves Donal had made so far counted for something, after all.

"And you two," added Bowman, addressing the twin sergeants, "keep talking to the Night Sister, find out anything else that might matter, and ring the same number I just rang to let me know, because that's where I'll be."

"Sir," said the twins in unison.

They left, one trailing the other, exuding competence.

Bowman was staring at Donal in a way that seemed quite unreadable.

"Former Lieutenant Riordan, you just met Sergeant Grimstone and Sergeant Grimstone. I take it you know the name?"

"Er… Actually, yes." Donal couldn't understand how this might be important. "I remember. Mage Lamis. He's Lamis Grimstone. That's his actual surname, right? I only just heard him say so this morning."

Bowman would know that Donal's acquaintance with Lamis stretched back to Commissioner Vilnar's day. In fact Bowman had died when trying to open a hex-protected vault left behind by Vilnar, right here in HQ.

If you carried a paid-up resurrection policy on your person and you did in fact have to die, then dying in this building wasn't a bad option, in terms of medic mages arriving in time to bring you back.

Too long dead, and you could only return as a revenant, an abomination that no law-abiding mage would have anything to do with. So speed mattered, for attaining zombiehood.

"Is that the only significance of the Grimstone name for you?" asked Bowman.

"I wouldn't have called it significant at all," said Donal. "They're related to the mage, these two sergeants?"

"Cousins, in fact, although they're a generation younger. Extended families aren't that neat in terms of timing birth years. And you still don't know what I'm talking about, so never mind."

"Commander Bowman, whatever this is, let's talk about it later when the city is safe. Who's on extension 52976? And are we going to meet them, or are they coming here?"

But Bowman was already moving towards the office door, with that same kind of transition to movement that characterised Donal's own habitual motion when he wasn't worried about disconcerting ordinary living humans.

Silver blankets with embroidered runic borders covered the dead officers in the open-plan area, not so much tidying their appearance as emphasising their newly inanimate nature.

An hour ago they'd been living individuals with childhoods behind them and current loves and fears and frustrations, and were now – if Tristopolis did survive the Void Threat – simply lumps of meat, of dead flesh insulating the all-important bones that were destined for the reactor piles.

The flesh was simply waiting to be stripped away, quickly and efficiently, by quicksilver shrikes in the preparation chambers.

Soon enough, necroflux resonance would replay – over and over – in chaotic configurations formed from the interference patterns of memory and emotion laid down in every skeletal bone, so that each reactor, with its stacked bones from a thousand deceased individuals in every core, would become and remain a resonance-cavity hell: kaleidoscopic perceptions and reactions replayed in an ongoing maelstrom of energy.

Bowman didn't even spare the lumpy bodies a glance, as he led Donal past them and out to the bank of elevator shafts. He stopped by one of the larger shafts, where there was plenty of room for him and Donal to step in together, side by side.

It took longer than usual, but soon enough a large wraith rose up inside the shaft and manifested enough tangible mass to support and clasp the two zombies who stepped inside.

"Thirty-seventh floor, if you please," said Bowman.

Acknowledged.

Donal nodded as the wraith fastened around him and Bowman. "Thank you."

The wraith bore them downwards with no further words. The movement was slow and remarkably careful, perhaps because of the increased risk of something happening to the building, given all that was occurring today.

"Hey," said Donal as they descended. "You ever hear the term *redblood*?"

"Not often. I see no reason to insult the non-resurrected."

"*Is* it an insult? I never even heard the word before today."

"Would you have been insulted in your first life, if a zombie called you by that name?"

"I have absolutely no idea, Commander."

"So maybe it's not an insult. *Hey, walking reactor fuel.* Maybe that's the way to insult the non-resurrected."

Well at least Bowman had acknowledged the dead officers' existence up above. Or maybe he hadn't. It was hard to understand the context.

"You've developed a weird sense of humour," said Donal.

The shaft walls still slid slowly upwards, relative to them.

"I agree. I've been working on it, and I still can't get it right. You seem a lot closer to your original self, Riordan, or at least to an ordinary redblood personality of some kind, than I've been to mine. Since resurrection, I mean."

"I... Right. I guess it's different for different people."

Their descent slowed until they were buoyed in the shaft, suspended without moving. They were level now with a lobby floor, and the opposite wall was marked with numerals carved from mammoth bone or similar: XXXVII.

Bowman had made no move as yet. "You've probably not been here before. Certainly not since its refurbishment. Be careful not to trigger any activated defences."

"Maybe I'll just follow two yards behind you."

"I think that might be best." Bowman's tone was entirely serious.

He stepped out first.

"Thanks," muttered Donal to the wraith, and followed Bowman.

Behind them – Donal glanced back – the wraith slipped downwards in the shaft without a word.

Bowman led the way between rows of inlaid heptagrams and heptacles that sparked on the floor as he and Donal passed. Translucent swirls of movement indicated wraiths circling shark-like inside the solid floor and walls and, when he looked up, the ceiling overhead as well.

Then he was inside the working area.

Viktor Harman rose from behind a desk. Unusually, he was in rolled-up shirtsleeves, which made the twin Grauser pistols in his shoulder holsters, one beneath each arm, more obvious than ever. Along with his height, the breadth of his shoulders, the hardened stubble-covered features and ironic eyes behind the usual round, blue-lensed glasses.

"You picked an interesting day for a homecoming," he said.

"Homecoming?"

"The old task force. Hafthorr is running it himself."

The long room – almost devoid of people, but cluttered with furniture and equipment – looked like a cross between a normal detective team office and Kyushen Jyu's laboratory, with maybe half a tonne of hardware pinched from Brian Fixtovax's armoury.

Viktor's desk was decorated with protective strips of white behemoth bone inlaid with steel runes, and on its top lay a grime-streaked hexzooka smelling of recent use, along with two seven-finned rocket shells glowing with soft orange auras.

Back when Laura was in charge of the task force, it had been a small team working in a very ordinary environment.

"Er," said Donal. "Who's Hafthorr?"

"That'll be me," said Bowman. "To people other than soon-to-be Dr Harman here, my first name is Commander."

"I thought your name was Pel."

"My middle name. I stopped using it when I came back." Bowman tapped a hand over his heart. The motion revealed that he wore his watch on his right wrist, and it was just like Donal's. In his case, it showed he had half a day remaining before he needed to recharge his heart.

Assuming the city still had power by then.

"Harald and Ruth are out and about." Viktor's gravelly tone revealed nothing about his feelings. "Coordinating response teams. Or Ruth is. Harald's on some kind of escort duty. There's a lot of weird stuff happening out there."

The soon-to-be-doctor business was new to Donal, and on any other day he would have asked about that. But soon-to-be-anything would turn to came-to-nothing if they failed to save Tristopolis.

Behind one of the desks rose a pillar, bearing a nonagonal dart board on which someone had fastened a blue-and-white photo of Harald Hammersen: young features, white hair, gentle eyes and subsisting on a diet mainly of flower petals. In the photo, he was stoically accepting an award from Commissioner Sandarov, doubtless for some act of improbable courage under fire: he was an ex-Marine and one of the deadliest men that Donal had ever had the privilege of serving alongside.

Seven black-fletched darts had pierced Harald's picture in various amusing parts of his anatomy.

I really have missed this.

At the far end of the room, a bulky man with stone eyes – sniper implants – raised a hand in greeting, and Donal waved back. It took a moment to remember the guy's name – it was Kresham, one of Bowman's old crew from Robbery-Haunting – by which time Kresham had returned his attention to the broad vellum map in front of him. It stretched across a framework of slender bones that could have come from anything.

Violet flames were moving on the map: some kind of tactical visualisation of the changing situation on the ground.

There were three other plainclothes officers busy at a variety of tasks. Donal recognised none of them.

At the far end of the room stood Bowman's office, with mother-of-pearl walls and pebbled glass half-windows, protected by jagged runes similar to ones Donal had noticed only once before, and recently: on the large protective box that Kyushen had produced at St Jarl's, the one that Donal had carried into the building after popping Drad, the obsidian skull, into the box.

The door to Bowman's office stood open, revealing a hooded figure sitting in a visitor's chair, slumped with tiredness but recognisable straight away: Mage Lamis.

Donal steeled himself. If Lamis was here and not with Kelvin, that meant either that the medics had taken over Kelvin's care completely – keeping him breathing or healing him enough so that he could breathe by himself – or Kelvin was gone.

Either way, two of the city's strongest mages were down and out – at best, they were both simply too weak for action – before anyone had really attempted to face the Void Threat directly. The earlier events in Möbius Park hadn't been anything like a full-on confrontation.

If the secondary, indirect threats were this bad, then the primary was too huge to—

Lamis raised his hooded head, and turned towards Donal. His lips didn't move, but his sepulchral voice sounded in Donal's mind all the same.

"There's always a way, for those who make the sacrifice."

Bowman carried on without pause, entering the office and circling behind his desk. Donal followed because he had to, making no reply to Lamis's remark about sacrifice because even now, with everything that was happening, revealing that a mage's voice could manifest directly inside his head was something to keep private.

The other occupant of the office wasn't actually there.

Donal stopped dead, staring at the human-shaped volume of darkness that stood inside Bowman's office, well away from the open door. He was scarcely aware of Bowman closing the door behind them.

Bowman, Lamis and the shadow shape – a human-shaped nothingness – and Donal, were sealed in the office.

"Who are you?" Addressing the manifested nothingness directly.

Something about the pressure against Donal's ears and the deadness of his own voice implied they were insulated in here. No one outside the office, not even Viktor in the working area outside, knew about this apparition: Donal was almost sure of it.

"My name is irrelevant." The voice reverberated: deep and male but so distorted that there was no telling what the original tone was like. "I am part of an order whose name is also irrelevant."

"Seriously?"

"An order that I formally joined on the same day as Arrhennius Vilnar, over twenty years ago." The shadow shape paused, as if allowing for its words to sink in. "The Commissioner intended on inviting you to join us, Donal Riordan. He had plans for you."

That part rang true. But still...

"I've only your word for that." Donal looked at Lamis, who remained slumped in the visitor's chair. "Don't tell me. You and the old Commissioner were part of the same secret-handshake club."

Below the wraparound shades, Lamis's mouth twitched in what might have been a smile or a grimace of pain. "We were, in fact."

"Well I don't have time for rituals and oaths, and I sure as Hades ain't dressing in a robe for anyone." Donal was a Lower Danklyn boy at heart, toughened by his years at the orphanage and the unforgiving discipline of the Sisters of Thanatos, and sometimes you had to wield that blue-collar attitude like a weapon. "And I'm not discussing anything with a stranger I can't even see."

"Are you so sure I'm a stranger? Perhaps we've met already, in more normal circumstances."

Anger could be controlled. Donal deliberately caused it to strengthen his voice. "Tell me everything now, or get the Hades out of here. Your choice."

"Then I'll take the second option." The blackness began to swirl and evaporate and slowly fade out.

And was gone.

Donal turned to Bowman, who'd been standing statue-still during the whole exchange with the shadow shape.

"Don't tell me, Commander. You're part of this secret gang as well. Does the current Commissioner know? How about Entity Resources? Or is this the kind of thing that results in instant dismissal when people find out?"

"I've not been fully initiated," said Bowman. "And I don't know that person's true identity any more than you do. But I wanted to show, well, not quite bona fides, but enough for you to see that it's not just me and Mage Lamis cooking up a small conspiracy here."

Donal shook his head. He'd been the one to drag Lamis into all this, hadn't he?

But Bowman had turned to Lamis. "It seems Riordan is wearing a ring on his right hand, one that I'm led to believe you can see."

"An interesting choice of words." Lamis's voice was sepulchral as ever.

"I can't see it, and neither can your two cousins."

"Ah." The wraparound shades were focused on Donal now. "The white wolves have done more than I realised. You understand, they are playing a long game on a timescale of centuries, which is what our own little order is all about. Tracking them, trying to foresee…"

He stopped and simply breathed, wheezing a little. Given the effort he was making just to talk, what he was saying had to be important.

But timescales of centuries meant nothing when the Void Threat was on its way back to the city, which might not even survive that long if the various entities from below HQ continued to panic and escape and smash everything, the entire structure of Tristopolis, as they scrabbled away for safety.

"Bowman. What do you want from me?"

"I want you to help me convince Lamis to accept help," answered Bowman.

"*What?*"

"I'm not a mage, and neither are you. And Kelvin is out of it for a long time, if he even pulls through. We need someone who can call on serious mage resources, and she's already been here today, seeing Commissioner Sandarov."

"Because I'm out of the… picture… these days." Lamis punctuated his words with short gasps. "Only… reason."

"You need medical help," said Bowman.

"No." Lamis held up a hand, frowned, and sat straighter in his chair. "I'll be okay."

"We're not getting help from the Order." Bowman was staring hard at Lamis, clearly struggling for a way to convince him. "Not the kind we need right now. We need her, Lamis."

"I don't think she—"

Someone was thumping on the door. Bowman hesitated for a second, then turned away from Lamis and pulled the door open. "What's wrong?"

It was Viktor, eyes hard behind the round blue lenses, looking scarier than ever. "Radio from a patrol car that got sideswiped off the road. One of Harald's escorts. He's getting close but something's picking off the escort vehicles. Donal?"

"I'm with you."

Bowman said: "I'll mobilise the tac teams and follow."

Viktor was already jogging towards the elevator shafts, where a grim-faced Kresham and two colleagues, all clad in flak jackets and bearing large-calibre rifles and glowing ammunition satchels, were stepping into the grasp of wraiths and beginning their descent.

Donal no longer carried a badge but clearly today's events pushed all the normal rules aside. He felt an urge to grin – despite everything – as he matched Viktor's pace, but it was the atavistic predator behaviour of baring teeth, not actual civilised humour, that drove that urge; so he kept his expression hard and serious.

But still he felt a thrill as a wraith materialised and he stepped into the cold shaft and let the wraith carry him down.

He passed the descent time double-checking his Magnus and the spare rounds he carried, and wishing he'd been able to pick up extra, all the while knowing that firearms, even with hex-doped rounds, might not be up to the task.

Not today.

Here we go.

He spilled out into the ground floor lobby at the same time as Viktor, slightly behind Kresham and the other two.

Wondering what the Hades they were running out to face.

TWENTY-NINE

Seven shallow, broad steps of marble led down to the vast main entrance-lobby, and Donal simply jumped from the top step, sailing all the way down to the floor and landing in a squat from which he bounced up and forward into a sprint, leaving Viktor far behind and overtaking Kresham and the other two detectives.

"Hey, Lieutenant—" called Eduardo, his torso as always rising from the upper surface of the tall granite block that acted as a permanent reception desk as well as forming the lower, greater part of Eduardo's hybrid petrimorph form.

It was nice to be recognised, even if the rank no longer applied, but Donal was already past him and reaching the great bronze-and-steel doors that had started to swing open, creating just enough space for him to pass through without slowing down.

He went fast down the big outdoor steps between the twin rows of glowing pillars and onto the sidewalk, noting the unusual sparsity of traffic with nothing at all in front of him, and he ran right out to the centre of the broad, long boulevard that was Avenue of the Basilisks.

Winged gargoyles were circling far overhead, dark grey shadows against the deep purple sky, but none that he could count on for help.

His eyesight was better than it had been in his former redblood life, so he was able to make out the distant limo with its bone-motorcycle escort – Harald on his Phantasm IV, the sight bringing a real smile to Donal's lips – and the two patrol cars following, one of which leapt up in the air in exactly that moment, followed by the other car spinning and swerving off to one side and smashing into a gothic storefront: Mooningdale's, by the look of it.

The big entity chasing them gradually resolved into an orange-purple shape, ridge-spined and talon-clawed and yellow-eyed, with fangs of what looked like diamond, becoming visible not just because it was drawing closer, but because its former near-perfect translucency was coalescing into normal, ordinary matter.

Not good.

Apart from the normal matter part.

Which was good news, in the sense that physical impact should have an effect, the problem being that the Death-damned thing was simply huge.

Donal drew his weapon slowly, swivelled to a side-on stance, and raised his Magnus one-handed, arm extended, as though preparing for a static-target session on the range.

By the time he was ready to fire, Viktor and the others had already stumbled into place, taking up support positions, one of them muttering a prayer to Saint Magnus, the Slayer of Evil, while making the Sign of the Axe before swinging his rifle up to his shoulder.

Donal aimed high, plotting the shallow parabolic path to his ever-nearing target, and fired at its left eye: three shots with minute adjustments for decreasing range as he brought the heavy Magnus back from recoil each time.

Sniper rounds boomed from Kresham and his two colleagues, while Viktor stood still with each fist holding a Grauser at the ready, waiting for the huge thing to get close enough for his favourite weapons to make a difference.

Donal wished he'd thought of taking the hexzooka from Viktor's desk, but there hadn't been any time to waste and now there was none at all as the thunderous avalanche of automatic Grauser fire spewed into the approaching creature's legs and the bone motorcycle was swerving to a halt, pointed towards the steps of HQ, with Harald crouched low upon its back.

The approaching limo, dark burgundy and trimmed with black and boasting serious black fins, was hammering straight towards Donal so he had to break stance and run to the side as the vehicle screeched past but with smoke pouring from beneath the wheel arches as the driver braked hard and swung it to an emergency halt and tumbled out, a big guy with a large belly swinging up his own automatic rifle and joining in the weapons fire.

Maybe the beast faltered a fraction before opening its diamond-fanged maw wider than ever and dropping forwards, straight for the limousine.

No.

With no idea who could be instead but understanding they must be helpless, Donal sprinted for the rear door, praying to Thanatos that it remained unlocked, not needing to worry on that score as it popped open just before he laid his left hand on the handle and wrenched it fully open.

A white-haired woman was reaching out, still caught in the act of opening the door from inside.

Oh, no. Not her.

He hauled her out, knowing that she was frail enough with age for such movement to hurt her, but needing to get her clear before the chasing beast simply smashed the limousine into oblivion.

The big chauffeur, still firing his automatic rifle, was an ex-cop called André Mordeaux: Donal recognised him now.

And the woman, Professor Helena Steele and mother of Laura whose zombie heart beat in Donal's chest, went with Donal's motion, letting him drag her away from the car, intent on keeping hold of her platinum-headed walking-cane, which might have cost them a split second but not enough to count as the big beast hammered down with one claw, trying to swat them into nothingness but missing, although the blow smashed into the tarmac hard enough to break the road into rubble.

From the steps of HQ swarmed a pack of TPD deathwolves, howling their hunting cry, while behind them a team of armoured SWAT officers opened up with their heavy sorcerous weapons fire that split the air with blue ravening lightning.

The creature reared up and roared at them, and swiped hard, smashing several of the glowing pillars by the HQ entrance steps, even as the deathwolves went for its legs and began to rip them open, purple ichor spilling out, visible even from here.

One of the wolves, cream-coloured and small but clearly ferocious, sprang up the great creature's nearest leg and body like a mountain goat ascending, and made a final leap to snap its jaws shut, biting into the side of the creature's neck, aiming for the carotid artery or its equivalent in this thing, and just about getting it.

"Put me down." Professor Helena Steele's voice was crisp, patrician and commanding.

"You need to get inside." But Donal allowed her to stand by herself, all the same.

Thanatos damn it.

He began to take aim again with his Magnus, but beside him, Helena had already raised her cane, and white lightning was dancing around its platinum head and tip, and her eyes were glowing with the same white brilliance that was steadily increasing, until Donal had to look away in order not to end up blinded.

White nova-light, bright enough to light up the buildings on either side of the great boulevard, accompanied the crack of sound and the coruscating blast that arrowed straight into the huge creature's skull, while the tiny-by-comparison deathwolf released its grip on the thing's throat and dropped clear.

The massive corpse dropped flat onto its front, the great head hitting the road jaw first, the yellow eyes growing opaque and, in a matter of seconds, frosting over into a dull, lifeless grey.

Silence and floating dust filled the street, as the normal darkness resumed.

Donal looked at the woman who might, in a different world, have become his mother-in-law, and swallowed as involuntarily and nervously as a redblood might.

"Sweet bleeding Thanatos," he said.

Helena Steele looked at him for a long, judgemental moment. And then, surprisingly, she smiled. "Fancy meeting you here, Lieutenant Riordan."

"I'm not actually—"

"Of course. I remember. I think I'll just call you Donal."

"Er, thank you, ma'am."

She looked over at her driver, André. "Are you in one piece?"

"Sure, Professor. Are you okay?"

"Right as quicksilver rain." Her expression darkened. "I'm afraid your friend hasn't been so lucky."

Viktor was already holstering his Grausers as he ran over to the bone motorcycle, the Phantasm IV on which Harald still lay slumped, unmoving. His clothes were torn, and both he and the Phantasm were streaked with what looked like soot.

"I'm sorry," added Helena. "I couldn't deal with that creature until your SWAT people weakened it. When I was younger... Ah. Never mind."

Donal wanted to help see to Harald, but he had to remain by Helena's side. If Harald had been trying to escort her here safely, then this counted as achieving Harald's mission objective, which for an ex-Marine was always what counted most.

"The crawlspace dimensions are totally impassable now," she went on. "A maelstrom. Do you understand what I'm talking about?"

"Sure," said Donal. "Layperson's explanation, right?"

"Something like that. If I said that I'm beginning to understand what Laura saw in you, you might think me condescending. But perhaps I do understand, all the same."

Donal nodded, accepting the near-apology. It was already far more than he might have expected.

Wraiths rose up from the road surface – one of them might have been Aggie, but it was hard to be sure – and three of them part-coalesced around Harald's slumped body and lifted him slowly upwards from the Phantasm IV whose headlight glowed a soft, plaintive shade of green.

Bowman said something to the largest wraith – yes, Aggie for sure – as they floated towards the open HQ doors, carrying Harald. Donal could only watch as they continued inside, and out of sight.

"He'll be okay," said Helena. "Provided the city survives."

And if it didn't, they were all done for. That went without saying.

Bowman came over, stopped, and greeted Helena with a kind of abbreviated bow. "Professor, thank you for coming back here under such circumstances. Although if I'd realised the danger—"

"Don't worry, Commander. That beast isn't from beneath the police department's cellars. It's something else, and at some point I'll determine exactly what it is."

Bowman looked at Donal. "The elevator wraiths have instructions to treat you as a senior ranking officer. Perhaps you could escort the Professor to my office in the task force room."

Zombies were good at clamping down the betraying minutiae of redblood body language and vocal subtleties – Bowman maybe more so than Donal – but Professor Helena Steele most likely understood that there was more going on than anyone wanted to say out loud for now.

Still, she simply nodded and reached out with an expectant hand, a gesture that Donal took too long to recognise. Then he holstered his Magnus and crooked his elbow so that she could take his arm, and he escorted her towards the steps of HQ as if this were a banquet of the high and mighty and she an honoured guest, maybe the guest of honour, and never mind the giant dead creature with newly opaque eyes and wrecked patrol cars further down the street, or the broken pillars partially blocking the steps in front of them.

Avoiding the wreckage, they climbed steadily, and passed between the great bronze-and-steel doors. A blood-streaked deathwolf stood there, looking up at Donal with its tongue lolling, while several of its fellow pack members stood nearby, quiet but alert.

Its fur was cream, and some of the blood was its own, but most of it was ichor already darkening from purple to black as it dried.

"Give me a moment," murmured Donal to Helena, and halted. To the deathwolf, he said: "You're one of FenSeven's sons, aren't you?"

"Yes-s-s-s."

"Is he still okay?"

"Old. Ok-ay."

Donal grinned, an expression that deathwolves always understood. "You have his courage. Respect to you, and say hello to your father for me."

"Yes-s, Do-nal."

Helena raised an eyebrow as they continued inside. Perhaps it was just as well that Eduardo – Sergeant Eduardo Kolemann – was busy talking into his desk phone, so that he could only raise a hand in acknowledgment as Donal passed. Catching up with old friends and colleagues was something for another day.

He just had to help make sure that there were more days for everyone to enjoy. Part of him wanted to simply cut loose and return to Mel any way he could and then try to get out of the city, the two of them, but the odds of success were marginal if not zero. Here, he might achieve something.

The third elevator shaft along was wide, with a wraith almost as large as Aggie floating inside, so Donal stepped into its coalescing form with Helena beside him, and asked for the thirty-seventh floor, please.

Again the raised eyebrow from Helena. Not everyone was polite to wraiths as a rule – very few were, in fact – but whether Donal's automatic courtesy impressed or disturbed her, he simply could not tell.

And wasn't sure it mattered either way.

The wraith carried them steadily upwards.

THIRTY

Heptagrams and heptacles blazed brighter than before as Donal led the way to Bowman's office, steering Helena who kept her grip on him – her frail-looking hand still grasping Donal's crooked arm – and he might have thought her a vulnerable old lady if he hadn't seen the immense destructive power she had wielded just now, whiter and brighter than lightning, conducted or controlled but not generated – he was pretty sure – by the slender walking-cane she carried in her other hand.

The wraiths swimming inside floor and walls and ceiling kept a wary distance, as though they, too, understood that Professor Helena Steele was far stronger and more significant than her age and elegant appearance might suggest.

She stopped dead at the sight of Lamis rising tiredly from his chair inside Bowman's office. Her old-lady fingers tightened on Donal's forearm. "What is my brother doing here?"

"Your… brother?"

"So no one told you. And isn't that just typical."

"Probably. I'm sorry."

"Well, I'm here now. Keep your head down, Donal, if things get fiery between us."

He wondered how literal her warning might be. "There are worse things happening outside. Remind Lamis of that, Professor, and he'll remember his priorities. I'm sure of it."

"As you've just reminded me? Very smoothly done. So come on."

They entered Bowman's office, where Lamis stood to one side, making no attempt to touch Helena, and leaving the way clear for Donal to conduct Helena around the desk, where he swivelled Bowman's chair for Helena to sit down on.

"Thank you," she said, with a momentary twinkle in her eyes as she took her place on the most comfortable and commanding chair in the room.

It wasn't just courtesy or even irony on Donal's part. Nothing else was good enough for her, not by a longshot.

"Be careful." Lamis's deep voice echoed like the catacombs where Donal used to run in what seemed like the distant past. "My sister has a way of snagging and co-opting people's loyalty without them even noticing how their thinking has changed."

"Noted," said Donal. "And you should sit back down, Mage, and stop trying to pretend you're in better health than you really are."

"It's fatigue, not illness."

But he looked old and unsteady as he lowered himself back onto the visitor's chair, before tilting his chin up and appearing to stare through his wraparound shades directly at Helena.

Her clear grey eyes stared back. Flinching wasn't part of her body-language vocabulary, not from what Donal had seen so far.

"Where is she?" Her voice was hard as well as cultured now. "Do you even know?"

"You're her mother. Too bad I need to remind you of that fact."

The air between them appeared to shiver, and even with his zombie acuity Donal couldn't tell if the effect was psychological – a trick of his own perceptions – or whether Helena and Lamis were already threatening each other with real energies on some level.

Bowman entered, and Donal hadn't even sensed him approaching. This encounter felt increasingly unnerving.

They're obviously not talking about Laura.

No, they're talking about my sister.

Donal's entire body locked down, as if ice had cascaded through him. Words from Laura – his sweet, dead Laura whose heart beat inside his body even now – had sounded clear as anything in his mind.

Are you still here, inside me?

No answer.

He had thought that whatever remained of her, if anything, had blended with and merged into his own self at the deepest levels, long ago.

Bowman flicked a glance in his direction, as if he'd sensed something from Donal, but not understood what it was.

Trying to gather his thoughts, Donal stared up at the stationary ceiling-fan he'd not paid attention to before. Its scale-covered vanes were marked with delicate scratches that spelled out sentences or verses in archaic Proto-Surinese script: indecipherable to Donal, but echoes of a callous, bloody culture and twisted, dark forms of hex that no one these days, from everything he'd heard or read, would dream of resurrecting.

It was a hint that more than the obvious was happening here.

"I note," said Helena from behind the desk, "that we're not in the

Commissioner's office. Is he alright?"

"He is," said Bowman. If he felt annoyed at her co-opting of his chair, he'd buttoned down the feeling. "And at some point he'll learn that you're in the building, Professor, if he hasn't already. But I thought you and Mage Lamis needed to talk directly."

The lines in Lamis's face deepened.

And Helena's features hardened in a similar way. "You've taken this on yourself, then. So who are you, precisely?"

"Commander Hafthorr Bowman, ma'am."

"Hmm." Her flint-hard gaze fastened on Donal. "Perhaps you can tell me what's going on here."

She must know he couldn't, not really, although the things he was in the dark about were maybe different from the things that she didn't know. But guessing games wouldn't help with a deadline looming.

Lamis said: "Kelvin used a coherent vitaenergetic transfer to boost my last translocation summoning. It's caused a fourth-phase degradation in his… Well. You know. And I'm sorry. He was still alive, the last I saw."

For a moment, seeds of nova-white luminescence shone in Helena's eyes, then she sagged back in her chair. In Bowman's chair, which creaked.

"It was Kelvin's idea, not Lamis's," Donal found himself saying. "He took Lamis by surprise."

"He would." Helena's voice was old and tired. "Surprising even my smart, omniscient brother."

Lamis said nothing.

Bowman glanced at Donal, who gave a sort of micro-shrug, the kind only a fellow zombie was likely to pick up on.

Letting Bowman make the play.

"Professor?" said Bowman. "We need to get mages to St Jarl's in force, the best in Mordanto and as much support for them as possible. Riordan here had an encounter with white wolves that—"

"I'm stepping down," said Helena. "As of now, if you'll give me a moment."

She tapped her cane, spoke ghastly words from a tongue Donal had never heard but which turned even his zombie spine to ice, and the cane sparked red and that was that.

With a sigh, she sank back, looking smaller as if dehydrated in a matter of seconds.

"What did you just do?" said Donal.

"Put Mordanto in more capable hands than mine, thank Thanatos. Revoking my power of veto and allowing the regents to choose whoever they think best." A sad pause. "I'd hoped young Kelvin would take over from me in time, but *my* time has passed and he's not yet ready, and the chances of his recovery from a fourth-phase degradation are minimal at best."

With every word she spoke, Donal's stomach felt more hollow, like the time that Aggie – back when she was Gertie – had dropped him playfully down an elevator shaft and took her own sweet time catching him and slowing his descent.

"I should have resigned before," added Helena. "But there. It's done now."

Stepping down in the middle of an emergency was unthinkable for a senior officer in the military or law enforcement, but mages were a law unto themselves, and the mechanisms for transfer of power remained invisible to outsiders.

Of course, junior officers taking over when their commanders fell, well, those stories were the stuff of regimental and departmental legends.

"Will your successor follow your suggestions about St Jarl's?" said Bowman.

"You'll have to ask him," answered Helena. "Are the telephone lines still intact? I had to travel here by car, remember, with the escort that the Commissioner provided. Or... Wait. *You* ordered the officers to fetch me here, invoking Commissioner Sandarov's name without his knowledge."

"Yes, ma'am," said Bowman. "And with good reason. He'll maybe fire me later, but I'd rather that than have the city destroyed and all of us with it."

All that talk about maelstroms in the crawlspace dimensions. Perhaps the landscape as seen by mages was already a battlefield or disaster zone in the same way that actual streets and buildings were due to become rubble or worse, all across Tristopolis.

"Commander." Donal held up his right hand, with the red-glowing ring that he knew Bowman couldn't see. "I've got to get to St Jarl's, with someone who can make use of this thing. No more talking."

"Can you reach Collosso from here?" said Helena. "I mean, are the roads relatively clear? Because my cane's entanglement was a one-off message, the final emergency signal through the chaos, and I'm now completely out of touch with everyone."

"Say what?" Donal had reverted to Lower Danklyn manners, but never mind.

"L'Institutio Collosso. You need to get there." Helena looked calmer now. "Professor Alkador Stern will be there, but not for long, because he'll be getting ready to leave for Mordanto, where he'll be taking over."

Lamis shifted, reacting to the name but not in any way that Donal could decipher.

"You blame me." Lamis's voice went deeper than ever. "But not that fool Stern. And you think he'll make a good conflict commander?"

"On the latter point, I do not. And on the former, I blame you because you lied to Alkador, and Victoria backed you up, pretending she had my blessing and authority."

Bowman, who'd clearly sent Harald to Mordanto to fetch Helena under false pretences, claiming the authority of Commissioner Sandarov, flicked a glance at Donal, who nodded as a gesture of support.

Helena turned to Bowman. "My replacement is not a fighting mage, but he is the quintessential survivor. If anyone can save the population of Tristopolis through sheer guile, it's him."

"And will you tell him about Donal and—"

"I've no way of communicating with anyone now. And I told Alkador Stern just this morning that he'd never take over from me, not under any circumstances. And my reversal isn't exactly an act of kindness, not today. So I'm the last person he'll take advice from, Commander." She looked at Donal. "You, he might pay attention to."

Wonderful.

Lamis was out of it, Helena was out of it, Kelvin probably wouldn't survive, and even Harald had looked in a bad way down on Avenue of the Basilisks, while all the dangers they'd faced so far had been side effects, secondary considerations before the Void Threat really did its worst.

Donal looked out at the open plan area where only one detective was left, talking urgently into a phone, but perhaps it was just an internal call. Where Kresham had been working earlier, the vellum map remained tautly spread across the bone framework it was fastened to, and purple flames still moved on it, exactly as before.

Tracking the danger zones, on the basis of... what? Radio patrol cars and municipal scanbats did the trick on normal days, but today the accuracy of any incoming reports had to be questionable.

Still, the map was better than nothing.

"I've got an idea," said Donal.

He realised Bowman had been saying something, but stopped now.

"You can try calling Collosso" – Donal pointed at the map outside – "while I check that thing, and make a phone call to the duty sergeant. Then I'll be on my way regardless."

"How are you going to manage that?"

But Donal was already walking out.

Taking action now.

THIRTY-ONE

The Vixen hung suspended once more, but this time she was right-side-up and it wasn't her idea: no filaments or tendrils – extruded from her tyres or anywhere else – were responsible for holding her in place.

This time it was angular exoskeletal legs, twenty-nine of them unfolded from a dank, stinking ceiling, each leg ending in a pointed claw that pierced her bodywork painfully, and simply held her here, high above the broken flagstones that formed the old coach house floor.

No one came here normally. The creature that had melded into the stonework between ceiling and rooftop, its exoskeleton merging imperceptibly into ancient sandstone, was the only permanent inhabitant. Its twin rows of dark convex eyes were ranged across the ceiling like lamps or portholes, but the polyrachnid creature was neither trapped nor helpless: it could break free and roam loose if it felt the urge; but as part of a solid building in the grounds of Collosso, it felt safer than it had for a century.

So long as people fed it regularly, that was. Which they did: living food for the most part, of pretty much any size or kind.

Or so the mage-novitiates had told her with knowing smiles and giggles, back when the Vixen had been Victoria and acquainting herself with the buildings and regulations and way of life that pertained in l'Institutio Collosso, the place that had literally made her who – or what – she was today.

That had given her the life she'd asked for, and might now snuff out that life entirely, assuming Collosso and the city of Tristopolis survived the coming threat at all.

Earlier, she'd almost made it as far as the outer gates, and she'd felt hope surging through her pistons and transmission as she gunned her acceleration, but then the gates had slammed shut before her and she'd sprayed gravel as she handbrake-turned, headed back where she'd come from, then braked to a halt.

The two unwary, careless mages who'd intended to kill her shortly before, well, she'd dealt with them readily enough and felt no regrets. But the ranks of young mages who poured out of the main building's side doors and came for her now, in that moment, they looked innocent and scared: a fear she could taste on the air that she pulled in through her carburettors and manifold; and whatever the youngsters had been told she was, they saw her as an enemy that had to be captured at all costs.

She couldn't use lethal force against them, not when they were innocents, even though she couldn't hope to force her way through them without that level of impact.

Alkador Stern, I hate you.

Guile, deception and persuasion. He was a master of all three.

And of hiding in the background while others faced the consequences of carrying out his commands.

So she allowed the young mages-in-training to bind her with propulsion and compulsion hexes, and to lead her to the old coach house beyond the rustwood copse where even the bloodghouls feared to go, where they led her inside and waited until the polyrachnid had finished stinging her and taking hold of her and raising her aloft.

And then, with relief more than triumph written on their faces, the youngsters had exited the coach house, swung the doors shut from outside, and headed back to lecture theatres and laboratories and spellcasting pits, to judge from the diminishing voices, and the empty, cold silence that followed.

Only then did Alkador Stern make an appearance, and even so, he brightened in place as a holomantic image standing approximately on the flagstones – not quite lined up correctly – and not his actual, physical self.

"Well, my dear. I seem to have outmanoeuvred you and your mother and even, as a little jape, that fellow who carries your dead sister's heart inside him. I get a promotion, a considerable step up before retirement, and... Well, you know, I could go on, but boasting is such a bore, don't you think?"

There was a great deal she had to tell him, and not just to vent her rage, because whatever he'd tricked her into doing, the result was a looming threat to Tristopolis and Thanatos-knew-how-much of the world beyond, which seemed like the opposite to any half-sane person achieving their ambitions.

But the polyrachnid had injected some necrochemical cocktail of toxins into her hydraulics that locked her solid, unable to manifest her thaumoplasmic form or perform any of her other esoteric tricks. All she could do was narrow and brighten her headlights at him, and crank up the intensity further.

Which might have been effective, if only to achieve momentary blindness, had a physical human being been standing there below her suspended self.

In his holomantic projection, Alkador Stern merely laughed. "I guess you could toot your horn, assuming you have one. Other than that, dearest

Victoria-as-was, I'd say you're entirely helpless here."

She growled, bringing her engine to life, then coughed as her ignition cut out and she hung in place, silenced and stalled and yes, humiliated.

"My little pet will take its time with you, my dear." The smile on Alkador Stern's face might have been charming in a high-class social setting. "Perhaps I'll return and chat again, while you're still compos mentis enough to understand my words."

It chilled the Vixen, the thought of her mind disintegrating as she slowly fell apart, dissolved and absorbed by the polyrachnid that held her captive. Already the pain from all twenty-nine puncture points was overwhelming.

How many days could she suffer like this before the end?

I need to get away.

A tidal wave of agony washed over her as two sections of her bodywork tore further open by a hand span, and when her surroundings wobbled back into focus once more, only empty flagstones formed the floor.

The projection of Alkador Stern was gone.

Maybe there's a way to stop the pain.

Human prisoners experiencing brutal incarceration did it all the time: hanging themselves, cutting their wrists. Maybe she could—

No. Never.

Life was always worth fighting for.

She would hang on, for as long as she could.

Pain piercing her all around, but she would fight until the final overwhelming conclusion.

After a while, she became delirious, then a jolt of agony and ripping bodywork – just one wing tearing a little more open – paradoxically snapped her out of it and back into rational awareness.

She had no idea how much time had passed. Her onboard clock, its hands formed of what had once been her own human finger bones, had stopped at some point. Maybe when the polyrachnid's toxins poured through her system, or some short while before, when the mass of young mages had bound her with unbreakable hex.

Still unbreakable?

Not any longer perhaps, but the wearing-off of the earlier spells couldn't help her now – not in this reduced state.

The world seemed to recede in every direction. Maybe she ought to give up, after all. Her previous resolve meant prolonging the pain, not actually achieving anything that might help her break free, or at least warn other people about Alkador Stern.

It's no good.

That realisation seeped deep inside her chassis and chilled her engine block, and made everything hurt even more than it had already.

I've messed up absolutely everything.

At which point the doors to the coach house blew inwards, and a pale woman clad in a jumpsuit was standing there. She looked up at the Vixen, her expression grim.

"Don't worry. You're going to be alright."

Her eyes began to glow an eldritch green.

What the Hades?

Above the Vixen, from its position within the coach house roof, the polyrachnid let out a thin, frightened mewling.

Knowing what was about to happen.

Green lightning coruscated everywhere, sheets and bolts of blinding energy, and that energy flared enough to crack the air itself, loudly and repeatedly and almost enough to drown out the death wails of the creature in the roof.

Its legs thrashed as they ripped free of the Vixen's body.

Strange hollow relief, coldness and pain in her wounds – the holes around her bodywork – as she dropped, knowing her suspension wasn't up to coping with another impact, surprised as her descent slowed as if time itself were congealing or the atmosphere had grown softly viscous.

Her tyres touched lightly on the ground, and she was almost herself once more.

When the green light faded, the polyrachnid's twenty-nine legs hung straight down from the ceiling, limp and lifeless, while dark ichor spilled like water from leaky pipes and spattered on the flagstones.

The woman in the jumpsuit walked directly in front of her, in full view of her headlights. "My name is Federal Agent Chambers, and I need your help."

For the first time in a long while, the Vixen wished she had kept the ability to laugh.

The federal spellbinder smiled, and placed her hand on the Vixen's front wing, and nodded.

Clearly, she understood.

THIRTY-TWO

Donal rode down the elevator shaft, held by a grim and silent wraith, feeling hard and determined himself. In his jacket pocket, he carried a folded vellum sheet sealed with something that looked like black wax but felt like metal; and he hoped it would do some good.

Against hex barriers and entities who climbed out of the crawlspace dimensions, his own abilities counted the same as those of any random human plucked off the street: as nothing at all.

While he'd been examining the tactical map in the task force office, Lamis and Helena had apparently worked together to write a technical description of the situation in St Jarl's and the nature of the Void Threat as they understood it. It had been Lamis who solemnly handed the sealed, folded document to Donal.

"No one's managed to get through to Collosso, by any forms of communication," Bowman had said. "And if you don't get there soon, then Professor Stern will presumably be en route to Mordanto in any case."

"I've taken that into account," Donal had told him. "I'll use the same way into Collosso that he'd be likely to take, except he'd be travelling in the opposite direction to reach Mordanto."

It was clumsily worded but Helena and Lamis both nodded as if they understood.

A ghostly three-dimensional apparition of a head had been floating above Bowman's desk, conjured into place by Helena. Donal had never seen such a thing before, but he had pointed at it almost casually, as if it were an everyday occurrence.

"That's what Stern looks like?"

Jowly, patrician features.

"Indeed." It was Lamis who had answered.

Nods and abbreviated farewells followed, and within a minute Donal was out of the office and heading downwards in the wraith's capable grasp.

"Thanks," he said as they drew level with the ground floor lobby.

He stepped out and the wraith shifted neither up nor down, but straight back horizontally into the shaft wall, disappearing from sight.

Abandoning its duty? Donal hoped not, but he couldn't really blame it.

Down the shallow steps to the main lobby, where he stopped a good distance from the granite block that served as the duty desk as well as Sergeant Eduardo Kolemann's lower body.

Immobile. There was no shifting Eduardo out of here, not easily, if everything went to Hades.

Donal looked up at him. "Is Harald Hammersen's Phantasm still outside?"

"Like I said on the phone, Donal. As far as I know, it ain't going nowhere."

While examining the tactical map upstairs, Donal had called down using the desk phone that presumably belonged to Kresham. He hadn't seen Kresham since returning inside the building.

"Okay, Eduardo. Thanks."

He started to head for the giant bronze-and-steel doors that were slowly swinging open.

"Hey, Donal?"

"Yeah?" He stopped.

"The phone lines are down almost everywhere, and I just heard even the patrol cars' radios are failing."

"Hades. It just keeps getting worse."

"So… You think we're going to get through this one?"

Donal shook his head. "I really don't know."

"Right. Good luck, my friend."

"You too, pal."

He went out onto the main outdoor steps where five of the normally glowing pillars now lay broken into huge, dull pieces. There was no sign of the deathwolves, but they must be ready nearby: that much, he was sure of.

Out on the roadway, with its knuckle-jointed parking stand extended, stood the Phantasm IV with its headlight barely glowing: a soft, sad violet glimmer of luminescence, no more.

Donal paused a moment.

It has to be done.

And he made his way down the steps towards the bone motorcycle, knowing it formed his only chance of reaching Mordanto in time – if at all – in today's chaotic conditions.

Provided it decided to allow him to ride it.

And if I'm capable.

It sure as Hades wouldn't be easy.

But the Phantasm remembered Donal well enough, and they both knew that Harald wouldn't be out of the infirmary any time soon; and when Donal laid both hands on the Phantasm's bone fuel tanks and spoke softly, relating everything he knew along with his intentions, the engine growled into life, vibrating beneath Donal's hands, and the headlight brightened to a fierce, piercing orange.

And so began his hellride.

For the first fifty yards it was a clear, slow ride, avoiding potholes and craters and blackened rubble strewn across the Avenue of the Basilisks. Few vehicles or pedestrians were in sight: everyone else was hunkered down or attempting to get out of the city, and Donal wished them luck.

They passed a particularly wide crater before the Phantasm began to growl without Donal having to twist its throttle. It had already altered its saddle shape to suit him, and he felt he could trust its instincts.

He looked over his shoulder as a tendril flicked out of the crater behind them and whipped itself around him and the Phantasm in one fast motion, and the Phantasm tried to surge forwards but the tendril held and then began to lift them both, bone motorcycle and zombie rider alike, clear of the road surface.

While a mound of gelatinous flesh rose from the crater, its giant single eye focused on its captured prey.

"I can't do anything." Donal spoke through clenched teeth as the tendril tightened around him. "Can you?"

The Phantasm whined its engine, spinning its rear wheel uselessly, and tried to morph but failed, because the tendril was that strong.

Done for already?

Still within sight of HQ, with the journey hardly started, and already they were—

An orange explosion split the lumpy entity apart – its head, if you could call it that: the central mass – and the tendril flopped away, slick but loose as softened rubber as it slapped against the road.

Lifeless now.

Behind the crater where the entity had risen, a tall figure was standing, with twin holstered Grausers beneath his arms and a smoking hexzooka positioned on his right shoulder. He waved left-handed before lowering the weapon, then turned and headed straight back for the main HQ steps.

"Thanks, Viktor."

Donal lowered himself over the Phantasm's fuel tank, tightening his grip on the handlebars. The Phantasm would know Viktor Harman better than it knew Donal. Its engine note deepened, as if feeling more settled knowing that this was more than a lone mission, or at least that the mission had the backing of another friend of Harald's.

They launched forward.

For a split second he glanced down at the Phantasm's speedometer, but even as he did so, the dial polarised into dark opacity, and Donal grinned as he got the message.

It was the motorbike's way of saying that whatever its choice of speed, he didn't want to know.

He grinned, despite all that was happening and the seriousness of the stakes today.

"Go for it," he called against the slipstream.

The Phantasm accelerated harder.

Canyon-like walls of renowned, quintessentially Tristopolitan dark towers flowed past on either side, while the air battered Donal's face and he had to squeeze his eyes almost shut, but it wasn't air pressing against his mouth that produced a second grin.

It's where I belong.

On the edge, and risking everything.

The ride became a blur of fast manoeuvres punctuated by stretches of smooth, redlined speeding: dodging crashed vehicles and dazed pedestrians and in one spot, approaching a twistabout near Brookvale Maw, an untidy pile of seven unmoving golems, who seemed to have dropped in place for no apparent reason.

Power vibrated through Donal's body, the wind was cold and hard against his face, and every time they banked into a turn it seemed his paradrenalin levels climbed even higher: even a zombie could grow addicted to this.

Fewer wild entities arose as Donal and the Phantasm travelled further from Police HQ, although the great wall of fire seemed to be burning higher than ever in the distance, far across the city.

Sometimes Donal steered, but mostly it was the Phantasm under its own volition, reacting very fast indeed to obstacles and moving dangers. Had it been Harald riding, then human and motorcycle would have formed a temporarily composite being, near enough: a joining of minds and possibly of the actual energy flows of thought.

Which made it an honour for Donal to be accepted at all, particularly since the last time the Phantasm had taken another rider, it had been an ensorcelled detective – acting under powerful compulsion – who had nearly destroyed both the Phantasm and herself, under the pretence of going to Harald's rescue.

But Harald lay in the infirmary now, and he wouldn't stand a chance if the Void Threat reached the city with destructive intent, no more than anybody else: everyone was at risk. And the Phantasm seemed to understand that in its bones, just as deeply as Donal.

Hence the wild acceleration even beyond his expectations.

No truly violent confrontations since the creature that Viktor had taken out with the hexzooka, but a hellride of sorts all the same.

They almost went flying on the descent of a spiralling ramp from the Clockblade Flyover where it merged onto Morbcrunch Parkway, because entire chunks of road were missing: not so much broken as simply dissolved in parts, leaving no traces.

Donal had no idea what that was about.

But the Phantasm dodged and banked and got them onto clear, unbroken roadway, at which point they howled along in a straight line, faster and faster, all the way to the pseudo-countryside that was bordered on the far side by the Worriesome Loop: an extended area that was too large and wild and dangerous to be properly termed a park, but which lay bounded by the extended city, all part of the gothic urban expanse that formed Tristopolis.

Soon they were speeding in apparent wilderness with black iron trees on either side and an occasional glimpsed bloodghoul, which didn't seem right: not this far outside the boundaries of Collosso proper.

Then they arced through a stand of blue steel trees across which several tattered forms were draped, and they were already past when Donal realised he'd just seen the remains of slain bloodghouls hanging from the branches.

Not what he'd expected.

What the Hades happened here?

The gates hung almost off their hinges, twisted and blasted outwards, as if something had escaped from Collosso rather than fought its way in.

They entered, keeping to the centre of the lane: whether this was a road or driveway, Donal couldn't decide. The whole thing had to be a third of a mile in length.

As the Phantasm slowed, approaching the dark castellated buildings of Collosso proper, Donal noticed a broken sign half-attached to posts that themselves were bent out of shape.

L'Insitutio Collo
Chrd. 6429
per dolor ad c

Dazed young mages-in-training, some of them wounded – although not seriously, as far as Donal could see – were wandering outside the buildings or hugging each other or simply staring into space with empty, shocked eyes.

The Phantasm rolled to a gentle halt, and extended its parking stand.

"Thanks." Donal pressed his hand against the top of the fuel tank. "I'll find out what's going on."

Two student mages, a young man and woman, approached Donal as he dismounted.

"Are you a police officer?" asked the man.

"I'm on TPD business." Donal gestured at the other students and the broken sign. "Tell me about this."

The young woman sniffed. "We had a bad thing here. It's our fault, and we've done evil."

"You don't know that, Cheryl." The young man started to reach out to her, then lowered his hand. To Donal: "We imprisoned something earlier and then it broke free, and the thing is, all the stories about it are confusing."

This might be significant, but Donal's priority had to be reaching Professor Alkador Stern and telling him everything he knew, handing over the document describing the Void Threat and showing him the ring that still glowed on his right hand, a ring that only he and mages could see, which apparently meant something important.

He figured geometry and weird dimensions had something to do with it, most likely. But that was as far as his speculation went.

"Not just the car." The young woman, Cheryl, sniffed. "The polyrachnid living in the coach house that way. That wasn't right."

Donal shook his head. "I need to see the mage in charge here. Professor Stern. Can you take me to him?"

"He left," said the young man.

That had always been on the cards, even with the route that Donal had chosen, but with luck he could catch up with Stern en route to Mordanto... provided he knew exactly which way he'd gone.

"Does Stern have an assistant? Someone who can tell me which way he went?"

"I-I don't know." The young man gulped. "There's not... It's just us. No faculty, no other, er, staff."

Something had been bothering Donal subconsciously, and that was it. Only young student mages were milling about in the aftermath of some startling event, when the people set to look after them – *in loco parentis*, to use the legalese – should have been here to take control.

"I haven't visited before," said Donal. "But this is like a residential college or academy, kind of thing. Am I right?"

"S-sure."

"Including the tutors, professors, whatever you call them. They live here on site, I'm guessing."

"Some of them. I don't... I think maybe half of them, sir."

Donal liked the *sir*, not because he enjoyed the title but because in the absence of solid information, having someone compliant and actually helpful might make the difference between victory and defeat for everyone.

"I need to find Professor Stern fast, and I missed him on the way here by not guessing the right route" – he gestured back towards the Phantasm – "and if I have to guess again, I might get it wrong a second time."

"Sir?"

"So I need to talk to someone who can... Look, can anyone contact Stern en route? You or any of your friends here?"

The young woman, Cheryl, wiped her eyes with the back of her hand, and gave a final sniff. "All the compactified dimensions are filled with cascades and turbulence right now."

"She means," said the young man, "the usual mage forms of communication are blocked."

"And translocation is difficult too," said Donal. "I know."

"Not difficult, sir. Impossible. It's been that way for hours."

Not impossible for Lamis drawing involuntarily on Kelvin's powers, but difficult enough. For the first time, Donal realised that Kelvin must have made the sacrifice while expecting almost certainly to die.

"Lead the way inside. I need to talk to someone senior." He glanced back at the Phantasm, and raised his voice. "If anyone tries to interfere with you, I'm authorising lethal force."

The Phantasm didn't need his permission, but its headlight blinked scarlet all the same, acknowledging the message. At least half of the students looked startled; none looked inclined to argue or otherwise protest.

"What's your name, son?" he asked the young man.

"Er, Tatsu, sir."

He wasn't young enough to be Donal's son, but that wasn't the point.

"Okay, Tatsu. Get me inside the building."

The young woman, Cheryl, said: "Use the south-east fire door. It's nearest to Professor Stern's office."

"But it might be locked again," said Tatsu. "From the outside, we won't be able to—"

Donal raised his hand. "Guys. You've no idea how urgent this is."

"Sorry. Tatsu's right, we should go in the front way."

"Alright. Both of you – Cheryl, Tatsu – we're all going in together, okay? And you'll see me through any wards or other defences designed to keep strangers out, because we do *not* have time to waste getting the usual permissions."

As they walked towards what appeared to be the main doors, silvery auras strengthened around Cheryl and Tatsu alike, and they took positions to either side of Donal, walking him between them.

Perhaps it was just as well that he'd thought about potential defences against strangers entering the premises.

The doors were encrusted with runes as expected, but once he had crossed the threshold, the coldness of the air inside surprised Donal. A black-walled foyer stretched further and reached higher than outside appearance had suggested.

Not painted, but polished black marble inscribed with columns of golden script, like monuments to the fallen at military academies. No doubt places like this bore a similiar burden of history – and embraced duty based on past achievements – just as soldiers learned the stories behind their regiment's honours, the tattered banners and badges that hung in places of honour.

Less shooting and more book learning, though, in a place like this. Soft options for soft lives.

They passed out of the foyer and into a silver-lined corridor in which flakes of white glowing light were floating. All that silver looked ancient and polished and once again, imbued with the weight of decades if not centuries past.

"Sir?" said Tatsu.

Donal had stopped dead.

History. And names.

That was one of the things about being a zombie. All that subconscious processing that remained available for conscious analysis afterwards if required.

"Back in the foyer," said Donal. "Were those inscriptions actually names? Of former Collosso mages who died?"

It was Cheryl who answered. "Only the ones who perished in sorcerous scenarios, unless they were notable alumni. Then natural deaths count as well."

The minutiae of remembered observation were subject to conscious recall right enough, but this was too important to get wrong. Donal was almost certain about what he'd seen, but he needed to check again.

And that was a lot of names dying in what Cheryl called sorcerous scenarios. Maybe Donal had been wrong about them leading soft lives.

Especially if they turned out like Kelvin, or Lamis with those blasted pits for eye sockets.

"Can we go back for a few moments?" he said. "There's something I'd like to take a closer look at."

He went back to the foyer, with the two young mage-students hurrying to keep pace.

"Are the names inscribed in chronological order? Most recent deaths at the bottom, kind of thing?"

He already knew it couldn't be like that, because he remembered what he saw, but he wanted to confirm his suspicions.

"Alphabetic, by surname," answered Tatsu.

"But there's no gaps for new entries."

"Ah. The names shuffle downward and along, for inserting new names when people die."

"In solid marble. Right."

But this was a mage academy, after all. He almost changed his mind about checking what he'd seen, but vacillating had never been his style, in any phase of his existence.

Out in the icy cold foyer once more, he turned and tilted his head back until he was looking at the dead mages' names beginning with the letter *C*, and in a few seconds he found the entry he was looking for.

Chaltintropovin, Baladradian Xavier ~ born 6582 ~ died 6607

Donal had learned a long time ago that coincidences happen, and that it could be dangerous as a cop to assume that every civilian was lying to you, because the whole point was to protect those very civilians from all the bad stuff happening out there.

But sometimes the odds of an innocent explanation were laughable.

"That name up there?" He pointed. "Died only last year. Baladradian Chalintropovin. I don't suppose either of you knew him?"

"Everyone knew Bal," said Cheryl. "He was Professor Stern's apprentice-in-waiting, and he was really nice. It was a terrible thing."

Donal wanted to ask why they hadn't abbreviated the name to Drad, but he forced the impulse down.

No one would describe Drad as really nice, either. Not the Drad who'd talked to Donal. But the white wolves had said that Drad was only part of a nine-strong composite these days, which went far beyond the normal effects of trauma.

Not to mention the possibility that one or more other components of that composite might also have been human originally: the wolves had been ambivalent on that point.

"Baladradian tried some really advanced solo conjuring," said Tatsu, "that was way beyond his grade. In Professor Stern's study, while the Professor was out. He was the one who found Baladradian. It… Cheryl's right. It was awful."

"Hmm. This solo conjuring. You know what it was about?" said Donal.

"It's hard to explain in simple terms—"

"Did it have anything to do with the crawlspace" – Donal glanced at Cheryl – "I mean the *compactified* dimensions?"

"Well, yes." Tatsu blinked. "How could you know that?"

"I'm on Tristopolis PD business, remember." Donal looked along the silver corridor. "So, absolutely no members of faculty in sight, while all your pals are outside with no one in charge. Something's really wrong, isn't it?"

Worse than he had thought.

"They're in the Senate Room, most likely," said Cheryl. "All of them."

"We can take you there," said Tatsu. "Although neither of us is actually allowed inside."

Rules and regulations, even on a day like today.

"Lead the way, my friends."

Hoping they would get the chance to mature in peace and become whatever kinds of mage matched their young potential.

Them and everybody else.

THIRTY-THREE

They reached the Senate Room in good time, given the size of Collosso's buildings. Long corridors, lined in metal or marble, formed the route; statues of worthy mages from the past occupied alcoves; the walls featured landscape paintings that sometimes depicted scenes in altered realities where even glancing at the geometry seemed to twist the mind; and the occasional sprite flitted past, unlike any Donal had ever seen, glowing an oddly disturbing shade of indigo.

It wasn't Mordanto. But it wasn't an ordinary place of learning either.

They reached a curved corridor – judging from the visible portion, the whole thing formed an ellipse – and a set of black metal doors in front of which two witches were standing guard, with amber amulets glowing at their throats.

The big elliptical hall bounded by the corridor would be the Senate Room, no doubt. The presence of witches felt surprising, but that only went to show how little Donal knew about mage culture and training, when you got right down to it.

"You can't go in," said one of the witches.

"They're in conjunction trance," said the other.

Donal looked at them in turn. "Conjunction trance."

"Yes."

"Exactly what it sounds like."

"Like a group mind," guessed Donal. "As if individual mages aren't bad enough."

Donal sensed Tatsu's surprise at his words; but Cheryl snorted, suppressing a laugh.

"They're not protecting this place," she said. "We're on our own outside, all of us."

Meaning the student mages, clearly.

"It's an extended shield," said the first witch. "Guarding Professor Stern while he's on the move."

Donal nodded. It made tactical sense. Especially since no apparent danger was facing the student mages milling around outside the buildings here.

"But the compactified dimensions—" began Cheryl.

"Aren't involved." The second witch formed a mudra gesture which caused Tatsu to nod in recognition. "The effect extends from here, unbroken, through the macroscopic dimensions. Which is why it's taking every mage on site to join their efforts together."

"That's hard," said Tatsu. "If the Professor travels far enough from here, it's actually really dangerous for the people projecting his protective shield."

"Can they guard him all the way to Mordanto?" said Donal.

Urgency was building up inside him, the desire to run outside and leap back onto the Phantasm and commence another hellride; but you can't reach the target before you understand where it is: he'd learnt that lesson a long while ago, back when scrapping in the schoolyard, and his weapons were his fists or whatever came to hand.

The witches looked at each other.

"He's not headed for Mordanto," said the first witch.

"You should have waited at St Jarl's," said the second.

"*What?*"

"You have the trace of that place upon you."

"And much else."

Tatsu cleared his throat. "Um, excuse me?"

The witches turned their gazes on him, and he swallowed.

"The thing is," he added. "Maybe if the officer can follow, he can do something about the entities chasing Professor Stern."

"He's failed before," said the first witch. "There's a resonance trace of the car upon him also. A fainter trace."

"And of the woman," said the second.

Donal turned his attention to Cheryl. "Can you explain what they're talking about?"

"I wish." She gave a soft shrug. "No one even believes me when I tell them she was a spellbinder. I mean an actual federal spellbinder. She blew everyone aside as if we were nothing."

"They wear suits and dark glasses," said Tatsu. "Everyone knows that."

"I know she could have killed us all, if she wanted to."

The corridor seemed to swirl about Donal, but it wasn't some hex effect: it was the realisation that he'd missed the most obvious line of questioning.

"Don't tell me," he said. "A pale woman in a jumpsuit."

"Er, yes."

"And… The car. What kind of car, exactly?"

"It was black," said Cheryl. "With fins, you know?"

"A Vixen," Tatsu told her. "They're classic."

"And they're chasing Professor Stern? Helping him, or attacking him?"

Tatsu and Cheryl clearly had no idea. The two witches were staring at each other, as if everyone else had ceased to exist.

It seemed to Donal that they didn't really know what was going on.

Then the second witch bowed, put her hands to her neck, and removed her amber amulet, which she held out to Donal. "The Phantasm will know what to do with this."

Of course they would know about the bone motorcycle outside. They were witches, after all.

He took the amulet in his right hand.

"For tracking Professor Stern," said the first witch. "And it'll let you walk out of the building without needing an escort."

"We're worried about the Professor," said the other. "Very worried, in several ways."

"You think…" Donal hesitated. "Is it possible for a mage like Professor Stern to become ensorcelled?"

He'd been a victim himself last year, as had the Guardian, Hellah's brother Klaudius, back at HQ today. Previously, he would never have thought to even ask such a question, not regarding a senior mage.

"We don't know. But there's something not right."

"Uh-huh. Newly not right," said Donal, "or has something been going on here for a while?"

Sometimes the cynical rule applied. Sometimes assuming the worst of civilians did in fact give you the most accurate picture of events.

The witches exchanged glances yet again, but neither of them answered.

"Never mind." Donal raised the amulet in his hand. "Thank you for this."

There was a prickling sensation, and by instinct he shifted the amulet to his left hand, farther from the ring inset with three red ellipses, and the effect faded almost to nothing.

Mages, witches and wolves. As bad as each other, the lot of them.

But he was grateful for the help, all the same.

"You're welcome," said the first witch.

"And good luck," said the second.

Donal nodded.

It was time to get out of here.

Less than a minute later, he was bent low on the Phantasm's bone fuel tank, hands on the grips and squinting against the slipstream as they banked into the turn beyond the ruined outer gates and headed out along the road where once again he could see the ragged remnants of newly killed bloodghouls hanging from the branches of blue steel trees.

The Phantasm thundered beneath him, generating massive power.

Merged into the spinal area in front of the saddle, the amber amulet softly glowed, signalling information that meant nothing to Donal, but told the Phantasm all about the changing location of Professor Stern en route to St Jarl's.

An effect that would last exactly as long as the conjoined Collosso mages' extended shield that encompassed Stern and presumably the vehicle he was travelling in – Donal should have asked what it was, but it was too late to turn back now and put more questions to the witches – which increased the jeopardy.

If it dropped, that shield, then not only would Stern's safety be compromised, but the Phantasm would lose the ability to track him.

Maybe his safety doesn't matter.

Not if his pursuers meant him harm, and if they happened to be Federal Agent Chambers and a Vixen whose involvement gave some kind of clue as to the apparition that had looked and sounded just like his dead lover Laura and which, when it boiled down to it, set all of this in motion.

Or not. It was the start of *his* involvement, that was all. The real story went back as far as last year, at the very least.

Everyone back at Collosso thought that Stern's promising apprentice, or about-to-be apprentice, had died in some sorcerous accident a year ago; but Baladradian Chalintropovin, trapped as part of a composite mentality within the obsdian skull, remained in some sense alive.

I've even talked to him, for Death's sake.

And the white wolves had called that composite entity the Summoner, which implied it controlled or at least enticed the Void Threat into the real world in the first place.

At a T-junction the Phantasm banked the opposite way to before, and within a mile they were hurtling along the Worriesome Loop, where strange beings that were neither wraiths nor ghouls and which no one ever discussed were flying here and there, sometimes passing into the solid road and surfacing once more, engaged in a never-ending dance whose significance remained unknown to everyone.

Except that today was different.

I'm not liking this.

Today, as Donal and the Phantasm passed along the road, each of the apparitions in turn ceased its flight and hung in place.

Silent, as if watching.

Or mourning a tremendous loss.

There was nothing he could do, except continue riding.

THIRTY-FOUR

Three times, they nearly died on the third and surely final hellride of the day. In each case, something burst out of the solid road surface or a roadside building – much of their journey being through proper Tristopolitan districts or else along the raised flyovers where the traffic was far less than expected, because of the dangers everywhere: fleeing the city wasn't an obvious choice when released entities were flailing around in panic and fury already.

Only if you knew the Void Threat was returning, and coming straight for the city. Then you'd want to get out of here regardless of any other risk.

Twice it was the Phantasm's reactions that saved them, twisting away from tendrils or limbs bursting from the road. Once it was Donal, adapted to the speed, spotting a manifestation bursting from a roadside diner shaped like or actually formed of the top half of a thirty-yard-wide skull, and jerking the handlebars just right, with the Phantasm responding, trusting him.

No wonder Harald was so attached to the motorbike.

There were other dangers besides the sudden eruption, including a maddened cloud of firesprites made dangerous by sheer panic, as near as Donal could tell; but he and the Phantasm reacted to those appearances in good time, leaving them behind before any of the sentient ones could react. Soon enough, they were out of the city's normal environs, and onto a familiar dark road arrowing between forests of black iron trees, eerie in the orange beam cast by the Phantasm.

Nothing moved in the deep purple sky overhead.

Nor could he see any other vehicles ahead, but the amber amulet continued to pulse against the Phantasm's spine, and Donal trusted it to track the signal properly.

Too much of a head start.

Even at this tremendous speed, the Phantasm couldn't make up the time. Soon enough, they were hammering through the open outer gates of St-Jarl-the-Healer's and decelerating along the gravel, spraying stones as they turned sideways and skidded to a halt.

St Jarl's wasn't really visible, except as a shadowed outline.

"It's bad, Riordan." That was Federal Agent Chambers, standing next to the black finned car she'd clearly arrived in.

A very familiar-looking Vixen.

"I can see that," said Donal.

What he could actually see was a silver-and-black dome, no doubt the same one as before, but grown much larger now: huge enough to encompass most of the buildings.

One of the hospital wings protruded, but from earlier experience, that wouldn't offer a way inside: the barrier could pass through solid walls and floors and ceilings, even while preventing the passage of anything else.

"Alkador Stern is implicated," said Chambers. "He tried to kill the Vixen. Who wants me to tell you she's really, really sorry, by the way."

Donal looked at the car. When Laura was alive, the Vixen had lived with her, in the sense of having a reserved spot in the parking garage of Darksan Tower, many levels below Laura's actual apartment. And Laura had driven the car – or ridden behind the steering-wheel, which might or might not be the same thing – and had told Donal that the car was also her sister.

But there'd been no time for her to explain the sense in which that might be so, not before she'd died her final, true death right before Donal's eyes.

Laura's sister.

Any anger he'd been holding inside him melted away now.

"Laura was the best," he said. "Simply amazing."

"The Vixen thought the Night Sister might be worthy of you." Chambers shrugged. "They were friends, and she used to drive Felice to the cemetery on a regular basis, apparently. Until the time they realised you were missing from your grave. Not an everyday story."

"No, I suppose not."

"She put Sister Felice in touch with the shady guy, the dealer, and he sold the skull to Felice. But the dealer's also dead now, and it wasn't the Vixen who did it. Or did you know this already?"

"What is this, a briefing?"

"So what, you don't reconnoitre and plan it out before walking into a kill zone?"

Donal glanced at the dome. There was something inside, just inside, perhaps close to the main entrance.

"That's Stern's vehicle," added Chambers. "The barrier didn't expand until he walked inside the building, which we arrived just in time to see happen. Up until then, the barrier was the same volume as when we left this place this morning. When I still had a pteracopter to fly."

"Thanatos, it seems like a month ago."

He continued to stare at the dome.

"What is it?" said Chambers. "What do you see?"

"You do your own navigation when you're flying, right?" Donal held out his hand like a blade, pointed at the middle of the dome. "Would you say that's a north-north-easterly direction?"

"Of course." As if everyone had an exact compass sense inside their head.

"Which is exactly the direction the Void Threat was travelling in, when it headed out to sea. Before it reversed direction and started coming back, along exactly the same line."

There was a flicker of green light in Chambers' eyes. "You mean it's not really aiming for central Tristopolis. It's headed straight for here."

"Which won't stop it destroying whole chunks of the city on its way."

"Okay," said Chambers. "I'm glad I waited to talk to you. Now please stand back while I do something about this."

"Hang on a minute." Donal held up the same hand he'd pointed with. "Do you know about his apprentice, Chalintropovin?"

"Whose apprentice? Stern's?"

"Right. The heart of that dome thing is the same obsidian skull that she" – he gestured towards the Vixen – "made sure came into my possession… It contains a, what, composite mentality sort of thing, and one human part, maybe the only human part, is the mind of Baladradian Chalintropovin, who supposedly perished while conducting a solo experiment unattended, back in Stern's office or lab or something in Collosso. Everyone else in Collosso thinks the guy died. His name's on a list of the dead, for Thanatos' sake."

Chambers bit her lip. For a federal spellbinder, that was the equivalent of an emotional meltdown. "Okay, that is significant."

"So is this, apparently." He waved his hand so the ring sparkled. "Non-mages can't see this thing. The ring, monitor device, whatever it is."

"Oh, really… Okay, you're right. That changes things."

"In what way?" said Donal.

"When I go inside" – Chambers gestured towards the dome – "you're coming with me."

"Me and my big mouth. No other help around?"

"If any of my colleagues are inside the dome, they've formed protective sub-fields of their own, most likely. Purely defensive. From out here, I can't tell for sure."

"And everyone else?"

An entire hospital full of staff and patients.

"I've no idea what state they're in."

"Thanatos," said Donal. "So it's just the two of us."

"You and me, pal."

At that, the Vixen gave a plaintive toot, while the Phantasm emitted a soft, almost subsonic growl.

Chambers placed a hand against the Vixen's door. "The four of us, then."

Donal looked at the Phantasm. He couldn't have explained his certainty, but he felt the motorbike's implacable determination to break through the dome barrier and face the threat inside.

"Wait," he said. "Federal Agent Chambers… How come you ended up at Collosso? Lamis was translocating all of us to Police HQ, but you somehow went your own way."

Maybe he was getting the technical terminology all wrong, but he was pretty sure his meaning was clear. Especially to someone as smart as a federal spellbinder.

"That was thanks to you, Donal Riordan."

"Say what?"

"I followed the quantal entanglement. From your heart" – Chambers pointed to his chest, then at the Vixen – "straight to her."

"But I've never… Oh. Sisters. Right."

"Not just that. She was there when her sister Laura was resurrected, which is why… Well, you didn't know that, clearly, and that part doesn't help with what we've got to do right now."

"Which is get inside that dome thing, right?"

"Right."

"And if it doesn't bounce us back or kill us," said Donal, "and we get inside, then what do we do?"

"Same as usual, of course."

"Which is…?"

"We stop the bad guys, or we die. Preferably the former."

"What happened to reconnoitring and drawing up an actual plan of attack?"

Chambers frowned at the gravel in front of them and all around as it began to tremble. A vibration seemed to climb up through the soles of Donal's feet and into his guts.

"The Void Threat," said Chambers. "I think it went deep underground, and increased its speed. Might save the city for now, so that's a good thing."

"How long do we have?"

Chambers shook her head. "This is our one and only chance."

Donal checked his holstered Magnus, for all the good it might do.

"I'm ready," he said.

"Okay."

He headed for the Phantasm at the same moment that the Vixen popped open her door for Federal Agent Chambers to climb back inside.

This was going to happen fast.

THIRTY-FIVE

Donal had forgotten about the folded, sealed document inside his jacket, but there was no time to show it to Chambers now. It probably wouldn't reveal anything she didn't already know.

The Phantasm did more than growl beneath him: it was gathering more power than he would have thought possible.

A silvery ribbon of light seemed to coalesce, leading towards the point in the dome beyond which stood a suggestion of a shape, which Chambers had said was Professor Stern's vehicle.

The shield. The extended shield…

Leading away from the dome surrounding St Jarl's, a silvery ribbon of light appeared and kept on shining, growing narrower with perspective and disappearing among distant black iron trees; but Donal would have bet that it stretched much further than that: all the way back to l'Institutio Collosso. And that it had existed all along, but was only now becoming visible, thanks to Chambers.

It was too late to ask her.

But: federal spellbinders.

If that connection to distant mages helped offer a way through the barrier, he was damned sure that Chambers didn't need him to point it out.

The Vixen manoeuvred herself so that the silver line passed longitudinally through her, and Donal was just starting to congratulate himself on guessing correctly – that this was their route through the barrier dome – when emerald green fire rippled along that silver thread, from the Vixen all the way into the dome.

We have to be on that thread.

The Phantasm acted, leaping ahead on the gravel in front of the Vixen and curving into the path of the green-and-silver ribbon of light and accelerating hard even as the world started to vibrate all around them and when Donal looked back, there was the Vixen with Chambers inside, surrounded by that same emerald glow.

And the Vixen came onwards very fast, accelerating almost as hard as the Phantasm as they rode the fiery green-on-silver route into the barrier that rose before them.

Impact.

Donal howled as loudly as the Phantasm engine as they powered through a mind-twisting geometry-smashing dislocation in the stuff of reality itself and then they were through, into a blue-grey, misty world where all sound dropped almost to nothing and the air felt thicker than seawater as they rolled to a halt next to a long, silver-chased car whose rear door hung open, while a woman in an honest-to-Thanatos chauffeuse's cap sat slumped back in her seat, quite unmoving, her eyes milky and opaque, her breathing non-existent.

More bones for the reactor piles.

If the city survived the Void Threat that was almost upon them.

Beside Donal, the Vixen slewed to a scarcely audible halt. And the driver's door swung silently open when Donal pointed to the open St Jarl's entranceway at the top of the steps, then at the Phantasm IV he sat on.

Chambers' eyes continued to glow green in a way that was hard to look at as she dismounted, glanced towards the entrance steps, then swung her leg to mount the Phantasm behind Donal, her arms feeling strong around his waist.

Go now.

The Phantasm leapt forward, its sound muted in the preternaturally thick, insulating air, but with obvious vibrating power: Donal felt it in his bones. Conscious of Chambers against his back, he steered the Phantasm directly for the centre line of the ascending steps and then they were jerkily climbing them, faster than expected, and dropping to horizontal at the top and wheeling into the main ground floor corridor where the Phantasm turned at Donal's direction, very fast indeed, and there were frozen people on foot plus several collapsed on the floor, everything obscured with blue-grey mist, but the Phantasm managed to bank and loop around every obstacle without striking a single one, and then they were at the inner staircase leading down.

It seemed like another existence, but it was only this morning that Donal had ascended those very steps in search of a doughnut for Kyushen.

Chamber's arms tightened around Donal's waist as the Phantasm took them bouncing down the staircase, managing the turns at the landings with deftness, and finally they were down on the basement level corridor they needed.

Almost at Kyushen's lab.

Gotcha.

In the open doorway to the lab, a silver-shielded figure stood with arms raised, his thin receding hair floating in the charged silver aura that protected him: Professor Alkador Stern at last.

The Phantasm halted. Running straight into Stern would have been an option, but whatever his degree of complicity, he wasn't the real, present danger here.

Chambers slid off first, and was already halfway to Stern by the time Donal dismounted and followed her, wondering whether he should draw his Magnus, then deciding it would most likely do more harm than good.

Like wading through water while wearing lead weights: the air was thick and swirling, something to press your way through, but with no sense of buoyancy.

There were silvery cages of light locked into impossible geometric configurations and interlocking in ways that made no topological sense, yet clearly manifested right there, at the entrance to Kyushen's lab, surrounding Stern and trying, perhaps, to force their way inside the lab itself.

Within the lab, similar cages of greenish-black energy formed an approximate many-dimensioned sphere around the floating obsidian skull they'd come here to find.

Donal knew nothing of mage lore but something about combat. Boxing was mostly about fast, whippy action or explosive power, but grappling, like climbing, sometimes required a more static form of strength. He felt, deep inside as he stared at these strange cages and mazes of energy or something, looking vaguely reminiscent of struts and girders supporting complicated bridges and the like, that they represented the more static opposing forces being brought to bear by Stern on the one side and the Drad-composite on the other.

There might be other, dynamic forms of confrontation taking place simultaneously, swirling attacks and defences and counterpunches and all the rest, invisible to one poor zombie detective struggling totally out of his depth.

And when Chambers took up position next to Stern and stared into the lab and directly at the skull, green fire added to blazing silver as the energy cage or whatever the Hades it was began to brighten and solidify, so that Donal would have sworn the struts were metal under bright spotlights: hard and durable and very, very strong.

There was an opening in the greenish-black cage of light surrounding the floating obsidian skull.

Drad. Summoner.

The energies were increasing and it felt like an imminent explosion but if Donal understood things right, they needed Drad to send the Void Threat back, which meant destroying the skull was surely the last thing they wanted.

Unless Chambers or Stern can work with a composite mentality when it's disembodied.

Donal shook his head, heedless of the air's unusual resistance, frustrated to have come so far and not know how to help in a struggle taking place within arm's reach.

Within striking distance.

Well, quite. And a knockout wasn't death, was it?

He tightened his fists and looked down, because his right fist was surrounded by a scarlet glow. Most of the arcane stuff remained beyond his understanding, so he was going to have to go with this: interpret colours as identifying energy sources, brightness as strength, and take everything else as it came.

What more could you expect from an orphanage boy from Lower Danklyn?

He took a step forward, and the dark air thickened in resistance.

Not going to be easy.

Neither Chambers nor Stern was glancing in his direction: enveloped in green and silver energies and totally absorbed in the struggle which currently seemed to be an impasse because neither side was giving way; and if the Void Threat reached here while things were like this, they were done for.

Another step.

Increased resistance from the air itself.

Again.

It was hard against his face and chest, against his limbs as he tried to push forward once more, but faltered.

Mel will die if I don't do this.

And he burst through the greater resistance and he was at the greenish-black maze or cage of energy-stuff and the obsidian skull might have been grinning but there was no way to tell as a lifetime of training brought energy from the big toe of Donal's right foot upwards through the kinetic chain of muscles – legs and core with forward and rotational movement together – and the arm and fist were almost an afterthought but accuracy and precision counted just as much as power and his right cross drove through the selected opening in the cage and the point he'd aimed for was the far side of the jaw, not the surface he struck, so his punch travelled on and the torque spun the obsidian skull in place and even without a soft physical brain to shake up the effect remained the same.

The greenish-black light cage flicked out of existence and the skull went sailing through the air and bounced off the floor and hit again, rolled and fetched up against the wall.

Close to the prone form of Kyushen Jyu.

The opacity of the air began to fade, along with the unnatural viscosity and deadening of sound.

The silver and green energies had disappeared also. Stern was soaked in sweat and wobbling. Federal Agent Chambers, looking crisp and fresh as ever in her pilot's jumpsuit, took hold of his arm to keep him upright.

Donal went to Kyushen, knelt down and reached for the neck, intending to check the carotid artery for a pulse, but in that moment Kyushen groaned.

No sign of him opening his eyes, but at least he wasn't dead. Donal looked up at Chambers and grinned.

"Take the skull," she said. "And we'll go check on the Vixen."

Stern still looked about to faint. His face was lined. Whether he was an exact contemporary of Helena Steele, Donal didn't know; but for sure, Stern wasn't a young man.

It was surprising he'd faced a threat like this by himself.

Drawing on other mages' energy.

Donal wondered what state the faculty mages back in Collosso were in – whether any at all still survived.

When Donal reached left-handed for the skull, he realised his other hand was no longer glowing. The ring and its three red ellipses looked like a normal piece of jewellery.

He hooked his fingers inside the empty eye sockets and stood up with the obsidian skull dangling.

"After you, Federal Agent Chambers."

"I should think so. Come on, Professor. Let's go for a little walk."

"Y-yes..."

An engine growled into life in the corridor outside. By the time Donal had followed Chambers and Stern out of the lab, the sound of the Phantasm from the stairway was receding. Heading up to ground level to check on something, most likely the Vixen.

Stern's strength seemed to be returning as he climbed the steps with Chambers' help. By the time they reached the main ground floor corridor, near the entranceway with the impossible five-sided tiles, he was able to walk by himself.

Fallen members of staff were picking themselves up from the floor. Those who'd been frozen upright were rubbing their eyes and working their mouths and attempting to regain normality.

Chambers led Stern outside, and Donal followed. They stood on the top step together. Chambers waved at the Vixen, who blinked her yellow headlights and beeped in soft acknowledgment.

No sign of the Phantasm.

Stern ran his fingers back through his white hair. A silver-haired man in a black medical coat was climbing the steps towards them. Someone important in the St Jarl's hierarchy, no doubt.

Brushing himself off after coming around while lying on the gravel, most likely.

Stern took half a step forward.

"I'm Professor Alkador Stern." With some kind of mudra gesture that probably meant something among magekind: "I'm the new head of Mordanto and I've broken the threat, I'm happy to say, along with some assistance provided by—Ow!"

His arm swung behind his back, then the other, and a click sounded as yellow metal handcuffs snapped shut. Black runes on the cuff bracelets seemed to glow, if that was possible.

Maybe he planned all this just so he could be the heroic saviour of the city. To make Helena Steele step aside from Mordanto and turn himself into everyone's favourite mage when he shut down the skull and thereby sent the Void Threat back to the dimensional space it belonged in.

Not going to happen.

"You're under federal arrest," said Chambers. "You have the right to keep your mouth shut, or die."

For a second, Donal thought Stern was going to say something. Then he subsided and his posture weakened.

The medical man stopped, looked Federal Agent Chambers straight in the eye – which took some kind of courage – and said: "Thank you, ma'am. I need to check on my staff but… thank you, so very much."

He started when he saw the obsidian skull dangling from Donal's hand, and gave it a wide berth as he circled around them and went inside.

"Professor?" called Donal, guessing at an appropriate title.

The medical man halted in the impossible doorway. "Yes?"

"Dr Kyushen Jyu was right next to the skull in his lab when everything went to Hades. He's still alive, but that's all I know."

"Thank you. I'll go check." He went inside.

Chambers tugged Stern. "Let's go examine your car. Figure out who killed your driver."

"I assure y—" Stern stopped.

Because: federal spellbinders.

They descended the steps in silence.

As they reached the gravelled forecourt, the Phantasm came steadily around the corner of the building, bearing a Night Sister. It took Donal a moment to recognise her: Sister Amber, who'd been in some kind of relationship with Harald Hammersen for some months now.

"It's alright," Donal called out. "Harald's alive. He's in the infirmary back at HQ, not here." Hoping that was still true.

"Oh, thank Thanatos."

The Phantasm halted, and Sister Amber just sat on its saddle, taking it all in.

"We did it." Donal grinned at Chambers. "Nice work, Federal Agent Chambers."

She started to say something, then emerald light sparked in her eyes.

All around, the gravel began to shake.

"No! Look!" Sister Amber pointed to the forest of black iron trees outside.

An exploding forest.

Oh, Hades, no.

And bursting soil, as a huge shape reared upwards, eclipsing half of the deep purple sky, and its form was dark and eldritch and filled with nameless energies and just looking upon the thing was frightening.

The Void Threat was upon them.

THIRTY-SIX

Donal spun around to Sister Amber, who was still sitting on the Phantasm. "Round the corner where you came from… Did you see any pteractopters on the ground?"

The feds had arrived in force this morning, but he had no idea how many had departed while his day had gone crazy in Tristopolis.

"I… Yes. Two around the—" She pointed.

Donal raised the skull and looked at Chambers. "I think we need to be high up and as far from the hospital as possible when we do this."

"Talk about blunt instruments." But Chambers was already leaping into the Vixen, and Amber was sliding off the Phantasm as if the bone motorcycle had shrugged her off – which it probably had.

The Void Threat was huge and rearing high into the sky but it hadn't come down on St Jarl's yet and Donal thought he knew the reason why: the obsidian skull's composite mentality was still out cold.

But wouldn't stay that way.

"Go," he said as he mounted the Phantasm.

They were fast but the Vixen had a two-second head start and screeched around the corner ahead of them, spraying gravel like a wave, and the Phantasm followed suit, even faster than earlier.

There. Pteracopters, on the ground with their rotors still.

How long to start one up?

His thumb was hooked hard into one of the skull's eye sockets, his fingers stretched to hold onto the Phantasm's handgrip, and it wasn't ideal but letting go of the skull might kill them all so he kept hold all the same as the Phantasm arced to a halt, next to the Vixen.

Chambers was already out and running to the nearest pteractopter.

The Void Threat was tall and huge, turning this way and that.

Questing.

Wanting to reach the Summoner.

Just need to delay a tiny bit.

He almost fell inside the pteracopter cabin via the left-hand opening, with Chambers already in the pilot's seat to his right, and he'd been about to ignore the safety harness but Chambers gestured and everything snapped into place, necromagnetic fastenings all secure, and the motors were already on with the rotors beginning to swing around overhead.

It was smaller than the other 'copter. This cockpit was only just big enough to hold two people – plus one skull – and with open sides rather than hatches, which made the safety harness more important than ever.

Definitely more manoeuvrable than this morning's ride: with luck it might be faster too.

"Emergency fast lift," said Chamber. "Hang on, Riordan."

Donal pulled the obsidian skull against his chest, just as his ring began to blaze red once more, and a muffled voice said: "You're suffocating me, you fool."

"You don't breathe, Drad. Remember?"

Something massive crashed beneath them.

What the Hades?

A maelstrom of green fire beneath the pteracopter was flinging them upwards, pressing Donal down into the seat, while Chambers' left hand flicked across controls as the other worked the control stick or whatever it was called, joystick, right, and then she had both hands upon it and they were high above St Jarl's already, with the pointed rooftops and pseudo-battlements far below, but still nowhere near high enough to see the Void Threat's head clearly.

Assuming it even possessed such a thing. Donal thought he'd glimpsed something like eyes and one or more mouths, but this was a many-dimensioned creature in the ordinary world and he wasn't sure anyone knew the rules for sure, not even mages.

Perhaps not even federal spellbinders.

"What's going on?" Drad's voice, from the skull.

"You were Alkador Stern's apprentice." Donal had to shout above the pteracopter's noise. "He put you in this skull, to summon an entity from the void."

"I… Yes. Pretty much."

Leaving out the part about joining his mind to others, but they were in a hurry here.

"And it's here," said Donal. "That entity. And you need to send it back."

Something made the pteracopter buck to one side, but whether it was a Void Threat limb or turbulence or something else, Donal couldn't tell. He was holding the skull between both hands as if intending to crush it, and his right hand was blazing with red fire even brighter than before.

Strong wind coming through the open side of the cockpit on his left.

"You can send it back, right, Drad? Baladradian? You're the Summoner, after all."

"Send it… Yes."

Hard to hear the words, but this was their chance. From this high up, as Chambers continued an ascent faster than should have been possible, the Void Threat looked even more frightening than before.

Not just shape but… intent.

As if every particle of its being ached for the destruction of organised ordinary matter wherever it found it.

"Do it, Baladradian. Send it back."

"Can't…"

Donal wasn't sure he was strong enough to crush the skull, but the desire to do so was flooding through him. "You have to. You were human once."

"The others… won't let me."

Then Donal did something that was probably insane. He pulled the skull against his chest left-handed, and spoke into the blazing ring upon his right fist.

"If you want to help, now's the time." The white wolves hadn't really said they'd help; but they hadn't refused, either.

The pteracopter lurched.

"This is as high as we go," said Chambers. "I'm heading straight for that thing's eyes. Collision course."

And her own eyes were emerald glows once more, which Donal should have expected.

"Do it," he said.

They flew towards the Void Threat, very fast.

Something was crawling on his hand.

Thanatos.

The ring was wriggling, moving like a spider.

"They won't let me," moaned the skull. "The others won't let me stop the Summoning."

Things were changing fast.

"Get close," Donal told Chambers. "But twist to one side at the last second."

"You must be kidding."

"I know what to do."

Chambers bit her lip. "Then do it."

She pushed the joystick forward and the Void Threat was growing huge before them while Donal wrenched the still-moving spider-come-ring off his hand and squeezed it into place between the two empty eye sockets of the skull. Pinching the metal tight, so it wouldn't slip off.

It wasn't moving now.

"Yes..." said Drad.

"For Tristopolis," said Donal. "Now, Chambers."

She banked the pteracopter right, and Donal pulled his right hand back, fingers clasped around the dome of the obsidian skull, then threw it hard out the open side to his left.

It sailed in a parabola straight for the nearest eye of the Void Threat – if it was an eye: a dark opening onto nothingness.

For Mel.

A tenth of a second was all it took to draw the Magnus, and the pteracopter was already banking away but he had to judge the parabola just right and aim where the skull would be the moment it hit the—

Now.

Trigger finger tightening before the thought truly began.

An explosion of obsidian shards, tiny against the Void Threat's overwhelming, sky-filling presence.

And a screech and roar and bellow beyond sound and there were distant black trees flicking past because the pteracopter was spinning around a horizontal axis, tumbling chaotically in a way it was never designed to cope with.

It doesn't matter.

Because the way to deal with a vastly greater threat than you is to not mind dying, so long as the threat dies with you.

Or goes back to the unknown Beyond that lies beyond the void.

That counts.

Strategy straight from the orphanage schoolyard.

Works every time.

And blackness.

Then green fire everywhere, and what seemed to be hands armoured in white living enamel pulling him from the wreckage, the air cold against his face after the heat and impact.

"Hades, what are you doing? Zombies don't faint."

"Sorry, Agent—"

His world went away again for a while.

But he knew the rest of the world would be there when he woke up.

THIRTY-SEVEN

It was the oddest of gatherings: the second social occasion since the opening of Mel's Gym. Or the first, if you didn't count the opening-day barbecue.

They'd thrown open the windows of the deconsecrated temple, declared it a day with no training sessions, and invited the kids and parents along with the older boxers, and Donal thought the place still smelled of sweat and adrenalin but no one seemed to mind.

There was beer and whiskey as well as soft drinks, all the lizard crackers and scarab cookies you could hope for, and a surprising amount of cooked food fetched by the hard-bitten cops who also attended. It was a kind of party within a party, and they were still here after the boxers left: first the kids and parents, then the older fighters.

Two boxers did remain, but they were sociable and one was thinking of applying for the police academy, so they fitted in just fine.

Donal and Mel hugged whenever they had a chance, and grinned a lot, and laughed whenever someone made a smart-mouthed wisecrack, which was often.

Even Commander Bowman's smile was coming along: a bit more practice, and it might look as natural as a redblood's.

And everyone cheered and clapped when Harald and Sister Amber walked into the gym-turned-party venue, because this was the evening of his release day, after recuperating at St Greaves-the-Shield, because it was the nearest hospital to Avenue of the Basilisks.

Donal shook Harald's hand and clapped him on the back, just like everybody else. He gave Amber a brief hug and stepped back expectantly, but she shook her head, meaning: no news.

Sister Felice was known to have caught a train to Fortinium three days after the Void Threat incident, and no one had heard from her since.

Kyushen and Sister Lynkse had been invited today, but sent back a polite sorry-can't-come note. Donal hadn't actually talked to either one of them since that catastrophic day at St Jarl's; and no one had given him straight answers regarding Kyushen's mental wellbeing after all that had happened.

There was another guest here, mostly keeping to herself in the corner, but only Viktor even dared to come over to Donal and murmur: "You really did invite her here?"

"Sure I did."

"Thanatos, Donal. She petrifies me."

Him and everybody else, it seemed.

"I like her," said Donal, and waved.

In the corner, with her eyes shining – twin burning orange heptagons – and her blood-red skin glistening, Hellah waved back, and raised a toast with the glass she'd been nursing for a long while.

Because everyone scattered whenever she came back to the table for a refill, or at least, everyone apart from Donal.

Klaudius, her brother, was fully cleansed of ensorcellment and feeling well enough, back on the minus two hundred and seventy-third floor of HQ, to look after all the eldritch denizens by himself for a few hours.

They'd all been exceedingly well behaved, those dread beings, especially the ones who came slinking back from all over the Federation, Fortinium included, once the Void Threat disappeared back to where it came from.

Donal hoped Drad – Baladradian – had experienced some kind of release, even if it was only in the form of merciful extinction. No one could tell him for sure what had happened to the composite mentality Baladradian had been part of.

Viktor growled: "I'd rather your federal spellbinder friend turned up. And that's saying something."

Donal shook his head. "I like her too. She's on assignment, though."

Analysing, back at the spellbinder training and research academy in Klein Heights, the document that Helena Steele and Lamis had drawn up, detailing everything they knew about the Void Threat.

Hoping, as far as Donal could deduce, to at least create some kind of early warning system should anyone be stupid enough to summon something like the Void Threat again… or should such an entity simply decide to come to this part of reality of its own volition.

One good thing about no longer being a proper cop: Donal wasn't legally required to attend Alkador Stern's forthcoming execution, for the incidental death of his chauffeuse as much as for the murder of the dealer, Gregor Stevanovic, and all the deaths and injuries among the Collosso faculty mages.

As for all the other conspiracy charges and indirect causation of damage and deaths across the city, they were just the icing on the cake, requiring mandatory extension of the time it should take for the condemned mage to die.

But rumours were that with senior mages, the normal penitentiary execution chamber was nowhere near secure enough. Some secret location was being hinted at.

Donal didn't want to know.

"Too bad," said Viktor, meaning Federal Agent Chambers' inability to make it here today.

"Growl it like you mean it. Anyway, there'll be another chance when you're celebrating your doctorate award ceremony, right?"

"I don't do parties," said Viktor.

"You're here, aren't you?"

"Pretend I'm not. I'll just go over to talk to Hafthorr. Later, pal."

"Later."

Donal watched as Viktor headed over to Bowman. They clinked beer bottles together. Not often you saw either of those two relaxing.

Mel came up to him, and he kissed her pug nose.

"Come and talk to Hellah," he said. "No one else will."

"Apart from you."

"Yeah."

"I… Donal, she scares me."

He let out a breath. "Alright."

"But I'll do it for you, okay?"

"Okay."

With one arm around her strong shoulders, he led Mel around the practice heptagon to the corner where Hellah was standing with an amused smile on her blood-red features.

"Pleased to meet you, Mel."

"Um, likewise."

Twin heptagonal irises of orange fire turned to Donal.

"Time for some girl talk, my friend."

Donal grinned at Hellah. "You go right ahead."

He headed back to the others.

It's all very civilised for a party.

And it was okay.

This really was where he belonged.

Hellah waited until Donal was out of earshot, taking into account the enhanced sensory acuity of resurrected humans. Donal's partner Mel shifted her weight from side to side: perhaps a hint of boxing footwork struggling to come out.

"You've got a good place here," said Hellah, and sipped from her glass without really tasting the drink: some kind of sparkling wine from Illurium.

"Um, thank you."

"He's a good man, is Donal Riordan."

"Well. Yes." A twitch of defiant grin.

"But he doesn't know, does he?"

"Know what?"

Hellah looked at Mel's abdominal area deliberately, then into her eyes: a gaze that Mel managed to hold for two seconds before looking away, which was longer than most people managed.

"About your condition." Hellah's voice went as gentle as she knew how to make it, which of course wasn't much. "And he also thinks you're a standard human, doesn't he?"

"Ah..."

"Don't worry. I haven't told him."

"But you're going to." Mel blinked, clearly finding it hard to stand her ground.

Still, she was lasting in Hellah's presence far longer than most. Apart from Donal, of course, who seemed immune to the fear she caused in what seemed to be everyone else in the entire world.

Apart from her brother – and fellow Guardian – Klaudius, of course.

"No," said Hellah. "I think I'll leave that up to you."

"I… Thank you. I think."

Mel retreated to the partying group, and after a failed attempt, adopted a sociable expression once more, and turned so her back was to Hellah.

Who nodded, and sipped her wine some more.

Humans.

So soft, and yet so interesting.

From the far side of the gym, Donal looked over at her and smiled.

She waved back, and she was the one to break eye contact, in part because she wanted no misunderstanding: he was with Mel, and that was that.

It would be interesting to see how things panned out.

ABOUT THE AUTHOR

John Meaney writes thrillers, science fiction and fantasy. He has won the IPPY Award and been a finalist for the Locus Award, and for the BSFA Award multiple times. He has several series in progress.

His contemporary cyber thriller series featuring spec-ops cyber specialist Case and his fierce partner Kat, begins with Destructor Function and continues with Strategy Pattern.

On The Brink is the first in a new series set in the 1950s and featuring schoolteacher-turned-spy Paul Reynolds.

Near-future thrillers feature Josh Cumberland, an ex-special forces cyber specialist driven by family tragedy, in a near-future Britain wracked by climate change, a legalized knife culture and political corruption.

The Donal Riordan novels feature a detective in the city of Tristopolis, where the sky is perpetually dark purple, and the bones of the dead are fuel for the reactor piles.

The seven Pilots novels include the epic Ragnarok trilogy, which begins with alien influences on humans at the dawn of the Viking era, covers the birth of the digital age at Bletchley Park, and concludes with a galaxy-spanning conflict, a million years from now.

Outside the world of writing, Meaney is a lifelong martial artist, a computer consultant with degrees from the Open University and Oxford, and a trained hypnotist.

Visit John at www.johnmeaney.com for the latest news.

Made in the USA
Las Vegas, NV
31 January 2021

16845988R00138